Stevie Morgan – the creator of the 'Beloved and Bonk' and 'In the Sticks' columns for the *Independent* – is the pseudonym of Nicola Davies, a zoologist and children's writer. She lives in Devon with her partner, her two children, one dog, and varying numbers of bantams and Shetland sheep.

ALSO BY STEVIE MORGAN

Delphinium Blues
Fly Away Peter

STEVIE MORGAN

Checking Out

FLAME
Hodder & Stoughton

Copyright © 2002 by Nicola Davies

First published in Great Britain in 2002 by Hodder & Stoughton
A division of Hodder Headline
First published in paperback in 2002 by Hodder & Stoughton
A Flame paperback

The right of Nicola Davies to be identified as the Author of
the Work has been asserted by her in accordance with the
Copyright, Designs and Patents Act 1988.

10 9 8 7 6 5 4 3 2 1

All characters in this publication are fictitious
and any resemblance to real persons, living or dead,
is purely coincidental.

A CIP catalogue record for this title
is available from the British Library

ISBN 0 340 79231 0

Typeset by Hewer Text Ltd, Edinburgh
Printed and bound in Great Britain by
Clays Ltd, St Ives plc

Hodder & Stoughton
A division of Hodder Headline
338 Euston Road
London NW1 3BH

For Mays

With thanks to Simon, Joseph and Gabriel

The Myth of Sisyphus

Sisyphus was a character in Greek mythology condemned by the gods to push a huge boulder up a hill for eternity. His only rest came each day when the boulder rolled down the slope and he could walk, unencumbered, to the bottom of the hill before starting his labours all over again.

1

Just round the corner from Deacon Road Primary School, between 'Shorthouse and Shepherd' (suppliers of wheelchairs, bath lifts and motor-aided Zimmer frames) and Firth's newsagents (suppliers of sweets past their sell-by date and time-warp stationery such as Animal Friends Calendars 1981), Samantha should be enjoying a private Sysiphean moment.

The other mothers are enjoying theirs, as they disperse in all directions from the school gates, as separate and urgent as the splashes from a dropped pebble. It's not the demands of nine o'clock bosses or the breakfast washing-up that makes them hurry so, with hardly a stop to chat. Nor is it the weather sending them scuttling for the refuge of their cars and kitchens, because even though it is the first Tuesday of Wimbledon fortnight, the weather is dry and warm. They rush away, out of the desire to savour, without even the interruption of friendly conversation, the only time in their day when there is nothing that can be expected of them, there is nothing that they have to do. For the next few minutes, before they reach home or their workplace, they are free. They move quickly, walking fast or changing gear smartly at the green light, so that no one will guess that, inside, they are slacking; that inside their heads, nothing is going on but a blissful blankness of white noise, or perhaps, at the very most, a little light fantasy of the silken sand and fluffy cloud variety.

But Samantha, Mrs Dale Cassinari, does not enjoy having nothing to do. She finds her own peculiar variety of freedom in the all-absorbing effort of pushing the rock up the mountain. When there is nothing that she has to do 'now', she thinks what it is she has to do 'next'. When there is no one to expect things from her, she tries to expect things from herself. So, as she crosses the road, leaving the alarming displays of chrome commodes and yellowing kittens behind her, she concentrates hard on improving the sound her new heels make as they hit the tarmac. She tightens all her muscles and snaps her upper spine straight, pulling everything inwards as if gathering her whole physical being inside a fortress of control. She adjusts the way her shoes impact on the ground, imagining a glass crushed to dust with every rapid step. Now, each time her heels come down, they do so with a satisfyingly self-possessed 'click'. Looking at her watch she is pleased to find that she is about to arrive at work a whole minute earlier than is usual.

Dressed in his brown stock-man's coat George is already out front, mustering the wire trolleys like a squad of unruly recruits. He pleats his forehead and pulls his brows down, glowering at them, daring them to misbehave. Hearing the sound of Samantha's heels he looks up. His whole face lifts, and becomes as bright and flat as smoothed tinfoil. He taps his watch and greets her.

'Tad early today, Mrs Cassinari.'

'Just a bit, George. Must be my new shoes.'

'Ah yes!' he exclaims, his face even flatter and brighter as he grasps this little truth she has offered him. 'Yes! That'll be it.'

Samantha smiles back, acknowledging that only she and George could find the correlation between walking speed and new shoe leather logical and satisfying.

'Well, better get on, George.'

Smiling still, she walks on, leaving George to scold his trolleys and ponder the influence of new footwear on the world at large. The moment George began their customary morning exchange, Samantha lost the need to concentrate on the inter-action of sole and concrete. The day of providing for people's expectations has begun again, she has things to think about and things to do. The barricades in her mind can be left less heavily defended as she puts her shoulder back to pushing the rock.

Round this side of the building there are no windows. Only the little red security door in the huge metal wall, like a hole cut into a giant tin can. Samantha keys in the code and enters the fluorescent-lit interior with its smell of fresh Dettol. The little warren of staff facilities and managers' offices inside feel as if they are the changing rooms of an old-fashioned girls' public school. Fresh-looking gloss covers the partition walls, snot-green to waist height and dirty-vanilla from there up and over the ceilings. The brown shine coating the concrete floors could be fossilised Bisto from a thousand school dinners. It squeaks faintly underfoot.

This little suite of rooms and corridors is really Samantha's favourite part of Stayfleurs. The atmosphere, reminiscent of stable and enclosing institutionalisation, is comforting, and the perfect antidote for the public part of the shop. After a few minutes in here she will be ready for 'out there', perched at a checkout surrounded by white Melamine and saturated in light.

Samantha pushes open the door – in a deeper shade of green – marked 'Female Changing'. Inside is a room like the rest – vanilla, snot, Bisto, Eau de Dettol – with the little addition of a row of neat brass pegs along one wall, above a slatted wooded bench. No need for the security value of lockers: theft here is unthinkable. Like swearing in front of the vicar or the Queen having sex. Samantha likes that unassailable respect-ability. It's not that Stayfleurs looks down on the rest of the world, retail and otherwise, it's more that Stayfleurs wills the world into non-existence. Such a level of self invention is something she finds admirable.

Three of her usual co-workers are already preparing for the day's work. They are not what you'd expect to find at a supermarket check-out but then Stayfleurs *is* a *better class* of supermarket. It flatters its clientèle with a choice of three

3

flavours of couscous, a selection of unpronounceable breakfast cereals and two sorts of air-dried reindeer meat. This kind of thing attracts a *better class* of customer – people who look for the fingers on fish and sigh with boredom over Australian Chardonnay – and a *better class* of staff. There are no fat and feckless seventeen-year-old girls, nor droopy six-foot boys, giggling behind their acne with a packet of Marlboro Lights in their top pockets. Stayfleurs employs 'ladies' on its tills, women who would find the term 'woman' vulgar. Stayfleurs ladies typically date from an age when middle-class marriage was a profession. But like miners and steelworkers they have outlived the industry in which they began their careers. They work here to escape their houses – big and empty – and their husbands' egos – ditto. At nearly thirty, which she feels is virtually the safe haven of her 'middle years', Samantha is almost the same age as their daughters.

They turn and smile at her as she comes in, then continue to slip the navy uniform housecoats over their Jaeger skirts and blouses.

'Oh. I think I must be electronic,' laughs Claudia as the material crackles over her arm and her newly coloured purple-brown hair stands on end. 'I do wish they'd make these things of natural fibres.' Claudia is an Amazon of a woman in her late fifties. She resembles a large sinewy horse. Quite a length of arm sticks out from the sleeves of the largest coats Stayfleurs can offer. She must have been team captain of everything at school.

'You mustn't let a uniform put you off, Claudia, my mother refused to join the Salvation Army, all because she didn't like the hats. And she always regretted it.' Mary can afford to say this of course, because she is small and neat, and the navy coat with its cream piping rather suits her pale, faded skin and white hair.

'I had an uncle in the Sally Army,' says Claudia, patting her static hair into place: 'But of course the men didn't have to wear those frightful bows.'

4

'Oh well perhaps they *do*, you know, *nowadays*.' Mary rolls her eyes and droops her right hand suggestively at the wrist, but Claudia stares blankly, blushing with discomfort because she doesn't understand the joke.

'Oh for Christ's sake, Mary!' Liz, who has been rearranging her contact lenses until this moment, shuts her gold compact with a snap. 'Nobody makes jokes like that these days.' She tosses her head and stares contemptuously at Mary's rather lost-looking hand. 'I mean, don't you have any gay friends?' Liz, glamorously, brassily blonde, was an actress before Trevor swept her off her feet with his dentist's charm.

'Oh! Oh God! Silly me!' Claudia is laughing nervously now. 'Gay, of course. Queer. Oh I'm such a chump!'

This is the usual uneasy mixture of embarrassment and irritation, that never quite crystallises out into camaraderie. They're all too busy proving that they were really destined for better things than a supermarket, no matter how select.

Quietly tying back her fine brown hair Samantha has been waiting for five to nine, the moment when she needs to steal between their words and squabbles, to get them out to work. She knows what they need is a little distraction, a shared sense of mild outrage. It's easy to provide it. Samantha places her words into the little awkward silence that follows Claudia's blushes.

'I think that Philippa, you know the under-manager from head office we had last Christmas, she was gay.' This is a fat worm none of the ladies can resist; there are appreciative gasps all round.

'Anyway, Ladies. As usual I think you look lovely in your uniforms. Shall we get ready to do battle?' United by a common sense of delicious scandal and a little frisson of genuine shock, Claudia, Liz and Mary walk to their work stations smoothed and content, like fed hens.

So far, thankfully, it has been a difficult morning. Samantha has hardly drawn a breath in two hours or put more than three customers' goods through her till without interruption. It began with twin toddlers running amok on aisle B and engulfing the freezer in a tsunami of mayonnaise. Once they'd thrown the jars they were no problem, being paralysed with the enormity of their deed. But their mother hyperventilated with shock and had to be sat in the staff cloakroom with a paper bag over her head whilst Samantha rang her grumpy husband at the BBC.

'I'm calling from Stayfleurs, Mr Hannan. Your wife would like you to come and pick her up. Yes, I'm afraid it is quite urgent. There's been an incident with your sons and some mayonnaise.'

Then there was a run on the Norwegian dried reindeer meat. Half of this morning's elderly customers have put at least one packet in their baskets (the Classic FM morning DJ announced casually between 'Gymnopodie' and the 'Moonlight Sonata' that Lapps don't get Alzheimers). When its bar code was scanned the computerised tills buzzed bad-temperedly and flashed 'item not found'. Pensioners do not react rationally to computer glitches of this sort. They treat the bleeps and warbles of the discomfited till as an infringement of their rights as human beings, as indicators of the indifference of the modern world and the harbingers of final social collapse. Seven times this morning Samantha has had to leave her own till to calm an almost self-combusting punter at someone else's.

'I perfectly understand your concerns about the future of society, sir, but really this is just a small temporary fault and if you could bear with us for a few moments you can complete your purchasing.'

But not even Samantha's most professional charm can pacify two of Liz's customers. A pair of old gents of military bearing vow to write to their MP about this incomprehensible flashing bleeping delay, and demand to see the manager.

'Oh God. Mafeking all over again,' Liz breathes, rolling her eyes. Secretly Liz rather enjoys her barking elderly clientèle because they make her feel young.

Luckily Mr Geoffrey is exactly the right figure to deal with the Sandhurst graduates of '41. He is the result of some strange crinkle in the time–space continuum. He exists apparently as the thirty-eight-year-old manager of a modern supermarket, dealing effortlessly with computer stock control and business projection graphics. Yet he has clearly been lifted from a genteel department store somewhere in the 1930s. Samantha always thinks of him as wearing collar studs, and formal navy three-piece pinstripes. His Marks and Spencer's charcoal flannel sports jacket always surprises her. He obviously makes the same impression on Colonel (Rtd) and Lieutenant Colonel Smyth Parker (DSO); he is as they remember the managers of their youth. Although Mr Geoffrey says almost nothing – personal communication not being his strong point – his general demeanour does the trick. The Smyth Parker brothers soften in a mist of remembrance of buying school uniform at Dickins and Jones with Mother.

'The trouble is,' Mr Geoffrey confides to Samantha, as the brothers leave with a complimentary packet of shrink-wrapped Rudolph, 'these old army coves think they're still fighting Hitler. I'm going to get on to head office about this bally reindeer meat. Could you hold the fort down here? You are so marvellously diplomatic, Mrs Cassinari,' and baring his yellow teeth in what he believes to be a winning smile, he disappears through the doors behind the deli counter nervously readjusting his collar, his fingertips searching for the studs he left behind in a former life.

The tense atmosphere has got into the Ladies' fingertips, making them jitter inaccurately over the till keys, so that Samantha has finally had to close down her own till to devote herself full time to trouble-shooting with her master key for everyone else. Claudia is particularly disaster-prone this morning. Her awkward wrists stick out further and become pinker with every mistake. Inside that gung-ho jolly-hockey-sticks frame, beats the heart of a house mouse.

'I don't know how you stay so cool,' she says tremulously over her shoulder as she passes another trolleyload of cat food and gin under the little red scanning light.

Samantha smiles professionally. 'Don't forget the "f" code on that alcohol, Claudia,' she says.

'Oops. Silly me.'

'And the "Delicat" is a special this week, it should come through on two for one, code four three nine.'

'Oh. Oh. Right. I don't know how you do it. Really I . . .'

'Code four three nine, Claudia!'

Whilst Claudia witters over her codes Samantha steps forward. 'That'll be thirty-two pounds and sixty-three pence please, madam. Shall I give you a bottle carrier for the gin?'

What no one understands is how relaxing stress really can be.

The offending reindeer meat has been withdrawn 'On Orders' and a lunchtime calm has set in. All the oldies are back home, sitting down to their reindeer and wet lettuce; the toddlers are safely parked in front of *Sesame Street*, whilst their mothers drink coffee at the kitchen table and wonder what it was they did with their time before kids. The only punters pushing George's trolleys are passing sales reps looking in vain for a simple cheese butty, husbands who have promised to cook dinner, and women with Lists, shopping efficiently in their lunch hours. The Reps and Husbands wander the aisles with the same air of lost expectancy, hoping that some product will jump off the shelves and ask to be bought. The List Women cruise at speed, barely stopping to grab their usual items from the shelves, their heads full of the next six things they are going to do. None of them wants to talk as they come through the check-out. They notice her 'good afternoon' as much as they notice the bleeping of the till. She's not drawn to look at faces now, only the middle bits of shirts and dresses as they pass the plastic screen beside her.

Samantha feels it is as if all the people in the shop, and in the streets and houses fanning out for miles around, had turned their backs on her. The demands of the external world become faint, they don't hold her attention. Inside she tightens control, reining in her thoughts, but it's like being in the basket of a balloon and looking down to see that the ropes holding you to earth and home are being cut, one by one. She hopes for a customer with a problem. A query about the next delivery of Dublin Bay prawns or a complaint about the selection of dessert wines, a gastric attack requiring immediate navigation to the staff lavatory. Anything would do. Once, at a quiet time like this, a customer exposed himself to her, grabbing his sad purple penis and ordering her sharply to look at it. She had been positively delighted; the furore kept her busy for hours. But the pale blue eyes of List Woman look clean through her and out to the world. As the basketload of olive oil, wholemeal pasta, Quorn mince and mackerel pâté pass under her scanner Samantha feels the familiar unease of an unauthorised Imagination Leak occurring.

At first it's confined to the back of the shop, where the aisles begin to fade into the dimness of artificial light. Out of the corner of her eye Samantha can see that the shadows there are acquiring a kind of greenness. She can't help glancing that way between items to see that leaf shapes seem to be suggesting themselves, poking between the stacks of packets and tins. Then, a flash of movement catches her eye and she turns to glimpse a lizard's tail darting under the dried chillies. It seems that every time she turns her head a bright green gecko scuttles up the shelves, which themselves become taller somehow and then grow upwards quite unashamedly. Soon they are disappearing into a forest canopy that has spread high above all the aisles and is reaching for the front of the shop to feed on the light where the glass stretches from the ground to the roof.

The next List Woman to bring her purchases to Samantha's checkout is quite unaware of the slim green vine snake twining itself luxuriously through her thick red hair. As she checks the cornflakes, yoghurts, beans, marmalade, lavatory paper, frozen spinach, Samantha tries not to look up at what the snake is doing. But it is a particularly beautiful specimen; recently moulted, its lime-coloured skin has a little iridescent lustre, and its head is a perfect arrow striking boldly through the deep auburn jungle. The woman puts her hand up to her hair self-consciously checking that nothing real is drawing Samantha's gaze and knocks the snake to the floor. It takes some self-control not to leap up and see where it went: Samantha concentrates harder on the parade of objects filing past her on the conveyor.

'Did you know that these ciabatta rolls were two for the price of one?' she says, without looking up. But her voice seems ineffectual and the woman with the red hair doesn't reply. Which is just as well as the vine snake has reappeared, popping asp-like from her cleavage.

Imagination started as 'her secret weapon' against little Dennis Williams, with his tiny wiry body, huge black eyes and lashes straight and thick as a wallpaper brush. At eight he was at the peak of his career with an empire that stretched over all three tarmac playgrounds and halfway over the grass to the back of the Nissen huts. Life for Dennis would never be this good again and he was making the most of it. Kids just did what he told them to do. Enslaved by his wicked elfin charisma, they brought him sweets, toys, money and weaker children to torment. Samantha, tall for her age, too clever by half and stick-thin, was a favourite pastime. In the middle of a silent ring of fascinated supporters he made her stand. Dennis was smart enough to know that words were Samantha's currency, so he never spoke. Just walked around her, slowly at first, then dancing and making kung fu kicks and karate chops, only some of which made painful contact with her shins and arms and head. The game was to make Samantha wince, and cower even when she wasn't being kicked or hit. It became a regular feature of her day. Every morning playtime Dennis's lackeys would come and round her up. She took to standing in the same corner of the playground to wait for them, because it was worse when they came and 'found' her wherever she happened to be.

Then one day her imagination just kicked in, unasked, like adrenaline. She looked at Dennis's face and saw the most extraordinary thing. 'You've got spiders coming out of your eyes. Big ones.'

His eyelashes flickered, but otherwise he gave no clue that he had heard her. 'Ha! Ha!' he exclaimed chopping first the air, then her side.

'You have. Are you listening to me? You've got great big spiders just crawling out of your eyes and down your face.' Samantha could see clearly that first a hairy leg, five times the thickness of his eyelashes, would poke out, feeling around like a hand groping for a bedside-light switch. Then, the lump of the body would show under the lid, stretching the skin so that the fine veins showed like web. Finally, struggling to gain a purchase on the smooth eyeball, the whole arachnid wriggled out, only to be followed immediately by another, just the same. By now Dennis's face was almost obscured by them. The early arrivals were having to negotiate the tangle of his hair.

'They're all over your face now.' Her tone was completely flat, but all the same informative, like a newsreader saying that ten people were feared dead in today's train crash. Dennis stopped his circling, and looked up at her. She noticed that the neck of his jersey was greasy, and slack. A particularly fat spider squirmed its way grossly from under the lower lid of his left eye. Involuntarily Samantha's nose wrinkled and, in reply, a ripple of revulsion shivered round the ring of supporters.

11

They turned questioningly to Dennis, leaning in to scrutinise his face.

Samantha waited in the corner of the playground at the start of break the next day, but no one came for her. A week later Dennis was running errands for a big boy with red hair. Dennis was smaller than ever and his jersey had gathered a few more spots of grease and egg. He turned his head from her as he ran past, and she felt suddenly that she must sit down under the weight of the revelation that had just landed in her lap.

Now, Samantha feels she has no one but herself to blame for the fact that there is a snake between the breasts of the young woman who wants twenty pounds cash back please. Imagination may have come to her unasked in the beginning, but then she learned to let it happen, trained it to be strong. Used it at first just at school but later at home too when escape seemed the only option. It's her own fault that she never learned to control it better.

People don't know what they're talking about when they say 'a failure of imagination'. They think it means an inability to grasp things outside of the immediate material world, but Samantha knows the real meaning: that imagination fails you. However strong and clear it seems, it isn't. It's weak as water just when you most need it. It can't be trusted to protect you from anything that's outside your own head. It doesn't get you anywhere. It gets in the way.

But luckily at Stayfleurs nothing strays out of hand, not even Samantha's imagination. Something always happens that throws her runaway balloon a nice anchoring rope. And today it's George. Liz, just off her break, comes straight to Samantha's till, as the red head and the snake duck under a liana and leave the shop. Something has ruffled Liz's laconic exterior. She seems genuinely agitated. There is even a little flush in her nicotine-tanned cheeks.

'Mr Geoffrey says he needs you in the office. It's that poor creature George. He's practically foaming at the mouth.'

By the time Samantha pushes through the doors marked 'Staff Only' there isn't a leaf or a lizard left in the place.

George is sitting on the settee in Mr Geoffrey's office with his long arms wrapped around his own body, and rocking slightly to and fro. His face is a million creases. Mr Geoffrey leaps up from his refuge behind the large desk and glowing computer and comes towards her, sweating with relief.

'Oh, Mrs Cassinari. Thank goodness this happened whilst you were here . . .'

'I will still have to leave at three twenty-five, Mr Geoffrey . . .'

'Oh yes. But perhaps you could . . .' he trails off and looks forlornly towards George, still rocking and still staring into space. There is a short silence during which Mr Geoffrey looks expectantly into Samantha's face, before remembering that he is the one who needs to speak.

'Ah! Yes. You need to be "filled in". A boy returned his mother's trolley to the wrong place. The front of a line rather than the back. George moved the trolley to the back, and the boy returned and took it to the front. I believe this procedure was repeated several times. The boy became abusive. Erm . . .' Mr Geoffrey shifts his weight uncomfortably from foot to foot as if relieving the pressure of sore corns. This is testing his ability to relate to humans, rather than figures or computers, to the limit.

'And George got upset?'

'Well yes. He shouted at the boy, excusable under the circumstances. I don't think the mother will complain. I think she recognised that her child was rather in the wrong. Then he came up here . . . Well, as you see him now.'

'Would you give us just a few moments, Mr Geoffrey?'

He is out of his own office almost before she's finished speaking, relieved to escape.

13

Samantha sits beside George on the sofa.

'D'you think they'll make me early every day?' she says, stretching her feet out in front of her. 'I mean they won't be new tomorrow will they?'

George stops rocking. 'Well. Not new as such. Not new *per se*. As it were.' His voice is shaky but his diction is as distinct and tight as ever.

'It could be the style of course. So different from my old pair. It could be the style that's making me walk faster.'

'Well. That is certainly a reasonable and valid theory. It could indeed prove to be the style. It remains to be seen.'

For the first time since she entered the room George looks at her, blinking as if he has just woken.

'Would you like a lift home now, George? I'm sure it could be arranged. You have had a difficult day after all.'

'Ah. In that instance there would be no one to attend to the trolleys.'

'Mr Mullen from the deli counter would help out just this once.'

'Well. Yes. I am reluctant. It may endanger my position here. I may be seen to be surplus to requirements.'

'I'm sure that won't be the case.'

'No. No. Well. Home then. I think. A trying day!' George smiles at her.

'You just wait here, George.'

Mr Geoffrey took a little convincing that a taxi for George courtesy of Stayfleurs was 'appropriate'. So Samantha has had to run almost all the way to school. Her ponytail has worked loose and one bra strap is halfway down her arm. As she comes through the side gate into the infants' playground, hair is sticking to her neck and face and her right breast is wobbling visibly out of its cup. She feels hot and uncontrolled. But it doesn't matter that there's no time to adjust her hairstyle or her underwear, because when she sees her boys there's no room in her for anything but the relief of being their mum again. No room for trying to pull her mind into a circle of control, no room for supermarkets full of tropical rainforest and retired soldiers. She fills up with her children and all she must be for them.

She's late and they've stopped looking for her. She sees them before they notice her. Joe is holding his thick brassy hair off his forehead with splayed awkward fingers and swinging his blue sweatshirt in his other hand. He looks sticky and crumpled. Samantha can feel his hot little palms in hers even at a distance of twenty feet. Tony is standing beside him, quite still. As usual Tony has come through the day untouched somehow, clean and unrumpled. One hand rests lightly on Joe's shoulder. Only she or Dale would notice the delicacy and the tension in that hand.

They are standing with Joe's teacher, Mr Hastings, who was Tony's teacher when he was in Reception. Both of them are looking up to Mr Hastings with total adoration, like pet spaniels. Mr Hastings is young and rather handsome; he is always making his class laugh, and uses the same voice for talking to adults as he does for children. Tony's teacher Mrs Wiggins wears brown stockings underneath her blue sandals and plays songs on her guitar about how lovely the Lord is, in assembly. Tony says with contempt that she has a special 'slidey voice' for speaking to children. Mrs Wiggins doesn't mean to make anyone laugh.

The boys notice Samantha and launch themselves towards her at full pelt. She holds them in her arms, her eyes closed as if they had been apart for a year not just a few hours. She is their mother again; defined by the food she will give them for their tea, the cotton shorts she will iron for them to wear tomorrow, the way she will stand in their room and listen to their sleeping breath.

'Mummy!'

Yes, that's right. Mummy. She has a whole galaxy of

demands on her attention now and four little hands to rope her firmly to Earth. She is sensible, efficient, loving. Totally in control of everything. She could list their every pair of socks, as well as recite their favourite stories. She is Mummy. At this moment Samantha can imagine that she was never anything else. Certainly never a child. Certainly never a person with a mother of her own.

She retrieves her bra strap and ties her straying hair, then taking Tony's hand in her right and Joe's in her left hand, they cross the road, and start to walk home.

2

At first Dale's mother, Maria, disliked their house in Lancaster Road, for the same reason that Samantha loved it. She came to inspect their purchase just before they moved in, clicking her smart shoes on the bare floors, swinging her small hips testily. 'Nnnah,' she said through her nose, her customary signal of deepest disapproval. 'Why you not get deetat-shed house? Make a good impression for Dale business. Eh? Why this house? Pushed in corner. Nnnnah.'

She was right it was 'pushed in corner'. It was the part of an Edwardian terrace built in a long L-shape to fit the hilly curves of the Bristol suburbs. Number eleven fitted the crook of the L by being wedge-shaped, narrow at the front, wide at the back. All its rooms were irregular with no two walls of the same dimensions. This gave Samantha the distinct and rather delicious impression of being inside a giant china cheese keeper. Stepping from the dark narrow hall onto the wide bright patio felt like some sort of trick, like becoming part of an optical illusion.

Samantha felt a kinship with Number eleven, almost a kind of compassion for it, from that first day. The house was shaped by the space it fitted. Standing alone it would have seemed weird and out of place, but held up by its surroundings it had a definite and respectable identity as a fine family house.

But she didn't say that to Maria. Samantha could just see what her mother-in-law would make of that. 'You feel sorry for a house?' Maria would exclaim, stretching her eyes wide, her painted eyebrows diving under her fringe. 'Eh, Dale. I'm worried. That wife of yours, she is going loopy with baby, yes?'

Samantha liked to have Maria's approval, and she knew exactly how to get it most of the time. 'It's a good house for us, Maria,' Samantha told her. 'It has a secure garden, on a quiet road. And it's near a good school.' She stroked her round stomach, drawing Maria's attention to the approaching birth of her first grandchild. 'It's big, four bedrooms. It'll have five or even six when Dale converts the loft.'

Maria looked away quickly. 'Nnnah,' she said again.

But the vision of a brood of grandchildren to scold in Italian was too strong for Maria to resist. She opened and closed a few of the cupboards in the empty kitchen. Then shrugged. 'Maybe. Maybe. The kitchen is good. OK. Yes. I know it's not you choose this house. It's my Dale. He choose this house to spite me,' and then she grinned and chucked Samantha's cheek, and leaned down to address her bump. 'The little bugger. Hey, you in there, your daddy he still a little bugger.'

It wasn't spite that motivated Dale. There was no malice in the way he constantly contradicted his mother's wishes. It was simply a matter of survival against the virtually irresistible force that was Maria. To remain himself Dale had learned to become an immovable object. They were like a tree and a prevailing wind; the tree always turned the wind aside, but the wind shaped the way the tree grew. From birth Dale's instincts had made him resist Maria's all-engulfing persona. Something in his little spirit had warned him that here was a mother who would take a million miles if given half an inch. He wasn't an angry or difficult baby, screaming wasn't his style, but he exerted his will. At ten months he'd done with his cot so climbed out every night until Maria got him a bed. At a year, he took all his clothes off whenever she turned her back until she gave up trying to make him wear a coat.

He opposed her encroachment onto the territory of his personality with determination but also with a kind of under-stated delight. As he got older he savoured confounding

Maria's expectations over everything – from refusing to wear a collar and tie, to calmly announcing that he would not enter the family business. He would put money into it but that was all. Just as she had tried to 'educate' him to fit her model he began to look on his guerrilla resistance as a learning curve for Maria. 'It's good for her,' he'd say calmly when Maria had been shouting down the phone over something he hadn't done, 'one day she'll get the message that her way isn't the only way.'

Nothing was too large or too small to be made into a contradiction for Maria to rage over. Number eleven was just another opportunity.

'Mum's got a thing about terraced houses,' he said the day they put in the offer. 'She thinks they're common. Outside bog, coal in the bath, whippet in the kitchen. This'll show her how lovely these old places really are. Mind you, we could get a whippet, you know . . .' he grinned.

Samantha kicked him slightly in the shin. 'She's getting old, why can't you just be nice?'

'What? And break the habit of a lifetime?'

He was doing some small-scale confounding and contradiction the day Samantha met him in the cake shop where she worked. She'd seen him before. He often came in to buy pies or doughnuts at lunchtime, but Julie served at lunchtimes whilst Samantha smeared greasy marge over what seemed like a hectare or two of bread. But in the quiet afternoons Julie went out the back and smoked. So Samantha was alone in the shop when Dale pulled his builder's van on to the double yellows outside and ran in to order a cake for the next day. Under two centimetres of masonry dust he still looked good to her. Not tall, not short, but well proportioned, very square shoulders, very straight posture, serious eyes. She'd noticed his looks on other days when she'd been glancing up from another ten rounds of cheese and pickles. He moved with a kind of inexorable slow energy that made Samantha want to step back as he approached the counter out of a concern that he might simply step through it. His smile was total – eyes, mouth, cheeks, even his encrusted hair seemed to participate. So Samantha was disappointed when he ordered a huge cake with white marzipan covering and a tasteless message in pink icing.

'To Mum, 21 Today', he told her to write on the order. His voice was lower than she expected. Measured and slow, but rhythmic like someone playing a double bass.

'That's nice,' Samantha said, dutifully.

'I don't know about "nice"!' He smiled and raised an eyebrow in an expression that might have been disapproving or teasing, she wasn't sure. 'Pink icing? And that greeting? She'll hate it, it'll drive her wild!'

'Oh,' she said, 'I see.' But she didn't. She couldn't help being pleased that he wasn't after all the sort of person to put a twenty-first birthday greeting on a cake for someone who couldn't be the sunny side of fifty. But going to the trouble of getting a birthday cake that the recipient would hate was intriguing. Samantha could only imagine it as some act of vindictiveness. The way he'd said, 'It'll drive her wild', had a definite heat in it.

'Oh. What name is it?' she asked.

'Cassinari, Dale.'

He spelt his surname to her. 'It's Italian,' he told her, 'my mum, she's Italian. I'll pick it up tomorrow, yeah?'

Was this a clue? Did his mother make him take her name and not his father's? She wondered if he too was carrying some load of anger against his mother and for a moment her aloneness seemed less permanent. But she put the thought aside with the broken Eccles cake she'd take home for her tea.

But the next day as she packed the huge white cake in its box she couldn't stop thinking about Dale and Mrs Cassinari. Why would pink icing make anyone quite 'wild' and why would 'wild' be a good thing? Maybe he wanted her to have a heart attack so he would inherit a huge fortune. Maybe in their family 'hate' and 'wild' had a different meaning. Julie, the cake-shop manager, thought it was easy to explain. 'He's thirty if he's a day. Nice looking. No wedding ring. Right then, he's gay. That's what. All fixated on their Mas those boys. And that Dale, that's a poof's name, no mistake!'

'But he said she'd hate the cake!'

'Don't have to be a good fixation. Could be bad one. S'all the same. Lock up tonight, there's a love. I gotta fetch my Buster from football at 'alf four.'

Dale's sexuality or the thought of some strange vendetta in the Cassinari family had filled her head for almost the rest of the day, but when he hadn't turned up by a quarter to five she'd managed to think about something else for while. She was wiping down the cabinets and wondering if a person could survive on Eccles cakes and if her allergy to cream was a judgment of some sort when he appeared. He was still dusty but his hair colour and skin tone were discernible: Snow White's brother, 'black as ebony, white as snow, red as blood'. Not at all the olive complexion you'd expect from someone with an Italian mum. Not an Italian *dad* then, she guessed.

Back then, Samantha was always wary of any conversation that went beyond the price of a Mr Blobby novelty cake and ten cream doughnuts. So, in spite of her curiosity, Dale was almost out of the shop before she found the voice to blurt out, 'Why are you getting your mum a cake she won't like?'

He looked at her closely for a moment before replying, assessing if she would grasp the answer. 'I'm teaching her,' he said, 'that her way isn't the only way of doing things. And it's a life's work I can tell you. She's bloody stubborn,' and he looked down at his feet, smiling and shaking his head as he left. Samantha understood the heat she'd heard in his voice the day before was a variety of love. She shivered with envy at the thought of such fierce affection, and with the renewed sensation of her own isolation.

21

Out on the pavement she watched a traffic warden berating Dale for parking on the yellow lines, following him and shaking her notepad as he walked back to put his head round the door of the shop.

'Can you come to a party tomorrow? You can see the effect of the cake! Early. After work. I'll pick you up here?'

He was gone before she could say no, I'm not like you after all, I'm not who you think I am. What, she wondered, would her identity be without the width of a counter and a box of éclairs to define it?

Dale picked her up bang on time and was gallantly attentive and complimentary about her rather plain outfit. 'Navy suits you. Nice cardigan,' he said as he walked round the car to open the passenger door for her, as if she were a small child. He adjusted her seat, leaning over her to reach the lever on the side, but being fastidiously careful not to touch her. They set off, in silence. Samantha looked at the traffic and the shops sliding past. She hadn't been in a car for months and the novelty of it made her forget her nervousness. Then Dale began to talk and almost immediately she realised she shouldn't have worried about her identity, Dale had one ready-made for her: 'My-date-that-you-won't-approve-of, Mum.'

The party he was taking her to was the tea dance for his mother's birthday and also the celebration of the thirtieth anniversary of the opening of 'La Tavolino Verdi', Maria's Italian deli.

'She started it on her own,' Dale told her as he drove his neat little hatchback over the Downs. 'I spent all my life there as a kid. My mum still runs it, but she's got people working for her now.'

'Do you ever work there?'

'No. I've cut enough salami for my lifetime. I'm a sleeping partner.'

Samantha understood now why a British Bakery sponge covered in cheap pink icing would drive Maria 'wild'.

'My mother is a fine woman. She's tough. She brought me up and made a business all on her own,' he explained. 'But she has a set view on everything. Everything from the right packaging for *panettone* to what colour tie her son ought to wear. She thinks the whole world is like traffic lights where the colours always mean the same things. So all men without a tie are unemployed, all motorbikes are ridden by criminals, all doctors are saints. It's good for her to be contradicted. Surprised.'

What would make Maria crosser – the pink icing or Dale's new 'friend' turning up unannounced to her birthday celebrations in a navy twin set and a skirt someone's gran took to the Oxfam shop? Samantha considered getting out at the next red light and leaving Dale without a two-dimensional walk-on in his on-going drama with his mother. But Dale seemed so warm and steady, if he had a part for her to play so much the better. She sat back in the seat and relaxed. She understood absolutely about playing a part: she could do two-dimensional. Easy. Hadn't she been living as a cardboard cut-out for almost a year?

Maria was a bit of a contradiction in herself, the proprietress of an Italian deli who was thin as a stick, and dressed in a very English tailored suit. Perhaps for Maria, that contradiction was enough, making her desire conformity in the rest of the world. She looked very pleased to see Dale, but she didn't say so. She was also very surprised, which Samantha could only attribute to the presence of an unannounced girlfriend.

'You are very late, Dale. Hopeless boy.'

'Happy Birthday, Mum. Hope you liked your cake.'

'Nnnah. Dale!' She looked at Dale unsmiling, with her pointed chin drawn in and her arched painted eyebrows pulled down. He kept smiling then, very slightly, he shrugged.

Maria smiled at him. 'Hopeless!' she said. 'Now introduce me your friend!'

After ten minutes with Maria, Samantha could understand why Dale was so keen to contradict her expectations. She had so many of them. And once one set was displaced, a whole new phalanx of them sprang up in Maria's mind. Samantha had only to react to Maria's questions and watch a whole personality for herself forming behind the crows' feet. They sat together on the plastic chairs that lined the community hall walls, whilst seventy or so people waltzed in oddly matched couples – grandads and toddlers, pre-pubescent girls and their spotty cousins, mothers and their middle-aged sons. Dale swirled by with a hopelessly giggly ten-year-old partner, and smiled dazzlingly at his mother.

'You meet my Dale in some disco techni yes?' Maria spoke without taking her eyes off the dancers. 'Dale tells me he meets girls there.'

'No, Mrs Cassinari. I met him in the cake shop where I work.'

'Nnnah,' she said. Then she said slowly, 'Cake shop' as if the concepts of 'cake' and 'shop' were not only ridiculous but also amoral.

'I asked him about the message on the cake.'

'Oh. Very funny. Big joke. Nnnnaah.'

'I thought it was tasteless actually.'

'Yes?' Maria looked away from the dancers for the first time. 'Yes I did.'

'So. You live at home? Big snobby family in Sneyd Park, eh?'

'No. I don't.'

'You live with, students? Other unmarried girls, going out to pubs. Doing, I don't know.' Maria's shrug expressed a world of ills from drunkenness to illicit sex.

'No. I've got a bedsit off the Gloucester road. It's all I can afford. I don't go out much.'

'Where are your parents? You have run away from home yes?'

'No. They're – not around any more.'

'No! Terrible. Poor girl.' Samantha now had all Maria's attention. The disapproval had gone and was replaced with concern. 'Does Dale know this? You come and visit me any time you like. Don't bother about that son of mine. You come yourself. OK?'

'OK.'

She stood up and called over the dance floor, 'Hey, Dale, Dale! Come here. You know this little girl here is an orphan?'

Maria spent most of the evening asking a series of questions so specific and tightly constructed that Samantha had only to choose yes or no to see a profile of her life springing up before her as if on an actuary's computer screen. Female, employed, under 25, no surviving relatives. A series of polite 'nos' let Maria see that she wanted to forget about her past. At least that bit was true enough. Dale had left them together between dances and had hardly spoken to Samantha all evening, until he drove her home.

'Thanks for coming. At such short notice.' He seemed sorry, a little shamefaced even. 'It was a bit of cheek to ask you. You didn't know me from Adam really. I'm very grateful that you came.' He sounded almost formal, acknowledging perhaps that using strangers as pawns in a private sparring competition was pretty unpleasant.

'That's OK. I had a nice time.'

'Did you? Good.' He seemed genuinely relieved. 'My mother liked you, very much,' he said.

'And I liked your mother.' It was the safe response. Neutral but also true. Samantha had felt quite safe with Maria, because Maria would never see anything she hadn't constructed inside her own head first. Dale's teaching efforts would always go to waste. And Maria's general belligerence and constantly in-flamed righteous anger were entertaining.

Dale parked the car at the kerb outside Samantha's house at the very downtrodden end of a pretty downtrodden street. The glass of one of the ground-floor windows was missing and there was rubbish strewn across the path to the front door. Next door was a derelict building, roof half off, garden full of wet cardboard and a litter of needles and broken syringes spilling onto the pavement every morning. Dale was pointedly quiet, then he cleared his throat for a moment and asked, 'Which is your window?'

'First floor on the right.'

'Oh. I see.'

'It's OK really. It's cheap.'

'Have you been here long?'

'About a year.'

'Is it . . .' Dale searched for a word for a few seconds and finally found, 'comfortable?'

'It's. You know. Not too bad.'

Of course it was vile. Dale knew that. She knew that. But the most important thing about her room was that the landlord was like Julie who kept the cake shop: he didn't ask any questions. She had endured the squalor of it all pretty well, protected by a blanket of inexperience of city life bestowed by her country childhood: she had wondered for ages why the hospital was evidently dumping its waste needles in a ruin off the A38. But now the cold and damp, the wiring system that periodically made the entire kitchenette live, bit into her. The feeling that this was what she deserved was wearing off.

Dale leant closer. In the monochromatic light from the street lamp she could see the dark peppering under the skin where his beard had grown since the morning. This close, she could see that her role was no longer that of the disapproved date. There was no telling now what he might ask or expect to hear. She should, she knew, plead her early start and rush inside. But sitting in Dale's warm clean car she was filled with a dread of going inside to her clammy bedsit.

'I'd like to see you again,' he said. 'I really would.'

She smiled a tight smile, Maria's questions had been so easy,

Dale's might be too hard. 'But if your mother likes me, that rather defeats the object, doesn't it?'

'No!' He drew back a little, smiling the total hair-involving smile. 'No, *I* like you, that's what matters to me. Anyway, Mum liked you in spite of her expectations. So she's learned something. That's the whole point of getting up her nose. Anyway, getting up my mum's nose isn't all I do with my life . . .'

Samantha relaxed a little: that seemed to be a cue! He wanted *her* to ask *him* questions. He was moving closer not to see her better, but to show her himself.

'So what do you do with your life then?'

'I work. I go out to the pub, I go to films. I read. I do a lot of reading. Books about architecture, buildings, engineering. But mostly I work really.'

Another cue! Samantha was warming to this. It was as easy as yes or no. 'What's your work? You're a builder or something, aren't you? I've seen your van.'

'That's me! One of those wide boys who whacks up a breeze-block wall and charges ten grand for it.' Dale had turned suddenly sad and fierce. He sat up and looked out of the window. Samantha didn't know what to say; she began to gather herself to leave the car.

'Don't go. I'm sorry. I just hate that word "builder". It's what people call those prats who work on construction sites. It's not me. That's not what I do. I restore houses. I can make ruins come back to life. I can see the beauty through all the dry rot and fallen plaster, all the crap that people do to old houses, I can see right through to what they're meant to be.'

There wasn't a trace of his mother's Italian accent in Dale's voice. He had the slightest Bristol burr, and a little sloppiness about his consonants cultivated to irritate Maria. It wasn't the sort of voice that says things like 'beauty'. The words seemed almost embarrassingly revealing in his mouth, caressing, proud and yet self-conscious. Samantha knew that Dale had told her

something he perhaps never told anyone else. She could imagine Dale, the last to leave a site at night, conjuring his vision of
period loveliness in the face of twenty years of dry rot, damp
and DIY. She could see him, looking over the day's work and
smiling. Patting a piece of stonework before leaving it behind,
imagining the life of a building springing up inside its rejuve-
nated walls underneath the Anaglypta, and polystyrene tiles.

She knew that feeling of holding onto an idea, a dream; it
wasn't like relying on something solid like a person, something
that went on existing without you, something that could talk
back. Relying on a dream was lonely, it required constant
effort: forget your dream for a second, and like Tinkerbell it
would stop existing. She wished she could explain to him how
she knew and understood the tone in his voice, but she had to
stick to her cues.

'I'd like to see one of the houses you've done up,' she said.

'You would? The house I'm working on is just up on Cotham
Brow. It's empty. I've got the key. It's not ten yet. After, we
could go for drink?'

Samantha looked at Dale's face, full of the quiet energy that
had rolled up to the cake-shop counter. The evening had
changed her into more than another part of the Maria education programme, more than the orphaned girl his mother had
invented. Dale leant and kissed her, like a cousin, on the cheek.
Samantha felt, just at that moment, that a person could not
survive on Eccles cakes for ever, nor sleep next to a wall with
black damp growing over it. Whatever they might have done.
'Lets go then,' she said.

Dale got her a second-hand dehumidifier that fixed the damp in
her room. He re-wired the kitchenette and got her an electric
kettle – 'So you can make me a cup of tea when I come round.'
She came home from work one day and found he'd redecorated
and laid a new carpet. He'd pop in after he locked up the house
he was working on, usually with a take-out, or they'd go to the

cinema and come back to the bedsit afterwards. Dale told her about his childhood, the deli, his mum and how she saw things.

'She just wanted me to fit in. To be some sort of pillar of society. To take over Tav's one day or, better, maybe be a doctor or lawyer. She sent me to school with the kids of doctors and lawyers. But school never did it for me somehow. I got bored. All I wanted to do was mend buildings. I did the tiles on our old house in Seneca Street when I was twelve. I bunked off school whenever I could and I left at sixteen. Went to learn how to cut stone.'

Once she asked him about his father. He shrugged. 'It was a holiday romance for him. He was even younger than her. She got pregnant. Her dad chucked her out so she came to England to find him, and never did. I think once she was here she didn't really try. That's all I know. She would never even tell me his name. End of story. I used to wonder a bit about who he was. Not now. He's not interested in me so I'm not interested in him.'

Sometimes he made a narrative of bits of his life, animated, funny, and coherent: stories of the antics of his workers, the peculiar habits of some customers, things Maria had done in the past. He spoke of what he wanted, and what he planned, but never what he really felt. And it suited Samantha to keep that little space between them; it kept her secrets. She could love him just as easily from a safe distance.

Dale was building their relationship one room at a time, like a house. All she had to do was walk in, comment on the wallpaper, sit on the chairs, cook on the stove, take her prompts from the decor. After a few weeks all that was left to build was the bedroom.

Samantha knew that Dale wanted to have sex with her. She imagined that he had slept with his previous girlfriends, although he never talked about them and she never asked directly.

'Who did you used to go to the pub with and things, Dale?' she asked once.

'Oh. Blokes from work. Girls you know,' and rather than admit that she didn't know, and that 'girls' sounded a little vague, she didn't ask any more. What Samantha did know was that sex was what couples did, when they were alone together.

She told him that she was twenty-two, nearly twenty-three. As a twenty-two-year-old woman Dale would expect her to know about sex. But all she really knew about was kissing, so she and Dale kissed. She liked kissing. She'd done kissing with boys from school. But the other cues Dale offered, the hand on her breast, the fingertips slipping up her skirt, she couldn't take. She didn't know what came next when she could choose what to do, when she was a consenting partner. When Dale began to hold her too tight, to pull her leg between his thighs, it reminded her of too much. How could anything loving be that hard? How could something so like a cosh, or a gun barrel, do anything good? She froze and pushed him away, her heart racing, her stomach turning. He never made any comment but every time he grew more sad, and left more promptly.

So Samantha made a practical decision. Like the decision she'd made to move to a city and work in a shop. In all other ways being Dale's girlfriend got easier and easier.

They'd fallen into a sweetly homely routine of evenings in and out together. As Dale's girlfriend, she felt safe. She wanted to go on being Dale's girlfriend. But real girlfriends had sex with their boyfriends, so she had to find a way to have sex with Dale. She booked a Monday off work to give herself two whole days and nights for research. On the Saturday lunchtime after work, she rang Dale's mobile to say she was ill and was going to bed. At least that part was true: she curled up with a pocket edition of *The Joy Of Sex* and a pile of broken Eccles cakes.

It didn't take that long to read, once she'd got over the desire to giggle at the amount of hair there seemed to be in all the pictures. Samantha read it four times, as if she were studying for an exam. By Monday night she had found a way she could have sex with Dale. Not a particularly attractive position, nor a foolproof technique for oral sex. What she had understood was that she could be in control. She could make Dale feel all the things he was supposed to feel, and yet give nothing of herself away. If hers were the wandering fingers and straying hands, she could remain completely hidden. The fact that sex was as strange to her as speaking Japanese might be, as frightening as facing the Devil, would never show. She was going to be the one to design and build the bedroom of their relationship.

On the following Tuesday she drank alone for the first time in her life: a miniature bottle of gin in a glass of squash, before Dale came round. She put on the long strappy nightie she'd bought in her break, and spent half an hour changing her mind about wearing knickers underneath. It was Dale's good luck that he arrived at a moment when she had resolved 'off' for the fourth time. She kissed him awkwardly but with determination as he walked through the door. When she slid her hand inside his flies he was too busy seeing stars to feel her shaking.

'What happened?' Dale asked, incredulously, afterwards.

'I just needed to trust you.'

'I thought that you were scared. That you were a virgin.'

'Oh no! I definitely wasn't one of those!' said Samantha. It felt odd telling the truth.

Two months later, Dale took her to Bali for a week and told her about the girl of his dreams, the girl he wanted to spend all his life with, the girl he wanted to have his children. He described 'Dream Girl' with great conviction and in some detail. He explained that *she* was that girl. Samantha was glad to be told, as she would never have recognised herself from Dale's description. She was pleased that she had concealed herself quite safely inside Dale's expectations. She only wished there was a way to show him the tenderness and compassion she felt for the Dale who patted old stone and talked to houses, who smiled so totally, who seemed so grateful to be kissed. But it was too risky. So she looked out at him from deep cover, and wondered if he'd ever know that he was loved in a way he didn't expect.

They got married in a little makeshift temple on a beach. They had bare feet and each wore a white sarong. Dale smiled so much she thought he might break with it. They needed no form of identification for the ceremony. Dale laughed and teased her because he knew how sensitive she was about her passport photo; even he'd never seen it.

So just like Number eleven Samantha has come to fill the space provided. And now every time she sees the house appear as they come round the corner from school, she gets a pang of affection for the place. As if the house knows what they have in common. And, seven years on, they have more in common than ever, because Number eleven is looking more like a prosperous family residence, than its more conventionally shaped neighbours. The front door is glossy blue, the windows clean as gin, and every tile, stone and gutter in perfect condition. But Number thirteen has peeling paintwork and a torn cardboard box in the window. Number nine has subsidence affecting its bay and a dog turd on the paved front garden so enormous, it could almost be an art form.

Maeve, from number thirteen, rushes out as she sees Samantha pass with the boys. Her greyish knickers are showing above the waistband of her long crumpled skirt, her daughter's tie-dye T-shirt only just accommodates her large, unfettered bosom. She has bare, dirty feet and her roots are showing.

'Oh God, oh God, I'm *so* glad I caught you.'

'Hello, Maeve!' says Tony. 'Look what I made in school! It's an elephant.'

Samantha is always slightly worried by how much Tony

seems to like Maeve. How can a child so fastidious find someone whose breakfast crumbs are often to be seen in their hair, so attractive?

'Lovely. Lovely, Tony my sweet,' Maeve croons rapidly, 'but I need to speak to Mummy. OK?'

At least Joe is always suitably reserved in the presence of Maeve's rambling, unkempt body and loud plummy voice. He snuggles in to Samantha's legs and puts a thumb in his mouth.

'I've got a batch of carrot cake in the oven and the trip's gone again!' Maeve is almost wailing with distress. 'Would you be a *dear*? Pop in and do the switching thingy for me?'

'Yes, of course, Maeve.' Samantha is gracious, even though it is the third time in ten days that she has had to do this service for Maeve. 'Come on, boys, we're popping into Maeve's house for a mo.'

'Weeeeee.' Tony zooms ahead, and in through the purple front door. Joe unpeels himself from Samantha's leg enough for her to be able to walk as if she has a bad case of elephantiasis.

'Oh Joe! Jo-e!' But he doesn't stop clinging. He can tell she's secretly pleased that he finds the uncarpeted, bike-filled hall rather threatening.

Maeve is doing her usual apologetic twitterings, and Samantha is patiently (and ever so slightly patronisingly) explaining (again) that the trip switch is HERE, and ALL you have to DO . . . is . . . THIS. The light in the hall comes on, and the fridge in the kitchen audibly shudders awake.

'Oh, you're so *brave*!' Maeve exclaims in wonder and gratitude. 'Anything electric just gives me the jidders!'

Samantha smiles. She's given up telling Maeve she could do this for herself. Now she just enjoys feeling that she – supermarket assistant without an A level to bless herself with – is more capable than Maeve – who has two degrees and a part-time solicitor's job.

'We're going, Tony.'

Tony emerges from the kitchen with Maeve's black cat,

33

Archimedes. The cat is looped over his arms like a vast fluffy bean bag and looks, as usual, as if it has no internal skeleton. Tony hugs the formless animal bundle to his face and wheedles, 'Oh! Can't I stay?'

Before Maeve can invite him to sample the carrot cake, Samantha cuts in firmly. 'No, Tony, Daddy's coming home tonight and we've having a special tea.'

Tony and Maeve exchange a decidedly complicitous glance. But there is no arguing with that tone. He and Samantha, with Joe still attached, leave.

The door of Number eleven closes. It's solid and heavily draught-proofed so it makes a sound like a bank vault shutting. Once inside, carrot cake, invertebrate cats and limpet imper-sonation fall away. The boys click into routine. They struggle out of their shoes and race up the stairs ahead of Samantha.

'Bring your clothes into my room, boys,' she calls, but she doesn't need to tell them. They do it every day. Still racing, they wheel into Samantha and Dale's white bedroom both making racing-car noises: Tony's are quite good, the 'nneeeeaww' sort of sound a McLaren makes out of a bend at Le Mans. Joe's are rather more 'brmm bbbrrmmm!' like the 'car noises' made by the out-of-work actors presenting tots' TV. They break abruptly and screech to a noisy halt by the high double bed, grinning and squirming. They are both clutching a neat square of folded garments, the play clothes that Samantha puts on their beds every morning before they leave for school.

'Get ready then!' Samantha tells them. They each put their clothes on the bed and step back theatrically.

'Where's your clothes, Mummy?' says Joe.

'I'm just getting them.' Samantha turns to the cream-painted tall boy, and slides drawers open soundlessly. She splits cubes of folded clothing inside like a card shark cutting a pack, removes a folded garment and reforms the cube. She piles a pair of beige shorts and a lemon T-shirt on the bed opposite the boys' clothes, then steps back. They all look at each other and smile.

'Tony's turn to say today,' Samantha announces. Joe squirms some more and claps his hand to his mouth. Tony gives Samantha a look that his brother doesn't see. 'I'm too old for this really, but I'm doing it for Joey' the look says.

'On your marks,' says Tony, 'get set . . .' Tony looks all round the room, then, 'GO!'

They all begin to undo buttons, wriggle out of tops and socks, the boys panting with effort. Only Joey talking to himself under his breath says anything. He is giving this race his all. At five, dressing and undressing is a trial. Arms don't come out of sleeves reliably, and getting terminally stuck inside one of his own garments seems like a definite risk. Joe's undressing is very physical. It takes a lot of space because he bends and stretches, reaches out and over and back, jumps up and down even in the effort of shedding one skin and getting another.

'Oh no!' he breathes as he finds that his little Thomas the Tank Engine underpants have come off with the elasticated waist shorts.

Tony's strategy is different now that he can handle almost any button, and even troubleshoot zips for himself. He's working on technique. Slyly he watches the economical way Mummy, a grown-up, slides her zips and takes her arms out of her blouse, smoothly, without rumpling the fabric. Doing it that way saves time at the end, because you can't say you've finished until you fold the clothes you took off.

Samantha is proud of her invention of this race. She paces the unzipping and hanging of her skirt, the unbuttoning of her work blouse, so as not to be first today. She has to be first sometimes to keep Joe interested in the unpredictability of winning. Already Tony doesn't need this to be a race. The satisfactions of speed and neatness are almost enough for him. In a year, less perhaps, Joe will get to that stage and the changing game will have to stop, having taught them all it was meant to. Samantha thinks of that day quite sadly, because she will miss the quiet intimacy of the three of them standing together in their underwear.

'Done!' Joe shouts triumphantly. He's got his T-shirt on the right way round for the first time in a fortnight, and he's managed to approximate folding his school shirt pretty well.

'You beat me, Joe,' says Tony untruthfully. He doesn't smile. Letting Joe win is right but doesn't yet feel good.

'Me too!' says Samantha.

'I'm the winner!' Joe is delighted with this evidence of his maturity and dances round the room. There is something generous about Joe, his victory somehow includes his brother, so Tony feels that he can't say that Joe didn't fold his shirt really properly. But Samantha knows he needs her to notice that. So whilst Joe is still dancing about, she catches Tony's attention and rolls her eyes as she pointedly refolds Joe's crumpled top and shorts. Now, Tony smiles. Glowing with pleasure, he runs to grab his little brother's hand and prances round the room chanting, 'Joe's the winner!'

Samantha sees how much they are learning, from T-shirts the right way round, to elementary human relationships. She pushes down the tiny ripple of sick panic that runs across her heart from their every step toward autonomy; she knows it's foolish, they'll be making demands on her for the rest of her life, they'll always need her, she tells herself.

'Come on, boys. Put your clothes away and we'll go down for drink and a biscuit.'

It's still warm at five thirty and the boys are quite happy getting their cars clogged and buried in the sand pit. Samantha decides she can allow herself another few minutes' intensive snipping, cutting back the invading forces of next door's garden. Keith and Felicity in Number nine have taken to rowing as a full-time occupation – they are at it now, hissing at each other near an

open window upstairs somewhere – so their garden is completely out of control. Tendrils, fronds and shoots of all sorts
are continually scaling the wall and poking into Samantha's
territory. They should know better; the moment any plant
strays to her side of the wall, it's chopped. She cannot endure
unchecked plant growth, it's too stimulating for her imagination. Dale wanted space to grow things when they bought the
house, and went on about all the plants that could grow in
Bristol's mild climate.

'Exotics,' he said, 'that's what we could have. You know,
tropical palms, like the ones they have in Torquay. They look
great in small town gardens like this.' She didn't tell him that
Cordyline australis, the Torbay palm, wasn't a palm at all but
a member of the *Lilliacae*, like gladioli are. He wouldn't
expect her to know things like that. But when he started
going on about climbers and arches and making a 'jungle' for
children to play in, Samantha had to do something. She
showed him the leaflet about the parasites in cat faeces. Unless
they paved the garden, she said, it would be not so much a
jungle as a giant cat toilet. Archimedes and some of his down-
market buddies were yowling on the wall at the time, for
which Samantha was grateful. The thought of his little baby
boy being blinded by such a thing so affected Dale that he
brought a concrete mixer and a lorryload of stone paving over
the very next morning.

So now Samantha's garden is concrete with four little square
islands of compost. She grows flowers in these, lobelias,
petunias, things that look limp-wristed and unthreatening.
She plants them in neat geometric patterns, chequers of blue
and white, concentric squares of contrasting pinks. This she
feels gives the plants the right message: 'No getting ideas of
your own in my garden.' When they die down in autumn she
rips them out, and savours the blank earth all winter. This year
she has grown a few herbs – parsley, thyme, basil – because
herbs are meant to be cut back all the time. Dale has got used to

her minimalist gardening, and these days he's too tired after work to bother about what's in the garden when he slumps in a deck chair with a beer. When the boys want to run about on grass, she takes them to the park. Its keeper is rather old-fashioned and still grows a succession of bedding plants in straight lines. Samantha has never noticed a weed there or even a French marigold out of alignment. It is very restful.

'Cooo-eeee, cooo-eeeee.' Samantha is distracted from dislodging a sowthistle from between two paving stones by the sound of Maeve calling over the low part of the wall that separates their gardens. 'Cooo-eeee. Bo-oys!'

'Oh, Mother! For God's sake. Can you be like, less *sad*?' That's Callendula, Maeve's highly pierced fourteen-year-old daughter. 'I mean "cooo-eee". For God's sake!'

'Oh all right. You call then.'

Maeve and Callendula haven't noticed Samantha crouched by the wall, and the boys are too engrossed to hear anything. Samantha stands up. 'Hello,' she says tentatively, as if she's heard something but isn't sure what or who, definitely not an adolescent daughter expressing her irritation for her embarrassing mother.

'Oh there you are!' Maeve is leaning over the top of the wall, but Callendula elbows her out of the way, as the low part of the wall is just one person wide. Callendula has on a purple velvet top, too hot for a summer day and is in her usual full 'alternative' regalia – scarlet dreadlocks, eyebrow, nose and lip rings. Callendula smiles angelically at Samantha.

'Hi, Mrs Cassinari!'

'Hello, Callendula.' For some reason Samantha cannot fathom, Callendula has taken to her since she turned fourteen. She leans over the wall at every opportunity and always calls her 'Mrs Cassinari'.

'Mrs Cassinari, what GCSEs do you think I should do?'

'Mrs Cassinari, did you know that dreadlocks never actually need washing after the first year?'

'Mrs Cassinari, did you find childbirth painful?'

It must be incomprehensible to Maeve.

'Mum and I were wondering if the boys would like to come and see Archimedes. We didn't even know he was pregnant, but he's having kittens in my bedroom.'

'And there's the carrot cake of course!' Maeve twitters from out of sight down in the garden. Samantha is about to explain again about the early tea with their father, but it's Tony's turn to cut in. The word 'kitten' has some consciousness-piercing quality that 'Cooooo-eeee' clearly doesn't, for the boys have both left the sand pit and come racing to the wall.

'Kittens!' they say together. 'KITTENS!'

'Mmm, little tiny ones. Newborn and he's still having them.'

'WOW!' Tony is speechless, but Joe is sceptical. Even kittens may not be enough to make him brave the terrors of number thirteen.

'I thought boys didn't have babies,' he says suspiciously.

'They don't,' Callendula announces eagerly, 'Archimedes is a girl!'

Joe makes no comment but sticks his thumb in his mouth and turns into a leg limpet: kittens might have been believable but Archimedes, a girl? No. That's too much impossibility for Joe to cope with. But Tony would go in search of kittens born to a plastic dog at this moment.

'Can I go and see them, pleeeeeeese.'

'Go on then. Run round to the front door,' Samantha says. Letting Tony go is the right thing but it doesn't feel good, so she's a little curt when she turns back to Callendula. 'Please make sure he's back by six! I'm expecting Dale home, and he's been away all weekend.'

'Oh yes, Mrs Cassinari!' Samantha can't help feeling that Callendula likes it when she speaks sharply to her. As the girl jumps from the wall she throws up her arms and reveals the studded leather bracelets she has taken to wearing on both wrists.

'C'mon, Joe. Let's get Daddy's tea!'

Having Mummy all to himself is better than fictional kittens any day. Joe is standing on a chair with a bowl of dried beans and pasta in front of him on the worktop. He stirs vigorously with a huge wooden spoon and talks to Samantha.

'I'm making boff-hoffie pie, Mummy. What are you making?'

'Smoked haddock soufflé, darling. Daddy's favourite.'

'Are Tony and me having that too?'

'Mmm-mmm. And some of Granny's shop bread and some of Granny's shop oil.'

'Yum. D'you want to taste my boff-hoffie pie?'

'Yes please. Lovely, mmm.'

Samantha is enjoying herself again. She knows she is a very convincing cook. She can picture herself at this moment, the woman smiling at her small son and folding egg white expertly into a sauce, with a soft clop clop sound. But Joe doesn't smile back. She can see he's about to ask one of his big questions. Joe is very serious about life and the universe right now. Starting with the exploration of his first Continent: Mummy.

'What would you eat if you could have anything in the world?' says Joe. His question is so direct, so full of desire for a real answer, that Samantha finds it unsettling. She feels a blush rising up her throat.

'Oh. I don't know. What would you eat?'

'I'd have Granny's *tartufo negro*.' Joe is already a likely successor to the Tavolino deli empire, a gourmand at five. The only Italian he knows refers to food – *prosciutto*, *bresaola*, *scallopini*, *gelati* – he savours the words, rolling them round his mouth. He says *tartufo negro* again as if he could taste the chocolate and ice cream.

'But what *would* you eat, Mummy, really?' Joe has stopped

stirring now and is looking up at Samantha as if his life depended on the answer. It's so hard to lie to a child.

'Oh um. Smoked haddock soufflé!'

'No! That's Daddy's favourite. What's *your* favourite?'

'Oh. Um.' Samantha is flustered, she has been caught without an answer of her own. 'Chocolate cake!'

'No, Mummy, that's Tony's favourite.' Joe's mouth is very straight now and his eyes could cut a hole in a pane of glass. Samantha can't meet his gaze. She turns away to put the soufflé in the oven, prematurely. It'll be ready too early now, will go leathery and fall.

'I don't know what my favourite is,' she says as she turns back, but Joe's gone. She can hear him tipping Lego aggressively onto the playroom floor.

It was all downhill after that. Dale rang from his mobile just as Joe trapped his finger in the playroom door. Between technological inadequacy and full-volume screaming all she heard was something about 'body plasterers' and 'fate worriers'. He wouldn't be home until after 'hen flirty' or even 'larf never'. Then, when she went to retrieve Tony she found the number thirteen household in crisis: one of Archimedes' miraculous kittens had apparently been stillborn. Everyone was jammed into Callendula's witch's bower of a bedroom, ducking the festooning Indian throws and trying to see through the incense. Maeve sat on the floor whimpering slightly and dabbing her eyes with a corner of her skirt. Malcolm, Maeve's tall and uncoordinated husband, was stepping back and forth over the cat and kittens, dripping TCP from a damp cloth. His huge uncontrolled feet threatened death by crushing with their every move. Tony crouched between Archimedes and Callendula looking from the live kittens then to the apparently dead one in Callendula's hands, as if he were watching a long volley on Centre Court. His eyes were stretched open, his face caught between tears and smiling. Only Callendula was doing something sensible: she wiped the pinprick nostrils clean then gently blew into them through pursed lips. Samantha was reminded of a picture in one of the boys' books, of a girl in a crown kissing a frog. She was wondering what might result from puckering up to a dead kitten, when the tiny body shivered, alive after all. Malcolm stopped dripping and Maeve went quiet as they waited for another sign of life. The tiny mouth opened and the smallest mew in feline history came out of the shell-pink space. Maeve and Tony burst into tears.

The kitten was christened – Lazarus of course – and Maeve invited the boys to breakfast the following morning to see him again. Tony said goodbye twice to all the other kittens and Archimedes. By that time, the soufflé was more of a sort of rubbery Spanish omelette. The boys wolfed Tavolino's ciabatta moistened with olive oil and pushed the yellowish lumps of eggy fish round their plates.

'Is this Daddy's favourite?' said Joe.

'Yes.' Samantha braced herself for more third degree, but all Joe said was, 'Why?' and shunted another bit of soufflé onto his fork.

'D'you think Lazarus would like to eat mine?' asked Tony hopefully.

'Lazarus can only eat his Mummy's milk, darling.'

'But he hasn't got a Mummy!' said Joe.

Tony rolled his eyes. 'Archimedes is his Mummy, Joe,' he explained patiently.

But Joe was determined to defend his vision of how the world was from Tony's cool logic. '*Archimedes is a boy*. He can't be a Mummy.' Joe spoke with laser-like intensity, his anger building behind his eyes. 'Just having kittens doesn't make him a Mummy.'

'Of course it does!' As usual Tony's response to anger was mannered calm, affected rationality. As usual it only made Joe more passionate. As usual Samantha couldn't think how to manage these titanic clashes of opposing personalities.

'No it doesn't!' Joe threw down his fork, and stood up. 'He wasn't a Mummy to start.' Tears welled up in Joe's eyes. 'You can't just *make* yourself be something.' He looked from Tony to Samantha. 'And you can't just *pretend* about favourites!' Then he stomped upstairs and picked up a little bit of routine: his nightly job of running the bath for himself and his brother.

It's gone 'hen flirty' now. Probably beyond 'larf never'. Samantha has exhausted nearly all the tasks her house and children can provide. She has bathed her boys – singly tonight – read them stories and kissed them to sleep. She has washed up, ironed, hoovered, taken a chicken out of the freezer and darned two pairs of socks in front of an hour's worth of mindless TV thriller. She is tired enough to sleep, but she stays up, waiting to be Dale's wife when he comes home. She likes to be his wife, and he likes her wifeness. She sees herself sometimes as a happy portrait looking out at Dale through holes cut in the canvas of the eyes. Occasionally she wonders if they are both standing behind portraits – a picture of a husband and a picture of a wife facing each other over the heads of real children.

She wanders around downstairs plumping cushions and picking specks from the carpets. She turns on lamps and admires the vistas over sofa arms and table tops, the pearly half-reflections in the paintwork. These rooms are her creations, cleverly concocted by Samantha, the Taste Magpie. She picked the bones of a hundred magazines quite clean to get this look, stolen from the town houses and country homes of Julians and Jocastas, Tottington-Smythes and Delaney-Norrises. She tracked down the bargain fabric places in warehouses off odd industrial estates and learned how to bid at furniture auctions. She chose all the colour schemes, soft sage and old rose, butter cream and melon-flesh yellow, web grey and pudenda mauve. Each object, every square foot of wall or floor has its own little history: the Knole sofa, now the colour of a lightly mouldered strawberry, she found brown and sagging in the corner of some auction rooms in Portishead. Dale brought it home for her on his truck. She got it reupholstered in material that she noticed tumbled in a crate outside a junk shop in Montpellier, that turned out to have been the ex-curtains of a castle in Monmouth.

These still-life stories have helped to construct Samantha's world, they are part of what defines her, what proves her to be herself. Her rooms reassure her tonight, after Joe's unsettling outburst. You *can*, they tell her, *make* yourself into something, aren't they themselves the proof of the self that she has made? Calmer, she goes upstairs with an armful of clean towels – all bright white. Folding them is another comfort, a kind of mantra. She stares blankly through the spare room window as she runs her hands over their fluffy roughness.

Out there the falling dusk is drawing the streetlights into the air, bleeding brightness above the lines of rooftops and darkening gardens. When they first moved in, she didn't like to be alone with this view. It was like the quiet of Stayfleurs on a Tuesday afternoon, sometimes it made her imagination take over. Ten minutes of staring idly like this over Lexington Gardens, towards the bike shop on the corner of Berkeley Road, was enough, back then, for her to see the whole of downtown Bristol clothed in Central American lowland rainforest. It was worse at dusk. The trees could creep in subtly from St Mary Redcliffe and Temple Meads, the blue-green canopy blending at first with the urban haze. Only when the crown of some rainforest giant – a kapok tree perhaps – appeared two hundred feet above City Road, would she notice that the orange lights along Stokes Croft had been extinguished and that howler monkeys were chorusing above the dimming hum of traffic. The huge trunks dwarfing the lampposts and the Victorian façades, the inscrutable continent of leaves, were beautiful in a way that was only painful. Their apparent reality only taunted her, showing again what she could never have.

But worse than what she imagined, was what the view from

the window made her remember. Those successive curves of roof lines, climbing and descending the city's gradients, reminded her of the ploughed furrows, working up and down the hills, at home in Suffolk. She remembered how in autumn, stubble fields surrounded her parents' house, falling away in slow arcs and crescents from the end of the garden to the horizon. Then, the ploughing tractors would come, turning the gold and green of the cropped fields under the clay. She felt, that year, that they were dragging the darkness in rows of six behind them, the plough shares cutting winter free from the soil. As each bright field was crossed out with lines of dead earth, a lifeless chill seemed to crowd closer. Then, the frost came and set the furrows like bars, shutting out the softness of living things. Always before the landscape had been her friend. Even in winter. Stripped of crops and greenery, the shape of the land was clearer. It had an honesty that touched her, like the unashamed nakedness of a baby. The land in winter shared its secrets: the hidden nests, the mouths of burrows, the bones and withered flesh of kills made under the cover of summer leaves.

But that December, the fields, lanes and hedges had no heart. Their faces set against her, with mouths shut in a hard line. They drove her back into the house, where it was always some Godforsaken Sunday night. She would hear the blackbirds' alarm calls signalling dusk in the garden, but inside the windows were already black. Granny Pearl would be waiting to be served her tea, hovering in the hall. She'd shift her false teeth rhythmically over her gums and twitch with irritation. On the other side of the kitchen door Dad would be making sandwiches, with tinned ham and lumps of butter too cold to spread. The strip light buzzed over him and he would whisper 'Samantha', over and over under his breath. In the sitting room, Mum would be on the sofa, very flat and still. The dismal emptiness of Sunday night religious programming would project onto her mum's face, like a treatment ray. It cured nothing and only filled the sick woman with the sense that there was no

God, and no afterlife, and that the indifferent Universe gaped from Harry Secombe's singing mouth. Upstairs, doing homework alone, Samantha would feel all the fear and silence seeping up like damp through a wall. How she had longed, that December, for a climate where death had no particular season and the dead were rapidly recycled as the living.

She'd come to a city to escape those winter furrows and that longing. And she had done it, finally, by adding time to the distance between her and the past. Now Samantha has memories of her husband and her children, and her suburban life, to keep her from the landscape of her girlhood. Looking over the rooftops as she folds the last few towels, she remembers the last time she looked over the rooftops and folded towels. Or Dale dozing on the patio and rocking the pram with one outstretched foot. Or the day the boys had their first climbing frame. Or the fairy lights strung all round the garden walls at Christmas. Or the last nub of the boys' snowman left after a thaw. Or Dale filling the paddling pool with the boys waiting solemnly in their little trunks. Nearly a decade of other sorts of days filled with Tony and Joe and Dale and all they need and want has pushed the imaginary rainforest and the memories of East Anglian winters far under the surface of her life.

She is not the girl who left the frost-bound Suffolk landscape. The proof of that is all around her and in her and now, too, walking through the front door of Number eleven. Dale comes straight upstairs. 'I'm home!' he calls up to her, not too loud, he knows she'll still be awake.

She meets him on the landing. He doesn't reach out to her or embrace her. He never does, never has. Instead he kisses her on the cheek, lightly, almost distractedly, and for a moment he holds her face in one rather dirty hand, so gently she can hardly feel the roughness of his calluses against her skin. This is Dale's habitual expression of affection, small, understated, and infinitely precious in its constancy and long repetition.

'I'm so late! Sorry. Bloody plasterer didn't turn up and then the lorry with the slate on it got stuck in the lane. I spent four hours digging him out of the hedge. Steve's doing tomorrow though. I'll go back up day after tomorrow.' He allows her to hug him for a moment and leans infinitesimally against her but only for a fraction of second before he breaks free.

'I'm so knackered.' He rubs his hands through his hair and Samantha switches her attention to practical caring, the brand of affection that he finds more acceptable.

'Come on, get to bed then!' Samantha pulls him slightly towards the bedroom.

'Bath first. I'm filthy. I'll go and run it.'

'Cup of tea?' She knows he wants one, she's already at the top of the stairs.

'Phoor. I'd kill for one.'

'I'll bring you one up. Anything with it? I made fruit cake at the weekend.'

He leans over the banister to answer her, 'Love some. Thanks for waiting up,' then he smiles his total smile. 'Angie. My Angie.'

3

'What d'you think about taramasalata?' Louise is sitting with her skinny legs very crossed. She is hunched over them, leaning on her elbows and chewing a pencil end. Her pointy folded-ness reminds Samantha of a pair of dividers. 'I mean, tarama-salata could be a kind of cross-over thingy. You know, like Geography?' The inside of Louise's head is like a tornado in a library, pages from Dickens fly past next to headlines from the *Daily Star*. Louise's connections are hard to follow and im-possible to predict. Most people don't pay enough attention to Louise ever to understand what she's talking about. But Samantha likes having to concentrate.

'At school,' Louise explains, sitting upright now and sipping from her mug, 'they used to say it could be a science or an art. So if you couldn't cope with *e* equals *m c* whatever, or remember the future tense of *venir*, then you did Geography and it did for both. See?' She smiles and raises her eyebrows hopefully.

Louise and Samantha constitute the Catering Sub Committee of the Deacon Road Primary School PTFA. This afternoon, a Wednesday, Samantha's day off from Stayfleurs, they are sitting in Samantha's kitchen and discussing the menu for the next PTFA event, the annual Staff versus Parents' Cricket Match and Tea.

'I understand the Geography part, Louise, but what's that got to do with taramasalata?'

'Well, it could do for vegetarians *and* meat eaters, couldn't it? I mean it's sort of meat, but not really.'

'It's fish eggs, Louise. I think that's meat.'

'Well, I don't know. I mean some vegetarians eat eggs, don't they? *And* fish. So taramasalata is the best of both worlds. It's a cross-over in two ways really.' Louise suddenly looks very happy. Her insight into the double-crossing nature of taramasalata has given her a moment of pleasure – her tornado mind may be confusing to outsiders but she, at least, enjoys the way it blows things around. Samantha decides that the vegetarians could eat both cheese options so taramasalata is neither here nor there. Which is kind of Louise's point anyway. 'All right. We'll do ham and salad, cheese and pickle, cheese and tomato *and* taramasalata.'

'Great.' Louise scribbles in her notebook. 'Mixture of granary and farmhouse white, sixty more rounds than last year. Settled.'

'And I'll do the cakes as usual, shall I?'

'Oh. Well yes. Of course.' Louise looks up, momentarily scandalised: even her brain couldn't come up with the idea that *someone else* might 'Do The Cakes'.

'Your cakes are half the reason people come to the Cricket Tea. They're a sort of tradition now.'

'Hardly that, Louise.' Samantha turns away to refill the kettle and to hide the pleasure that Louise's compliment gives her. But she knows it's true. Her lemon sandwich, her chocolate gâteau, her coffee and walnut cake, her fruit loaf, her Swiss roll and Battenburg – they compensate for rain, they celebrate sunshine, her cakes are the very soul of the whole event. They crown the tea table in the pavilion; they melt in the mouths of the righteous members of the PTFA, like manna. They are the Host, the Body and Blood of the English Family Summer.

'More tea, Louise?'

'I'd love to, but it's Barney's swimming lesson and I didn't bring the "you-know-whats".' Barney is Louise's six-year-old son. He is charming and bright, a friend to both Tony and Joe, but he rules Louise's life like a fascist dictator. The 'you-know-whats' are the only brand of biscuit that Barney will eat. Without them to fuel his stroke he might as well puncture his own arm bands. And with Barney's obsession with success in general, and swimming in particular, Louise might as well slit her own throat. This is why she refuses tea. She must drive across the centre of town to buy 'you-know-whats' before picking Barney up from school. But before Louise can pick up her shiny angular handbag, Samantha is up on her little kitchen steps, reaching for a yellow tin, stored on top of the units.

'I've got some "you-know-whats". I got them when Barney came here after school. There's a whole lot here unopened.' Samantha hands the flat purple and white packet to Louise.

'Angie! You are a Saint! There's only one place you can get them!'

'Mmm. I know. The Post Office Stores on Coronation Road.'

Louise is speechless with gratitude and admiration; she can only beam and wrap her legs into a reef knot again.

Wednesdays for Samantha can be difficult. No matter how tightly she plans to pack her day, there is often some unexpected hole in her schedule. She tries to keep some chores in reserve, something meaty and absorbing like a cupboard to tidy, but it's not always possible. So sometimes she can find herself with nothing to do. At times like that she's reduced to re-ironing sheets, or changing the labels on the frozen food.

Today it looked as if everything was conspiring against her. First Tony persuaded Joe to come with him to check on Lazarus, and have breakfast at number thirteen. They got themselves dressed and disappeared *with Dale's blessing* whilst she was in the shower. So there was no need to fuss over their clothes, coax them to eat their vitamin pills and drink their juice. She did Dale a cooked breakfast to make up for some of the loss of tasks, but then he began to dismantle her day too!

'I'll drop the boys at school,' he said over his fried egg. 'It's on my way. I've got to go to a couple of reclamation places the other side of Stroud. I'll be finished there by twelve so I can do the shopping, pick them up after school and take them to swimming too.'

Dale had just emptied most of her day. She'd done so much housework waiting for him last night that there was nothing to fill it with. Samantha was irritated, but she smiled calmly and refilled his tea cup. 'That's OK – I'll do the school run, and I'm all set to do the shopping and take them to swimming lessons. You just get straight on with what you need to do.'

'No, I want to do it. I'll be away again for the next three nights. I want to see them. And it's your day off. Relax!'

He patted her bottom gently but she snatched herself away. 'That's not the point of my day off.' She pulled his breakfast plate away from him. 'It's not *for* relaxing. Wednesdays are for doing the food shop, catching up with housework, so I don't have to do it at weekends.'

'OK. No need to get cross. I'm just giving you more time for housework then.'

Samantha knew she'd lost. Her only chance of restoring her itinerary lay in trying to get Dale to storm off without the boys. But he'd grown so placid that it was almost impossible to manipulate him in that way any more. Worth a try all the same. She tutted as she piled up the plates. 'You've left your fried bread again. I don't know why I bother!'

'Neither do I really.' Dale sipped his tea unruffled. 'I've never liked fried bread, I've never eaten it, but you always cook it. It's a mystery. Some kind of ritual?' This was where Tony got his ice-cold response to Joe's temper.

Samantha found herself getting hot-faced in spite of her plan. 'No. It's called a Full English Breakfast – bacon, eggs, mushrooms and fried bread. That's what. It's not a Full English Breakfast without the bread!'

'So what?' Dale shrugged. 'What does that matter?'

It wasn't working. He was oblivious to the way he'd wrecked her day, and it infuriated her. 'It's like pizza without anchovies!' She was almost shouting now, standing frozen, with the plate and its offending bread congealing in the middle.

Dale was just getting more logical. 'But suppose I didn't like anchovies? I'd just leave them.'

Samantha could feel tears wanting to form behind her eyes. What did Dale know about the dangers of dead time? Did he ever wonder why they had a colour-coded label system for everything in the freezer? For a chip of a second Samantha felt she would tell him about vine snakes in the hair, encroaching rainforest and the remembrance of winter fields. She stomped to the sink and yelled over her shoulder instead. 'Yes, but the pizza's still *made* with them.'

Dale followed her as far as the kitchen door. 'Ah! There you are!' he said. 'It *is* a ritual. You don't care if I don't *eat* the fried bread as long as you *cook* it!' He smiled in triumph at his own reasoning. Seeing that smile, Samantha was reminded of the confounding birthday cake, and Dale showing through his layer of masonry dust. It wasn't his fault that he didn't understand her world. She'd made it that way. So she smiled back through the holes in the canvas and wondered how to fill the spare hours of the day.

Dale turned to find his keys and leave. 'Post's come!' he called from the hall. 'I'll take it – looks like work stuff. I'm getting the boys. Have a nice day off.'

So it could have been a very tricky Wednesday. Louise wasn't due to arrive until ten, but by nine all the breakfast things were cleared and Samantha was outside in the garden, forlornly searching the boundary with number nine for overnight shoots to snip. She was wondering if Dale would consider it too strange to completely replant her four little beds, when the phone went. She dived inside.

'Oh, thank God you there!' It was her mother-in-law.

'What's the matter, Maria?'

'Marcella phoned a sickie.' Marcella was Maria's newest

assistant. She was a massive, handsome bull of a girl, a great Titian beauty in skin-tight jeans who could shift twenty-kilo crates of olives with a single jewelled pinkie. Samantha suspected that she had been chosen, at least in part, for the entertaining contrast she provided to Maria's avian proportions. She also had a loud and lively grasp of young persons' vernacular, which Maria was beginning to pick up.

'She says that *no way* she gonna make it in 'ere today. I have a big delivery coming, also big *big* lunch party, antipasto order to get out . . .' Maria trailed off, she wasn't good at asking for things. She couldn't even accept a direct offer of help, she needed to be persuaded. Dale would never collude with Maria's inability to admit any sort of defeat. He drove her to ask, and ask nicely. If Maria had complained of Marcella's absence to him, he would simply have said, 'Bad luck, Ma. I can't think how you'll manage alone.' But Samantha could always see Maria young, skinny and exotic with her little son clinging to her hand. A foreigner with a bastard child in mealy-mouthed 60s Bristol: only her stubborn self-reliance had kept her alive. So Samantha was happy to press her assistance on Maria, especially when the alternative was ironing tea cloths.

'Would you like me to help?'

'Oh! But it's your day off! No, no, no.'

'I'm not doing anything, Maria. Really.'

'Well. I don't know. You have a job, you have the boys and Dale. It's a lot you know. You should rest.'

'I hate resting. I'd love to help.'

'Well. Well.' Maria sighed hugely. 'OK. I guess, if you sure. Really sure.'

'Yes I'm sure. But I'll have to go about two.'

'Nnnah. Oh. That's not so good. But OK. I can manage around that.'

'I'm sorry I can't stay longer, Maria.'

'No. No, that's OK.'

By the time Samantha had phoned Louise to move their

meeting to the afternoon, a cab was waiting to take her to Tav's. Maria must have ordered it before she rang.

Tavolino Verde has become an institution for the middle-class community that surrounds it. If you know about 'Tavs', then you are one of the club. Your preferences in newspapers, books, films, clothes, children, furnishings and partners can be predicted to be within a certain range of liberal acceptability. Tavs is part of the social landscape, and 'having a Tav' has a meaning for all age groups. On a hot summer day, Mummies, home from the office, promise their kids 'a Tav' on the way home. They pull up in their Volvo estates and whilst the children eat *tartufo negro*, *gelato grosso*, or little pots of *tiramisu*, their mothers chat to Maria, and buy a 'Tav' dinner: *canaroli*, saffron, Parmesan. On Saturday mornings Dads are dispatched for 'a Tav' for lunch: they shuffle in, blurred and uncombed, to buy *ciabatta* and *focaccia*, Ascolane olives, *soppressata*, *mortadella*, *prosciutto*. Children buy 'Tavs' with their pocket money – a *gelato* in summer, a slice of *panettone* or a Florentine in winter. Lovesick fifteen year olds treat their objects of desire to 'a Tav' – a box of dark chocolates, or a mozzarella sandwich to share on the bus into town.

Tavs has been there for so long, that it has spun its own special myths: *ratafias* bought from Tavs are reputed to be especially accurate at predicting the sex of babies. A lighted wrapper floating to touch the ceiling means the birth of a boy, one that turns to a tissue of carbon and flutters down before it's over the candlesticks, a girl. So, for as long as most people can remember, Tavs' ratafias have been the present to give a newly pregnant woman. Tavs' chocolate *gelato* is said to be a sure-fire aphro-disiac, so synonymous with sex that 'chocky Tav' has become local slang replacing other nastier words like 'shag' or 'fuck'.

More generally Tavs has come to be associated with all things pleasant, celebratory and romantic. A perfect holiday, a roman-tic day out, a well-struck deal, a successful examination paper would all be described by local residents as 'good as a Tav' or even 'better than a Tav sandwich'. In spite of the class profile of its customers, to shop at Tavs is about more than showing that you are one of the 'club'. Tavs is the living embodiment of the axiom that the way to any human being's heart is through their stomach. All of which is very good for business.

For an establishment with such a big place in the local psyche, Tavolino's is tiny, squeezed between an estate agent's and an ironmonger's. But Maria has made sure that she makes the most of the small available space. For some years now the whole of the shop front has been plate glass, from floor to ceiling, with a glass door at one side. The interior is painted the colour of double cream, and lit so that no corner escapes a bright pearly glow. From outside you can see everything, both sides of the counter, and all the goods. It looks like a particularly enticing theatre set, a world of homely magic which you can join just by stepping through the almost invisible door. The dramatic appearance is added to by the particularly wide pavement in front of the shop, which acts like an empty downstage, or perhaps a wide frame for a perfect picture. There is no logo on the plate glass, only a symbol on the door the size of a ciabatta roll: the outline of the little green picnic table which was Maria's very first 'counter' on her stall in St Nicholas market thirty-five years ago.

As she steps out of the cab Samantha can see Finnian wrestling with a large wicker basket full of anchovy jars at the front of the shop. His sleeves are rolled up above the elbows, exposing his pale arms, and his hair is sticking to his forehead. Finnian has been Maria's manager for years. He is an essential part of the Tav stage set, as much of a fixture now as Maria herself. He is tall, soft and white like dough, without being fat. He has dark red hair, as thick and curly now in his thirties as it was when he came to Maria, a forlorn university drop-out. He has the lilting remnants of a Cork accent, in spite of the fact that since he left at sixteen he's never been back: it wasn't, he says, 'a good place to be queer in'.

Maria, in an orange shirt-waister and matching shoes, is arranging the morning's bread delivery at the far end of the shop. Samantha can see by the way they don't look at each other that they've already had a row this morning. They are both, separately, very pleased to see her, but the air between them is frosted like a still day in Greenland.

Maria calls, 'I do the bread. I be there, just minute OK?'

'Hi,' says Finnian, unfolding over the anchovies to lean and kiss her on both cheeks. 'Glad you could come.' He rolls his eyes and pinches in his nostrils. 'You know what she's like when she gets in a paddy.'

'Shall I help with this basket?'

'No, I'll manage. Could you finish the display cabinet for me, and serve if anyone comes in.'

'Fine!'

Samantha knows the routine in Tavs quite well. Over the years there have been other small crises in Maria's staffing arrangements and Samantha has always been happy to fill in. And of course Samantha came to Tavs after leaving Julie's. Maria insisted on it as soon as she began going out with Dale.

'In that cake shoppe,' she said, 'you will learn nothing. With me, you learn all Italian food. Everything. Eee-ver-ry-thing. *And* I will pay you more.'

It was a very attractive offer. Samantha was beginning to feel that if Julie told her the details of one more night of passion ('I dunno, girl, they says size don't matter but that's 'cos they've never 'ad a biggun') she would bury her head in the margarine tub. But working at Maria's might require the filling in of forms, the signing of names so Samantha feigned reluctance.

'That's so kind of you, Mrs Cassinari, but I don't know . . .'

'Look. Come and try. See if you like it. I pay you cash, eh? No commitment.'

The following Monday Samantha had got off the bus at the

stop just across the street from Tavs. It was a dark and greasy winter morning and the little deli stood out like a candle in a cave. Back then, the shop front was only partly glazed but still, every detail inside was visible. The cars steamed slowly in their rush-hour queues, and the bright and busy interior of Tavolino Verde was an irresistible draw to every eye. Julie's cake shop had been hidden in its narrow dark street, with the cars racing past too close to the murky window to notice anything. She'd felt safe in Julie's. But here? Who could predict what eyes might look out from this endless procession of traffic? For five minutes she stood watching the figures of Maria and Finnian moving inside, deciding whether to catch the next bus home. But what could she say to Dale? This could be, she told herself, a kind of double bluff. Who would think of looking for her in a place as public as a floodlit billboard? She jumped the puddles and crossed the wide pavement to her new job.

It was Finnian who taught her 'ev-er-ree-thing'. When Maria wasn't performing for her customers she was reorganising the stock rooms or crooning over the phone in Italian to some favoured supplier. Finnian spent the quiet times in the shop teaching Samantha how to think about food. He had all the fervour of the convert and had even learnt Italian at evening class; when he said *bresaola*, or *spaghettini* it sounded more authentic than Maria's pronunciation.

'Soda bread and Guinness,' he told her early on in her apprenticeship, 'you know I'm sure they're lovely and all. But I was raised on the chips and the vinegar from the shop next door so I thought the Saints had taken me the day I ate my first proper antipasto. Jeezus. First communion or what?'

His enthusiasm was infectious and his desire to share it unstoppable. He made her taste, smell, look and form opinions about what she liked and didn't like. He made her think about everything she did.

'Well, that's a nice arrangement of tins you have there. Why did you put the artichoke hearts at the bottom?'

'I know there's *porcini* in it, but what else?'

'Which balsamic's the older then, d'you think?'

He required her total concentration. She gave it at first because it distracted her from the eyes looking out from the crawling cars. But soon, learning the difference between '*cotto*' and '*prosciutto*', between '*toscano*' and '*sardo*', began to make her feel safe again. Like a caddis larva collecting sand grains for its case, she gathered the information Finnian gave her. Cheeses, hams, salamis, chocolates, pastas and breads encrusted her new persona along with Dale and his visions in stone and brick. The more she accumulated the more protected she felt.

All Finnian wanted of her was to fill her up with knowledge. It felt comfortable, sweetly familiar to be someone's star pupil again. Samantha's small life hadn't included a gay man. But she knew he was some human cocktail that she'd never encountered before, different from the gross divisions of humanity as 'men' and 'women'. There was a quickness, a fluidity about him, the way he spoke and laughed that didn't match the big soft body and the ginger stubble. He made her think of the poplar trees in her parents' garden, that shimmered, green then white in every breath of wind. She adored him.

Yet with customers she noticed, he was different. He chatted in the same engaging way, but the chat was padded with empty enquiries. 'What was the forecast for tomorrow? How did they plan to use the *farfalle*? Where did they get such a lovely jersey?' It was weeks before she realised how Finnian too was protecting himself. It was the most valuable thing she learnt from him – that the best camouflage is to reflect the image of the observer. She thought of the mirrored bellies of fish, their silvered scales making them disappear against the bright surface. Pretty soon she'd got the trick too.

'Such a brilliant jacket!' she'd chirp. 'How do you plan to use the buffalo mozzarella?'

She could look any customer in the eye and know that they'd never really see her.

Samantha had always been a good pupil, clever and quick. By the time she and Dale were married there were only a few times a week when Finnian could show her something new. This was just as well because when Dale had come home and told Maria he'd got wed on some remote beach she'd gone to Italy for a month in a fit of pique. Samantha and Finnian were such a good team that they could run things comfortably without her. But with no need to cram Samantha with more knowledge, or cope with Maria's imperatives and crises, Finnian found a new sort of question to ask.

'So, where were you born then?' he said one sleepy Tuesday morning.

Samantha woke up fast. 'Suffolk.'

'Ah! A country girl then.'

'Yes.'

'Are your family farmers?'

'No. They're dead.'

'Oh, I'm sorry, I had no idea.' That was as far as eighty percent of people ever got – gagged by their own embarrassment at uncovering two dead bodies in an ordinary conversation. Even Dale hadn't got a lot further. But Finnian had survived being called an abomination by his own mother, so death was a breeze.

'No, actually, I tell a lie there. I did know, because I remember Maria saying ages ago that you were an orphan. You know her and her melodrama. When did they pass on?'

'When I was little. I grew up in care.'

'In care. Huh, I bet that's a bloody euphemism and no mistake. What was it like?'

Finnian was now part of a tiny minority prepared to brave the possibility of being confronted with another person's pain. People only went beyond this point to find a convenient place to turn around; all she had to do was provide it.

'Just like you'd imagine, really.'

'I don't have that kind of imagination. Were you in home or what? Foster parents?' Finnian wasn't going to turn round. He needed the ultimate stop sign, the sight of a little red blood on a good solid stone wall.

'Look, I don't want to be rude or unkind, but I don't talk about it. Not to anyone. Not Dale even.' She'd never used such a tone with him before. All he'd seen of her had been the bright but inexperienced young woman, eager to learn, overcoming an innate shyness. It was like a hamster snarling.

'Well, I respect that of course.' He paused for a moment then spoke again, 'But you know it's not a good thing, to keep anything locked in the closet. Believe me, I know!' He looked at her so straight that not even a shoal of mirrored fish could have deflected his glance.

Maria came back with a crate of olives 'the size of Socrates' testicles', no pique and an enthusiasm for her new daughter-in-law. But even with Maria's fussing there were still too many opportunities for Finnian to go on asking questions. Samantha watched him sadly as he served, and knew that Tavs was just too risky a place to work any more. Morning sickness gave her the escape she needed. She didn't even have to make the decision herself. Dale found her throwing up before work one day and was overcome with protective instincts. He rang Maria on the spot and told her that his pregnant wife was not going to be in that morning or any other.

'Does this mean we can eat something English now?' he joked as he made her a slice of dry toast and tucked her back in bed.

She never went back to Tavs permanently because, with two of Maria's grandsons to raise, she couldn't commit herself to working for Dale's family business.

'I don't mind letting a supermarket down,' she told Maria, 'but if one of the boys is ill and I have to be at home, I'd hate to leave *Family* in the lurch.'

*

'So nice you come. On your day off too!' Maria is on tip-toe to embrace Samantha. She holds her by the shoulders for a moment so that Samantha can smell her hair spray, her perfume and the fabric conditioner that Judy her cleaning lady has washed the orange dress in. Maria whispers into her ear, 'You make Finnian better temper. He is never so nice these days as when you worked here.' Then releasing her, announces, 'That Finnian, he is getting to be a grumpy old queen!' She sends her most Italian film-star smile down the counter to him; he tosses his head and grins.

Turning away in mock outrage he calls back, 'You are a dried-up old has-been, Maria, and the Virgin herself wouldn't look at you. So it's a blessing I'm here to look after you.' The air thaws, a Technicolor cartoon spring rushes its tendrils all over the shop just as the first customers of the day come in. With six years of motherhood to shield her Samantha is very pleased to be back in Tavs.

It has been an unexpectedly lovely day with not a single spare moment since the morning in the garden. Tavs was busy providing the district with impromptu picnics, tennis suppers and toddler treats. The only time that Samantha and Finnian had to chat was used up in discussing the colour scheme in the cloakroom of Finnian's new house.

'I don't know. Really. If I've had one of those little tester pots I've had twenty. Robert wanted a really OTT thing. You know, purple damask and gold taps. But he's totally lost interest now. That man has the attention span of a gnat when it comes to decor! But I think "restful" you know? Lavender, pale lemon. What d'you think, Ange?'

With Louise's assertion that she should once again provide the cakes for the cricketers' tea, Samantha's next three Dale-less evenings are to be filled with baking and icing. At four o'clock, with Dale and the boys not due back for an hour a whole sixty minutes of empty space had opened up in front of her. But even that got filled. Felicity from number nine turned up on Samantha's doorstep not two minutes after Louise's departure. She was as usual perfect – a tailored suit, a smooth chignon, quietly expensive jewellery. Hard to imagine that this was the woman whose domestic party trick was throwing TVs through closed bedroom windows.

'Could I possibly just come in for a minute?' she said in a very small voice. She'd appeared like this before to borrow sugar, tea, coffee, staying for a minute of empty pleasantries then going back. Usually it happened moments after the shouting had subsided. But Keith wasn't home from work yet and everything had been quiet. She was deathly pale, tricky for a woman with skin the colour of damsons. She stepped into the hall delicate as a doe, and spoke in the same small trembling voice, 'I don't suppose you've got any dried sheets of lasagna have you? I think I'd like to make Keith his favourite meal.' She burst into tears. Samantha led her into the sitting room, made her drink some sweet tea and dabbed her eyes with cold water. Felicity stopped crying and adjusted the jacket of her suit and smiled. 'I'm all right. Just a silly minute.'

It was clear she wasn't going to offer any sort of explanation. 'Thank you, Angela,' she said. 'I'm sure I can trust you not to mention this to anyone. I don't want everyone in the street knowing my private life.' It was touching the way Felicity failed to realise that arguments at eighty decibels with open windows tend to render the private somewhat public. But Samantha reassured her and gave her a whole home-made lasagna from the freezer to take next door.

'You can come round any time you want, Felicity,' she told her.

Felicity would, she felt, be filling more odd corners of her time in the future.

So now it is ten to five. Still quite hot and gold outside. A chicken casserole is in Samantha's oven and the rice to go with it is measured out ready to cook at the last minute. Samantha puts a lick of lipstick on her straight determined mouth, a shade that tones perfectly with her cotton shift. She smiles briefly at the image in the hall mirror as she leaves. She'll walk to the corner of the street to meet Dale and the boys as they turn down the road to home. But as she steps out through the front door, Dale's car draws up to the kerb. He turns to speak to the boys and for a moment the three of them don't see Samantha. They are so alike now with their hair all wet and the pink scrubbed look from the swimming pool showers still on them. She is filled with a rush of passion for them all, a feeling unfettered and unplanned. This, *this* is her true life. This is the flowering fruiting apple tree, spreading into the light, the root stock to which it was once grafted, far below, buried safe under the brown earth.

The boys tumble out of the back seat and chase up the path and into the house.

'Am I forgiven for not eating fried bread?' says Dale as he locks the car.

'Yes, Dale. I won't even make it any more.'

They smile at each other as close to setting aside their portraits as they have been for quite a while. Then Dale reaches into the back pocket of his baggy jeans. 'There was this amongst the mail I took this morning. I thought it might be a PTFA thing. I know they give your address for all the committee members sometimes, yeah?'

He gives her a stiff brown envelope. Long and thin, an old-fashioned shape from the days of quarto paper and sealing wax. The address has been typed but the name written by hand. The good formal copperplate is as easy to read as any printed typeface, but Angela Cassinari stares at it for a long time whilst her blood screams round her head.

'Samantha Powell' it reads.

'Samantha Powell' it still reads.

'Coming in, love?' says Dale from the doorstep.

'Yeah. Yeah.'

'You OK?'

'Yeah. Just wondering who she might be.'

4

At two a.m. consciousness is a fish out of water, flapping on the surface of the great wild continent of the unconscious. Awake at two, you encounter a world as impervious to conventional logic as sub-atomic physics is to Newtonian theory. There are way more than three dimensions in your dreams and fantasies. Elephantine shapes of long-lost fears and unexpressed desires lumber down the shadows, and multicoloured fogs of memory roll in from the deep ocean of a zillion brain cells. Behind the little world of the daylight will is a living thicket where everything tangles together. Gripewater, dead bodies, playground bullies, baked beans, footballs, sand, your lover's skin, and the blue alien from last night's TV all meld into one insane cocktail. At two a.m. time goes anything but forward, the past and the future sit down like lambs and lions. At two a.m. we have nothing to protect us from the universe. It is the hour of least resistance, to birth, to death, to ourselves.

So at two twenty this morning Samantha is lowering herself down the stairs in her cream rose-print pyjamas and matching wrap. She is leaning her weight heavily on the smooth banister to avoid the creaky treads. No one would know if she switched on the light in the hall but the dark seems safer, so she feels her way to the living-room door.

A blade of orange street light is slicing between the imperfectly drawn curtains there. Falling into the black, it cuts a thin sector of the room from the huge darkness. But without the context of their whole selves, the lighted slithers of objects are strange and disembodied. The sofa is represented by a textured stripe, and the rug is reduced to a sequence of tone patches that couldn't be a pattern. In the polish of the mahogany table, the light blurs as if the wood had become molten. At one edge of this pool of brightness a pair of china paws show, apparently preparing to paddle. At the other is the long thin envelope. Only two of its edges show and the surface that stretches between them is just a faint bloom on the skin of darkness.

All evening and half the night Samantha has resisted the call of that envelope, pushing it down with tasks and busyness. She prepared perfect rice, 'every grain fluffy and separate' just like the adverts; helped Dale to bath the boys and made bubble beards and hairstyles; sat in the garden with a glass of wine and listened to Dale talk about the restoration of cornices and ceiling roses. She even managed a sort of sleep, with her eyes wrenched shut and her mind burrowing down out of the way. But at two she woke to find all the lurid possibilities that the envelope and its copperplate name had conjured, free, dancing round the bed like Dervish bears.

So now she is sitting on her Castle-clothed Knole sofa staring at the envelope's indistinct outline and trying to be calm. She tells herself that after so long she is safe. That whatever it contains can't matter. That it could stay unopened until morning or even for ever. It could be thrown away still sealed. She imagines the sound of the flip-top bin swallowing the envelope along with dregs of soggy cereal and spent tea bags. But even from the bottom of a landfill site she feels that it would glow like something radioactive, calling her. Against her will she sees a seagull on the rubbish tip picking amongst bin bags that are split like pigs' guts in an abattoir; the bird spears the envelope oddly with its beak and flies back towards Lancaster Road.

Samantha switches on the brass lamp with the dull rose shade. The heartless stripe from the street light dissolves. The room is warm, full of her and her acquired history. The envelope is surely just a practical problem. It can be assessed and resolved. She reaches for it and rips it open, flinching only a little at the loud tearing sound.

Like the envelope, the writing paper and the words are oddly archaic. Samantha reads them several times before they stop their jump and jumble, and settle into a meaning. The letter is not from any relative, nor the police, so the very worst has not happened. Something stranger than 'worst'. It is a solicitor's letter from the executors of the 'late Lawrence Spence'. The *late* Lawrence.

'The *late* Lawrence Spence desired that the house, gardens and glasshouse of Lime House be made over into your name.'

So much information in so few words. So many layers of meaning, and only the first of those layers is that Lawrence is dead, and has left her his house. Samantha looks up and around the room searching for something to steady herself – the china dog, the patterned rug, the gilt-framed mirror. But her lips are whispering on their own, 'The late Lawrence Spence. The late Lawrence Spence. Lawrence. Lawrence is dead.' It is after all still the hour of least resistance, and Lawrence always was hard to resist.

Sam had met Lawrence on a Sunday in April. As usual on a Sunday she had spent most of the day shut in her room doing homework. That Sunday it had been mostly chemistry. She always felt that there was really only just so much organic chemistry that a person could be expected to absorb in one sitting without having a sense-of-humour bypass. She enjoyed the way chemical sub-units fitted together like so many poppet beads but it was the naming that always made her giggle. 2–3-hydroxymethyl benzoate, 5–7-transtoluene-amyl-arsinate. Supposing Miss Lock the cookery teacher decided to adopt a similar system? Meringues would become tri-albumin-di-sucrose-floccate-oxide, or cakes might be di-ova-tetra-sucrose-farina-trans-marginate. Chemistry irritated her with its lack of imagination, and with its teacher Mr Lewis. He tucked his shirt into his knickers and never realised that pupils took bets on how much of his multicoloured Y-fronts would show above the waistband of his trousers. By five or six that day the daft names and the entertaining underwear had finally eroded her concentration. It was a gorgeous afternoon anyway.

'Going for walk. Taking the dog,' she called to whoever might listen, as she went out. Dad at least knew she was going, because she could hear him roaring from the den about slamming glass doors. Just like he always did.

Bracken bounced up the hill ahead of her, pushing his flat nose into the banks of new grass and making a 'wuuff' sound as he tried to sniff out baby rabbits. At the village sign she stopped and peered over the edge of the verge. Yep. There they were, the first cowslips of the year spangling the grass on the south-facing side of the ditch. Up to Lords Wood then. With this mild weather the first oxslips could be out. She knew that other people went to Lords to look at their botanical celebrity but the oxys, as she called them to herself, still felt like hers. A bit like having the Koh-i-noor diamond stashed away for your own private gloating session perhaps. Their clusters of yellow trumpets falling to one side of the stalk looked to Sam like clusters of shy kisses made solid, and turning modestly away. She knew just where to look for the earliest blooming plants because she mapped them for an O level biology project. But today she would just sit and look, drink in their odd loveliness and take it home to sustain her against her Granny Pearl's denture grinding and the thought of Mr Lewis' Y-fronts.

She and the dog, Bracken, set off down the green lane, the unmade cart track between the wide fields of winter wheat and barley. The landscape was deserted. Only the farmers and their vehicles came down here and then only on a weekday unless it was harvest time. Late on this bright spring Sunday the fields were empty. They made Sam think of huge faces turned up to the sky, calm and open. The ground was still wet enough to hold clear puddles in the ruts, tiny crystal worlds with silken mud at the bottom. Bracken's feet made a strange rapid plopping sound as he streaked past her, flexing his spine like a cheetah, full of the joy of speed. Of course he was a guarantee that they wouldn't see any birds. He disturbed everything. Only the skylarks were unperturbed, still singing in the slanting afternoon light. Tens of them. Twenties. Hundreds. Thousands perhaps, suspended fluttering, falling, climbing, and singing, singing, singing. Sam imagined an invisible net of song, connecting all the skylarks in the air at one time, a sort of magic meshwork stretching above the whole county. The light burned their tiny dots of bodies into the blue, so that it seemed that the sky itself was singing.

Sam turned left towards the wood, where the track widened as if it were an empty dance floor the moment before the band started to play. She called to the dog and looked back over the field for him. He wasn't in sight. Instead, out in the shimmering sea of green, four hares were boxing. First one pair then another rose from the wheat and battered with their front paws, heads thrown back. The sun was low enough to shine through the blades of wheat and the light outlined the hares' fur and accentuated the length of their ears. They moved with a quickness and abandon that made Sam's throat catch at the sight of such wildness.

Suddenly the dog burst between them scattering their chestnut backs helter skelter in all directions. One in a panic took off across the field towards her, passing close enough to the over-exited boxer to make him believe he had a chance to catch it. Both the hare and her dog were gone, over the track and across the next field before Sam could draw breath and call Bracken to heel. Turning her back on the wood and its oxslips she stomped after them, swearing.

She crossed three fields and from the top of the last watched Bracken's rear end disappearing into a thicket of trees surrounding a large house. She was on unfamiliar territory. Her walks always took her to Lords Wood, then home again. What road was that house on? She couldn't think, she just hustled down the hill furious that the dog had ruined her plans.

The thicket surrounded a high brick wall, crumbled in one place where Bracken must have gone through. The light was going fast now and everything below on the other side was dark, a black tangle of who-knew-what vicious brambles. But she was still angry enough to be foolish, so she jumped. It was a drop of less than four feet as the ground was built up on the other side of the wall.

Sam moved through the small trees still making for the house. The dog would no doubt be following his nose to the kitchen having lost the hare. From what she'd seen from the hilltop, she'd expected the dense thicket of overgrowth to go almost to the front door. But as she walked, the tangled chaos gave way to a subtle order as wilderness changed quietly to garden. The scrubby saplings were replaced by large trees, all vibrantly healthy and well shaped, perfectly spaced in a simulation of natural colonisation. Spring flowers, in pools and arcs and garlands of colour, scattered across the grass. A special stillness drew her on as she forgot all about the missing dog.

She came to a band of whitebeams coming into first leaf, with their pale buds lifted up like church candles. They dotted the shadowy air all around her, and glowing in the dusk below them were oxslips, fifty or more all in full bloom. The harmony of the whitebeam shoots and the oxslips was flawless, artifice made into a perfected version of the natural. Beyond the white-beam candles was the velvety emerald of a lawn. And around the lawn were tree ferns, big ones five feet high. Tree ferns! The soul and symbol of the tropics, of jungles and steamy heat, of bird sounds like chinking bottles and butterflies as big as dinner plates. Tree ferns were a shorthand for all the places Sam wanted to go and everything she wanted to do. Drawn like a hypnotist's patsy she walked out on to the lawn towards them. The trunks were still partially swathed in jackets of straw to protect them from the cold and drying winter winds, and last year's fronds dangled sadly from the top of the trunk. But nestling at the base of the old fronds were the silky heads of the new, curled croziers covered in silvery hairs. They looked as vulnerable as a foetus, and Sam reached out to touch with featherlight gentleness.

'So, another fan of *Dicksonia antarctica*?' A voice straight out of her mum's favourite TV dramas about nineteenth-century toffs spoke behind her. Sam snatched her extended hand back to her side and almost screamed. Like the Merchant in *Beauty and the Beast*, lost in the admiration of the garden she had forgotten entirely about its owner. Madly, she imagined he'd demand to be given the first thing she met on her return to her home. She had a brief, glorious image of herself wheeling Granny Pearl across the fields in a barrow. But not even a lonely Beast would stick more than a week of all the demands for tea, cake and the right sort of bacon. And here he was, 'The Beast', walking towards her, over the velvet grass. It was too late to run, or think of excuses.

'I'm sorry,' was all she could manage to say in her best and most precise speech, saved for formal occasions when the school camouflage of dropped 'aitches' and Suffolk burr were not required.

'Why? What have you done?' He was right next to her now. Smiling, apparently relaxed in the presence of this intruder on his property. He didn't look like a Beast. He didn't look much like anything she was used to. He wasn't a young man, like stringy Mr Volta the trainee PE teacher, or like fat Darryl who helped Mr Tofts do the roof on the garage last summer. He wasn't middle aged in the way dads were middle aged. He didn't have the used-up skinniness of Christine's dad, nor the look of a bag where everything had dropped to the bottom like her own father. His body had a tightness about it, a springiness that reminded Sam of a whippy stick. He certainly wasn't old, but then he did have a lot of grey in his dark hair. Not bald though. His clothes were a puzzle too. Faded blue jeans but worn with a crisp formal-looking shirt, white, with a button-down collar and neatly pressed. His shoes caught her eye. Men's shoes in her experience were like boats, big and awkward even when polished. But these shoes were neat and small. They seemed to hug his feet with only just enough leather to encase them adequately as if any superfluous sole or upper was vulgar in some way. He was, she decided, exotic, like the tree ferns, a non-native species.

'Um, nothing. I mean, I'm sorry I came into your garden.'

'Are you?' He had raised an eyebrow in disapproval. It moved up over the domed forehead like a small piece of perfectly oiled machinery. 'You didn't *look* sorry a minute ago. You looked quite pleased with my *Dicksonias*.' His tone suggested some sort of joke, but Sam didn't understand what it might be, it was too hard to read his languid upper class pronunciation. She smiled anyway, seeing that he wasn't really angry.

'I *love* tree ferns.' Her enthusiasm usually charmed adults, especially as she almost invariably knew more about her subject than they did. Her father didn't know a tree fern from a Brussels sprout. 'My dad only grows ordinary things like roses in our garden. Tree ferns are so *tropical* . . .' she gushed.

But the performance hadn't impressed the Beast. He still had one eyebrow raised and he did not smile. 'Well, no actually not all *so tropical*,' he said rather irritably. 'These are *Dicksonia antarctica* from a perfectly temperate region. They don't even mind the East Anglian frosts. What they don't like is drought. High rainfall is the key thing with tree ferns really. These are misted with water all through the summer.'

Sam could feel the blush rising up her throat. 'Oh,' she said trying to cover her ignorance. 'They aren't a species I'm familiar with.'

But the Beast was not going to let her off the hook. He looked at her with his peat black eyes and said, 'Really? Strange, as they're certainly the commonest form in cultivation.'

She gave up fighting the blush and studied her feet. There was a small silence.

'I'm being ungracious. You're quite right of course, they are synonymous with many tropical habitats. So tell me, why are you so keen on the tropics?'

'I'm going to be a biologist *when I grow up*—' She blushed again. Damn. At seventeen she had to get out of that phrase! She corrected herself and stood up straighter trying to regain some dignity. 'I mean, when I leave school and university.'

'Really? What sort of biologist? That's a bit general. You can call yourself a biologist these days if all you know about is the inside of a hamster's testicle.'

She grinned in surprise at him. She had never heard an adult speak like that. Brave again she trotted out her little party piece, her potted plan for the future. 'I'm going to study rainforest. Tropical rainforest. Probably Central America, Costa Rica perhaps. The plants mainly, but the ecological interaction between plants and animals I find interesting too.'

He threw back his head and laughed. The big adam's apple moved in the strong throat and the straight dark hair with its flecks of white fell away from his head a little making him look for a moment very young. But Sam was insulted, hot with anger all over again. She wasn't used to this response to her earnest expression of her life's dreams. Most adults were impressed into silence by Central America, let alone 'ecological interactions' and the pompous construction 'I find interesting'.

'It's not funny. It's very important. We're losing species faster than we can catalogue them!' She wanted to turn on her heel and flounce away. But you can't flounce through a birch thicket and over a brick wall.

'No, no.' He recovered himself and held up his palms in a gesture of apology. 'I'm not laughing at you at all. I think it's wonderful. Marvellous. An admirable ambition. I'd like to have done something similar myself. It's just that all the young women I've ever known have been more interested in silk underwear and lipstick than in tropical rainforest. Forgive me, I didn't mean to be disrespectful.' He stretched out his right hand and Samantha stared at it stupidly. No one she knew shook hands. She'd seen her father do it once with a chap from work, and the French assistant did it with the other teachers. Awkwardly she stretched out and grasped his hand firmly, determined not to seem like the limp sort of 'girl' who would trade a wild kapok tree for a pair of French knickers.

'I'm Samantha Powell,' she said, taking care to look straight into the black hole eyes.

'Pleased to meet you, Miss Powell. I'm Lawrence Spence. You have met a fellow enthusiast, Miss Powell. Plants are my passion. I have quite a selection of truly tropical species that I grow under glass. Would you like to see my conservatory?'

Lawrence's hand, light as a leaf, held on to her as he waited for her reply. Samantha hesitated, feeling herself on the edge of something, at some subtle transition point like the one between thicket and garden. Then the dog started up an unmistakable barrage of loud barking somewhere close by, and she drew her hand away.

'That's my dog,' she said. 'He ran in here and I followed him.'

'Sounds as if he has cornered a squirrel.'

Lawrence walked her to his gate with Bracken restrained on a lead he had provided. He stopped between the two stone pillars, as if there were some invisible barrier that barred his way. 'I won't come further than this if you don't mind, I've business to attend to as they say,' he said. 'But do come back sometime. I'd really love you to see the conservatory.' He turned abruptly and marched away, and again Sam was reminded of something robotic and non-human.

As she walked up the lane Samantha wasn't sure she'd take up the invitation. Then she remembered the fine leather lead in her hand, too good not to return to its owner. Lawrence always found a way to make you come back.

There is pale grey showing through the slit in the curtains and seeping around their edge. Outside birds are lisping into wakefulness. The world of up, down and sideways is back on line. Now tomorrow and yesterday are restored to their usual setting. There are bills, and deadlines, advertising and road accidents. If Lawrence was really dead, then she was safer than she'd ever been. She didn't want his house or the hothouse with all its whisperings or the garden. It could all rot, forgotten, lost to the world. She didn't need to give him a thought ever again. All she had to do was push the letter down in the dark along with everything else. Easy.

Above her there is the unmistakable creak that the bed always makes just as Dale is about to get out of it to go to the loo. Samantha flicks off the light and shoves the letter deep into the heart of the settee, well beyond the cushions, to the secret realm of metal springs and bound horsehair.

5

In spite of the drizzle Jack Mullen is leaning against Stayfleurs security door. His small pale frame has its habitual limp greasy look. How does someone so young manage to look quite so used, Samantha wonders. He is sucking a roll-up and exhaling slowly through his nostrils. As usual the smoke has a suspiciously spicy smell. As usual Jack is reluctant to step aside without some attempt at an exchange of words.

'Good morning, Mr Mullen,' Samantha says in her brightest and most business-like tone. Everyone else except George of course calls him Jack. 'Jack the Lad', Claudia quips occasionally, when he's made some mildly flirtatious remark to her on her way past the deli counter to her break. He is possibly the youngest staff member Stayfleurs has ever employed. 'I play golf with his grandfather occasionally,' Mr Geoffrey said on the day he was taken on, 'Jack was at Cambridge you know, before his, er, illness.'

Liz, rather closer to the family than Mr Geoffrey, as they share a cleaning lady, had a different perspective: 'Illness!' she said. 'Smoking pot during lectures on the romantic poets more like.'

'Well! Good morning, Angela Cassinari,' Jack drawls at her but doesn't move, 'and how is the Ice Maiden of Bishopston this morning? Frozen and impervious to my charms as always?' Normally Samantha would just smile sweetly and wait. After ten seconds of being completely ignored he would stand aside, his eyes on her like chewing gum stuck to a pane of glass. But this morning before she has the chance to notice and be surprised at her own irritation, she has spoken.

'*Mr* Mullen, I don't know if it's escaped your attention, but it is actually drizzling. And I am getting wet.'

'Really?' He cannot quite conceal his delight in having, after so long, got a rise out of her. He smiles his slow louche smile at her. 'I'm flattered by that remark, Angela.'

She feels herself blushing like a kid, but she won't look away from his slack face. He throws his stub into the bin by the door and stands aside at last.

'Time for us to *get to it*, I suppose. After you, *Mrs* Cassinari. I always like to get behind a woman.'

In the changing room Samantha tries to tighten all her psychological sphincters. She concentrates hard on the day ahead and what will be required of her. She listens to the pre-work chat around her, waiting for the lull that will allow her to round up her little work force for the start of the day. But all she can hear this morning is the detail of their conversation – small and sharp, it grates under her attention like sand in the eyes.

'Well, I told him at least now we know what it is.' Claudia is tucking her double string of pearls inside the neckline of her blouse. 'One has to be positive.'

'Forgive me, Claudia, but I don't think giving something utterly spurious a name *is* positive.' Mary has got her 'my-husband-was-a-GP-you-know' voice on. But she's chosen the wrong moment for it. The mouse in Claudia's heart turns to tiger when it comes to her sons.

'What *do* you mean, Mary?'

'Well, my husband says that there is really no such thing as ME. It's just depression. Or laziness of course. One of David's partners started with it, you know, last year. In the middle of a very important case what's more. David wouldn't have it *at all*.' Mary smiles indulgently at the thought of her dear son's toughness and resolve. 'Just told him to pull himself together and that was *that*.'

'Are you suggesting that my Richard is depressed or malingering?'

'No. Of *course* not, Claudia. I'm just giving you my perspective on ME. Perhaps Richard has something else instead.'

'Or perhaps all he needs is sex.'

'I beg your pardon, Liz!'

'Sex. Has your son had sex recently, Claudia? It's a simple enough question. You know young men and their hormone levels. I've never heard you mention a girl friend.'

'Ohh!' Mary is off on her favourite theory about the ills of modern society. '*No girlfriend eh?* Well perhaps it's another sort of treatment he needs. You and Richard *are* very close, Claudia, and that's supposed to be one of the things that turns them queer.'

'Oh for God's sake! Will you three shut up!'

Only a dousing from a bucket of ice water could be more shocking. The three women stop with their mouths open and their vocal chords still vibrating. They are struck utterly dumb and look towards tolerant, calm Samantha who never raises her voice to even the most abusive customers. She has her hand over her mouth and looks like the bridesmaid who broke wind during the exchange of rings.

'I'm sorry, ladies,' she says, 'I think it's nearly time.'

They walk to their checkouts silent, and smarting like burnt fingers.

For the first time in her retail career Samantha is not savouring this difficult morning. The drizzle has turned the attention of the Stayfleurs constituency to the emptiness of its store cupboards. The Hannan boys have been back with their mother and have clearly got a taste for Drama. This time it was two giant jars of organic pasta sauce that they launched across an aisle. Their mother is mortified. 'Oh, boys,' she whimpers. 'Mummy's very, very cross.' Mummy looking as if she's going to cry versus a gorgeous tide of red over a whole freezer cabinet. No contest, think the boys. They can hardly contain their excitement.

Samantha rings their father whilst their mother pats her eyes with wet tissues in the staff loo.

'Mr Hannan,' she says just as she rings off, 'why don't you just wallop your boys a bit more?' Samantha has never walloped her own boys, and has never suggested such a thing to anyone before. She has shocked herself once again this morning.

No sooner has the pasta sauce been cleared up, than the over-seventies with ambitions to become the over-nineties, turn out in force. They have finished Rudolph and are back to get Donner and Blitzen. What's more they have told their friends of the power of Stayfleurs' reindeer meat. Obviously it works or how else could they have remembered what they bought for supper over thirty-six hours ago? So all morning the shop has been awash with frail eighty year olds asking for brain-boosting Lapp delicacies. The vacuum packs are simply flying off the shelves. No other branch of Stayfleurs could sell as many. The other shops are in more fashionable areas inhabited by young professionals whose interest in enhancing brain function begins and ends with snorting a product line that Stayfleurs can't stock. Mr Geoffrey is beside himself with delight. He spent the whole first hour of trading standing by Samanthas till enjoying his triumph. His over-charged circuits crackled and made her skin prickle unpleasantly. Today it seemed she simply couldn't tune him out. But luckily his bleeper called him to the office before Samantha did more out-of-character snapping.

Although the reindeer was selling well, there seemed to be endless problems with other lines – a rash of burst bags of rye flour, suspicious bulges in some tins of artichoke hearts and some alarming green spots on some of the ham from the deli counter. Everyone has been directing queries to Samantha from the moment Mr Geoffrey scuttled back to his den. She has had to abandon her till for long periods to pacify disgruntled customers and find replacement products. All of which has made the other tills busier and created an atmosphere of tension.

Samantha is helping a mother of four to pack her purchases. The twin babies are sitting in the trolley like a pair of pink sugar pigs, hungry and grizzling. The smallest toddler is holding onto its mother's leg and hampering her movements, so that the transfer of every item from trolley to check-out is a twenty-second job. Meanwhile, the eldest toddler is running from till to till like a demon, leaving a trail of sweets and chocolate bars that he grabs, then drops. Just as Samantha is about to field the larger toddler, as he streaks past one more time, a small woman marches up to her. She is very elderly, encased in tweed, pearls and the several chords of her archaic hearing aids. She speaks as if addressing a junior groom who has saddled the wrong horse for her morning ride.

'I can't find tapioca pudding. Where is it?' she demands, addressing a point somewhere past Samantha's left shoulder. Samantha attempts to look her in the face, to give her the best chance of lip reading but the woman is not used to direct contact with the lower orders. She averts her eyes and shouts before Sam can reply. 'Tapioca, girl. Don't just stand there gawping at me!'

'Aisle four, madam. Next to the tinned soups and condensed milk.'

'What? What?'

'Aisle four. Next to condensed milk and tinned soup.' Samantha leans down a little, attempting to make communication possible.

'Speak up, you stupid girl!'

Demon toddler fixes on Sam's hand for some reason and begins to pull at her as if her whole body were a maypole string. The Lady in Tweed is turning a little pink. 'Will you answer me? Where is the tapioca?'

The child's pulling and the woman's shouting are as sharp as a needle to Sam's perceptions. She snatches one of the woman's hearing aids with her one free hand, and speaks into it at close range, like a football commentator at a match.

'Aisle Four. Next. To. The. Tinned. Soup. You. Rude. Old. Bag!'

She snaps the hearing aid back into position and in one movement grabs the toddler's ear. She drags him to the trolley and presents him to his mother.

'The next time you bring this dysfunctional little brat in here, can you make sure he isn't shit-faced on sugar?'

Under the circumstances Mr Geoffrey was very good about it. He didn't need to explain how serious the incident was, especially with the threat of official complaint already hanging over George. White and whispering with shock, he suggested that Samantha take the rest of the week off and come back on Monday. She agreed without a word. As she left, Jack Mullen was on his break smoking something legal this time outside the red door. He opened his mouth to wisecrack but she beat him to it.

'Don't you dare say anything, you pathetic little dope head. I could pick up one of your roaches out of that bin and even your grandad being on the square couldn't save your skinny arse.'

And now it's two o'clock, a whole one and half hours before her duties as Mother begin again. For once, such a gap in the day's schedule seems, if not quite welcome, then at least a good idea. She has ninety minutes to work out what is happening to her today and try to resume normal service. She felt nothing out of the ordinary as she left the house with the boys and walked up the road focusing hard on the day ahead. Everything that had flown out of the long brown envelope along with Lawrence's name had been stuffed back in. All was under control again. Yet somehow she had shouted at 'the girls', insulted a customer and given Jack Mullen the satisfaction of a reply. At some level invisible to herself something has slipped out under her guard and now she feels distinctly odd. And the oddest thing about the odd feeling is the absence of the usual anxiety and panic about any loss of internal control. Inside she feels a kind of comfortable blankness that is focused – in a blurred sort of a way – on a snippet from a natural history film that she must have seen on TV as a child. It repeats itself, in the way that the line of a song or an advertising jingle can lodge and loop, over and over in the mind. It shows the smooth white caps of mushrooms bursting with inexorable force through the hard crust of a concrete surface. It plays and replays, soothing, like a mantra.

Samantha considers going home. She could make a start on the cakes but that would leave this evening blank. She could walk on the Downs, but there's too much space there and anyway it's cool and drizzling again. Without a thought of a plan she wanders in to the large shabby shop that sells second-hand clothes for charity. She's brought the boys' outgrown dungarees and little jerseys here several times. The shop smells of the back of wardrobes and the bottom of tea chests. Usually she hates that smell but today it seems friendly, like warm bread or new leather shoes.

She is the only customer. The stooped skinny woman behind the counter eyes her suspiciously and Samantha can't be bothered to offer the reassurance of a charming smile. She simply looks away and busies herself with a rack of unseasonably heavy garments. A stained sheepskin coat, a dogs-tooth skirt in Crimplene, several puffy anoraks, in sizes large enough to double as accommodation for whole families of Inuit. And then, between two navy nylon blazers with nasty mock brass buttons, a little jacket that stands out like Audrey Hepburn in a crowd of New Jersey fish packers. Samantha caresses the material, steel blue, lamb soft. Cashmere, she thinks. *Cashmere*. She whispers it to herself. It's a word she hasn't said in a decade. It is a word that belonged to Bea. Her mother. When her mother said 'cashmere' it filled the air with perfume, with stories. Samantha leaves the shop and walks fast down the road. But the mushrooms have pushed through the pavement, and the cashmere, soft as mascarpone on the tongue, has done its work.

When she was a girl, Sam knew that other parents made up tales of dragons or cutesy animal adventures to amuse their kids. But Bea never had. Which was good because you can't tell a teenager about talking bunnies. Nothing particularly shocking or exciting ever happened in Bea's stories, but still Sam loved to hear them. They made her feel close to who Bea was, before she was ill, before she was old, when she could have been Sam's best friend and not her mother.

All Bea's stories began in the same way, with an outfit. Clothes were the set, the stage, the lighting, the atmosphere.

Bea would begin: 'It was the most gorgeous material, dove-grey *cashmere* with a little mauve check. In *mohair*. Very fine.' Her voice would have that special lisping, confidential tone, the words *cashmere* and *mohair* taking on a sacred, spell-like quality that could transport you to the fairy-tale world of luxury and idleness. Sam and Bea would be sitting together almost cheek to cheek; on the sofa downstairs with the telly off, or on Bea's bed, sometimes with Bea in it, everything but her voice as limp as a popped balloon in the wet. Never in Sam's room, because there was never anywhere to sit amidst the litter of books, files, paper, house plants and discarded clothes. Today they were sitting in deck chairs on the lawn, Bea wrapped in a nest of blankets even though the late spring sun was warm. Sam snuggled close to her mother, savouring the first time for weeks that they'd been together like this.

'Mauve,' Bea said, 'mmm. No, not really *mauve*.' Bea looked all around as if the colour could be plucked from the air to show her daughter. 'More a deep lavender. Do you remember those curtains we had on the landing? No? Oh. Well there, look! That wallflower, next to the lemon yellow and before the crimson. There. *That* was the colour.

'Anyway,' she continued, 'I made a skirt and jacket from a

Vogue pattern of Auntie Dilys'. I had to fiddle with it to get it to fit. I used to tailor things properly in those days, lined it and everything. And I cut it very close fitting.' She put a wiggle in her voice so that Sam would imagine her wriggling into the suit and coaxing the zip to close, then turned to Sam. 'Classic style,' she said patting Sam's cheek, 'it wouldn't look out of place now. If I still had it you could wear it, if you weren't so tall.' She turned away, looking into the air as if seeing herself in all her youthful glory, hardly believing that she had once been so lovely. 'I had to starve for week before I wore it the first time. And I stood up all the way to Gloucester station so the skirt wouldn't seat.'

Sam tried to see her mother as the slender upright figure, immaculately dressed and teetering slightly as she stepped from the train in her too-high heels.

'Roy was at the station to meet me. Imagine, I had this beautiful suit, little seal-skin handbag; I'd dyed an old silk hanky of Dad's the *exact* same shade of lavender as the check, for a little scarf at my throat. And grey suede shoes. Can you *imagine*? Grey suede shoes in *those* times? We hadn't long come off the ration. And all *he* said was, "Oh, Bea, you'll catch your death without an overcoat." I can laugh now but then! Oh! I didn't speak to him all day. We went to the pictures and he tried to hold my hand but I pulled it away. I made him take me to the station two hours early and told him I never wanted to see him again.'

This of course was supposed to be the real point of the story because, freezing in her close-cut classic suit on Gloucester station was how Ralph, Sam's father, first found her. 'At least *your father* appreciated it,' Bea said. ' "It's a shame to cover you up, but you *are* shivering," he said, and he gave me his coat. It was a very good coat, black, pure wool with a raglan sleeve and satin lining. Soft as butter, warm as toast.'

This point Sam knew was the end of the formal, ritual part of the story. Now came the interactive section. When Sam had been little, this was the bit that had told her about steam trains, roads almost free of cars, milk from pails not bottles and houses without electric light. But now her questions were different.

'Was it love at first sight then, Mum?'

'No. I'd known him for years. One of the village boys he was. The year above me in school. But I hadn't seen him in a while. He'd been away doing National Service then college. I suppose you could say that day was the first time I'd noticed him.'

'All right then, was it love at first notice?'

'Yes, Sam. Yes I think it was.' Bea sighed and looked away. When Sam had first asked these questions Bea had talked fondly about their courting, of long walks, and posies of wildflowers. But the contrast with their current state of siege was too painful now to remember the sweetness of the past.

Sam changed tack, back onto the safe ground of clothes. 'Did you wear that posh suit after?'

Bea smiled again. 'Oh yes. Lots of times. Your father loved me in it. In fact the skirt got ripped on a hedge one night when I was out with your father.' Bea smirked. 'We just nipped into a gateway for a little cuddle, you know.'

Yes, Sam did know about 'cuddling'. She'd been kissed first at fourteen, on a school trip to the Lake District. She and her friend Christine got off with two scouts from the campsite next door. She'd shared this with Bea when she got home, enhancing the Romantic theme, when in reality, it had all been much more about showing off to the other girls. Pretty Christine was the boy bait and as boys seemed to come in pairs – one handsome, one ugly – it worked well. Christine snogged the handsome one and Sam got his friend Martin, who wasn't that bad close up and under canvas.

What Sam didn't tell her mum was that from that day she had dropped any snobbery about appearance, because once you were snogging you had your eyes shut so looks didn't matter. So, even though at school Sam was considered swotty and weird, she never suffered the ignominy of having no one to take her into a corner at the end of a party. Being officially pretty as Christine was seemed to Sam a bit of a drag. She always had some boyfriend keeping her away from homework and her friends. And regular boyfriends expected a lot more than just a twenty-minute snog and a little grope. By the time they started sixth form Christine was on the pill and Sam a contented virgin, tipped for an Oxbridge place. What use, she told Bea, was a boyfriend to a woman who was going to spend her life in the rainforest?

'Well, that's true,' Bea said. 'You know how important I think a woman's independence is.'

'That's what I'll be. Independent. I'm not going to have children or get married. I'm going to be a biologist instead.'

'Good for you, poppet,' Bea said, but her voice carried a vein of doubt. It was certainly true that Bea's attitude to Sam's love life, or apparent lack of it, was ambivalent. Sometimes, when Sam came downstairs with her wet hair in a towel-turban and her face pink and fresh, Bea would look at her fondly and say, 'Lips made for kissing. If I was a boy I'd fall at your feet!'

But at other times, usually after reading of teenage pregnancies in the newspaper, she'd say darkly. 'Never go all the way with a boy, Sam. Never let a boy touch you. Not ever,' although she never specified what 'touching' and 'all the way' were. It was Christine who gave Sam a good idea about *their* meanings.

So, Sam avoided 'boys' as a topic with her mother and just smiled when Bea hinted at what she'd got up to with 'your father' in the farm gateways of the 1950s.

'Did you mend the skirt after that?' Sam asked.

'The material was just too fine to be mended.' Bea sighed. 'You know, I've never seen material like it since. And then? You couldn't get anything nice. I never knew where Mummy got it in the first place.'

Bea always referred to her mother as Mummy, or Ma. It was

another reason Sam loved the stories because they featured her dead granny, Agnes, whom she had never met. Dead Granny Agnes sounded a lot more fun than the live Granny Pearl who they lived with. In the one photo that remained of Agnes, she looked plump and pretty, poured into her clothes like a luscious milkshake filling the glass to the brim. She looked into the camera as if inviting you to step through into the frame with her, and have a laugh. There were smile lines round her dark eyes.

'She was such fun,' Bea always used to say, 'I'd put my feet in her bath and we'd talk for hours.'

Pearl would never have run a bath generous enough for anyone to even put a little toe in. She was always going on about how you could keep clean with just a tea-cupful of tepid water.

'Daddy would bang on the bathroom door sometimes. "How long are you girls going to go on giggling in there." Oh, how we used to laugh!'

'Just like us, Mum!' Sam said. 'Just like we laugh!'

And it had been true once. Sam and Bea used to laugh a lot. And Ralph, like his father-in-law before him, had loved to hear his wife and daughter 'getting the giggles'. But now in the summer when Sam was seventeen, there wasn't much to laugh at any more for any of them it seemed. Least of all poor Bea.

It wasn't as if Bea had ever been really well. There was always something putting her to bed, or sending her to hospital for a couple of weeks. By the time Sam was ten, 'Mum in hospital' was like an annual festival: not quite Christmas but not Lent either. Ralph took time off work to care for Sam whilst Bea was 'in'. It felt odd yet thrilling to be alone with Daddy, serious and fun at the same time. He burnt chips almost every night for tea, and ironed things that didn't need it, so that all the towels went from fluffy to flat.

At evening visiting time they'd both get ready solemnly. He'd put on a suit or a smart jacket and a clean shirt. She'd get bathed and changed into a frock, put on her newest pair of white ankle socks. Then she and Ralph would drive to the hospital, with Sam in the front passenger seat like a grown-up. They'd get flowers or magazines and grapes on the way. Then walk down the long corridors arms full, smiling at each other, with their shoes squeaking on that odd rubberised flooring. Sam never worried that her mother would die, because her illnesses seemed an ordinary part of things: there were lots of other mummies in the hospital so they couldn't all be dying. Ralph worried though, she could tell because he never mentioned Bea except to say something to reassure Sam.

'Now don't be surprised if your mother's a bit groggy. She's fine: it's the anaesthetic.' 'You're not worrying about your mother, are you?' 'She's doing very well. The doctor says she'll be home in a week.' And he'd pat her head with his awkward rough hand and try to hug her resisting body, that only wanted her mother's touch.

Yet, when Bea came 'out' he seemed angry with her. He'd snap at her if she tried to come downstairs for a meal, or tell her to get dressed if she'd just popped down to see half an hour of telly. At night, Sam would lie in bed and hear them rowing, snarling like dogs she thought. In a month or so it would wear off. They'd be back to normal. Bea cooking and cleaning. Ralph coming home from work and mowing the lawn. They'd eat and chat and watch telly. But gradually there were fewer patches of calm between the snarling, as the gaps between Bea's spells 'in' got shorter.

That, Sam supposed is why they ended up having Granny Pearl as a permanent resident.

'She can take care of you while Mum's "in",' Ralph said, 'and be here for Mum when I can't be and she's too weak to be left.' But really what Ralph wanted was a buffer, some sort of layer between him and Bea, between him and his anger about her chronic ill health. The moment Granny Pearl moved in she forgot that seventy-one really wasn't that old and that she'd been wallpapering ceilings in her own house weeks before. Pearl had she thought 'slaved' for long enough. Now it was someone else's turn to do the caring. A week out of hospital Bea was running up and downstairs getting Pearl's morning coffee and malted milk biscuits, salad sandwich lunch and cake and tea at four.

Afterwards, Sam thought of Granny Pearl's arrival as the event that marked the beginning of the end. Things had got bad before her, but after they were dire. Pearl made the house feel like shoes that no longer fitted, cold, tight and chafing. She grumbled about everything, and turned personal criticism into a kind of art form.

'Those trousers would be lovely on a young woman with nice legs, Bea'. 'You can't help your pot belly, Ralph. You've inherited from your dear father, God rest his soul.' 'Intelligence is all very well in a girl but I think grooming goes a long way, Samantha.' 'The curtains in my bedroom are very nice. If you like that sort of thing.'

She could change her colour like a chameleon to protect herself, one moment pink and puffed with her own opinions, in the next grey and slack in the face of any retaliation. 'I don't know what I've ever done to deserve being spoken to like that.'

Pearl could rival any RADA-trained actor in her rendition of the tearful retreat. Even after months of its repetition it still worked well enough to leave behind it a pall of guilt. Ralph and Bea spent so much time and energy in their conflicts with Pearl that they barely spoke to each other. Almost every evening Pearl sat triumphantly watching her favourite programmes. On either side of her on the sofa sat her son and daughter-in-law, silent, merely grateful for a moment's peace. Sam decided that it wasn't adolescents that were the cause of poltergeist activity but grumpy embittered old women – since Pearl's arrival, emotions jumped off the shelves like possessed crockery.

*

But there were still times when Bea and Sam could laugh.

'Sorry, Sam, no cornflakes left. She ate the last of them again this morning.'

'Oh! There was half a packet left yesterday!'

'I don't know where she puts it. She's so skinny.'

'She's probably shoving them up her jersey, so she can sell them back to us on Sunday when we've run out and the shops are closed.'

'Sam!' Bea tried to sound censorious but she was laughing too much.

Pearl came to live with them at Christmas, and after New Year Bea seemed to get weaker. Even without a hospital stint for more than ten months she was still asleep on the sofa every day when Sam got home from school. Then, one morning in the Easter holidays a single word extinguished the last flickers of fun in Sam's home. It escaped whole and intelligible from a muffled phone conversation in the sitting room where Bea sat with the receiver to her ear. A wickedly purposeful and busy little word, penetrating and pushy with no respect for anything. *Cancer*. Sam was transfixed. She crossed the landing and tiptoed downstairs. One look across the hall to her mother's face, still held to the phone, was enough. Bea turned away and kicked the door shut. But they both knew what she'd heard.

Sam didn't dare ask about this new invasion in her mother's body and Bea offered nothing. There were just the usual platitudes that Bea had always trotted out:

'Doctor says I'm doing well.'

'I'm feeling a lot better today.'

'Not feeling too bright. But a little rest and I'll be fine.'

Vague and euphemistically bright, like weather forecasts. Nothing it seemed was any different. Ralph and Bea still snarled and quarrelled, Pearl still whined and picked at people like scabs. Only the sudden spate of almost daily hospital visits and Pearl's one blunt indiscretion gave Sam any clue about what was going on: 'Your mother's very ill now you know. I've seen people snuffed out in weeks with cancer.'

Silence encased the cocktail of broken glass that had become home. Nobody spoke and nobody listened to her. She felt she had been handed this deadly information and then shut out. It was like being on the outside of a soundproof screen. Sam had never felt so alone. She sat on her bed at night stroking the leaves of her cheeseplant in the dark and asking out loud for her mother not to die.

On weekdays there were distractions: giggling on the bus with Christine and taking the piss out of her taste in music. 'Oh, God, look at his clothes. A white suit. UGGHH! And what sort of name is Al anyway?'

'The *Reverend* Al, *if* you don't mind. He's lush. Really lush. You don't know anything. He was the best in his day. A classic. All you ever listen to is Radio Four anyway.'

Standing up to spotty Mr Brett's sexist banter in physics lessons: 'Girls can't do physics, isn't that true, Samantha?'

'Course it is, Mr Brett. Just like people over eighteen never get acne.'

Battling with Mrs Farz's low horizons: 'All I'm saying is don't set your heart on Oxbridge. It's just very difficult to get in.'

'Look. Can I take the entrance exam in school or not? Yes or no?'

'Well. Yes but . . .'

'Thanks, Mrs Farz. Bye.'

And making sure that Elaine and her white stiletto-ed, blue eye-shadowed denizens were slapped down: 'Nice to see the same hole in your jeans as last week, Samantha Powell.'

'Nice to see the same daylight shining out your ears, Elaine Evans. How is the one O level re-take going?'

But at home the deafening quiet of the unsaid had only one antidote: another kind of unreality, dreams and fantasies of her future world as it would be when somehow the awfulness of 'now' was done with. So in her room with her homework, in the shower in the morning, walking the dog, she used the imagination that had called spiders from Dennis Williams' eyes, and made Elaine Evans disappear under her own fingernails. Sam imagined herself in the rainforest. No, not the rainforest, not that flat, academic word but 'Jungle'. She'd say the word out loud to herself. It sounded juicy, three-dimensional and savage. She saw herself walking on the forest floor, in the dim sage-coloured light, as if she were at the bottom of a great sea. Far, far above her the breeze blew the canopy into billows of green, saturated in sunlight and alive with birds and monkeys; but down here amongst the boles of the trees, as big and archaic as dinosaurs, there was a profound stillness. Here was the foundation of all the forest's diversity, here was the site of quick exchange between death and life; the plant and animal corpses were sublimated in this steamy crucible back to their elements. Then, from just beneath the rubbly surface of brown leaves and insect bodies, the trees snatched them back, and sent them rushing upwards into the clamour of light and sound. Like souls pulled from across the Styx and thrust back into the world. Sam could close her eyes and put her hand on the warm rough skin of a trunk and sense the sap singing under her palm; electric, alive, potent with tangible magic.

A chilly wind whipped over the wallflowers in the spring garden. Bea's lips had gone bluish, her skin the colour of yellowing whitewash. She shifted in her deck chair. 'I'm getting cold, and it's time for your gran's tea.'

'I'll do it, Mum. You go upstairs and rest before Dad gets home.'

'Thanks, poppet. I will.'

They went inside. Pearl was already in the kitchen foraging ineffectually. 'It's gone five,' she said, adding in her customary offended tone, 'you both know I like my tea at four. I am diabetic, you know. I have to have regular meals.'

'You're as diabetic as Shirley Bassey, Pearl,' Bea said wearily. 'Sam'll get your tea. You don't need to invent ailments.'

Standing in the kitchen looking out to the mowed lawn and the neat leylandii hedge, Sam escaped to her green world amongst the buttressed trunks. But even there that solitude had been turning into the same loneliness she experienced in the real world. Until the day Lawrence had stepped so lightly from behind a tree fern.

6

'You look as if you've seen a whole fleet of ghosts. Or whatever the collective noun for them is. A Wobble perhaps or a Scream.' The hand on her arm is for a moment incomprehensible, in the way ordinary furnishings are on waking in a hotel bedroom. It is the first thing in the external world that Samantha has been sensible to since the moment she blundered out of the charity shop. 'You're white as a sheet, are you OK?' The face looking anxiously up at her is at last recognisable.

'Oh, Louise!' says Samantha, suddenly flushed with relief that she can put a word to something in the scene around her. 'How lovely to see you!' She kisses Louise warmly on the cheek. Louise blushes with surprise at this unprecedented display of affection from her kind but usually unemotional friend.

'Oh! Well. Thanks. It's nice to see you too, Angie. Are you *sure* you're OK?'

'Mmm. Oh. Fine. Just feeling a bit, you know, under the weather that's all.' Samantha looks around at the adults huddled under umbrellas in little groups on the tarmac. It is a school playground. More than 'a' playground it is 'the' playground. She is here because of her children. But whether to drop them off or pick them up or spectate some infant drama production she's not sure. It seems to have slipped her mind for a moment. Tentatively she searches for clues:

'What time is it?' she asks Louise.

'It's gone twenty-five to. They're always late out on a Thursday.'

'Who are?'

'Oh guess who? Mrs Wiggins, as always. She holds everything up. Keeps them in for extra sandal appreciation or something.'

Samantha recognises that this is some kind of joke and smiles uncertainly at Louise. She is just about to ask who Mrs Wiggins is, when the big double doors open and a horde of children tumble out, like sweets from a spilled box.

And the two foremost little morsels look to Samantha and cry 'Mummy' simultaneously and run towards her. Two lovely little boys; the taller one pale with dark obedient hair, keeping his tartan satchel on his shoulder as he runs; the other more solid, hair a little bleached, skin a little tanned, approaching with the abandon of a small whirlwind. They are completely beautiful, and of course utterly familiar. And yet today, Samantha finds her eyes filling with tears because somehow this is the first time in her life that she has seen her own children. She kneels on the wet playground to hug them. Her tights will be ruined and the hem of her pale lemon skirt will stain in the dirt.

Joe puts his sticky hand on her face. 'Are you sad, Mummy?'

'No, darling. I'm not sad.'

'But you're crying.'

'I'm just tired.'

Tony pulls her arm. 'Get up, Mummy, everybody's looking.'

As Samantha gathers herself and her two rediscovered children, Louise hovers closer. Something about her friend is making her nervous. 'Um, Angela, I wonder. Um, is it still OK for Saturday? You know, the cricketing tea? Cakes. Tarama-salata. All that?'

'Oh yes. Cakes of course. I'd forgotten.'

'Oh,' Louise titters nervously, 'that's not like you!'

'Oh, isn't it?'

'So will you still do the cakes?'

'Of course. We'll start tonight. You can help, can't you, boys?'

There is a moment of disbelieving uncertainty. Joe and Tony are allowed in the kitchen *whilst* their mother cooks, doing pretend mixing with dried beans and pasta, but the real thing? That's surely for grown-ups only.

'What, and do *real* mixing?' says Joe.

'And put things in the *oven*?' says Tony.

'Yes! Why not?'

'Wow!'

'That's good then. Fine. Great.' Louise retreats, like a startled egret. 'Bye. See you tomorrow.'

'Right, boys. Shall we go home?'

They don't know what to say. Where else is there to go but home?

The interior of Number eleven is not looking its customary immaculate self for this time on a Thursday night. The play-room floor is still invisible under a layer of plastic bricks, toy cars and felt tip pens *without their lids*. In the front room, all the cushions are on the floor and piled under a canopy made of two pink sheets stretched between the backs of the sofas and held in place by safety pins and pegs. Amongst the cushions are plates with crumbs and crusts, peel and apple cores. It seems a tribe of miniature Bedouins has made camp and had a feast. The air in the kitchen is still warmed with the sweet homely scent of baking, but all the work surfaces are as jumbled as scrap yards. Bags of flour and sugar lean at odd angles losing their contents through open mouths and egg shells stuck with yolk adhere to the side of dirty bowls. Squalid as dirty knickers, margarine wrappers lie scrunched beside soiled wooden spoons. Splodges of cake mixture spot the walls, the ceiling and the floor. But some order has come out of this chaos: on the kitchen table under a sheet of muslin are a line of cakes, baked but not yet iced. Not one is round or square or any sort of normal cake shape: two teddies, a pyramid, an amoeba, and a hand. Their colours are unusual too – blue, purple and bright pink except for the one brown chocolate bear. It has taken a lot of activity to effect this radical change from neat orderliness. It seems odd that now the house is quiet, after so much has obviously been going on. But it is completely still, breathing out gently in the twilight, like someone who can finally undo the waistband that has been too tight all day.

Tony and Joe have had a wonderful evening. You can see it on their faces. Each wears a little moustache of chocolate cake mixture, and a delicate spotting of lurid food colour. They have fallen asleep on their parents' bed. They were bouncing on the mattress one minute and the next they'd run out of awakeness and dropped where they stood. Their arms are at odd angles and their legs slightly entwined. Tenderly Samantha peels off their socks and shorts, and rearranges their limbs a little. They don't stir, only smile in their sleep, like puppies twitching. She covers them with the sheet and stands in the twilight at the end of the bed looking at them. Her heart squeezes as she thinks how much they enjoyed this evening's release from routine. 'What do you want to do?' she'd asked them.

They knew immediately. 'Play with the toys and *leave them all out*!'

'Make an indoor tent!'

'Have all the cushions *on the floor*!'

They wanted things that Samantha's little rules didn't allow: spontaneity and mess. Most of all they wanted her participation. So she sat on the floor and played car crashes, ate toasted sandwiches in the 'tent' and showed them how to make cakes in the most un-cake like colours.

She leans now to kiss each chocolatey face and whispers 'thank you' to her sleeping boys; because she too has had a wonderful evening. She closes the door behind her and wanders into the spare room to look out over the rolling landscape of gardens and rooftops. In the summer twilight there are great trees gathering on the skyline, but she doesn't flinch or turn away. There is something comforting tonight in the inevitability of their spread. She can't fight it. At last the orange lights in the next street are extinguished by lianas, and she lies down on the smooth, cool bed. The expanding blank white of a huge mushroom cap fills her mental frame. There is almost no room left to wonder where this might lead her tomorrow.

'Phooooo!' Max from the garden centre sticks out his bottom lip and blows his blond fringe from underneath. 'I dunno how we're gonna do this.' His square shoulders are straining and his biceps are damp under the tight cap-sleeved T-shirt. They are on the path outside Number eleven, with a native of subtropical China, *Trachycarpus fortunei*, a Chusan palm, in a pot the size of a hip bath. It has a just-caught, untamed look about it with its five spikey fronds spread in alarm like the giant hands of a drowning witch. Samantha is enveloped in them, so busy imagining it silhouetted against an orange watercolour sky, that she doesn't notice immediately when Max stops lifting. She limbos out from under the leaves to see what's the matter. After two hours of manoeuvring large pots through Samantha's house and out onto her patio, Max's customer care is wilting. 'It's not going through that door. No way!'

Samantha looks from palm to door and back again. How can they have spent forty minutes wrestling this plant out of the van and up eight feet of path, without noticing that it is three feet bigger in almost every direction than Number eleven's front door? Max slumps against the wall. Surely, he wonders, his gap year could be better spent than this?

'Wow. Cool. What is it?' Samantha peers round the palm to see Callendula, out early of what passes for a school in the number thirteen household. She is wearing faded jeans and a turquoise fringed top that finishes just below her rib cage. Her perfect shell-white belly button is exposed and she is obviously developing the family bust. No one would say she was younger than sixteen, so Max is apparently within his rights to perk up quite considerably at the sight of her.

'It's *Tradycarpus fortenia*,' he swaggers, 'the Chewing palm. Handsome beast isn't it? Prob is it won't go through this lady's front door so we can't get it in her garden.' Callendula is unimpressed by the Latin name, or the arm muscles suddenly tensed although there is no lifting going on. She looks past him to Samantha and her palm tree.

'It'd go through ours though, Mrs Cassinari,' she says, 'our front door is a double one. And there's that old fence panel at the bottom of the wall. We could move it and get it in that way. Dad's in too, he can help lift.'

Normally Samantha finds offers of help unsettling; they necessitate a doubling of the internal guard. But 'normally' she's not filling her garden with a selection of plants that look as if they could have been flown in from the Amazon. With just the slightest internal twinge of discomfort, which dispels like a bubble of wind, Samantha says, 'Well, that's very kind, Callendula, if you're sure your parents won't mind?'

'Course not. No worries.' She's already bouncing up the road to open both front doors, and the sight of her neat buttocks are enough to make Max forget the weight of the pot.

By the time *Trachycarpus* has been navigated through number thirteen's hall, down the garden, through the gap in the wall, and up to Samantha's patio everyone concerned is much better acquainted. They have, by that time, been through so much together: setbacks and solutions, improvisations and discoveries. It's taken two banana loaves, twenty-three cups of tea, a bottle of lemonade, a roll of old carpet and some pram wheels to get this far. Plus the contribution of everyone at numbers nine to thirteen and Louise and Barney.

It is now after six. Tony, Joe and Barney are chasing round the pots dodging leaves and tendrils. Eight adults, counting Callendula, are in Samantha's garden toasting her palm, and reminiscing about their roles in its journey, like mountaineers after an ascent of Mont Blanc.

'I'd completely forgotten about the wall behind the fence panel,' Malcolm is saying to Max.

'Yeah, if Keith hadn't stepped in there we'd have been well stuffed.' Max downs his wine in one.

Keith beams and reaches a long arm out to engulf Felicity's shoulder. 'Yes, but Flick remembered about the railway sleepers . . .'

'I'm just sorry I couldn't help lift that's all,' Felicity simpers. Under her gorgeous ebony purple skin she looks as if she might be blushing.

'Oh yes,' Maeve pulls up next to Felicity and Keith like a suddenly breaking bus, 'have you done something to your back?'

'I know an awfully good, um thingy. Osteo whatever if you have,' Louise splutters.

Keith and Felicity exchange a look of powerful delight.

'Well,' Keith says slowly, 'it is pretty safe to to tell you now . . .'

'I'm having a baby in October.'

'We've been trying for a long time.'

'A very long time.' The shouting, the rampant garden, the flying tellies and the tearful lasagna are all explained.

'Oh how lovely. I'm very happy for you both.' Maeve is crying again. How she manages to be a solicitor is quite beyond Samantha's comprehension. Everyone crowds round Felicity and Keith congratulating and back slapping. Samantha refills glasses and says thank you to them all, for about the twentieth time. She had no idea that feeling grateful could be so nice.

Eventually the children brought the impromptu party to an end. Exhausted after another night off from routine they had to be fed and put to bed.

'What'll you do with all those plants, Mum?' Tony asked sleepily.

'I'm going to make a jungle in our garden.'

'Ooooh, can we have parrots?' said Joe.

'I don't think so.'

'Oh please?'

'We'll see. Sleep now, boys. Daddy's home tomorrow.'

Outside now in the light cast from the kitchen window, Samantha is wrenching up paving stones and revealing the good earth beneath. Here the huge purple spikes of giant *Echium* will reach for the bedroom windows, here the spiny pineapple leaves of *Fascicularia* will coat the soil like a pangolin's scales. She's planting canna lillies and Himalayan ginger. Campsis with its luscious red trumpet flowers will swarm over the walls. By August this selection of plants from all over the world will be a rampant bower, a little counterfeit of jungle. Dale was right all along, this south-facing plot is a perfect place for an exotic garden. She shudders at the memory of colour-coded lobelias and the four little holes in the paving.

Later, nails broken, sweaty and soil encrusted, she sits on the patio steps and looks at her new planting. The half-light doesn't hide the starkness of the bare soil, or the rather shocked appearance of the plants, not yet settled in their new home. But this new clearing calls the rainforest closer. Soon there is a whispering wave of a million leaves blocking out the streetlight. In the darkness under the fence panel something growls, then steps from the shadows. Samantha holds her breath as a jaguar sniffs delicately at the newly turned earth, then clears the wall in a bound and is gone into the thicket that has engulfed Keith and Felicity's back garden.

Louise and her catering Sub Committee helpers are in the pavilion kitchen buttering bread as if their lives depended on it.

'I'm so glad the weather's nice!'

'Oh, doesn't it make a difference?'

'D'you remember last year?'

'Oh, my God do I? I thought they were going to drown on the pitch!'

'It took Stewart three weeks to get over the cold he caught.'
'Come on, girls . . . shake a leg, they'll be in in five minutes.'
'Jesus! I haven't put the urn on!'
Samantha stands in the cool echoey space of the main hall, listening to their voices coming out of the serving hatch. She should be hurrying to lay out her cakes. The table is waiting to receive them, standing in pride of place at the top of the hall, draped in white cloth like an altar. But Samantha is not at all sure what people are going to say about the cakes this year. She loaded them into the back of the car quite confident about their unconventional forms and colours. But now, the thought of a purple amoeba with green icing and silver sugar balls in the middle of that virginal expanse of table cloth is too shocking – like the Pope giving his Christmas blessing in drag. She goes out to the car and looks at the cakes through its window. They are more like a piece of installation art than something you could eat. The pink hand has lost its hand shape somewhat, in the process of being iced, and the pyramid seems to have doubled in size since it was mortared together with layers of cream. The two teddies are still convincingly bear-shaped inside their rough furry buttercream. But the ordinary lemon sponges and chocolate and walnut cakes only serve to make the rest look even more bizarre.

'Goodness!'

Samantha has been so absorbed in cake anxiety that she has failed to notice the arrival of Louise by her side.

'Goodness!' Louise exclaims again and puts her hand over her mouth. *What*, Samantha thinks, *have I been doing? These cakes are like an insult. I might as well have made one with a middle finger sticking up from its centre!*

'Shall I just take them home again? It won't look too sparse if I just put out the normal ones . . .'

'What!' Louise takes her hand from her mouth to reveal the widest smile Samantha has ever seen on her face. 'Oh no! They're lovely. Really. I'm terribly impressed. Everyone will adore them. Come on, I'll help you take them in. They're, you know, very sort of Barcelona-ish. Like that sculpture park with the multicoloured monsters. Oh, *you know*.'

Samantha doesn't know, but she is reassured. Once more Louise has come up with the unexpected. 'Barcelona-ish' sounds like a good thing to be and anyway, it's too late to worry now, the players are crossing the field towards her. She scuttles to the table with the cakes that Gaudi, apparently, would have been proud to call his own.

'Taramasalata *and* purple blob cake? Mummy's a revolutionary, boys.' Tony and Joe giggle at their father's face in the rearview mirror even though they don't know a revolutionary from a stick of rock. Dale is laughing, but only with his mouth. He arrived late at the cricket match in his works truck having driven from the site that morning. His eyes were already dull and shadowed with something more than exhaustion and all afternoon as the match concluded and the last crumbs of cakes were eaten up, they have been sinking further into their sockets. But Samantha has resolutely ignored whatever is cooking behind Dale's face; like the boys, she is full of the surprise that Dale will get when he walks out into their new back garden. She has been trying to convince herself that the garden is all for him, because it's what he always wanted. It's what she will tell him anyway.

Outside the front door the boys pop like over-shaken lemonade.

'Mum, Mum, can we show him now?'

Dale looks from his wife to his children.

'Show me what?'

'Shut your eyes, Daddy,' commands Joe.

Samantha watches. With his eyes closed Dale looks different. Like an actor suddenly without make up, he is exposed, vulnerable. She notices how pale and worn he seems, how relieved to give his hands to his two little sons and let them lead him. Samantha is struck by the thought that perhaps, of all four of them, it is only Joe and Tony who really understand where this family is going.

Joe and Tony nod solemnly at each other. 'OK,' says Tony, 'open them!'

It is an astounding transformation even though the plants are still looking a little sorry today after the shock of their journey. Dale wanders down the central path, all that is left of the paved garden. An intermittent carpet of stiff pointed leaves like green icicles replaces the flagstones. Springing up from amongst it are big bold plants, like a series of living sculptures: long tongues of green; tiered layers of dancers' skirts on stalks of green bone; purple spikes, straight as metal, twining tangles of coils and springs. He looks back toward the patio, takes in the giant hands of the palm, and looks to Samantha, his face a frozen traffic jam of questions.

She knew there'd be questions, but she begins to answer before he asks. 'I can't remember what half of them are called.' It sounds like the lie it is, so she stumbles on to bury it quickly, 'I got it all out of Stayfleurs money. Money I've been saving. The garden centre recommended everything. They're all pretty hardy. Just one or two need protection in the winter, the *echium* I think it is. It'll all fill out a bit, the climbers will cover the walls by the end of the summer. The boys like it don't you, boys? And we can go to the park if they want to run about or play football.'

There is a little silence. The boys are still smiling though uncertainly now; Daddy is so quiet.

'D'you like it, Daddy?' Tony asks.

'Oh yes, I think it's fantastic.'

'Mummy said we might have parrots,' says Joe.

'Oh did she? Run inside a minute, boys . . . turn the telly on and see what the Test score is.'

Joe opens his mouth to dispute the dismissal but Tony, wise to the stillness in the air between his parents, grabs his brother, 'C'mon, Joe.'

Dale hasn't moved. He stares about him and at last turns towards her. The day Tony crashed his trike and was knocked out and Dale carried his unconscious, spectacularly bleeding child into casualty he wore this face: a mixture of pain, fear and incomprehension. They sat together in the waiting room, holding hands, saying nothing. She had never felt closer to Dale than at that moment, when the only thing that was real in the world was Tony's next breath. Now, she wants so much to tell Dale not to be afraid, to beg him to accept the surface of things as they are. There have always been questions neither of them asked each other. They have always acknowledged the safety of their positions behind their respective portraits. But making a jungle of the garden has somehow broken the rules, so that the questions stand in the air between them shouting.

'What made you do it? What about the cat poo?' he asks.

She moves towards him and takes a limp hand in both of hers. 'I did it as a surprise for you. Because it's what you wanted when we moved in.' She squeezes his hand and looks out at him, willing him to feel the love he's never been told about. But all he can see is something he doesn't understand.

'But why *now*? What's *changed*?'

How can she begin to explain? If she gives him even the smallest thread to pull, her whole life will unravel. She shrugs. Turns away and goes inside. 'Shall I make tea?' she calls from the kitchen. 'Cannelloni?'

They ate in the garden, on the patio beside the palm. Dale busied himself with the boys' jungle fantasies, imagining all sorts of animals peeking from behind the plants: lions, hyenas, giraffes, wildebeest. Samantha smiled and bit her tongue so as not to point out that none of the animals Dale suggested would be found in a rainforest. Dale finished the bottle of wine and stayed downstairs in front of the TV whilst she bathed the boys alone. They wanted to find animals in the bath so she risked revealing a little knowledge.

'The bath is freshwater, Tony . . . we can't have sharks in it. But you can have river dolphins, and sturgeons and anacondas.'

The thought of giant snakes under the suds got them far too excited so she sat with them until they fell asleep reading their current favourite bit of *Winnie the Pooh* over and over again, so that poor Pooh fell out of the tree into the gorse bush far more than was good for any stuffed toy.

Then the bathroom was dirty, and the linen cupboard needed a little tidy; it seemed silly to go downstairs and have to come up later to do a few little chores. But now it's ten o'clock and there's nothing left to do. Dale has been alone with the TV since seven. She should go down and sit beside him to watch some stupid film with exploding helicopters and oiled biceps. Dale might be coaxed back into faith in the solidity of the surface of things. She steps across the landing, resolved, but at the top of the stairs she turns back. A bath would be nice and quite a natural thing to do on a Saturday night. She locks the bathroom door, turns on the taps and peels her clothes off anyhow, careless as a snake sloughing. The mirror over the sink is misted and short but she peers in to see her face and naked torso. Pink skin, dark nipples, a narrow face in a dark frame. She rubs the vapour from the glass and bends closer, looking for cracks or the hint of a join. But what she sees is smooth, a single piece of work. Samantha wonders why humans can't be like plants, with their history captured in the way limbs and torso grow. Then the past could be simply pruned away.

There is a gentle knock. Dale whispers her name between the frame and the door.

'Angela? Angie? Are you OK?'

'Oh yes. I'm fine. Just having a bath.'

'Can I come in?'

Dale has never asked for this before. Their only physical intimacy happens in bed; at all other times they are as comfortable but as chaste as siblings.

'Please?'

'Oh, all right. Just a second.' She wraps herself securely in a towel and lets him in.

'Thank you. Can I sit down while you take your bath?' It isn't an unreasonable request for a husband of so many years but she feels awkward and shy.

'Well, I suppose so.'

'What's the matter?'

'Nothing. Nothing. It's just that you've never done this before. Seen me in the bath.'

'You've never made a jungle in the garden before!' He looks up at her defiant, and confronting.

'Don't you like it?'

'Yes I like it. But I don't understand why you did it now.' He looks at her unflinchingly, almost angry. Unstable, un-Dale like.

'What's wrong with doing it now?'

'Nothing. Nothing. I wonder why that's all. You know, with the purple cakes and everything. I wonder. What's happening to you?'

'Nothing's happening to me. What d'you mean with the purple cakes?'

Dale looks away from her, and slumps on his seat. 'Oh I don't know. I've had a horrible week.' He rubs a hand over his eyes as if wiping something aside, then looks up again, smiling, ready to try a new tactic to make things right.

'Are you getting in this bath or what?'

'Yes I suppose so.'

'I'll wash your back for you.' Dale is aroused, she knows by that tone. But he never makes the first move like this. That's her role, that's how it works for them; she starts it, she sets the pace, and she gives Dale all he wants. Her control gives her safety, keeps her untouched and unengaged. Sex is what happens to *Dale*, the nearest she's come to it is giving birth to her sons.

The bathroom is the only place where she is truly naked. She feels it now under her towel, vulnerable, exposed and real. Dale's desire feels threatening here, out of its usual context.

'So are you getting in?'

Reluctantly she steps towards the bath, holding the towel in place with both hands.

'Better take your towel off then.' In a single step he is beside her, unfolding first her arms, then the towel. He notices her shiver. 'I'll warm you, Angie love.' His hot hard fingers are all over her, squeezing her breasts, dragging over her thighs, cupping her buttocks, coaxing her legs apart. He is strong and insistent, taking the initiative that is usually hers, being in control. But her flesh is as dead as plasticine, and her heart gallops. She feels so frightened that she knows she will be sick. She ducks violently over the bath and retches. Gobbits of chewed cannelloni, like broken internal organs float in the hot water. Dale picks up the towel and drapes it roughly round her shoulders. She could make up some story about having felt ill all day, but it'll sound as convincing as everything else she tried this evening.

'I'm sorry, Dale. I'm really sorry,' she says. And she is more sorry than he can know that she can't explain any of this to him.

He is wearing the hospital waiting-room look again. 'S'right,' he says in a flat voice, unfamiliar in its lifelessness. 'Can't help how you feel. I'm done in. I'm going to bed.'

By the time she's scrubbed the bath free of dirt and probably two layers of enamel, Dale is just a dark hump on the far side of the mattress. She creeps into bed and lies listening for Dale's breathing, too quiet to be that of a sleeper. The huge flat sheet stretches between them like the entire Russian Steppe in mid-winter. Speech is unthinkable. Sleep seems unlikely. But she spent most of last night taking up paving stones and planting the garden, she has had less than three hours' rest in the last thirty-six. Soon she is struggling over a frozen plain, a mixture of sand and snow whipping her legs, Dale always just ahead of her somewhere in the twilight.

All night it seemed to Samantha she pursued Dale across continents of cotton percale until she heard him ask, 'Cup of tea?' Dale's voice was rough as if he'd been coughing all night. For all she knew he might have been. Samantha opened her eyes. The daylight in the window had a reproachful mid-morning sort of look to it.

She took the mug that was offered and gulped. Dale's face swam from the brightness, paler and more shadowed even than the night before. He was shaved, washed and dressed but still looked crumpled and used up.

'What's the time?' she asked.

'Half ten. You've been asleep for eleven hours.'

On a normal morning that would have been a shocking revelation; Samantha is always awake early and up. But all she said this morning was, 'Oh. Where are the boys?'

'Number thirteen. Looking at kittens with Callendula. She said she'd keep them for an hour.'

An hour. That was long enough to try to mend some of what she felt had broken before she went chasing over hundreds of miles of featureless white sheeted dreamland. Samantha willed herself awake. She reached to caress Dale's face then slipped her hand inside the neck of his shirt, feeling the wiry dark hair grate under her fingertips. On the beach in Bali so long ago now, she'd felt his chest hair like this; she'd found that suntan lotion wouldn't rub in through it.

'It's like trying to moisturise a Brillo pad!' she'd said. That made him laugh, she could remember it so clearly, his shoulders shaking and the laughter jumping from his throat in chunks.

Now he shut his eyes, and sighed at her touch, but then took her wrist and laid her hand back into her lap.

'I'm taking the boys to Mum's for a bit,' he said. 'She can pick them up from school and take them home. I can be there by six. I need to be in Bristol for a few days next week anyway.'

'What?' It was as if Dale was speaking backwards, like the malfunctioning tapes you hear on the radio sometime: 'nnyip snorp tedzzbe jnjabezis'. His words didn't seem to mean anything. She looked around the room bewildered: the smaller of their suitcases was packed. Three pairs of underpants identical except in size sat on top waiting for it to be shut: Goldilocks' Bears Go On Holiday; Daddy Bear's knickers, Little Bear's Knickers and Baby Bear's Knickers. Samantha was impressed that Dale knew where the boys' underwear was kept.

Dale spoke again but his voice was tight, each word emerging slowly as if struggling to free itself from some tide of glue rising in his throat. 'I think you need some time on your own. Some rest. Some time to think. And I do too. So me and the boys are going to Mum's for a while.' Samantha wondered if this was a bizarre manifestation of her over-active imagination. She scanned the room for signs of fast-growing plants or twining snakes. Nothing. Just the suitcase and the summer morning light.

'Why? I don't understand? Is it the garden?'

Dale couldn't look at her any more. He took her hand in his two and turned it like a pebble. 'The garden's part of it. It's been a bad week. The worst week. The worst month. Disastrous. The business is in trouble, Angie. Really big. Too many people owe me money. I've got thirty grand of outstanding invoices, I need to get ten grand's worth of materials to finish the Bath job and the money's just not there. I came back from the site yesterday to tell you we might have to sell the house. And you'd done that to the garden but I don't know who for. And now we'll have to sell.' He let go her hand and wiped his palm over his head, pushing some weight aside. 'Oh it's all knotted up in my head.' His breath was shallow, his face twisted. Huge fat tears began to roll down his face. His eyes pushed them out as painfully as babies. 'I can't cope with it

109

now. Not with the business and all, it's too much. Just too much.'

There was that backwards tape again: 'Nneep snnep djibyt dedshethel'.

He stood up and crossed the room to shut the case. Samantha sat very still. There was no air it seemed, breathing was taking all her attention, pressing her back into the pillows like a stone on her chest. Nothing was making any sense. Not her own behaviour, and not Dale's. Neither of them seemed to be themselves. Or at least not the selves they usually were to each other. All she could grasp was that he was leaving and taking the boys. She opened her mouth to speak several times but couldn't fix on what to say.

Dale was still crying and she was still not sure why. He stood by the bed but she could say nothing.

'I'll ring you,' he said, now almost choking. 'Or you can ring me. Or something.'

He didn't kiss her or say goodbye. Just took the suitcase and stumbled out, down the stairs and through the front door. She heard the boys bounce out of number thirteen and into the car.

'Where's Mummy?' Joe's voice was clingy and plaintive.

'Mummy just needs a rest.' Dale had regained that steady double bass vibration.

'Daddy, what's happened to your eyes?' Tony asked.

'Hay fever, Tony. They're really sore.'

The car doors slammed and her husband and her children disappeared out of her life, leaving her pinned by a vacuum to the bed. Who was she now?

Rest. That's what Dale said. She's had that all right. All day in bed with her arms around a pile of pillows. The Sunday sounds of the street outside drift in and out with wakefulness and sleep, like a gentle tide. She's slept a lot, a passing-out sort of sleep, from which she surfaces to find the same confusion, and like a seal in a storm goes down again to the bottom.

It's afternoon. Lawn mowers hum and children's voices chink across garden boundaries with a sound like morning milk bottles. Dale's words knock around the room as if they were coins left in a washing machine. They have formed themselves into many permutations over the course of the day losing meaning rather than gaining it. Other things bounce off the wall too: the old woman in the supermarket, the boys spotted with rainbow icing, the palm against the night sky, Dale pulling at her towel. She cannot make the bouncing, rolling feeling stop. Nothing can be fixed for long enough to seem real and even the bedroom is growing unfamiliar.

What she needs are the old remedies: tasks. She gets up and goes downstairs. The living room still bears the traces of Thursday night's encampment. She will, she says to herself, just tidy the cushions a little. But she knows where her hand will reach, deep into the horsehair heart of the settee.

The moment she touches the stiff slender envelope something shakes out of the last few hours; some of Dale's words at last have a meaning:

'The business is in trouble. I came back from the site to tell you that we were going to have to sell the house.'

The washing machine stops in mid cycle and all the words and images fall in a heap to the bottom of the drum. She looks around at the unequal walls of Number eleven. At this moment the old cheese-crock house is the only thing that is solid and real. It is the container for her children, her nest with golden eggs. Half of Dale's tears suddenly make some sense: he too needs this house, it's the proof that he provides for his family in the way his lost father never did. If she can save Number eleven he may not be washed away by hardy palms and purple cakes; she can mend Dale's faith in the surface of her smiling portrait and stop him feeling so bad. She can pull the solution from the envelope: Lawrence's house will buy a terrace of Number elevens. But the house can't be pulled out alone. Like Hope in Pandora's box it keeps bad company.

She catches sight of herself in the mantelpiece mirror. A tall thin woman in winceyette pyjamas with lank hair sits on an elegant sofa in a room lit by afternoon sun. She is holding an envelope rather unnaturally in her right hand. In that one picture Samantha knows two realities are contained: the present is the woman in the room, the past is the girl in the envelope. Doppelgangers, she's kept them apart in fear of some mutually assured destruction. And now they must touch. She fears to find which reality will be the stronger.

7

Samantha had prepared herself carefully for her visit to Lawrence's lawyers. She would find them buried in a sixteenth-century back street. There would be railings thickened with millennia of lead paint, a heavy front door, wide enough to take periwigs and crinolines. At least three brass plaques would stud the brickwork as she rang the doorbell. Inside, a faded rose of a receptionist, employed in 1968 for her pretty legs, would usher her to a dark oak-panelled room. An elderly lawyer in a three-piece black suit – Mr Geoffrey's elderly relative – would sit behind a desk with a green leather top. Gravely but impersonally he would ask her to produce proof that she was Samantha Powell. Every scene was stained the colour of tea or Cuban cigars, and Samantha moved confidently through them, softened and concealed in their tannin dark shadows. No one would be there to see her, no detective inspectors ready to reopen a long-dead case, no parent waiting for a glimpse of a vanished child. She clothed herself in an enforced rationality by picturing minutely the scene and how it would progress.

But the offices of Tucker, Fryer and Woodward didn't fit the picture. The taxi dropped her on a recently built estate apparently made from the plastic bricks in Tony and Joe's toy box. The little ticky-tack houses gathered round a square of green, so synthetic-looking that she expected to see a blue plastic cow with a painted flower in its mouth grazing there. The lawyers' office was at number three, with a vets' practice on one side and an ordinary house on the other with washing on the line and kids' bikes resting against the wall. Through the windows of number three Samantha could see desks and word processors, tiled floors and chrome tables in what would have been the living room. There was a natty little glass porch over the front door, and a large mock terracotta pot of pink geraniums beside the path. The comforting gloom of old streets and leaning houses was burnt off in the glare from the acres of double glazing. Immediately she could imagine police cars pulling onto the neat little brick forecourt and thought she caught sight of her father's green estate parked round the back. It was a struggle not to run. She walked stiff-legged up the road and spent half an hour being guided round a show home with a couple of newlyweds from Ipswich. She was grateful for their endless questions. While the agent told them about fitted carpets and gold bathroom taps Samantha reconstructed the scene in the lawyers to accommodate PVC window frames and mock-Victorian coach lights.

Samantha returned to number three with her perceptions shifted from Pepys and Dickens to Beezer and Disney. In the end the Legoland nature of T, F and W's offices helped to give the whole experience a kind of cartoon feel. She held back the thoughts of parental saloons and panda cars by imagining them like giant matchbox vehicles with little models of people inside. It was effective enough to let her walk calmly into the bright anodyne consulting room and sit at the black ash table as if the whole scene was happening to someone else. In place of Mr Geoffrey's uncle a young woman lawyer appeared, Miss Taylor, a cross between Jerry Hall and Roger Rabbit's girl friend. It all helped to maintain calm through a sense of total unreality.

Samantha watched her own white fingers pulling documents from the bag on her lap, like the tentacles of some deep-sea squid rummaging in the abyss. She heard her own voice explaining the link between Samantha Powell and Angela Cassinari. The lawyer's red-lipsticked mouth smiled, then moved to make words but they arrived at Samantha's brain some time later, in the way that the sky roars after the fighter plane has passed.

'There's no problem, Mrs Cassinari, you have all the documentation here,' the words announced from the now still mouth. 'In any case Mr Spence included reference to the use of your middle name as your Christian name and your married surname in his will.'

Lawrence *knew* she was Angela Cassinari? Samantha had assumed that the lawyers had found her; tracked her down through the card indices and dingy computer networks, the way they find lottery winners who don't claim or lost wives in films. The day she opened the envelope she'd imagined Lawrence grey and haggard giving them her name, her old name, and nothing more, not knowing if she could be found.

But Lawrence had *known*. Known all along where she was. Samantha shuddered as the room become coldly real. Here was the real executor of Lawrence's will sitting before her: no cartoon blonde but a woman in her early thirties, with bad open pores on the end of her nose, smelling of instant coffee and cigarettes. Samantha spoke, trying to sound businesslike and detached:

'Did Mr Spence give you any idea how he knew my address? We haven't been in contact for almost ten years. I just wondered . . .' Miss Taylor was off guard. Her face showed surprise and her voice was hesitant as she scrabbled to string the right words together.

'Forgive me, Mrs Cassinari. I assumed in the light of the bequest and the details Mr Spence gave us that you were . . . *close*.'

'What details?'

'Mrs Cassinari.' Miss Taylor blushed, caught out in professional indiscretion. She went on with great deliberation, 'I wasn't personally acquainted with Mr Spence, but I understand that he spoke warmly of you and your husband and children. I gained the impression that he was a close friend of long standing. He was, I understand, something of a recluse, not inclined to leave his home. I assumed that you had perhaps visited regularly . . . I apologise if I have offended you in some way.' The shutters went down on the lawyer's eyes. She would give nothing else away.

The red-lipsticked lips moved again, drawing Samantha's attention:

'Your signature here and here . . .?'

Her fingers took a pen, and moved it to make a signature: 'Samantha Angela Cassinari née Samantha Angela Powell.' The two names for the first time together on the same page. She stared at them whilst the blonde woman bent her head to write again. And then she was outside in the dry East Anglian noon, the deeds for Lime House in her bag and its keys in her hand.

Inside the old café on North Street it was comfortingly dim and familiar. Weren't those brown splashes on the wall the ones Christine's spilt coke made a decade and more ago? The proprietors seemed to subscribe to the Quentin Crisp school of cleanliness that dictates that after the first seven years the dirt doesn't get any worse. Samantha took off the dark glasses, and sat over a coffee trying to stop the ringing in her head. She had imagined Lawrence contained in the past, frozen in a cold winter afternoon, with the clock on the study mantelpiece stopped at the moment when a seventeen-year-old girl had walked from his front door. That was what had kept him in a separate world, part of a life that was nothing to do with Dale, Tony, Joe and Angela. But that had never been the truth. Although Lawrence himself may never have left Lime House, all the same he'd been watching and following. Running his sinewy hands over her life. She felt him now, pressing the breath out of her body.

She shut her eyes and wondered how many times in ten years a camera had clicked on her life? On her bedsit curtains, on the baby in her arms, on the boys' faces as they crossed the road to school, on Dale as he kissed her on the doorstep. Perhaps her father too knew everything. She imagined Lawrence's desk strewn with photos of the life she had begun to feel safe in. As she watched, a dark stain drew across each one, like blood seeping through a bandage.

Sam opened her eyes. Delivering the keys to an estate agent and taking the next train home just wasn't possible. Sprung free from the past Lawrence was suddenly more alive than ever. She had to know in her heart that he was dead, and without a body to bury, an empty house would be the next best thing.

She asked the taxi driver to be back in a hour, then got out of the car and stood in the time-travel landscape. This had been one of her favourite places as a girl. Two narrow lanes going to almost nowhere crossed in the cornfields. The two straight and invariably empty tracks marking out the waving acres of wheat or barley made this piece of cultivated landscape into something wild, deserted. She'd felt then that this was a taster, a little aperitif of the solitude and wilderness she would savour all her adult life. Now, as the sound of the cab faded over the hill she shuddered; it hadn't changed a bit. The barley still stretched from skyline to skyline, the green already gilding under the sun. A hundred yards away the same yellowhammer was still strung on the wire, winding in the reel of its hot dry song. Down amongst the stems even the grasshoppers were the same, they still shushed and chipped, their bodies desiccated as paper. The sounds measured out the silence and the heat, like the equidistant poles on a fence line. Lead-heavy, she turned and walked towards the avenue of lime trees that marked the approach to Lawrence's home.

Time folded. Angela Cassinari and Samantha Powell were side by side on the same page, on this lane on the same hot afternoon . . .

*

It is four but still too hot to cycle. She must have done five miles already at least. She knows she'll have to get used to temperatures much higher than this over the next few years. Every day perhaps she'll be walking alone with the sun slicing down to ground level like a hot knife between the trees. She sees herself, legs sticking out of khaki shorts looking sinewy and intrepid rather than plain, pale and skinny, a man's shirt tied at the waist, binoculars round her neck. She'll walk along a path with last night's rain rising as steam from the soil all around her. People don't get cancer in the rainforest. If Bea would only live long enough Sam could find her a cure, some plant distillate or extract of frog to make her yellow skin flush pink and get her laugh back.

She leans the bike against the bank and sits down. She thinks about the day, trying to flatten the creases out of it and lay it down. There had been the usual start: the sound of her father's electric razor buzzing in the bathroom and him singing some out-of-tune snatch of something, it always made her smile.

'O sole mio!' it had been this morning. Then she heard him walking about on the landing doing up his tie, and saying 'Samantha' out loud to himself in various different ways. 'Samantha. Samantha. Samantha.'

He'd always done it but she'd only just started noticing and now it was far too late to ask why, or explain that she didn't like it. What did he think when he said it? Of some little girl in a pair of flowery shorts and a sun hat, she was pretty sure. *His* little girl Samantha, who was nothing to do with her any more.

Samantha stayed in bed until Ralph had gone this morning because today had been another of Bea's hospital days. Sam had taken a day off school to go with her. That's what always happened now. Ralph didn't even mention taking his wife to Addenbrookes as he had two months ago. She took herself on the bus, and Sam went with her. Sam had heard them arguing about it at first.

'It's not fair, Ralph. It could affect her future. She wants to go to university.'

'It'll affect more than her future if I lose my job. I can't take any more time off.'

That was a lie. Ralph's boss had told Bea that whenever Ralph was needed at home he could take the time. Sam had heard Robert say it over a rare social Sunday afternoon tea. But Ralph ignored all that.

It's double biology now, Sam thought as they stood at the bus stop. She'd be missing double biology, a chemistry practical and physics today. How could she prepare for the Oxbridge entrance exams like this? What did Ralph care? 'Be good, sweet maid, and let who will be clever!' That's what he said whenever she mentioned University. She felt a hot wave of panic and resentment rise from her stomach as the bus pulled up.

'Can you take my handbag for a minute, Sam?' asked Bea. 'I need both hands to get up the first step.'

They sat at the back of the bus. Bea leant against the window and dozed a bit. 'You don't mind do you, Sam?' she said. 'It's just this radiotherapy makes me so tired. Still, halfway through now. Another two weeks. They say you feel better after it stops.' Bea used those giveaway words 'radio therapy' and 'chemotherapy' all the time. Today they walked through the plastic corridors to find 'Oncology' again. But they never talked about Bea's *cancer* and the fact that she might die. They sat waiting, Bea in her horrible hospital gown, and looked at the back copies of *Woman's Realm*.

'Look, Sam, would you wear that if I knitted it?'

'No, it's vile.'

'Humm. Well, I think camel is a very flattering colour. My mother had a beautiful camel-coloured coat. And matching gloves. Very classy.'

They were surrounded by other poor victims, all women, similarly brought low and humiliated by sickness. They all wore the same garments distinguished by nothing but a laundry mark, picked from the anonymous piles in the changing cubicles; like shrouds – one size fits all. There was an atmosphere of mute acceptance. As if their disease and its miserable indignities was just one more of the inevitable burdens of womanhood along with knitting patterns and recipes for left-over chicken. From their whisperings Sam gathered that their cancers were indeed particularly 'feminine': wombs and breasts brought nothing but trouble it seemed – burdensome husbands, wailing babies, tumours, pain, and death.

The patients hardly spoke to each other, as if by acknowledging each other's presence they would be admitting the possibility that this disease was reality. They sat alone, or with a companion in street clothes, pointing out items on the thin badly printed pages: pictures of Easter cakes with bright yellow marzipan chickens, grinning women in appliquéd aprons, and fat white babies with knitted booties. The stories printed between the overlit photographs told of disabled toddlers pulled from burning buildings, devoted husbands snatched by wives from the very jaws of death. The women sat reading and when they spoke their voices were like sighs, just reverential murmurs covering the time until they were called for their treatment.

'Mrs Powell?'

Smiling, Bea gathered her dressing gown and got up, 'Back soon, poppet. Watch my bag won't you?' and the nurse led her away. Whilst she was gone Sam paced the squeaky tiles and swore silently. She vowed, that she would never, *never* have *any* of this. No illness, no laundry marks, no nylon cardigans with homespun look, no portly husband or gap-toothed child. She was going as far as she could get from this, the designated 'Realm of Women'. She seethed that her mother should submit to it all so quietly. When Bea came back she wanted to shout at her, shake her out of the horrible white coffin lining, with its tied back that gave other people access to your body before yourself. But she just walked meekly to the cubicles, to wait whilst Bea changed.

'Look,' Bea said, pointing to her chest and laughing: 'I'm the Golden Shot!'

Samantha looked: there were three concentric circles, black and ugly, with Bea's skinny breast bone at their centre, red and hot like a knuckle of roasting pork. They had drawn a target on her mummy's chest and burnt its bulls eye red with their X-rays. Bea laughed again. Sam swallowed hard and stretched the corners of her mouth outwards, hoping her face would appear to smile. 'Bernie, the Bolt!' she said.

The bus seemed to take forever. Bea dozed again, nodding like a toy dog on a parcel shelf. Sam laid her cheek on the window and breathed in the coolness of the glass. But the hospital smell wouldn't go. The scent of the black marker on her mother's burnt skin and the faint mouldering of ancient magazines stuck in her nostrils like sick. She wanted to smash her head against the window until the glass broke. But Bea was propped against her side snoring very slightly. So Sam sat still and imagined a scream so loud it would cleave the road in two and sear the black tarmac to white.

They had to wait half an hour for a taxi home from Haverhill. Bea was so tired that she sat on the town hall steps amidst the crisp packets and last Saturday's confetti. She picked a tiny blue fragment from the ground, and held it up delicately between a finger and thumb. 'Oh look!' she said. 'It's a little bell! How sweet!' Bea's drawn face was lit up with genuine delight. 'Look,' she insisted, 'look! It's the exact same colour as blue sky and a *perfect little bell*!'

How could her mother take such pleasure in something so small? Sam was amazed and repelled. 'You're dying of cancer,' she thought, 'and you care about a scrap of trodden tissue paper?' She pretended hard to be looking out for the taxi but Bea was oblivious anyway to anything but the miniature wedding bell.

'Nothing like this when I married y'father,' she went on still staring hard at it.' 'People threw rice at us. Mummy collected it all up and made a pudding. She really did. Never got over rationing did your Granny Agnes.'

It was gone three when they got in. Granny Pearl's voice came thin and wavy, like an asp from her bedroom, 'Bea? Samantha? Is that you?'

Bea went a paler shade of grey at the sound of her mother-in-law's voice. 'Funny isn't it?' she whispered. 'I forget all about her when we're not in!'

'Don't bother about my lunch,' Pearl called tremulously, 'I've gone beyond hunger now.'

'You've got to hand it to her for performance.'

Bea smiled, but Sam threw her mac across the hall, furious. 'I don't know how you can laugh. I want to kill her!'

'Sam! She's an old lady!'

'She's a selfish bitch. Age hasn't got anything to do with it!'

'Oh, Sam, don't start. It doesn't help.'

'Why don't you get angry with *her*? Why are you snapping at *me*?'

'I'm not snapping at anyone.'

'Well maybe you should!'

'Sam! Stop it!'

'Stop what? *What*? I'm going out for a bike ride. Don't you *dare* make her *anything*.'

Sam slammed the back door and cycled fiercely up the hill, crying, sweating and swearing all at once, not aiming to go anywhere but away.

It's only now after resting in the sun that Sam knows that she's decided to seek out Lawrence again. She looks at the emptiness of the shallow valley and wheels her bike towards the lime-lined drive.

The bright lane meets the shade under the lime branches, drawing a boundary of light and dark. Sam pauses at the junction feeling the contrast of coolness and heat. The limes are in full leaf, their branches meeting over the drive, making a tunnel of sharpest green with the blue of the front door just visible at its end. Light streaks and puddles onto the ground beneath, enhancing the perspective of the avenue's length, with a receding mosaic of sand, shade and burnt-out white. It is tempting to Sam in the way that a lawn of new snow tempts footprints or a smooth lagoon tempts a swimmer. She rides her bike slowly down the cool dappled passageway, closing her eyes to feel the stripes of light and shade fall on her skin, throwing back her head to catch the flashes of sky and the first sweet scent of lime flowers. Then she shoots out into the sunlight, the house rises up before her, and Lawrence is standing in the open front door, sudden as a conjuring trick.

'Well well!' he says smiling. 'That was fortunate timing!' There is that strange unreadable languor again, a private joke against the world in every word. He runs down the short flight of steps to the drive, wearing the same faded jeans and perfectly laundered shirt. He is thinner than she remembers, more tanned and still he doesn't fit any of the categories of adult men, with which she is familiar. 'I was about to inspect the conservatory,' he says, 'I seem to remember my last attempt to show you around was hampered by a dog! Do you have time now?' It is as if it were two minutes since she last came instead of two months.

'Um. Yes please!'

'Good. Good. Why don't you just leave your bike here?'

'Oh. Yes. Right.'

Like a well-prepared tour guide he ushers her through a gate, telling her the names of plants as they go . . .

Sam has almost no experience of big tropical greenhouses. The ones in the University Botanic Gardens in Cambridge have been closed for renovation for several years. Greenhouses in people's gardens are usually the size of a corn-flake packet and full of sickly tomato plants. Christine's father had made a conservatory over the back of their house, with a roof of see-through plastic, crinkle-cut like chips. It now holds a welly rack and two washing lines and Christine's mum says it's a great place to dry things on showery days. Lawrence's conservatory contains no wellies or washing and instead of creaky plastic it has a glass roof, high as a chancel, domed as if a flying saucer has landed over the rafters.

Inside, the atmosphere is hot and weighted and seems to offer more resistance to movement, slowing everything down. There is a complex layered smell, spicy and fruited, sweet and fermenting. Sam feels she could wring out the richness from the air with her hands. Every surface is slick with fine moisture, and the floor is slippery. 'This was in ruins when I moved in. Plants didn't interest my father. They were my mother's domain,' says Lawrence. 'I had it restored but with a few more modern features, automated heating, watering and ventilation, that sort of thing.' He is swaggering slightly, walking ahead and pointing to things. Sam isn't listening. She is taking in full-sized palm trees, ferns, orchids, climbers. Everything twined and tangled, with no artifice of neatness. She half closes her eyes and sucks in the warm moist air.

Lawrence turns to see her standing like Saint Teresa before a vision of the divine; rooted, euphoric. He has never encountered anything like her before. At least not anything female.

'It's all a cheat really,' he says, briskly continuing with his usual guided tour patter, 'these plants are from all four corners of the sub tropics. Monsteras, Zingibers, Cyatheas, various orchids . . . They're all things that will grow readily in an intermediate house like this, where they can take a little air in the summer and don't need a great deal of winter heating. Suppose you'd call it a pretend jungle.'

Sam's eyes snap open, her attention focuses on his face with such sudden intensity that Lawrence flinches. 'You said "jungle".' She sounds shocked, accusatory. Lawrence laughs nervously. There is definitely something strange about this girl. Then she smiles, 'I mean the word "rainforest", it doesn't sound *wild* enough.'

Her face is so open, so naked that Lawrence is almost embarrassed. He looks away. Up in the roof he sees the sunlight spearing through the leaves and fronds, sharper than he's ever noticed it before. His speech becomes less formal and more hesitant. 'I'd never thought about it that way. When I was a child it was always called jungle. I've never called it anything else. But I do understand what you mean. You know real jungle is much, much better than this!'

Sam gasps with the intense desire to hear first-hand reports. 'Have you been? What was it really like?' He looks from the brightness above and is blinded again by the expression in her eyes. What is it about this girl? Not her looks: compared with his mother's pale rounded femininity this girl is rather mannish. And yet she does have a touch of, what? Delicacy? Those long thin limbs, that straight self-conscious hair, and the light in the face, in the eyes! Is it just that he meets no one these days in his house-prison? Or is there really a magnesium flame of intensity here, in her?

'Yes I have,' he says, 'often. Belize, Venezuela, Brazil, twice to Malaya, several times to West Africa. At the end of business trips you know. Some of these plants are things I brought back myself.'

He tries hard to regain his indifference and detachment, his lord of the manor benevolence. But her candour, her unashamed passion are compelling. She shares at least some of his fixation with plants. She even has a little knowledge. He's drawn to her, the way you are to deep clear water; you lean over the still surface to wonder at the way you can see all the way to the bottom of another world.

'Did you see really big trees? Buttress roots and things?' Sam steps closer, almost touching his chest with her pointed little breasts. He doesn't remember standing so close to a girl like this. When might it have been? Ten years ago? More? Her desire for his experience draws up the memory of the Malaysian dipterocarps. He never knew he'd noticed so much detail.

125

Closing his eyes for moment, his heart, like hers, beats faster at the very thought of them.

'Yes. Yes I did. Huge trees. They feel as if they're on another scale, as if one had stepped into some sort of land of giants!'

She gives a huge sigh, and rocks back on her heels, eyes closed, 'Oh, that's what I want to see. Really, really big trees, with trunks the size of a house.' She spreads her arms wide. 'I want to walk around their roots, where it's almost dark and then climb up two hundred feet to their crowns where it's all light.' Her head drops back and she looks up as if she were already reaching for the highest branch in the canopy. And Lawrence finds himself looking up too, expecting to see that intense blue sky and feel the heaviness of tropical sunshine, falling through the topmost leaves of a kapok tree.

Lawrence brings drinks to have on the terrace beside the conservatory. 'Pimms,' he says, 'really not that alcoholic.'

They sit side by side on the weathered wooden benches sipping their drinks and talking mostly about plants. Sam crosses her legs like a film star being interviewed and feels grown up and sophisticated. Lawrence asks about her ambitions, and out they fly, natural as butterflies around Sam's head. Lawrence could swat every one of them, because Sam is like every other idealist he's ever known, full of dreams and no concrete idea how to achieve them. His father, Fraser Spence, would have seen no use in this unformed girl, no reason not to strip her silly dreams to the bone. Fraser had always known how to achieve, had made every step of his own climb from a room over a wet fish shop to the gracious velvet lawns of Lime House. Fraser taught his son that ideas and dreams were a waste of time, and the folk that harboured them foolish. Dreamers could always be manipulated; dangle their dream before them and you could lead them to the very brink of hell. Faced with such people Fraser was gripped with the same feeling a fox must get in a shed full of clucking chickens – the desire to rip and bite and see blood on the walls.

But in spite of all his father's training Lawrence retained a soft spot for dreamers. His mother had been one. Margaret had lived for her flowers. She spent all her days in the heart of her flower beds. Lawrence learned to walk in amongst his mother's herbaceous borders, the plants towering above him, their tall stems raising shimmering petals to the sun. Down there, in the canyons of cimcifuga and phlox, achilea and knifophias nothing existed but the flowers, the blue sky and the sweet lisping voice of his mother telling of the secret workings of roots and the invisible capturing of sunlight. Sometimes afterwards, dwarfed in the heat of some tropical forest, Lawrence would catch a remnant of those lost days, a brief chiffon touch of that old bliss. Always, it was gone before he could even name what he felt.

So Lawrence listens attentively as Sam chatters on about species destruction and the loss of biodiversity. Somehow she imagines she will combat it all with a few scientific papers read by a handful of academics. He can imagine his father's distaste for such talk, the curled lip, the coldness in the eye. He experienced it himself as a tiny child when he trotted round the garden after his mother. Fraser didn't much like his wife Margaret, but she'd come with a fortune. Nothing he couldn't have made himself in a few years but an opportunity was an opportunity. Already thirty when she married and plain, Fraser expected that Margaret would at least be sensible. He never imagined that such a solid-looking woman could harbour such a frivolous obsession. Fraser Spence had no patience with such useless and unproductive activity. Flowers were for the soft, the weak, the self-indulgent and indolent. Lawrence's mother was barely cold in her grave when her flowers were removed and replaced with shrubs. Hard and undemanding plants that could be controlled with a pair of shears. The icy willpower of his father blew around Lawrence's heart, cauterising it, shrivelling its growth to nothing.

But now that Fraser is dead too, it is the pollen-light memory of his mother that has settled on him and drawn Lawrence back to wander in her garden. He replaced her flowers in the first year at Lime House, spending thousands to establish instantly the swathes and clumps that she had nurtured from tiny cuttings and rootlets. He feels protected here by Margaret's dreams. Cleansed somehow. The bitter acidity of his father's long influence is neutralised a little. Lawrence feels that if he stays safe at Lime House, he may become a better person. In time he may wear away the patterns ingrained by his father's long training: the taste for blood, the old reflex to manipulate and control, as habitual as eating breakfast.

But only in time. Lawrence waits for a gap in Sam's stream of words, and he leans forward to replace his glass on the tray. It is a gesture so apparently natural and casual, that Lawrence hardly recognises that he is about to manipulate an idealist yet again.

'It sounds to me as if you've planned things out quite carefully. Oxford, a doctorate, then fieldwork.' He notices how she glows under his praise; it's the perfect moment to deliver the well-aimed blow. 'But I think your only possible problem could be funding for your doctorate, and beyond of course.'

Lawrence can see that no one has ever pointed out the practical flaws in her plans, she has never met with anything other than blind praise or total indifference. She uncrosses her legs, a gauche schoolgirl again.

Sam has always believed that academic excellence alone will get her to the rainforest: her brilliance and suitability would be acknowledged, she would simply be 'sent'. It has never occurred to her that money could stand in her way. In one sentence Lawrence has flicked the 'off' switch on the hologram of her ambitions.

'Please, Sam, don't look so worried. I don't mean to pour cold water on your plans. Nothing could be further from my mind. I just wanted to know if you have a sponsor, someone who can support your research in future.'

'No. I don't have anyone.' Sam is blank with dismay.

'Well then. I think that's where I could come in. Given my interest in plants and my business contacts I think I could find you sponsorship. Maybe even some funding for a gap year trip . . .' he trails off, tantalisingly vague. 'I'll investigate things for you. We could discuss it further next time?'

Sam nods. He understands her speechless silence. In the space of ten seconds Lawrence knows he has taken Sam from despair to wild hope. He's not even sure himself why. He fiddles idly with the plant poking from the stone wall, and starts to distract her. 'I always tell Mr Jenkins to leave the *Cymbaleria* in the walls!' he says, giving her a chance to show off.

She grins immediately, and takes the bait. 'It's nearly my favourite Latin name *Cymbaleria muralis*!' Sam says. 'It sounds like the name of some fairy, The Princess Cymbaleria!'

'That's a shamelessly feminine and romantic viewpoint, Sam. I wouldn't have thought you'd have time for such things?'

'But that's how I remember Latin names – I have to give them some sort of story or character or I can't remember them. Unless they just sound nice like *Fraxinus excelsior*. I think that could be a spell. You know, you'd stand in front of a big rock-face and say it and the whole thing would open!'

Lawrence laughs quite genuinely. Sam blushes with pleasure. She has never made anyone except Bea laugh quite like that. If I look at him sideways, thinks Sam, he could be thirty, twenty-five even.

In his study Lawrence watches her reflection bending over the maps, her neck so curved and delicate, her face completely absorbed. He points to the areas where he's travelled in the past.

'All this is above the tree line. Incredible landscape almost four thousand metres up. Are you familiar with the *Masde-vallia*? No? Marvellous plants. South American genus of

orchids. *Masdevallia veitchiana* grows there in the rock cre-
vices. The most astounding orange with electric-blue hairs that
glint in the sun. I collected some very good specimens from
there!' Her intense attention is unsettling. It calls back the
memory of the orange flowers and his lungs burning with the
altitude so powerfully that he shivers. 'Quite a number of them
I remember, huge plants a foot or more across!'

'What did you do with them? The orchids you collected.'

He's caught off guard, still standing and panting over the
cowering plants on an Andean mountainside. He wants the
answer he gives her to be the truth. He thinks of it like that, as
truth, as he tells her, 'Donated to botanical gardens. That sort
of thing.' At that moment he wishes the smuggling of rare
orchids hadn't proved to be such a lucrative sideline. But the
truth is that it was. The truth is that the passion for plants
seeded by his mother was nipped by his father's chill, infected
with the impulse to use, and control. The truth is that Lawrence
has ripped and plundered and possessed what his mother and
this gangling girl hold to be almost sacred. Lawrence hasn't
blushed for thirty years as he blushes now. He's grateful that
the clock on the mantelpiece strikes loudly enough to be a
distraction.

Samantha looks up, startled he guesses at the time, but then
attracted by the clock itself. A perfect box of glass holds a little
golden tree, in whose branches a white clockface sits amid rows
of perfect miniature white blossoms, its hands are tiny rows of
enamelled leaves.

'It's so beautiful. I've never seen a clock like that before!'

'It's seventeenth century. Quite unique. It has two different
faces, Summer,' he turns the glass case through a hundred and
eighty degrees, 'and Winter.' The tree is gnarled with broken
branches, bare of any leaf or blossom. The clockface is black
and its hands two chains of withered leaves. Involuntarily
Samantha shudders at the obvious symbolism of the passage
of time leading only to death and decay. 'It's worth twenty-five

thousand pounds,' he tells her. Price in Lawrence's experience is what people want to hear most about any object.

But Samantha shrugs this information off. 'It's sort of sinister. I can see why you have the green tree side showing. Not the other side.'

'Oh, I turn it round sometimes. In memory of my father. He and my mother had a sort of silent battle over it. Each time Mother passed, she would turn the Summer face outwards. And when he passed Father turned it the other way.'

She gazes for moment, transported. 'Who won? In the end?' But she doesn't wait for an answer, she's already fluttering and agitated like a bird. 'I've got to go,' she says, 'I've been away for ages.'

'Do come again, whenever you like.'

She cycles away, with those long white legs, that wispy hair, catching the patches of light then shade under the limes. He runs lightly up the steps to the front door. 'Fraxinus excelsior!' he commands it, and smiles. As he puts away the maps and books in the study he tells himself he will take responsibility for realising her dreams. He will be her friend and mentor. Perhaps he could fund her studentship and research himself, why not? If she would accept he'd be glad to. It would be penance for all the logging concessions, the hydro-electric dams, the open-cast mines to which he has been midwife. Her idealism will heal him and absolve him.

'I *hope* she comes back!' he says aloud and turns the Winter face of the clock to the wall, hiding the knowledge, that he *knows* she'll be back. Her dreams are in his pocket.

Samantha stood just inside the shade of the lime trees looking down the drive to the house. Nothing but the breeze had moved in half an hour or more. The gravel was waist high in weeds and she could see that the front door was boarded over. The pink rambling rose that Lawrence had laughed about and always said was 'common' was finally getting its revenge and had grown over his study window. He really was gone. She didn't need to go any closer to feel the lack of him. She didn't want to look through the windows and remember any more. The taxi horn bleated and she fled down the road towards the sound. She slumped in the back seat and gulped the cool air streaming in as they slipped through the time travel countryside of her childhood. She ran ahead with Lime House like a trophy for Dale, already editing the sort of truth she would tell him.

But the past wasn't finished with her for the day because the taxi driver, being one of the last true locals in that part of the world, was taking a nice quiet shortcut. A route down a lane where only one house stood, almost invisible now behind an overgrown hedge. Years ago he remembered that the people who lived there had lost a daughter, though whether dead or simply run off he couldn't recall. So when the apparently exhausted young woman passenger yelled 'stop' at the top of her voice as they passed its gate he began to wonder who she was and why she wanted to stop here. He pulled in and she asked him to wait. But she didn't stay long. He only had time to smoke a cigarette and doubt his recollection of the tale of the disappearing girl before she came back and asked to be taken to the bus station. She tipped him a fiver over the fare, and he watched her walking away. Whoever she was, she looked tired enough for two lifetimes, he thought.

8

Samantha ignores the taxi driver's surprise. She leaps out of the car and runs towards her old home without thinking what she is doing, like a pigeon homing by instinct. She puts her hand on top of the gate – the old wooden gate that Ralph made – ready to push it open and walk round the hedge as if this were just the end of another school day long ago. Everything looks much the same, just a little softer at the edges, blurred by vegetation growth. She hears a young child's voice come through an open window, and wonders if she'd find her baby-self sitting on Daddy's lap in sunshine by the living-room window, pushing her bare toes into his hands and laughing.

She stops stock still to listen.

'Go on! Harder!'

The whole length of Sam's foot fitted easily into Ralph's palm. She braced her back against his chest and pushed his hand away using all the strength of one leg. 'Keep pushing! Go on, nearly done it! There!'

She could feel the warmth and roughness of his calluses under her pink sole. He took both feet crammed side by side into his hand. 'Right. Two legs against one hand. One, two, three, GO!'

She shut her eyes and pushed with all her might. He never let her win easily, she had to try right to the end, when her legs were stretched straight and her toes pointed between his fingers. Fully extended her legs didn't reach the end of his lap. She must have been less than two.

'Strongest girl in the world!' Ralph told her. 'You'll live to be a hundred. Women live longer than men you know, because women can cry and men can't.'

Ralph sounded so sad that Sam felt sorry. It wasn't fair to stop men crying, but she didn't have the words to say so.

That was just before Bea's first operation, when she was in hospital for the first time. But Sam never remembered that, because in those first years she was her daddy's girl. They were always together, out in the lunar landscape that the builders had left around the new house, trying to make it look like a garden. Sam jumped on the joins between the turves of grass in her little red wellies and wheeled tiny barrowfuls of topsoil to make a veg patch. She held strings straight so Daddy could plant long rows of carrots and peas, and wrote labels with her tongue sticking out of the corner of her mouth. They had a greenhouse then, and Sam would stand on a box so she could see over the top of the staging, and watch Ralph pricking out seedlings.

Every spring until she didn't need to stand on a box any more Sam spent Saturday afternoons in the greenhouse with Ralph. They had the radio on in the corner and they worked side by side without speaking, comfortably silent as dogs in the same basket by the fire. Sometimes in the mornings before breakfast, she would join Ralph on a little tour of the seed boxes, to see what had come up.

'That's the fastest germination for parsley I've ever known! Did you plant those, Sam?'

'Yes and the thyme.'

'Green fingers, my girl. Green fingers!'

They shared the excitement when the first tiny green shoots showed that seed had germinated and it never seemed less than magical.

Bea came into the garden like a visiting Royal. Sam would show her around all the things that she and Ralph had been doing: seedlings in the greenhouse, first potatoes in the veg plot, petunias and snapdragons in the flower beds. Sam was the official spokesperson and as she talked, Bea would smile at

Ralph over her head, and he would smile back. Sometimes, when Sam had been cooking with her mother she took things into the garden for Ralph to try, and Bea and Ralph would smile at one another through the kitchen window. Sam loved those moments; she felt that by being their words she held their hands in each of hers.

Those times trickled gradually away to nothing, evaporating like water in the sun. The easy atmosphere of the greenhouse on a Saturday morning stiffened year by year to an intolerable rigidity. The sweetness of a shared family life took years to drip, drip, drip away. Only the last dregs were left after the summer of 'The Scottish Holiday' when Sam was fourteen. Afterwards that's how Bea and Sam referred to it; like actors refusing to say Macbeth, no one ever said 'The year we went to Scotland, or 'That holiday we had near Skye', it was always darkly 'The Scottish Holiday'.

Bea had been ill, but insisted they should still take their holiday as planned in a tiny caravan on a lochside, an hour's drive from the nearest loaf of bread. It was wild and beautiful with red deer passing the windows every evening and naïve little brown trout jumping onto Ralph's hooks every morning. But Bea's health wasn't up to the kind of communion with Nature that she and Ralph had shared and enjoyed in their youth. The fifty-yard clamber over rocks and heather to an earth closet and standing in a stream in the rain for hours wore her to greyness in two days. She huddled in the caravan in her sleeping bag and waved through the windows. As Bea grew visibly paler, Ralph grew more determinedly jolly.

'Nothing wrong with your mother that a nice bit of grilled trout won't cure! Come on, Sam, these fish won't catch themselves y'know!'

But after four days Bea was getting incoherent with pain and cold, and Ralph panicked. Sam had never seen her quiet father flustered before. Never even heard him say 'Damn'. So when, outside the caravan, he hissed, 'We've got to get her home tonight, or she's going to fucking die on us!' she felt as if she had been punched in the face.

They loaded the car in silence, Ralph throwing things into the boot with a ferocity that made Sam bite her lip and tremble. Bea got worse. By the time they set off she was groaning and semi-conscious on the back seat, Sam was rigid and terrified in the front. The darkness seemed to stretch for ever, and Sam felt locked inside it with her mother's groans and her father's curses, mesmerised by the headlights and the windscreen wipers. Ralph drove so fast Sam felt they would all be killed but she was too numb and miserable to care.

They got home in a dawn drained of any colour or warmth and put Bea to bed. Ralph dug out the flower beds the same day. He demolished the greenhouse too, smashed it in ten minutes with an axe. Sam crouched behind her bedroom door and cried.

'No time for this nonsense any more,' he said when he came in, 'not with your mother the way she is.'

There were no days to spend with Ralph in the garden after that. He mowed the lawn on weekday nights, scowling like a demon and if Sam tried to help with the veg patch at weekends he snapped at her if she made the slightest mistake. He took to standing at her bedroom door from time to time and shouting at her about her untidiness.

Yet he still seemed to harbour a longing for those sweet Saturday afternoons. She heard it in his voice every morning, when he said her name aloud over and over again to his reflection as he shaved. At first it made her sad, and then it made her angry. How could he go on saying her name like that, as if he hadn't pulled down the greenhouse and become an old cuss overnight? How could he pretend he loved her when he'd pushed her away?

Later that same summer when Bea had seemed to be sinking fast, Ralph took time off from work to care for her and Sam played at Christine's house a lot. One morning Ralph called her into the kitchen after the doctor had been.

'Sam,' he told her, 'Mummy's very ill.'

'I know that!'

'I mean, she's iller than we thought.' He reached forwards and took Sam's hand. She hung back, keeping the distance of her arm between them, daring him to say more. She wouldn't hear her mother condemned by that fat GP, with his nervous piggy eyes.

'We'll be all right, Sam, just the two of us. We'll be all right. Won't we, us two?'

She snatched her hand away with such ferocity she scratched his palm, and ran out without looking back at his face. It was no excuse that he didn't understand what he'd done.

The fat, smoking GP was dead in a year, but Bea rallied. In the years after 'The Scottish Holiday' her health was like a yo-yo, and Ralph's strategy for coping became avoidance. It became easier and easier for him to ignore Bea's relapses as Sam grew old enough to take on the burden of nursing her, and running the house. By the winter of what they believed might really be her mother's final illness, Ralph was coming in late every night. Sam didn't bother to ask why. He'd just say 'pressure of work' anyway. He'd perfected a relentless plastic cheeriness that gave the house an atmosphere of unpleasant surrealism whenever he was in it.

He beamed as he came through the kitchen door when Samantha was cooking their meal.

'Ah! Samantha, Samantha!' he sang. 'How was school today, my little chickadee?'

'Fine. Why don't you go and say hello to Mum?'

'And the bus, that was on time was it?'

'Yes, Dad. It always is. Go and see Mummy.'

'How's your Gran? I'll just take her up a little sherry on my way to get changed.'

And out he drifted humming 'out of my dreams and into your arms' from *Oklahoma!*

He bought another telly and took to watching it upstairs in his bedroom in the evenings. 'So I don't disturb your mother,' he told Sam conspiratorially. So Sam sat downstairs with Bea in the evenings whilst she watched the TV in the old sitting room where she now had a bed. Sometimes Sam did her homework down there too, so that Bea wouldn't be left alone. Just before he went to bed himself Ralph would pop his head around the sitting-room door and smile impishly at Bea and Sam, before producing two mugs of sickly sweet cocoa and a mound of cheese sandwiches. 'You have to keep your strength up, Bea,' he'd say, putting the tray of sandwiches on the table by the bed and kissing his wife on the cheek. 'Night night, love,' he'd say and leave, humming, without waiting to hear her speak or even looking at her properly.

'You should put all these in the freezer,' said Bea looking at the doorstep sarnies, 'then you could give Bracken a feast sometime. You've never liked cheese sandwiches, and I'm not going to be around to eat them.' Her tone was blankly commonplace. Sam packaged up the sandwiches and stuck them on the bottom shelf with last year's frozen gooseberries that no one really wanted. She felt as if she was shutting her heart in with the ice and the dark too.

Bea got weaker every day. The pain and the drugs filled her whole world. Day and night lost their division and Bea drifted in and out of the same twilight twenty-four hours a day. At night in her room Sam could sense Bea awake and suffering downstairs. Sleep was impossible so in the weeks before her entrance exam Sam studied until three, listening out for any sound from Bea's room. Sometimes she'd hear a suppressed sob or groan and go down to find Bea wide-eyed, in agony, biting her lips so as not to cry out. She'd put on the light, fetch them both a drink and sit holding her mother's clammy hand.

'Get me my pills,' Bea would say. Sam had taken to hiding

them, leaving Bea just a few within reach during the day. 'Sam, just give me all of them. I can't stand this pain.'

'The dose is two every six hours. I've only got a day's worth left anyway.'

'Sam, please. Please.'

'No, Mummy.'

'Please.'

'Oh, take four then.'

'Let me have all of them.'

'Mummy, please don't ask me that.'

Granny Pearl had hit on a new attention-seeking role: The Self-Sacrificing Matriarch, Suffering in her Final Years for the Benefit of her Family. She began to insist on doing everything for herself, wedging herself in the kitchen alongside Sam, making a single portion of cheese on toast whilst Sam made an evening meal for everyone else.

'Sure you don't want spaghetti Bolognese, Gran?'

'No, no. I can't have you cooking for me whilst you're catering for your poor mother. I'll just have a little snack.'

Whilst Sam was at school in the day she started to 'take care' of Bea.

'She flutters around when the nurse is here,' Bea complained, 'stands and watches whilst I have my injection. It's humiliating enough baring my backside without having her as an audience. Then if I try and sleep in the afternoon she comes in here and rattles the curtains until I wake up and pay her some mind. She's driving me mad, Sam.'

'It's no good me saying anything to her, Mum. You know what she's like.'

'Yes. I know. Floods of crocodile tears and she'll go on in her own sweet way doing what she likes.' The humour and resilience had gone from her mother's voice, she now simply sounded desperate.

'I'll stay home tomorrow, Mum, and keep you company.'

'Oh, Sam. It's your entrance exam soon . . .'

'It's two weeks yet. I can catch up.'

At weekends the only oasis of brightness was the supermarket on Saturday mornings. Sam had taken to going with Ralph to supervise the weekly shop after two weeks of having nothing in the house but cheese and cocoa. She found the rows of products cheered her up, and deciding what they needed made her feel grown up and responsible. Away from home Ralph's gossamer-light hold on reality beefed up a little, and he would sometimes suggest something sensible like a chicken that they could roast, or frozen fish. But most of the time he would walk beside her as she pushed the trolley and suggest things they might buy, or go on little forays of his own, returning with endless products which Sam quietly put back.

'Ah, Sam, chocolate teddy bears! You used to love those when you were little. Shall we get some?

'How about some nice cream horns? That might tempt your mother. Half the problem is that she doesn't eat enough, you know.

'Look! Disposable cutlery! Now that's what we need. Scented drawer liners. Marvellous!'

One Saturday, after Bea had begged to be given the whole bottle of pills, Sam tried to talk to Ralph on the way home from the supermarket.

'Daddy, at night when I get up for Mummy, she asks me for more pills. You know, she asks for more than she should have.'

'She gets confused, Sam. She forgets how many she's supposed to have.'

'No, it's not that. She wants . . . she's asking me to give her all of them. You know, because of the pain. Could you talk to her? Could you get up for her?'

'There's no need, Sam. It's all right. I know you're coping brilliantly with her. I'm so grateful. I'm proud of you.'

She could smell his fear, through the false brightness, the

terror that here in the car where he couldn't get away she would say something really blunt, like, 'Mummy is going to die soon,' or 'Mum wants me to kill her, Daddy'. It was like being faced with a rabbit pleading for its life. She could never bring herself to deliver the *coup de grâce*, but she was left with a sticky ooze of contempt on her heart so that when they unloaded the shopping and she noticed several bottles of sherry, she wanted to hit him as he said:

'For your Gran. Her little treat.'

Sam didn't argue. She knew who it was getting through a bottle of Harvey's Bristol Cream every night.

In those snot-grey weeks of November leading up to her entrance exam Sam swam in an internal tank of misery and exhaustion. She sat up hour after long hour, staring at her books, with the print and formulae floating free of the pages. As her careful revision plans unravelled and her preparation schedule fell apart, she saw the single foundation of all her dreams – an Oxbridge place – slipping away. It was like standing back in the playground, waiting helplessly for Dennis Williams to do something awful to her. But just as her imagination had helped out with the spider-exuding eyes, this time it cut in with an elaborate fantasy about the ability of examiners to sense her talent through what she feared would be her poor exam performance. She imagined them poring over her paper, seeing the flashes of brilliance and reading between the lines to see the exhaustion and worry, perceiving quite clearly her ability and commitment. It would still be all right.

The night before the first paper Bea had been sick until three a.m. It had taken Sam an hour or more to change the sheets and get her back to bed. Bea had looked so ill when she left that Sam feared to find her still and cold at the end of the day. As she walked into the freezing examination room, Sam could think only of her mother's corpse, alone with Pearl rattling the curtains fit to raise the dead.

She sat on the bus at the end of the week of exams, cold through with weariness. Each paper had felt more like a dream than the last. She could scarcely remember what she had been asked to write. Her ability to discern triumph or disaster was addled. The glass of the bus window chilled her, and she found herself shivering inside her duffel coat. But just as a climber with exposure feels warm as he slips into a coma, so Sam's emotional hypothermia triggered a fire in her imagination, smelting self-doubt into a new certainty. She was glad no one at home remembered to ask her how it all went. She sealed herself inside her fantasy and on Saturday afternoon when the house was quiet she escaped to the one place where fantasy could be real.

'Going for a bike ride!' she'd yelled as she slammed the back door. And in fifteen minutes she was freewheeling down the drive of Lime House.

It wasn't that she and Lawrence had become confidantes. He told her nothing of himself directly beyond the fact that 'a nervous complaint' meant that it was virtually impossible for him to leave his house and garden. It sounded romantic, almost like something out of Hardy and fitted with the hints and insinuations he slipped her about his globe-trotting past and his business empire maintained from the study at Lime House. And she didn't tell him about having to hide her mother's pain killers, or her father's mounting pile of empty sherry bottles. She didn't tell him about the cold and the nausea in the examination room either. When she visited Lawrence, Sam played the part of the person she wanted to be, and over the months she had got better and better at it. Being with Lawrence was like being able to visit her future, her adulthood, far away in the remote rainforests of tomorrow. As far as Lawrence was concerned she was a success about to happen, the sick mother she'd mentioned in passing was already an unimportant feature in her past.

When Lawrence answered the door Sam always got the brief impression that he had been standing behind it waiting for her to knock. She knew it couldn't be true. Although his 'condition' made him a prisoner of his own grounds he still must lead a busy life. The world must come to him when she wasn't there, old friends, business associates. Surely? His study was full of machines and telephones to allow him to keep up with his business interests even in the middle of the Suffolk countryside. Yet there was that moment as she arrived when the house seemed too still, as if everything had simply been switched off since her last visit.

'Sam! My dear girl! How lovely to see you!' He kissed her cheek and took her coat; the reception was always the same. 'It's so frightful, this dark and cold. Can I get you a hot drink after your freezing journey?'

'No, I'm fine really.'

'In that case . . . The *Phalaenopsis* is flowering!'

'Oh. Let's go now.'

Samantha's enthusiasm for his captive jungle made Lawrence smile. She invariably wanted to rush straight to the glasshouse and see whatever had come into bloom, seeded, or leafed or ailed since her last visit. She wanted to know everything; her questions only stopped when there was something new and particularly lovely to see. Now, she was speechless.

'It is rather wonderful, isn't it!' Lawrence was proud of this specimen. Not that they were a particularly difficult species but this plant was such a trouper, flowering two or three times every year, and always once in deep winter like a blessing. Sam walked underneath the arching spikes of moon-white flowers, each one as big as her palm.

'It makes me think of a wedding dress. Or new snow. That white is so pure. I've forgotten where it's from.'

'South East Asia. I bought in the Philippines ten years ago. I had it in the conservatory in Chiswick for a long time.'

'What pollinates it?'

'Samantha! You know I'm simply a *gardener*. Horticultural

143

botany does not allow for the existence of other organisms! *Biology* is your department. But it is called the moth orchid, so that could be a clue.'

'I wish I knew.' And feeling her frustration, her passionate desire to acquire knowledge, Lawrence too wished he knew. That was the effect she had on him, infecting him with good desires, worthy ambitions.

'I've a surprise. Somebody else in bloom. Look. . .' He led her to the opposite corner of the glasshouse where an epiphytic orchid had put out a spike four feet long and covered with frilly yellow and brown flowers. It was magnificent, mad, almost ridiculous in its extravagance.

'What is it?'

'*Oncidium papilio*. I thought I'd lost it. They're quite extreme sorts of beasts these. They can flower so vigorously they kill themselves. It put out five, six foot inflorescences two years ago. This is the first time it's flowered since.'

Samantha leant against the trunk of the tree fern which supported the orchid. She looked up under the mass of blooms. 'Wow!' she said. 'I'd love to see this in the wild!'

'Knocks all those vulgar hybrids into a cocked hat, I'd say!' Lawrence too leant against the mossy trunk to look up at the plant.

'I wonder why it does this suicide flowering?'

'Suicide flowering. Very good, Sam. I like that. Well . . . worth risking your all for love, don't you think?'

'That's about as daft as my Princess Cymbaleria, Lawrence!'

'All right. Another theory. This plant lives in a habitat where the right conditions for setting seed are very unusual. So when those conditions . . . whatever they might be . . . occur, then the right strategy is to go for bust.'

'Yes. That sounds much more scientific!'

'Almost biological one might say! And the next thing you'll ask is what *are* the right conditions. Well, I have no idea.'

They looked up at the plant in silence. It was often like this. An exchange of information, of hypotheses like coupling computers, followed by silent contemplation of some part of Lawrence's plant collection. And then tea and books in the study.

But on this dull winter afternoon the silence went on. Sam went on leaning and looking, the tiredness of the week settling on her like dust. She wasn't sure how long it took her to notice that Lawrence's arm was just millimetres from her own. She could feel the faint touch from elbow to wrist where their shirt sleeves were rolled up. Lawrence's little finger crooked over hers and clinched it in a miniature embrace, a touch that was witty and light, but unmistakably sensual, intimate. Here was something a world away from paternal cheek-kissing, shoulder-patting and coat-taking. Here was the touch from an equal: another adult, testing the ground. It reminded her of swimming in the sea as a child and reaching her feet for the bottom to find only deep water. But she didn't need to panic, this was just another scene from her future, something that happened like this between grown-ups. She didn't need to fear, or to offend Lawrence, just gently step away. She drew her hand from his and stood up, making an effort to smile.

'It's like visiting Summer coming here,' she said.

'It's like Summer visiting me actually, Sam.' He took back her hand and she wriggled her fingers playfully as if running the keys of a piano, trying to escape his grasp, pretending it was an insignificant game.

'It's always Summer in the rainforest.'

'It's always Summer here when you come.' He held her hand in both of his now, and touched the fingertips with his lips. His eyes looking at her over the horizon of her own knuckles were hard as glass, as dark and unreadable as deep space.

'Perhaps you'd better escape and come to the jungle with me, then you'd have a double Summer.' She pulled her hand away more purposefully.

Reluctantly he let it go and said, 'Or perhaps you'd better stay here and then Summer would never go away.' Lawrence wasn't smiling, his expression had an intensity that Sam didn't understand. She felt an emptiness open up beneath her, into which she could imagine herself falling.

'Can we have tea now, Lawrence?'

'Yes. Yes, of course, I've been neglecting my duties as host.'

She got in after six. Ralph was making sandwiches and Pearl was stirring a packet of soup into a saucepan of water and making a huge clattering noise with the spoon. 'Samantha, Samantha.' Ralph took her hands and waltzed her around the room singing.

'How's Mummy?'

'One round or two, Samantha?' Ralph said.

'You could share my soup, cockaleekie!' chirped Pearl. 'I don't mind going without.'

No one asked where she'd been.

A splinter from the gate pricks Sam's hand. Looking more carefully she can see it isn't the one Ralph made. She closes her eyes again for a moment remembering her reluctance as Ralph waltzed her round the kitchen. How she loathed him at that moment! But looking at his face in memory, from the perspective that time and experience have given her, she can see the terrible fear and grief etched there. He was trying to make things better somehow, to bring some light into their dark tight little world.

The child's voice is coming closer, its little feet crunch the path beyond the hedge.

'Max! Max, come here!'

Another second and Max's mother will catch sight of the strange white-faced young woman standing transfixed at her gate. If Max and his parents are in residence here, then Ralph certainly isn't. For the time being that's as much information as Sam wants. She takes her hand from the gate and runs back to the taxi.

9

Bristol welcomes Samantha home at one in the morning with a warm greasy mizzle that shines on the empty tarmac of the roads and smudges the street lights. Breathing is like inhaling a wet dishcloth. She feels disjointed, bent the wrong way at the neck, the hip and the knee like a pipe-cleaner figure, after sleeping wedged against the bus window. As usual the taxi driver doesn't know her road and has to be guided. He seems so clueless that as he leaves her at Number eleven she imagines him wandering lost in the back roads of Bishopston for the rest of his life. She closes the vault-like front door behind her, and stands in the darkness. The Lime House deeds in her bag don't seem to offer the universal solution to her problems that they did when she started her journey home. Somehow they have to be explained to Dale, but she's not sure how. Perhaps inspiration will come with the daylight. She kicks off her shoes and is about to go upstairs when she hears the unmistakeable sound of a sob coming through the closed door of the front room.

Sitting on the sofa in the light from the street lamp is Dale. He is cradling his head in his hands and crying, completely unaware that she is in the room. Samantha has never seen Dale cry. He looks stripped bare, even more vulnerable than the day when the boys led him by the hand into the new garden. Samantha feels the terrible responsibility of her long deception. What can she say to him now?

'Good news and bad news, Dale! The good news is that I've inherited enough to bale out your business and the bad news is that I'm not who I told you I was.'

Tenderness and fear rush through her. There is no time to

think or plan a part to play, she must just step into the unpredictable reality of the night.

'Dale. I'm home.' He looks up slowly, groggily, as if he might be dreaming her. He's been caught unawares, just as she has. Both of them here in the dark room, without their portraits to stand behind. They feel shy, almost as if meeting for the first time.

'Oh, Angie. I didn't hear you come in.'

She sits down beside him.

'How are you?'

'Oh. You know. OK.'

'How are the boys?'

'Fine. Mum's been great. She hasn't asked anything.'

'Shall I draw the curtains? Put the light on.'

'No. Let's just sit here in the dark.'

'OK.'

'Where have you been?'

'Oh, Dale. I don't know where to start.'

'Just tell me who he is. That would be a start.'

'So you know about the will then?'

'What will?'

'Lawrence's will. That's who *he* is. Was. Lawrence Spence.'

'Was? So he's died?'

'Yeah. That's why I've got the house.'

'What house? When did he die? Were you upset?'

'I'm not really sure. I was glad when I heard.'

'What?'

'Dale, we're not talking about the same thing, are we?'

'I don't know. I'm talking about your—' He came to dead stop, his voice clogged so that the next words were squeezed out of a tight throat, 'Your affair. Your lover.'

'What affair? I'm not having an affair.'

'Then why were you sick when I tried to make love to you? Why have you been so different?'

'Dale, I'm going to put the light on. I want to see you properly and I want to show you something.'

Samantha swishes the curtain closed and puts the smallest lamp on. The room springs to Technicolor life and Dale blinks like an owl at her. She feels much braver, now that the partial reality she will give Dale is better than the fiction he's been constructing for himself.

'So you aren't having an affair? I'd sooner know what's going on . . .'

'Dale, I'm not having an affair. I'm not in love with anyone else. All that's been happening is nothing like that. Nothing. There is only you. You and the boys. Nobody else.'

He stands up white and unsteady and holds her so tightly she's ready for a rib or two to pop. 'I can't stand the thought of losing you, not on top of everything else.'

'Dale?' she says into his shoulder. 'Dale? I do have a lot to say.'

He releases her, 'So do I.' He looks guilty, worried. 'There's a lot I need to tell you about the business. About the house.'

'Well, what I've got to tell may help with all that.'

'You go first then.'

'I don't know where to start.'

'Tell me something good first. Give me the good news.'

Good news. Bad news. Perhaps after all that is the way to do it!

'The good news is that I've inherited a house that's probably worth, I dunno, a lot of money. Twice what this is worth at the very least. A lot more maybe.'

'Oh my God!'

'So that should sort out the business and let us keep the house?'

'Yeah. I should say so. God. Angie. You don't know the weight you've just lifted . . .'

Samantha has that expanding sensation of white mushrooms filling her brain. After so long keeping the facts on a lead, it's going to be a relief to let them go. The tricky part is the few she must still keep quiet and under control.

'Wait, Dale. You haven't had the bad news yet.' She holds his hand and takes a deep breath, like a cave diver about to plunge into cold water unsure where the next source of air might be.

'My name wasn't Angie Dawes when you met me. It was Samantha Powell. Angela was my real middle name. I was younger than I told you, just eighteen, not twenty-four. My parents didn't die when I was a baby. I've never been in care or a foster home. I left home at seventeen and I didn't want to go back. The man who left me the house – Lawrence – was a friend, without children of his own to leave it to.'

There is silence. Dale lets out a long breath, lets go of her hand and rakes his fingers through his hair. 'Well, that explains how you look so young. I was beginning to wonder if I was just aging extra fast.'

'I'll be twenty-eight in two months.'

'Jeesus. And this bloke knew where you were and your parents didn't know?' Dale's face is scrunched into creases with the crying and with struggling to understand so much so fast.

'I didn't know that he'd found me until I got the letter from his executors telling me he'd left me the house. It was shock. All that purple-blob cake and the garden, it was all sort of shock. And that was more what I used to be like, before I left home.'

'A purple blob?'

'No! A bit wild. I was going to be a botanist, and ecologist. Whatever. I was going to study rainforest, jungle, all that stuff.'

'If you'd changed your name and age, how did Lawrence find you?'

'I don't know how he found me. I don't know if he told my parents. I don't think so.'

'Because they would have come looking?'

'Yeah. Maybe. Maybe my dad wouldn't want to see me any more.'

'Why?'

'Because I ran away.'

'What about your mum?'

'She's dead. I think. No, I'm sure. She was dying when I left.'

'But you don't know?'

The pace of Dale's questions is getting out of hand. Inside Samantha can feel a dangerous abandon. She reins it in, takes a deep breath and answers slowly, 'Yes I do know. She had weeks to live, the doctor said.'

'But she was alive when you left?'

'Yes.' It's not so hard to say this with conviction. It's not quite a lie.

'What happened? Why did you leave?' Dale takes her hand again. She can see the marks of the tears on his face and the dark shadows left by the nights of worry he's had. She wants to tell the whole truth. But the best she can do is some of the truth, enough truth to take away the shadows and the tears, and keep herself safe.

'It was my mum's illness really. And the way my dad was about it and about me. I couldn't stick it any more. All that and my gran, and failing my entrance exams. I think I was nearly going mad.' That, at least, is nothing but the truth . . .

The weather in the run-up to Christmas that year was particularly dismal. It never got properly light after the first week in December. The sky had been replaced with polystyrene ceiling tiles of uniform grey that seemed to suck the warmth from the earth below. Everything was cold and blank. The only colour in the landscape was the red of the tractors labouring up, and down, carving the fields into straight lines. Christmas loomed closer, inviting as a torture chamber. All its tinsel imagery of home, hearth and happiness looked like a sickening parody to Sam. She couldn't see how she was going to manage Christmas Day with Bea glassy-eyed on the camp bed and Pearl and Ralph swigging sherry in front of *The Review Of the Year*.

Every morning as she stood waiting for the school bus she got the feeling that the Evil God Christmas was stealing the brightness from the world around her, reducing it to a dimly lit monochrome. Even the interior of the old school bus began to look cheerful and inviting. As Sam climbed into its mustard-coloured light each morning she entered another world. For the first few minutes of every journey she felt self-conscious, as if her home life was printed on her like newspaper headlines:

SAM SPENDS NIGHT WATCHING GROANING MOTHER
BEA ASKS FOR A WAY OUT AGAIN
MAN SINGS *OKLAHOMA*! WHILST WIFE CRIES
GRANNY EATS DOG'S SANDWICHES

She had to make the transformation from her real self to her school self and every day it was harder. Every day that she managed it, she felt she had somehow betrayed her mother by laughing and joking whilst Bea lay ragged and limp as wet newspaper.

At the end of the last day of term she dropped into the bus seat beside Christine who was scribbling notes from an art book open at the Max Ernst page. 'I'm going to get all my homework done before Christmas Eve. Then I can raid Dad's drinks cabinet and watch crap films until New Year.'

Sam looked at the reproduction of the picture. 'The Elephant Of The Celebes' read the caption. It showed a distorted elephant-like beast constructed from an industrial boiler being beckoned by a female torso. The colours were flat and cold and conveyed a feeling of purposeless desolation.

'That's what it's like at home these days,' she told Christine.

'What you mean, headless women and elephants with heads on the wrong ends of their trunks?'

'Yeah. Pretty much.'

'You coming to John Woodbury's eighteenth-cum-Christmas party? You've done the exam. It's the end of bloody term. You can slack off a bit now, can't you? Oh God, Sam. You're going to say no, aren't you? Why? What's happening at home?'

The next question would be about Bea, Sam could tell. But everything at home was just too big to talk about, like trying to do the Sistine Chapel in wax crayons. 'I am slacking off. Just got to stay home and keep the Celebes Elephants in order. You know how it is, you leave them to their own devices for half an hour and they'll grow buffalo horns on the ends of their trunks. You can't be too careful.'

'So you're not coming then?'

'Don't think so, Chris.'

There was absolutely no sound in the house. Not even a welcoming 'wuff'. Bracken had been sent to live with a work colleague of Ralph's when Bea couldn't cope with a big dog in the house any more. Samantha put her bag on the kitchen table and wondered what today's silence might mean. The usual significance was a napping Pearl and a dozing Bea. That meant she could talk to Bea without Pearl interfering. There were other possible meanings: the worst option was a dead Bea and a dozing Pearl, the best a dead Pearl and napping Bea. The latter was unlikely because Pearl still looked as if she would outlive Methuselah. Sam tiptoed into the sitting room. It was Bea's bedroom now as she was too weak to get up and down stairs and liked to be near the life of the house. And as far as possible from Pearl's centre of operations upstairs. Sam saw at once that Bea was still breathing. The second-best option then. Probably.

'Mum? You awake?'

'Hello, love. How was school?' Her words were faint, but distinct, like a very distant lighthouse on a clear night. A good sign. When the pain was bad it blurred her voice and her thinking.

'Oh. Like school. You know, teachers, lessons.'

'That bloody health visitor's been again today. She told me about the meek inheriting the earth.'

'She shouldn't be allowed to thrust her beliefs down your throat.'

'No, she shouldn't. Especially with a haircut like that. If that's the standard of coiffure Jesus accepts in his followers then I'm glad I'm not one of them.'

'You'll go to hell saying things like that!'

'I'm going there anyway. Always liked a good bonfire.'

'Cuppa?'

'Go and check on your gran first?'

'Do I have to?'

'Yes.'

Pearl was asleep in her armchair by the window, peaceful and apparently as blameless as a baby. Mercifully she was neither snoring nor dribbling. Sam closed the door and hoped she'd go through to morning. Or the next century. There was a sudden cry from her mother's room and Sam threw herself down the stairs. Bea was crumpled beside her bed, panting and blue around the lips.

'Put me on my back,' she managed to say.

'Shall I ring the doctor?'

Bea shook her head. 'On my back,' she panted. Awkwardly, like moving a piece of furniture with no handholds Sam turned her. Bea pursed her lips and tried not to cry out but a little scream of pain managed to force its way between her teeth. She gripped Sam's hand and lay fighting with the agony inside for a few minutes. At last her colour returned a little and she spoke. 'I was feeling a lot better. So I thought I'd try and get to the loo alone without the chair. Stupid. Stupid.'

'Yes, Mum. Stupid stupid *stupid*, I'd say. Shall I get you back into bed?'

'Oh Sam,' Bea began to cry, 'I need to change my nightie. Can you help me? I'm so sorry.'

Sam didn't mind Bea being soaked and filthy, she didn't mind the smell, or having to scrub the carpet. What bothered her was Bea's silence and the way the tears emptied onto her cheeks as if nothing would stop them.

When Bea was finally back in a clean bed she said, 'If it's going to be like this, I don't want to go on. Sam, just give me all my pills to take, won't you?'

Sam had no idea how to answer. 'Don't be silly, Mum,' she said, 'don't be silly,' but she felt that Bea's request was a long, long way from being silly, and that some last line that heralded only the finish had just been crossed.

Pearl didn't sleep through until the next century. She was up early the next morning. Sam could hear her pottering around the kitchen, in what sounded like an uncharacteristically purposeful sort of way. She heard Pearl take Bea a cup of tea and make toast for Ralph. Sam hurried out of bed to witness the unprecedented phenomenon of Pearl doing something actually useful.

'Good morning, dear, cup of tea?'

Sam could barely speak with the shock of seeing Pearl smiling, charming and voluntarily doing something for someone else instead of for effect. She had her best travelling clothes on too, the turquoise twin set and the green tweed skirt.

Ralph cleared his throat and took a swallow of tea ready to make an announcement. 'Your gran's not going to be with us for Christmas, Sam,' he said as if informing a seven year old that the shops were completely out of toys and there would be no possibility of even Santa getting hold of any. Sam was so surprised she managed by accident not to look delighted.

'Oh. Where are you going, Gran?'

'My sister-in-law Lydia in Brighton. She's alone this year, and I felt I couldn't be selfish and spend Christmas with my son when she was on her own.'

'I'm taking Gran to the train on my way to work.'

Sam couldn't work it out. Pearl had never liked Lydia and hadn't been to visit her once in the three years since Pearl's brother Ron had died. But as she left Pearl said, 'I won't disturb your mother, just to say goodbye. I'm sure she's resting,' and Sam realised that Pearl too had noted that crossing of a 'last line'.

Sam remembered the injured mole she'd picked up last summer; all its fleas and ticks had jumped off onto Sam's bare arm. Pearl was just doing what any good, sensible parasite would do – she was quitting while her host was still warm.

The macabre significance of Pearl's departure went right over Bea's head. She was delighted.

'If I'm having Christmas alone with my husband and my daughter I'd better start looking more respectable. Give my hair a wash, Sam, there's a love?'

Sam wheeled her into the shower room downstairs and improvised a salon from the tiny sink and a large measuring jug. Leant back, with the soothing warmth spreading over her scalp, Bea could escape for a while and pretend that illness hadn't conquered her world.

'We need to get you some smart trousers and new shoes,' she said, 'and a good coat. We'll go in the January sales. We'll have a girls' outing.' Bea sounded so bright that Sam could have believed it would happen. But Sam could see the parched skin, yellow as peeling paint. She felt the sparse coarseness of the grey hair under her finger tips. Bea had weathered the years of illness well but the cancer had sucked the last beauty out of her pale luminous complexion and her dense silky hair. Now Bea's very skull seemed fragile, compromised, and Sam felt that without the utmost care her fingers might crack its surface. She massaged the lather into her mother's scalp, tenderly, coaxingly as if somehow she could draw the loveliness into the visible world once again. Sam curled the little tufts of hair around her fingers trying to get them to hold a pretty shape as she blew them with the hair dryer. But the hair didn't have the heart for that sort of thing any more, and fell sad and flat. 'Oh, it's so nice to feel a bit smarter!' sighed Bea. 'Let's have a look then, Sam, like they do in a real hair-dressers.'

'I can't get the mirror off the wall, Mummy,' Sam lied. 'You'll just have to take my word for it. It looks really nice.'

'Oh come on, Sam. Just unhook it. It's not attached or anything.'

Reluctantly Sam did as she was told, wishing she could have thought of some better excuse to keep her mother from the truth of the reflection.

Sam held the mirror and Bea peered in. 'Oh God!' she said. 'Oh God. What's happened to me, Sam?'

There was nothing Sam could say. There was no denying that the skull was clearly keen to be free of the flesh of Bea's face. Silently Sam returned Bea to bed and sat holding her hand without a word passing between them.

The final retail frenzy of Christmas had set in. Already at ten a.m. on Christmas Eve the streets of Cambridge were filled with a collective hysteria of acquisitiveness, as people rushed from shop to shop with mouths as straight as pokers. The back catalogue of Christmas number one hits leaked from shop doorways and mixed with the town band's renditions of carols, creating a kind of aural oil slick. The sound clogged Sam's brain as she wandered miserably through malls and precincts trying to think of something to buy her parents: a new recording of *Oklahoma!* for her father perhaps? Or an ostrich suit? No long books for her mother, or gloves for warmth on country walks, or even chocolates to make her sick. All she could think of was sherry glasses for Ralph, so that at least he wouldn't swig it from the bottle. And for Bea a set of children's glow-in-the-dark stars and moons so she would have something to look at in the deep nights. After an hour of miserable wandering she settled for those and rushed to meet Ralph at the car park.

He was staring into space with the radio on and a huge expensive-looking carrier-bag on the back seat. He looked lost. For the first time in months, years almost, Sam remembered the Saturdays in the greenhouse, his smile over the top of the sea of tiny seedlings as he'd said, 'We need Mummy to come and inspect don't we, Sam?'

She leaned over to squeeze his arm when she got into the passenger seat. 'Hello, Dad.'

'Hello, my little flower. Didn't see you coming.'

'We should get home.'

'Want to see what I bought first?'

He lifted the carrier onto her lap. Inside in a swathe of white tissue paper were two hats. One was felt, the colour of wood smoke with a big soft brim. The other was a stiff boater shape, covered in a cloud of lemon chiffon. They were hats for big occasions, Autumn racing at Newmarket, a formal wedding in May. Hats for a social life Bea might once have dreamed of, but had never had, and now never would. Sam felt the blood go from her cheeks almost before she knew she was angry. The hats symbolised all of it: all the cheese sandwiches in the freezer, all the Saturday mornings in the supermarket, all the sherry bottles, all the avoided conversations. Every last bit of Ralph's head-in-the-sand behaviour rolled out of the hat bag in a white-hot mass and ignited, burning off the tenderness and pity she'd felt a moment before. It was several long seconds before she could look up at Ralph and speak. When she did her voice sounded odd and unfamiliar as if it was coming from a different place from normal.

'And when the bloody hell do you think your wife is ever going to wear those?'

Ralph's face set in a half-smile, as if the wind had changed and fixed his expression.

'What planet are you on, Daddy? She's dying. She'll be dead by Easter. She's in so much pain she can't move most of the time, or even talk, or think. She keeps begging me to give her all her painkillers.'

Ralph sat so still and quiet that the ticking of the dashboard clock was suddenly audible.

'And all you can do is ignore it all and buy her posh hats!' Sam shoved the carrier with the hats inside onto Ralph's lap. She had never spoken to her father like that, never raised her voice to him. Certainly never sworn. She stared ahead of her, shaking, wondering what would happen next.

'Let's get home,' Ralph said, and he nosed the car out through the streets where the messy cocktail of 'Winter Wonderland' and 'Silent Night' was coming down over the town like rain.

Sam hadn't noticed when she fell asleep. She had screamed into her mattress with a pillow over her head for a long time, then lain, too tired to cry, listening to the tiny popping sounds coming from her bedroom radiator. When she woke it was dark outside. She wanted some comfort, something to remind her of a time when Bea and Ralph and she were happier. She raked off all her clothes, clammy with sleep and unhappiness and took out the old blue velvet dress that Bea had bought her for her sixteenth birthday. It was a little too small now but its softness was like a baby's blanket against her skin. Sleepily she reasoned if she went downstairs in this they could all remember something good and today could be somehow healed over. Then Ralph was at the door knocking.

The sound was so insistent that Sam was afraid. She leapt to open it. 'Is Mum all right?'

'She's sleeping. Sam, St Hilda's rang, the admissions tutor wants you to ring before six, tonight or any time after Christmas, she said.' Ralph was completely detached from the importance of his message. He could have been telling her that there was pasta for tea or that Christine had rung to say hi. He clearly didn't understand Sam's desire to interrogate him.

'Oh God. What did she say?'

'Just to ring.' He shrugged.

'Did she know you were my dad?'

'Yes, she asked if I was.'

'And she didn't say anything about a place? About passing?'

'Nothing. Just to ring her. She didn't sound like there was a rush or anything.'

'She didn't leave any message?'

'Why don't you just ring? I'm popping out to get the turkey from Hundon. Mr Berry said he'd hang on to one 'til five.' It was almost funny that Ralph was off to buy a huge turkey; perhaps he was developing an affinity for others of his adopted taxonomic group. Mr Berry's birds were renowned for being the size of ostriches. He clumped downstairs, leaving her stunned at her bedroom door.

Samantha felt as if she'd been plucked out of a dream and placed into a new dimension of absolute sharpness and clarity. It was obvious to her now, in the way that the existence of gravity was obvious, that she had failed her exams. If she'd passed, St Hilda's would have said. It was only ever bad news that people were reluctant to impart. Good news you could entrust to anyone's telling. Bad news was a responsibility that you couldn't pass on. They wanted her to ring back to tell her that they were very sorry but her application had been unsuccessful. They would wish her luck in her A levels and her attempts to get in somewhere else. She'd failed. It was all over. The whole jungle dream. All her ambitions were just a juvenile phase, junk to be thrown out with the old Barbie dolls and the Lego bricks. Her life felt over before it had begun.

Dale has his hand on her back, warm and strong and steady. There is a greyness around the edge of the curtains and the sound of a milk float passing the top of the street. Samantha is holding her own temples as if stopping her mind from spurting out onto Dale's lap. She hasn't finished. She wants to tell him as much of the truth as she can.

'I'd failed my entrance exam, otherwise the Admissions Tutor would have told my dad I'd got a place. I couldn't bear to ring and hear it, hear her say the words. I sat in my room for a long time. I thought about the rainforest. About how it would smell with the heat and wetness drawing the scents out of the leaves and flowers, the bark and the dark roots. I thought about the mist caught in the branches at dawn and how bird sounds would carry on the air then. I thought about how it would feel to know it, to be able to name and recognise everything I found there, for it to be my home. I thought about it as hard as I'd ever thought. And I felt it all peeling away from me, the way that Sellotape does on a wet surface. I couldn't get my dreams to stick to me any more. I'd lost it all.'

'But you couldn't be sure you had failed. And anyway, you could have tried again or tried another university. Or just saved the money and gone there!'

'I was seventeen. I was three quarters of the way round the bend with my mum and all. It didn't occur to me to try another way, another university or reapply to Oxford. It was like I'd been set some test, like something out of Greek myths – a trial of my worthiness. And I'd failed. I'd proved I wasn't good enough. I went downstairs to see my mum, she was in a lot of pain. And all I could feel was angry. Not sorry for her at all. Angry with her for being ill and angry with Dad for being hopeless. She started asking for me to give her all the pills in the bottle again. Really begging. Then I knew I just couldn't stick it any more, without my dream to keep me going. I couldn't stand it. I left her crying out and I went upstairs. I didn't know where I would go, I sort of imagined getting on a ferry and going somewhere so I took my passport and my birth certificate . . . Mum had them in her dressing-room drawer for safety. I took my building society book and my warm coat and I walked out of the door.'

'You didn't say goodbye to her?'

'No. No I didn't.' Sam sobbed. She had never told anyone even that much. Gently Dale took her hands from her head and gathered her up to his chest.

'Oh, my love. My love,' he said.

She lay against him with an ocean of tears flowing down her face.

Inside her, the story ran on through its real ending. She closed her eyes and saw Bea's face grey on the pillow.

'I can't stand this, Sam. Please just give me all the pills. Please.'

Sam had felt so cold, so empty. Bea had sucked up all her dreams with her years of illness, with her months of dying. She looked at Bea's paper-folded face, the black socket of her mouth moving to plead and she shivered with a chill of revulsion. This almost dead creature had taken her chance of life, snatched a whole green world of jungle from between her fingers. Her heart cracked like a glacier in a dry frost; inside she reached absolute zero.

'All right. All *right*. If that's what you really want.'

She fetched the tablets from the hiding place inside a cereal packet and tipped them slowly into her palm. 'One, two, three, four, five, . . .' She'd counted them out, pressing each one into her flesh, imprinting it with the winter in her soul before submitting it to Bea's greedy mouth. Bea had taken them all, gobbling them like a starving peasant. Perhaps she had believed in her daughter's compassion. Perhaps she didn't see the murder in Sam's heart. Perhaps she just didn't care any more.

As Dale held her, Sam remembered the terrible long moments as Bea slipped from consciousness and her breathing seemed to fade. Her panic, and desperation to quit the house before Bea's last breath could be drawn. She saw in her mind her own hysterical flight to Lime House, weeping and staggering in the tomb-cold darkness. She remembered Lawrence's sudden strength, sinewy as a strangler fig, wringing her out. She had walked away under the naked frost-glittered lime trees, a different person, metamorphosed into something that was no longer herself.

10

'Mrs Cassinari, Mrs Cassinari!' George hails Samantha as she stands at the security door in the side of the tin sandwich box that is Stayfleurs. He rushes up to her, his square face pink with hurrying. 'Our theory concerning shoe design, vis à vis walking speed. I fear it may have been a little hastily constructed.' It has been more than week, a lifetime in some respects, since Samantha has been to work. She stares at George blankly for a moment, and his features begin to pucker, pulled together by a drawstring of disappointment. Just in time to save George's hurt feelings she remembers their odd conversation in Mr Geoffrey's office.

'Yes, I think you're right. On reflection, I think the key factor is newness rather than design: quality of sole-grip, heel traction; that sort of thing?'

'Yes! Yes! Of course. Blindingly obvious when one engages wholly with the knotty problem!'

'I think we've cracked that one, George.'

'I believe you are correct, Mrs Cassinari!' Beaming with delight, George nods respectfully at her and goes to retrieve escapee trolleys from the other side of the car park.

Behind the red door nothing has changed of course, how could it in such a few days? The floor is still Bisto brown, the air still full of Dettol. Yet today for the first time Samantha finds the atmosphere is not comforting, but dull and claustrophobic. It is hard to focus her attention on the hours ahead; nothing seems able to draw her concentration.

Seeing her co-workers helps a little. They are pleased that she's back but tentative, wary of another outburst.

'How are you, Angela?' Mary asks. 'Are you recovered?'

'Yes,' says Claudia, 'you didn't seem to be quite yourself last week.'

Only Liz stands back as Samantha comes into the changing room, steadfastly peering into her powder compact mirror. 'Oh for God's sake, leave the poor girl alone, it's bad enough being back at work without you two slobbering all over her.'

Looking at the three women as they put on their navy uniforms Samantha is struck by how attractive and intelligent they look. She stops her own preparations for work and gazes at them. 'What did you all do before you worked here?' The women exchange nervous glances, but they are rather flattered that Angela, with her odd new atmosphere trailing about her, wants to know.

'Wives and mothers, darling!' says Liz. 'The world's most demanding role apparently. Certainly used my RADA training and that's no word of a lie!'

'I was a fully qualified SRN,' Mary drew herself up to seem taller than her five feet, 'but I was more useful as John's receptionist when he set up his practice. Then the boys came along . . .'

'Tony always told me I was too dim to work, so I never got a job. Married him straight after Oxford,' said Claudia, adding in her best hockey-captain voice, 'I probably was a bit of a flake, but I got a better degree than he did, a two one in English.'

'What the hell are you girls doing working here with qualifications like those?'

There is no time to answer as Mr Geoffrey's voice alerts them to the fact that it's almost nine, something which has for once escaped Samantha's attention.

In her absence Mr Geoffrey has increased their stocks of fresh venison and venison sausages, because he says that venison is almost reindeer anyway. The various problems with bar codes and bulging tins have been sorted out and there is a smooth brisk passage through the tills all morning. It's been busy with customers queuing five deep and more arriving by the minute. Normally, it's the sort of morning that Samantha relishes. But loosening some of the bonds around her past has allowed the home guard of her mind to stand at a permanent 'at ease'. So in spite of the tasks demanding her attention, great trunks have sprung up behind the rows of waiting customers, one so large that it spans almost two whole aisles. The back of the shop is in deep shade, the floor covered in fallen leaves and patrolled by skeins of ants. An agouti grabs a mango from the fruit and veg counter and scuttles back into the undergrowth gathering around Jack Mullen's deli counter. Samantha's old ambitions, tattered, a little musty but still trailing clouds of glory stir at the sight and smell of even this imagined forest. Once again she can see herself measuring, collecting, observing, learning. Samantha's heart turns and turns like a leaf in the wind. When it comes to the time for her break she almost runs outside, dodging through the lianas that threaten to cover the 'Staff Only' notice on the door.

Outside it's an ordinary summer day, with the sky almost bleached of blueness by the sun. The metal sides of the shop are hot enough for a barbecue, so she sits on the wall near the delivery bay in the shade taking deep breaths. Jack Mullen, skulking in for his 'one to eight' shift, joins her to finish his fag. He lifts the cigarette to his permanently sardonic mouth but today it's something else she notices. His wrists, thin as bird bones, betray him: tiny, vulnerable and adrift.

'Well,' he begins his habitual leer, 'Mrs Cassi—' but she cuts him short.

'Samantha, you can call me that.' She holds out a hand to shake. 'Sam if you like.'

'Weeell,' he makes one last attempt at maintaining his lust-lizard persona and then gives up. He takes her offered hand, 'Jack, well no, John actually. Pleased to meet you, Sam.' His real smile is quite sweet, like a shy five year old.

'John, why don't you go back and get your degree?'

'I was, well you know. They all know in there.'

'Go somewhere else, do another course.'

'Can't face it.'

'Can you face being here when you're forty?'

'What can I do? I messed up, Sam. Big time,' he says quietly, 'I can't go back. I'll just mess up again. I'll be OK here. I can cope.' He throws his cigarette down and watches his own foot crush it to dust. When he looks up he's back in character. 'Gotta go. Catch you later, *Samantha*.' He slithers through the red door and is gone.

John is twenty-two. He doesn't know how long life lasts. He can't see that he will outlive his temporary decision 'to give up' in the same way that Claudia, Mary and Liz have outlived theirs. Samantha herself is only beginning to know how things don't last, how even the past changes once you're not in it any more. Quite suddenly she decides that she's had more than enough of Stayfleurs. A supermarket was OK for Angela Cassinari but for Samantha Powell it is never going to be enough, even if it does sell two sorts of reindeer meat.

Within fifteen minutes she has resigned with immediate effect, leaving Mr Geoffrey mouthing like a landed goldfish. She leaves through the front of the shop, waving to the three 'girls', neck-deep in customers. George is getting a row of trolleys to stand to attention at the entrance.

'Off early, Mrs Cassinari?'

'I'm leaving, George. I'm not going to work here any more.'

'Mrs Cassinari! I am more disturbed by this news than I can express!'

'I'm sorry, George, I'll miss you. But I'll pop back and say hello. I'm only round the corner.'

'What will you do?'

'I'm not sure, George.'

'A grey area then.'

'Yes. That's it, a grey area.'

The garden of Number eleven is a sun trap, and all Samantha's exotics are looking very happy indeed. On the kitchen table is a fat white envelope with Angie written in Dale's hand. She squeezes the letter and smiles. After the weekend they've had together this could be the first love letter he's ever sent her. She takes it out onto the hot patio and lets the sunshine soak into her body before she unfolds it. She sniffs the paper: it smells of Dale-ness. Sam feels a longing for him, his closeness, his body, that she's never felt before. She shuts her eyes and the memory of Friday's dawn comes like hot dew settling on her skin.

She'd clung to Dale long after the last parts of her story had run their course again in her mind. Her cheek was against his shoulder, his chin sandpapery with stubble was against her neck. Neither of them moved, but a subtle awareness of the change that had come about seeped through them both as the light grew stronger in the world outside. Sam was completely relaxed, not holding herself as she usually did, just a fraction of a millimetre away from Dale, guarding herself against intimacy and the risk of discovery. She leant all her weight against him, her arms slack and soft under his. And he in turn held her, rather than letting himself be held. In that simple shift of emphasis they could both feel that all the usual customs of their embraces were reversed. There was a vital pulse of new possibility waking inside them.

Sam took her head from Dale's shoulder, and raised her face waiting for him to kiss her. His mouth had a passion, a gentle insistence that was entirely new. Always before she controlled, giving to Dale, encouraging him to lose himself in her, never letting go of herself for a moment. Abandonment had always carried a risk of exposure, even after long familiarity with sex had laid to rest the fear and disgust Sam had first felt. Now, Sam let herself be soft, fluid under Dale's touch. His hands

167

caressed her, smoothing her, opening her, finding her shapes and her responses, for himself, for her. She felt she was being unfolded, and with infinite care, spread wide, so that the sweet slow burning sun of sensuality reached every part, burnishing all to ignite.

Afterwards they had lain on the floor incredulous, holding each other in a kind of wondrous shock. At last Sam said in a voice straight from her seventeen-year-old self, 'Wow! Can we do that again?'

Dale was no longer part of the outside world to her. He was inside her, a part of her, close enough now to rip her apart if he wanted and for the moment far too close to see clearly. Finally, she felt, they had both stepped from behind their portraits, and she shivered to find that Dale wasn't quite as she expected him to be. She unfolded the letter. It was exciting to see so much of Dale's large angular writing all together. Like finding a new part of him. But frightening too, as it reminded her that there was so much of him she'd never known about . . .

Dear Angie,

I never asked you if you minded still being called that. I could get used to Sam. It doesn't matter about the word. I don't call you a word inside myself anyway, you're just you. Especially now.

What can I say about the last three days? When you came home the other night, Thursday?, everything looked so bad to me. I thought I'd lost you, that you were just going to leave me. I thought the business was gone. And I found that everything was OK. Not just OK, but wonderful. Better than I ever imagined. It's like finding you again in the cake shop, except that now I really understand what I found that day. A huge beautiful, multi-faceted diamond.

I'm all over the place. I don't know what order to say things in. There's so much to say.

I don't understand everything that's happening with us yet.

I'm still reeling. Making love this weekend was like, well no. It wasn't like anything. It felt like you'd never let me make love to you before. It felt, equal. Real. I don't know how to say it. It felt deep. That's it, deep. Important. God, I can't wait to get home. (Sorry, I nearly made you late taking the boys to school!)

I have to think of something practical now or I'll still be here when you get in from work!

I'll go and look at Lime House today, I'll get there by this afternoon, M25 permitting. We can get the loan secured against its value now to tide the business over. By the sounds of things it's probably in our best interest for me to do the work on it, then sell it ready done up. But I'll only know what's what when I've seen it properly. We'll need to go to the solicitors later this week. I'll be back as soon as I can, Friday. Thursday maybe.

There's still so much to talk about. You've got to do your rainforest stuff, Angie. I loved the way you talked about it. And think about your parents. It's really hard but maybe you should find them.

Angie, there've always been times with you that I've felt there was something more behind your eyes. Something beyond the person who does all she can to care for me and the boys. I never asked what. I just swallowed what you told me because it was easy. I told myself that you didn't want to talk about your past. But that's not the real reason I never asked. Not if I'm honest. The real reason is that your secrets gave me the excuse to keep mine. And now I don't want there to be secrets between us any more.

I feel lucky, like a lottery winner today. Nothing to do with your inheritance. It's just you. I only hope I'm good enough for you as you really are.

All my love,
Dale

PS: If anybody calls for me, no matter what they say, just tell them I'll be home in a few days and to call at the weekend.

Sam had always thought that she knew the secrets Dale kept about himself. She'd always seen the person who patted houses as if they were old pets, and kept the boys' first shoes in the bottom of his toolbox. Were there other secrets to know? It was exciting to find new things in her 'old' husband, exciting to reveal so much more of herself to him. But frightening. Supposing he still had as much to tell as she did?

Sam folded the letter and held it tight against her body, willing him to be as good and true as she'd always seen him to be. She leant back and looked at the blue sky through the pointed frond fingers of the palm. High above her a little flock of parakeets flew south towards the Mendips. Imagination again? Or escapees from a cage with real bars? She couldn't tell.

'Why can't we sleep outside, Mummy?' Joe is tired and dangerously petulant. He and Tony love their new garden and have taken to playing complex imaginary games about being explorers. Joe with his love of foreign-sounding words has even learnt the Latin names of some of the plants.

'Because it gets cold in the middle of the night, Joe.'

'But we'll be under the duvet, Mummy.'

'We promise to come inside if it gets too cold, Mummy,' Tony chips in his reasonable argument.

Samantha sighs. A month ago they wouldn't have dreamed of requesting something so outrageous, but they've adapted to the new spirit of liberalism surrounding their mother. She looks out from the patio to the network of gardens beyond. It is hard to imagine some child-stealing criminal climbing their way over so many garden walls to harm her sleeping boys. She can see how much fun a bed under the palm trees will be for them.

'OK.'

They can hardly believe their luck. They run in to gather cushions, pillows and teddies.

'Can we have choklit bissskits in bed?' Joe calls from their bedroom window.

'No you can't!' Sam says. She has to keep some sort of hold on the reins!

Samantha has resisted the temptation to sleep on the play-room sofa to keep watch over the children. She lies awake in the middle of her own bed staring at the ceiling. She has spent an hour wondering with no conclusion and no particular focus what she will do now that Stayfleurs feels like the edge of a hole rather than an horizon. Just as she's drifting into a pleasant but unhelpful dream about flying over the forest canopy with her family, like Peter Pan trailing the Lost Boys, the phone rings. It will be Dale ringing from a hotel room. She pulls the handset under the covers with her to hold his voice close to her warm body in bed.

'Hello, Sweetie!' Samantha breathes sleepily into the phone. A small black beat of intense silence meets her voice, a slither of a moment but enough to make her throw off the covers and sit up, awake, alert and reaching frantically for the switch on the lamp.

'Thank you, Mrs Cassinari. I didn't expect such a warm reception.' It is an old voice, worn down, feeble. But the accent is cultured, the tone velvet with a mannered politeness which only serves to emphasise an underlying desperation. It's not a voice Samantha knows. She runs to the window of the boys' room with the phone, and cranes her neck out of the open window.

'Who is this?' Looking down she can see Joe and Tony curled together in the moonlight.

The voice is at least not that of a kidnapper. It continues slow and a little faltering, 'I don't think we've met.'

Calmer now she knows the boys are safe, she tries to regain control with a little righteous anger, 'Do you know what time it is?' she says hotly.

But the Voice is still unhurried, 'Oh yes, I know the time but I wanted to be certain to catch you in.'

Samantha shivers and swings away from the window. 'What do you want?'

'I wonder? Could you perhaps pass a message to your husband. Just tell him I called?' Before she can draw breath to say more, he's gone.

Samantha runs out to the boys. 'I've just heard a weather warning. There's a storm coming, you'd better get inside.'

She tucks her sleepy sons into her own bed to keep them safe and close. She lies between them, still hearing the Voice. The voice of a person at some sort of edge, ready to lose control. Inside her a nasty little trapdoor of doubt opens, and she wonders what secrets Dale really needed an excuse to keep.

'I can't believe we're planning the end of term, Barbie, already. I have absolutely no idea where this month has gone!' Louise's legs are trying to knot themselves as usual, but with their owner sprawled in a deck chair it's hard for them. They twine and untwine repeatedly before finally settling for snaking their way round the sloping legs of the chair.

'Just whooshed away like lemons!' Louise smiles beatifically and looks to the end of the garden where Barney has taken over as head of the Tropical Exploration Team of Joe and Tony.

'D'you mean lemmings, Louise?'

'*Lemmings?*'

'I thought because they whoosh over cliffs.'

'No. *Lemons. Whoosh. As in lemon sorbet. You know!*'

It's not worth saying that she doesn't know, because after the longer explanation that would ensue, the rules of Louise's mental association football still wouldn't make sense to anyone but Louise.

'I adore what you've done to this garden! What prompted it, Angie? I mean, it's so different!' Louise is having one of her moments of clarity, rare but utterly piercing. Samantha is pinned by the blue eyes, that say quite clearly that they know the garden signifies far more than a design decision.

'Oh, I don't know. I've just got more time now the boys are bigger.'

'Oh yeah! Sure!' say the eyes. But they look away, they can see it's the only explanation they're going to get. 'Well I suppose we ought to get down to business,' says Louise reaching for her notebook whilst her legs do another little rearrangement of themselves.

The Tropical Expedition is enjoying a supply stop. Tony and Joe are showing Barney how to make peanut butter and Marmite sandwiches, a skill they have recently been allowed to hone unsupervised. Outside, the Deacon Road Primary School PTA Catering Sub Committee have moved on from a discussion of per capita sausage consumption and age-specific pizza toppings, to the misdeeds of Louise's recently ex-husband.

'I've got a new accountant, Louise, he said, very creative, he said. You won't get anything!'

Louise has no idea where her next, or any other, mortgage payment might come from: she has no job, because her CV goes straight on the reject pile when employers note that the last time she worked was just before Barney was born. Understandably under these circumstances she's getting a little tearful. Sam is about to make some unfavourable comparisons between the ex-Mr Louise and various forms of pond life when the phone rings.

'It'll be Dale. I'll tell him to call back. Here, take these tissues.'

She takes the call in the kitchen where a second round of peanut butter is being distributed over bread, hands, arms and the table top.

'Hi, Dale?'

There! That fragment of silence again. Speaking as eloquently as it did the first time. Then, an intake of breath at the other end of the line and the Voice speaks with a wasp-trapping sweetness, 'Mrs Cassinari. Mr Cassinari – Dale – isn't home?'

'No.'

There is a hiss almost like a suppressed curse. The voice wavers, struggling to keep its civil tone, holding back some piece of information that wants to escape. 'Could you then kindly pass on my message? That I'm very, very anxious to speak with him. Soon.'

She doesn't bother with the pretence of asking 'who shall I say called'. With the last syllable the phone is dead in her hand. It feels clammy and her heart is racing. She wipes her palms on her jeans and then calls Dale's mobile. 'This is the Vodafone recall service for . . .'

'Phone me, Dale. Soon as you can.'

She settles the boys in front of the TV and cleans up some of the peanut butter before she's calm enough to return to Louise, who has a pink nose and has used up all the tissues.

'Sorry I was so long. Crisis with the expedition team.'

'Is Barney being a pain?'

'No, he's lovely. Look, why don't you stay tonight? The kids will love it and you can drown your sorrows?'

Louise just beams and starts crying again, 'Thanks, Angie.'

'That's OK. You're doing *me* a favour. Really you are.'

The phone hasn't rung for two days, except with Louise's call to say that she'd got over her hang-over. Samantha takes the boys to school and picks them up at the end of the day, but inside her things are getting out of proportion. The voice of the nameless caller is wandering around in her brain leaving doors open everywhere. One minute she can convince herself that he is just a disgruntled customer with a leaky down-pipe, and the next he's a Mafioso with a deadly hold over Dale and his business. She cleans the house from top to bottom and reorganises the freezer as if she were still holding back the full-strength tide of her past. She tries to think about her 'future', about what she can do with her reawakened dreams and ambitions but her attention keeps wandering to the phone.

When she finds herself standing beside the phone for the fifth time in a single morning, wondering if it will vibrate visibly before it rings, Samantha decides it's time for more effective distractions. She takes nothing but her door key and almost runs all the way to Tavs.

Finnian is pulling down the awning as she arrives.

'Well! To what do we owe this rare pleasure?'

'I've finally got sick of Stayfleurs. I wondered if I could come and be useful here for a bit?'

'Can you ever be useful? Maria never told me you were coming, it would've brightened my day considerably!'

'She doesn't know. I mean I decided just now.'

'Right.' Finnian is perceptive enough to know that something unusual is going on, but will wait for the right moment to find out what. When he sees Maria's reaction to Samantha's arrival, he knows that whatever it is, it's pretty big. Maria runs the length of the shop, embraces her daughter-in-law, and bursts into tears. She hasn't seen or spoken to Sam since the day Dale turned up on her doorstep with two boys and a suitcase.

'Finn, Finn, Angie and I, we have a little coffee. We'll be back soon, OK?'

'No problem, Maria.'

With the upheavals of the last week Samantha has forgotten to ask Dale what his mother knows. The way Maria has taken her arm and is so solicitously offering her a coffee in their tiny office, Samantha wonders if Maria suspects her son of being banished for wife-beating. Samantha takes a restorative gulp of coffee, but before she can speak Maria takes her hand again. 'Angela. You are like my daughter. Yes?'

'Maria, thank you!'

'Dale, when he come to my house with the boys. Ahh! Nnnnnah! I think "what has that little bugger of mine done now?" He didn't say anything then. But after, he phone me. Told me everything, all about you run from home. Your mum is dying. About the big house that guy leave for you. You don't need to tell me nothing.'

'I feel I lied to you, Maria. When we first met. I told you . . .'

'Don't matter what you told me. Everybody has some lies, yes? I have big lies I don't tell nobody. But I am still Maria, I am still like your mum, OK?'

'OK.'

'Good. I worry about Dale's business. He say it's bad. I don't want you to waste your money on Dale's business if it's goin' bust.'

'It won't go bust. It's just a bad patch. Cashflow. The house I've been left can help that.'

'You and Dale OK?'

'Fine. He's gone to Suffolk to sort out the house I've been left.'

'OK. Then what are you doin' here?'

'I've given up my job in the supermarket. I don't know what I'm going to do in the long run. I just don't want that dead-end job any more. Can I work at Tavs for a while?'

'Music of the saints and angels! You know who call this morning, just when you arrive? I didn't even tell Finn this yet. That Marcella tha's who! Say she's going to live in Cornwall with 'er boyfriend and sell surf boards. Ppfff! Can you work here? You wanna start now?'

The boys love it when Samantha works in Granny Maria's shop, so they endure sitting quietly whilst Sam stays on and helps with the rush of business between four and closing at five thirty.

'Hey, boys, Granny going to invite herself for tea,' Maria says, pulling down the blinds, 'so you pick what you want to eat, eh? And, Angie, you find us a good bottle of wine.'

Finnian's happy to be left with the last of the chores. 'I'm meeting Robert at the Anolfini at six thirty – something soulful and subtitled he wants us to see together – I haven't time to go home first anyway.'

Maria and Samantha walk along the wide pavement towards Lancaster Road, with the boys running ahead of them like eager pups in the woods.

'You and Dale, you going to have more babies?'

'I don't know, Maria. Two is fine.'

'Two. Nnnah! Is nothing. If I had a husband I would have ten!'

'Ten grandchildren in Tavs eating free ice creams? Where would your profits go?'

Maria laughs and slips her arm through Samantha's. 'You always make me laugh, Angie. But hey. Dale told me, Angie is not your name. Is Samantha. Very pretty name.'

'I think my father chose it. But Angela was my middle name. And I've used it for so long now . . .'

'I wished I change my name too, when I come to England.'

'Why?'

'I didn't want Papa's name after the way he treat me. Nnmah. So bad. He throw me down the stairs to the street when he found I am pregnant.'

'But you didn't change your name?'

'No. I came here. Bristol. Big, wet, grey. People who don't smiles. I start my business and Cassinari is a good name for business.' Maria shrugged.

'And an easy name to trace if Dale's daddy wanted to find you?'

'Hah! No. I *know* Dale's daddy don't want to find me.' Maria's face is suddenly closed and dark, the dancing eyebrows low and straight. Then, like a passing cloud the darkness is gone, and Maria is laughing at the boys climbing on the wall of Number eleven. 'Dale don't know about me and his daddy,' Maria says. 'What he don't know won't hurt him.' And she smiles her dazzling smile, so that Sam feels this secret is somehow a present, a silver charm, a symbol of trust.

*

Maria has added her own expert selections – wild boar ham, bean salad, stuffed peppers and rich cheese bread – to the boys' standard favourites of *bresaola*, *caponata* and *provolone*. They eat in the kitchen with all the windows and doors open and the soft muggy summer air rolling over them.

'Is a new one for you to try, boys: *fagioli con gamberetti e bottarga*.' Maria puts a spoonful of the salad into each of the boys' waiting mouths.

'Lovely, Granny,' says Joe through his chewing.

'I like the bean part and prawn part but not the other part,' says Tony.

'*Bottarga* . . . oh but that is the best, the eggs of the tuna, *tonno*. And now you have to say it. Ready?'

The boys falter through *fagioli con gamberetti e bottarga*, with Joe rolling the 'r' of *gamberetti* with obvious pleasure.

'It's a big word for such little prawns, Granny.'

As they eat, Maria tells the story behind each dish, polishing the bare facts to brightness with her passion and experience. '*Prosciutto di cinghiale*, this is the ham of the wild boar. Is very fierce. Is the beast that attacked Odysseus when he was a young hunter. This is made by my friend who has boar in the woods near his house. He works with *cinghiale* so long he look like boar. Last year his wife have a baby, and I thought it would be born with stripes like *cinghiale bambini*! Now, Tony, you try this olive. Good? You know when Adam lay dead, there were three trees sprouted from the seeds in 'is mouth. The cypress, the cedar and the olive tree. Imagine that, three big trees with their roots in a skull.'

The boys run out to eat their chocolate bars in the garden leaving Maria and Sam to savour the more adult pleasure of figs and mascarpone.

'I'm going to plant a fig tree in the garden. It'll be fine on that south-facing wall.'

Maria isn't really listening, she's waiting to talk. 'You know Mr Belling next door is giving up? He's got a bad heart, he can't work no more.' Maria has never got on very well with the proprietor of the ironmonger's next door to Tavs. In all his fifty-seven years the most adventurous thing to pass Mr Belling's lips has been a pork sausage. He still regards Tavs as a temporary fad and a hotbed of subversion. But Samantha can tell there's more point to Maria's observation than mere *schadenfreude*. 'So he won't need his shop, and the lease will be up to grabs.'

'Are you going to take it?'

'Maybe. I need new challenge. I don't want just expand. I'd like to do something bit different. A real Italian bakery. I'm fed up with chasing that Guy. You know, last week I ring him, "Where is my *focaccia*, Guy, I have a big order here." He says, "Oh Maria, you can have it tomorrow, I forgot to start the dough . . ." and then blah blah excuse. Always! Nnnh! In the autumn I go home to Italy and I find a good baker. A young person who wants a big start.'

'I think you'll make a fortune, Maria.'

'Maybe. It's big money I need. Got to rip out all that Belling crap. Put in special oven. Twenty-thousand pound, maybe more. I got some little money. But well, I had big expenses this year. Nnnah.' Maria pauses, pushing a last dollop of mascarpone about her plate. 'You know, Angie, I'm no good to ask things. But I think this is good idea. I think you're right, it will make a fortune. But I need money to do it. Money, nnnahh, I don't have so much . . .'

'And you'd like me to invest some of my inheritance?'

'That's it. Invest. I do it all proper so you get profit share and all. Maybe you could take over Tavs with Finnian while I do the bakery?'

'The money's yours, Maria, as soon as I get it. And I'll work in Tavs for while, but I've got a lot to decide.'

'That's good enough answer for me. Now, another glass . . .'

Samantha stands at the sink with her rubber-gloved hands idle in the suds. Why hasn't Dale rung back? Maybe his mobile isn't working. But the whole of West Suffolk can't be a dead zone. She wants to hear that the voice that escaped the phone and is scratching at her peace of mind is not important, just some bloke with problem stonework or a kink in his flashing. She wants to be sure she already knows all Dale's secrets.

Maria comes downstairs after reading the boys at least four stories. 'Ah, those boys. I love those boys! That Joe he will learn Italian like this, ppht. Easy.'

'I'd like that. I can't speak anything apart from English.'

'Ah! You manage my shop with that Finn and he will teach you.'

'Don't hassle me, Maria!'

'Not hassling. Teasing. Is different. Now where is your cloth? I help dry up.'

'Maria, has Dale rung you this week, whilst he's been away?'

'Dale ring me? Are you crazy? He didn't ring you? How long?'

'Three days.'

'Three days. Nnnah.' She takes a plate from the draining board and walks, with her testy hips swinging, to the cupboard. 'He's a bugger that boy. Don't worry. Maybe his phone is bust.'

'Maria, what was Dale like, before he met me?'

It takes no more than a second for Maria to master her reaction yet still she nearly drops the plate. 'What you mean? He was a little bugger. Same as now.' She shuts the cupboard and turns to take Sam's face in her hands, smoothing her cheeks with both thumbs. 'That Dale. He is a little bugger. But he is a good man. A real good man.'

'Thanks, Maria. I know. I know.'

The two women, suddenly close to tears, hug, then break apart to finish the chores.

'D'you want to stay the night, Maria?'

'No. I like my bed. Call me a taxi?'

Samantha seeks the blankness of the spare room after Maria

has gone. She watches the few late traffic lights track over the ceiling. She and Dale had made love in this room just a few days ago and the lights had moved over the pale paint work in the same way. Then they'd made her feel peaceful, lulled – she felt she'd beaten Pandora, and kept the worst things from the box of her past under the lid. Now the lights make her anxious, and the lid of her box, and of Dale's too, seem menacingly ajar. Dale's 'secrets' cast grotesque shadows on the wall; how could his healthy business have foundered so fast if not through some corruption? Outside of this house, away from her and the boys, Dale could be anybody, involved in anything; a victim or a predator. The lights race unpredictably down the wall, another stops halfway, there are gaps between them of varying length. She tries to count them to get to sleep, one, two, three but there's no pattern, no rhythm to soothe her. The numbers run away with her like the pills metered out onto her mother's palm and soon the shadows of her own secrets are dancing on the bedroom wallpaper. She gets up at last, draws the curtains and falls asleep with the bedside lamp on.

11

'I've brought some carrot loaf!' beams Maeve when Samantha answers the door. 'Managed to get it baked without the trip wotsit going! Malcolm's coming in a minute, he's just finishing his meditation.'

'He's here already, Maeve. Perhaps he levitated or something. Anyway, go on through to the kitchen. Everyone else is here.'

Eight people are sitting round Samantha's kitchen table with mugs of hot tea to ward off the chill of the rain. It's another committee meeting, not the PTA this time but the Lancaster Road Street Party Committee. All the residents who helped to get the giant palm tree into the back garden of Number eleven are there, plus three of the students from the big tatty house on the corner.

Maeve puts the cake in the middle of the table, edging Samantha's fruit cake out of centre stage. 'Carrot loaf!' she says in a stage whisper which drowns out Keith's words for a second. She sounds as though she expects applause. Two of the three students would be prepared to applaud any sort of food and wonder if it would be OK to tuck into the loaf and the cake whilst Keith is still speaking and everyone else is paying attention.

'So then, in conclusion,' says Keith, 'although we've got away with closing off the road this year, next year's going to be really tricky.'

'Thank you, Keith.' The third student is a business and tourism major called Julie. She sees running meetings as something she can put on her CV. 'I think we should run through what needs to be done tomorrow and on the day itself, yeah?'

'Josh at number thirty-eight'll help me put the crash barriers up at noon on Sunday,' says Keith. 'I'll pick them up tomorrow and store them in his alley.'

'Crash barriers!' Maeve is horrified. 'Did we have those last year? I mean, it gives all the wrong signals. Couldn't we have ribbons or balloons or something?'

'A string of pink ribbon isn't going to stop a joy rider in a Mazda at sixty, Maeve.' Keith is severely irritated that his meticulous attention to health and safety regulations has been entirely ignored by Maeve, who cuts herself a slice of carrot loaf and looks hurt.

'Perhaps we could decorate the crash barriers?' suggests Julie, quietly congratulating herself for her ability to think laterally.

'Of course,' Keith is really quite flushed with irritation, 'I wasn't suggesting we left them looking like prison bars, for God's sake!'

'Right.' Julie's neat lipsticked mouth is pulled tight as if she's just sucked a lemon. 'That takes care of security issues. Now the barbecue? I think that's your department, Spider.'

The large sprawling politics student, Spider, is caught with a mouthful of cake *and* loaf; all he can do is look desperate and shake his head vigorously.

'What d'you mean, no!' A note of unprofessional, almost domestic, ire enters Julie's voice. She could be standing in the kitchen of their shared house yelling over the empty bean cans and the greasy pan left in the sink.

Spider swallows fast. 'I said I'd help run the barbecue. Not like set it up.'

'Fine,' says Julie with a definite sub text of 'I'll-see-you-later-Spider-you-useless-div'.

'Um,' says Malcolm, fiddling with the bridge of his glasses, 'we usually use our barbie. It's big enough. The one we use on

Woodcraft Folk camps actually. I'll set it up, if Spider could lend a hand. Just outside our place, Spider?'

'Yeah, cool.'

Beside Spider, the other student Jon (who's doing Women's Studies as it might offer him the only chance he's likely to get to pull,) clears his throat. 'Umm,' he says as if trying out a new sound system, 'I'll like take care of the sounds. You know, put my system outside. Or in the window. People can just bring me, like, tapes of what they want to hear? OK?'

'Good! Now, drinks?'

'Two trestle tables outside our front door?' Felicity pipes up sweetly, pencil poised over a neat little notebook in case anything needs writing down. 'And I've got lots of paper cups left over from a do at work.' Keith smiles at her adoringly as if she had just formulated the recipe for the elixir of youth or offered the foolproof solution to world poverty. No one would ever guess that six months ago they were throwing crockery at each other over the breakfast bar.

The music, the barbecue and the drinks stand are all taken care of. Samantha offers to go to the Cash and Carry and get the meat for the barbecue. Maeve says that there are very good Quorn patties available these days and so, the ritual contest of carnivores versus vegetarians begins.

'I personally had to throw away sixty-three unsold veggie burgers last year,' says Keith, 'and we ran out of *beef* burgers and *pork* sausages after forty-five minutes. It just doesn't make economic sense to buy half a ton of *Quorn patties*!'

'Well, the real solution,' retorts Maeve, showing some sign that she might really be a lawyer, 'is to give people no choice. Meat eaters can after all eat vegetarian food, whilst the converse is not the case!'

The phone rings. Gratefully Samantha tears upstairs to take the call in peace. She considers too late the possibility of picking up the receiver and cutting the call off, as it might be the phantom ringer again. She can already hear the voice at the other end of the line. It's Dale, brimming with excitement, his inexorable energy powering down the phone at her. All he wants to tell her is bank managers, roof repairs, authentic leading and Victorian tiles. All she really wants is to know when he's coming home.

'Where are you?'

'Bury St Edmunds. I'm in a pay phone, the mob's bust. I managed to drive over it!'

'Clever!'

'Angie! Listen . . . The house looks fabulous from the outside. I could do wonders with it, I really could, Ange. I can't tell you . . .'

'When are you coming home?'

'Not yet. After the weekend. I'm going to have to miss the street party. I'm sorry.'

'What's taking so long?'

'Oh. There's just a lot to do.' It's a vague answer and Samantha hears the tiny silence which is the sound of Dale coming up with something more specific and convincing. 'I'm trying to get as many quotes done for the work on Lime House as I can. I've had a couple of estate agents look at it, and as it stands it'll fetch six hundred thousand, at least.' Dale is back on truthful ground now, she can tell by the enthusiasm in his voice. 'So it's up to you to decide, you know sell now, or do the work and then sell for more. I think we could make maybe another fifty or a hundred grand if we do it up.' He's ready to expand on this but Samantha isn't interested just now. 'Dale,' she says, with a tightness in her voice that makes him pay attention, 'this man keeps calling. Won't say his name. Just says to tell you he called. He really scares me. He sounds, I dunno, sinister.'

Dale goes quite still at the end of the line. 'Posh voice? Old?'

'Yeah.'

'Bugger. *Bugger.*' Dale pauses and sighs. This is not reassuring to Samantha. 'I'm sorry. I'm so sorry. Look. Don't worry about it. He's harmless. There's nothing to worry about. Just put the phone down whenever he rings. I'll be back soon. I'll explain then. I've got no more change. I love you. Don't worry. I'll be home very soon.'

Harmless is how her biology teacher described a hornet that flew against the inside of the classroom window. 'Oh, it's quite harmless really.' It was the size of a Cuban cigar with a buzz like a Harley on full throttle and a sting like a Mossad stiletto.

Downstairs the meeting is breaking up. In the hall Callendula is chatting to Jon and Spider. 'Wicked!' she says, and they smile shiftily at each other.

'Bye, Angela,' they say in their best Addressing-Grown-Ups voices as they slope out, with the same bony, loose-limbed sway that Friesians have on their way to the milking parlour.

Keith and Felicity are holding hands like the Start-rite kids and being subjected to Maeve's opinions on birthing pools. They don't seem to mind, as they revel in anything to do with babies and pregnancy. Felicity has taken to wearing Lycra to show the world her hard-won bump which already looks as if it could be holding triplets. Samantha can imagine them reading birth manuals and baby-feeding texts to each other in bed at night.

Julie is telling Malcolm about her job prospects in 'the business sector'. Malcolm is looking at the clipboard clutched to her chest and the way her cleavage peeps enticingly over the top. As she leaves Julie briefly squeezes his forearm, telling him she valued his contribution to the meeting. Immediately Malcolm plunges into panicky but rather exciting fantasies of telling Julie's heaving bosom that they can only be friends, that a physical relationship is impossible. Julie sails out, internally quoting from the 'Get To The Top' manual: 'Eye contact and arm touching can be among the most valuable of management tools'. Practice makes perfect, she tells herself.

The cheese-wedge house has been host to many scenes like this in the past. Samantha has always been happy to host meetings, busying herself with providing everyone with what they need and expect – drinks, food, opinions – and yet staying safely untouched and unengaged by it all. It's all been another bit of her 'portrait', meticulously painted to give her camouflage and a disciplined occupation for her thoughts. And at the end of the evening she always refuses the offers of help or company, preferring to maintain her safe separateness. So she's only herself to blame for the fact that tonight everyone leaves without offering to help wash up or stay and chat. But tonight she wanted them all to stay, to drink more tea, maybe move on to the whisky and finish every last scrap of cake. She wanted to hear them talk about their kids, their jobs and their worries, to gather clues about how other people collect up the pieces of their lives – rows and loving, business sectors and sticky bean cans, burgers and Quorn patties, murky past and uncertain future – and make a whole. Alone in the kitchen with carroty crumbs and dirty mugs, she settles for a practical solution to her present anxieties: she unplugs the phone, and sets the burglar alarm.

Sunday morning rain gets Maeve twittering with anxiety. She's out before ten knocking on doors in search of tarpaulins and tents so, for a while, the collective irritation of the residents of Lancaster Road threatens to draw a worse storm down on the Street Party. But as people emerge after their first cup of coffee and a little restorative toast, the clouds at ground level and above the roof tops dispel. Sunshine dries the pavements and slants through the trees, casting jaunty continental-looking shadows onto the road. The austere crash barriers are decorated with an assortment of balloons donated by Mr Pradashie's print shop – pink ones bearing the words 'Spirit of Sixty-Six', yellow ones with a faultily printed logo that looks disturbingly phallic and blue ones saying 'Hoppy Birthday Dvid'. Spider and Malcolm are striking up an unlikely friendship over the hot charcoal, and a band called Urban Tarmac Suckers are playing their hearts out through Jon's 'system'. Impromptu stalls of all sorts are springing up in people's front gardens as the residents of Lancaster Road begin to have confidence in the weather.

Eric Donaldson, the widowed French teacher at number seventeen, has covered a picnic table with shoe boxes filled with gooseberries with the sign 'Help Yourself' pencilled on the back of an empty cornflakes packet. Callendula has draped a sheet over the brick wall of number thirteen and is laying out her home-made bead and wire jewellery for sale. Margaret and Edith, the retired anthropologists at number six, have baked cakes and scones and have them neatly arrayed on starched cloths and china plates with little jars to receive 'contributions to charity'. Everyone is bringing chairs and tables, cushions and rugs out into the street, and the under-tens have formed a single collective entity which tears up and down the road beside itself with excitement. Jon sensibly changes the music, putting on a tape Eric handed him, labelled 'Charles Trenet.' It's a long way from grunge and garage, but the light tenor voice and the tootling orchestrations seem well suited to sunshine and the smell of burning Quorn burgers. He shakes his head and laughs at how much he likes this sound redolent of 'gamine' girls in fifties' frocks and men wearing straw boaters: 'Wow. Wicked, Eric! Can I borrow this tape? I reckon it'd sample brilliantly!'

Perhaps it was just the level of participation, every door in the street open, everyone outside talking, eating, drinking. Perhaps the sun and the steamy heat made people feel a little less British, but from the very start the Lancaster Road Street Party had a certain chemistry to it. Spontaneity is normally difficult for the English; it might involve interaction with people one hasn't been introduced to, or a course of events one cannot predict. Yet sometimes, when the sun shines they can be different from their ordinary rainy-day selves and the repressed spirit of play, fun and mayhem can suddenly burst out. It's a chain reaction too – gathered in a group above a certain critical mass it can give rise to a collective ability to party quite outside the bounds of the National Character. The Sunday of the party was one of those times and from the first flipped burger there was a kind of slow crescendo building: the street was ready for something, anything, to happen.

It really started with Spider getting the gang of under-tens to dance in a ring to Baggy Trousers. His huge skinny frame draped in even more enormous clothing hypnotised the children into losing their inhibitions and following him round in a roving conga of outrageous movement and mime. Then, kids grabbed their parents, or any other adult who was close to learn the routine and join in. Samantha was pulled into the circle of manically dancing children by both Joe and Tony.

'Pull your trousers out like this, Mummy . . .'

'Then flap your shirt . . .'

'And grab your hair . . .'

'Make a nasty face, Mummy, like this. See?'

'Oh, Mummy, pleeeeese . . .'

Samantha was reluctant to join in, because 'Angie' didn't dance. Angie'd watch Dale doing joke-dancing with the children or the occasional ironic jiggle with Maria or with someone else's older wife. Sam, however, had rather enjoyed throwing herself about at school friends' parties with shameless if rather uncoordinated abandon. Since then dancing had become dangerous, like sex: potentially too revealing. But with so much already revealed, and safe in the mass of other jiving bodies, Samantha felt liberated. She let the boys coax her at first, following their lead, tentatively swaying and turning. Then she was leading them, making up new moves and new steps, that they copied with laughter and delight. And it felt so good! She threw her head back, shaking her hair like a mane, and noticed flocks of macaws bending the TV aerials with their weight, and epiphytes sprouting in profusion along the ridge tiles.

'Hey, boys! Can you do this? See how far down you can twist without falling over!'

Callendula led Eric from the last of his gooseberries and soon he was wiggling his bottom with the six year olds. The street filled up, the music got louder and the joint jumped – Madness, Charles Trenet, Abba's Greatest Hits, The Chemical Brothers, it didn't matter what it was, everyone just moved to it. People from other streets came and joined in. Cars passing the top of the closed-off road pulled over. At five o'clock a salsa band on their way home after a competition in Birmingham leapt out of their van and set up in the tatty garden of the student house. They played until the surrounding roads were blocked with cars and everyone had danced holes into their shoes and kinks into their spines. Just as the curious fever of spontaneous pleasure looked as if it might spread across the whole city, the clouds cracked open, spilling cold water onto the revellers' heads and the police arrived to restore everyone to their normal wet-day selves.

Samantha and the boys had danced for what she realised now had been nearly six hours, solidly. They'd been possessed with a kind of manic joy that brought each new second into existence bright and burning, making the moment that had just passed fade to non-being. Now Samantha is sitting on her bed. Her body feels like a car that's been borrowed and then returned with the tyres bald and the clutch gone. Her feet are almost too sore to stand on and her head is three times its normal size and weight. The boys collapsed, whimpering with exhaustion almost the moment that the rain and the sirens came to break the spell. She would also like to collapse but she realises with some regret that she is too hungry and thirsty to sleep. She wraps her poor feet in two pairs of Dale's biggest fluffiest socks and goes down the stairs on her bottom.

The kitchen clock shows nine and outside darkness is just beginning to cover up the remaining litter lying limp on the wet tarmac. Samantha pads around her kitchen wincing slightly with every step, but the warmth of the floor tiles and the glow of the kitchen in the falling twilight are comforting. She takes a sweatshirt of Dale's off the airier and wriggles it over her summer dress, now her aches and blisters are hurting in a cozy way. She opens cupboard doors foraging for some indulgence to eat – possibly out of its packet – at the kitchen table. Broken Eccles cakes would fit the bill perfectly but she hasn't eaten those since she left her bedsit. She settles at last for chocolate biscuits dipped in hot tea. She licks the melted chocolate off the crumb and curls her legs up onto the chair, reflecting on how exactly like three am it feels. There's a sudden shuffling outside the door and the sound of whispers. Maeve has probably tripped her circuits again cooking supper and she's come round with Callendula for moral support to ask Sam to do her magic trick. Samantha smiles: that's OK. Having danced cheek to cheek with her to 'No woman no cry', Samantha feels a bond of solidarity that will carry her through at least five more trip-switch incidents without irritation. She sucks her sticky fingers and waits for the bell to ring.

A key turns in the lock, the front door sighs open and Samantha knows it's not Maeve but Dale home early! The voices on the doorstep are suddenly quite clear as they move into the hall. Dale's voice and two others, a man and a woman, obviously manoeuvring luggage into the hall.

'Thank you, Dale, I can manage really,' says the woman.

'Shall I take that from you, dear,' the man says to her.

Shaking, incredulous, rigid with shock, Samantha hobbles into the hall to the sound of their voices. The visitors are instantly recognisable, in the same heart-stopping thunder-flash way that God's face would be, peeping at you in your coffin. Samantha stares and they stare back. Standing there with her skinny brown legs stuck into a bulbous mass of sock and her body enveloped in faded orange cotton, Samantha, the grown woman, looks just like the gangly kid they remember. The three of them are caught in a swell of time that builds over the moments to a wave, it crests and breaks, washing the daughter across the carefully chosen pile of her hall carpet into the arms of her father and her strangely, incomprehensibly miraculously alive mother.

12

It is more than an hour before anyone can speak properly. There are many different sorts of tears to be cried. Ralph seems to suffer most, his sobs pulled out from deep inside as he holds his daughter, his wife or simply covers his face in his hands. But at last the three of them can sit calmly, taking in each other's faces and sipping the sweet tea that Dale has quietly produced.

Samantha can't stop staring at Bea. Bea is not simply alive, but is pink cheeked and blooming, even a little round. Her hair – now completely white – is cut in a short straight bob, with a wispy fringe to just above the dark and striking eyes. She wears a short-sleeved cotton safari suit the colour of cornflowers and neat brown sandals revealing a row of toenails painted bright pink. She sits erect and elegant with her legs folded together to one side. Even her teeth look better than ten years ago. Certainly a lot better than a corpse's. She is essentially the same warm lively woman that was always there under the illness. But the details of Bea's appearance are not at first what Samantha notices. Initially all Sam's attention is focused on the simple fact that Bea is alive. It is so huge a fact and yet so simple, so obvious and commonplace. The fear, the guilt and the grief that have made her emotional life into a fortress for ten years collapse. Not noisily, explosively like a cooling tower under the influence of dynamite, more like the massive melting of an ice cap in a sudden Austral spring. It is an almost physical sensation, as if Sam has a sand-castle in her stomach that the tide is washing flat. The word *murderer* that has branded her soul loses its power like a retreating thunder cloud. She's left blank and shaky, staring at her parents and trying to take in reality.

Bea is simply a healthy version of herself, the self that Sam always talked and laughed with. But Ralph is transformed into something that Sam only gradually begins to recognise. Physically he too seems to have improved with age. His paunch has gone and a healthy leanness has replaced the old sag. He is wearing jeans and sandals with no socks. There is even a copper arthritis bracelet around his right wrist which gives him a slightly bohemian air. He stands straight, and when he sits his posture is open and relaxed. There isn't a trace of the old stoop and hunch and his speech is slower and more flowing. He's come alive.

Gradually, something more than their obvious health and good grooming strikes Samantha. Bea and Ralph look like *people*, not simply her parents. They had of course always looked like people, but at seventeen, she had been too young to notice. She hadn't understood what her leaving could do or mean. Now she can't think where she will begin to explain and apologise.

Bea is the first to brave the hard task of starting to speak. Leaving the deep-water questions for later when they might be ready to be asked and answered, Bea begins with a little paddle in the shallows. 'You know, Sam, you've grown a little bit. I'm sure you're taller.'

'Still a skinny ribs though!' says Ralph.

'You both look so well.'

'We've just been to Portugal for a week, staying with a friend of your mother's.' What friend? Bea and Ralph didn't have friends! Portugal or any other country might as well have been Jupiter when Sam was at home.

'Dale rang us the night we got back,' says Bea, 'then he came round and spoke to us. He had a very hard job convincing us you'd want to see us.' Bea tries to keep her tone light, but her voice is shaking already. She turns to Ralph for help.

'We'd come to accept that you wanted to be left in peace,' he says.

'We understood how you felt. That you'd had such a bad time at home . . .' Bea looks forlornly at Ralph, pursing her lips, her eyes filled with tears. Samantha wants them to shout and be angry, to call her selfish, to call her cruel, to call her what she's called herself all this time, a killer. But there isn't a scrap of anger to be found between the two of them. They look at her with such gratitude that Samantha has to look away out of shame. Far from coming to her with retribution they've come for forgiveness, and are afraid that she will reject them again.

Bea is crying anew and takes Samantha's hand in her own. 'We're so sorry, Sam. When I was ill and Ralph couldn't cope. It was awful for you. I never blamed you for leaving.'

'I've felt all this time that I failed you.' Ralph is sobbing.

Samantha is dazed, how can they be apologising to her after what *she* did? It doesn't make sense. All she can do is blurt her apology and hope they will listen. 'No, no, I'm sorry I ran off. Now I've got the boys I know how frantic you must have been. But in all this time I never tried to contact you.'

'Oh, Sam, don't. That's not even true. You did keep in touch.'

'We always knew you were all right. Because of your Christmas cards.' Ralph's words make no sense at all to Samantha. She stares at him stupidly. He interprets Sam's tearful bemusement as the confusion born of overwhelming emotion and he goes on, 'It meant the world that you sent those. Every Christmas. Even that first Christmas. We knew you were all right.'

'When you wrote to tell us about the boys being born . . .' Bea is crying too much to go on, she simply rummages in her bag and pulls out a weathered envelope. 'I've kept them with me every day.'

Sam takes two cards from the single envelope and opens each

in turn. The first has a glitter-strewn robin on the front. Inside a typed message is pasted: 'Happy Christmas, Mum and Dad. Hope you're well. Dale and I had our first baby this year, a boy called Tony. Best wishes, Sam.'

The second card bears a reindeer with mistletoe woven through its antlers. The same style of typed message appears inside: 'A brother for Tony, little Joe born without a hitch this year. I'm well. Hope you are. Sam.'

'I don't know what we would have done without those cards,' says Ralph, 'I really don't. They were our lifeline. They made us able to go on.'

How can she tell them that she didn't offer them even this tiny scrap of compassion? That if she had known Bea was alive, she would have come home? That guilt, fear and cowardice kept her away? It will only make the pain of their separation worse, through having been unnecessary. Sam sees immediately that bearing that knowledge in her heart, privately, is her new penance. All she can do is hug her parents and tell them how glad she is that they got the cards, and how glad she is that Dale came to find them and bring them to her.

It's too late and they are too exhausted for much more talk. The bare facts of Bea's recovery and Ralph's return to reality, their move from the family home, Ralph's early retirement and Bea's new career as owner of a vintage clothing shop are run through like a news bulletin. Granny Pearl's death two years ago in a car accident is only slightly elaborated. Dale takes their bags to the spare room and everyone cries again a little as they kiss good night on the landing.

'What time do the boys go to school?' asks Bea.

'Oh. Day off tomorrow,' says Dale, winding an arm around Sam's shoulder. 'Yes definitely. Day off all round.'

Sam flops onto the bed as soon as the door is closed. Dale comes to sit beside her. He looks tired but the same as always. Yet he is not the same as he was a week or a month ago. He has produced the unexpected from the personality she always viewed as simply dependable, he has shown a third dimension she never noticed. She reaches up and touches his face as if discovering his profile for the first time.

'Why did you do this?'

'It seemed wrong not to. Wrong for you and wrong for them. Aren't you happy?'

There's still so much to lie about, she wants to give Dale as much truth as she can, so Sam thinks carefully before answering. 'I'm *glad*. I've got my mum back from the dead. There aren't words to say what that feels like. But it's all too painful to be happy about. But I am very glad. More peaceful, more at peace. But it feels weird. Not real yet. It's so big. I feel better because Mum's alive and worse because I never contacted them.'

'But you did. They always knew you were alive and OK. Because of the cards. Why didn't you tell me about the cards, Sam? All these years . . .'

'I don't know, Dale.' It seems the safest thing to say, safer than telling one truth to Dale and then expecting him to lie to her parents. 'I don't know. Why didn't I tell you the whole story anyway? I'm sorry.' Sam is crying now, sorry that still she has to lie to Dale.

'You were just a kid when you left home. When we met. It's OK, Angie. He smooths her face, wiping the tears from the corners of her eyes with his fingertips.

'How did you find them anyway?'

'Determination. Just like tracking down an authentic Georgian door or something. Would have been easier with their address. *Why* didn't you tell me about the cards, last weekend when you told me everything else? Oh I'm sorry, love. I mustn't keep asking.'

'I dunno,' she says, which seems close enough to her real feelings, 'I dunno.' Sam reaches up and winds him in her arms. 'You didn't tell me all your secrets did you?'

Dale holds her, but says nothing and in his silence turns a little more of that unfamiliar profile towards her. Sleepily, half dressed, they squirm bit by bit under the duvet together.

'Who was that man, Dale? Who kept ringing up? Scared me!'

'He's nobody. It's nothing.' He scoops her up, holding her close. 'It's nothing to worry about.'

She is not convinced, but she lets Dale persuade her out of her clothes and into a languid and caressing lovemaking that drops her, soft as a leaf, into sleep.

It's going to be hot again today. Shorts weather. Samantha reviews her neat stacks of summer clothing and wrinkles her nose. She pulls out a pair of slightly frayed white denim shorts and a blue vest.

'You haven't worn those in ages!' Dale has woken up and is propped on an elbow watching her dress.

'No. I haven't. But I can be officially twenty-eight now, so I'm entitled.'

'You look gorgeous. You make an old man very happy.'

'Oh yeah? Well, get up, Methuselah, 'cos we need to be around when the boys get up and meet their granny and grandpa raised from the dead!'

'I'll be down as soon as I've put the batteries in the pace-maker!'

Sam runs downstairs feeling light, and efficient, equal to the emotional day ahead.

Bea and Ralph are up already, sitting hand in hand on the patio. She calls good morning from the kitchen door and they leap up, and rush towards her and kiss her good morning the way they did when she was little. The memory is so sharp that Samantha's eyes prickle. Bea grins through tears and Ralph coughs a lot and takes a turn around the echiums, clearly resolved not to cry like a woman today. Sam watches him sadly; she has no idea what to say or do. Arriving at normality is going to take more than a fried breakfast.

'He'll be all right in a minute. Really he will. And I'm fine. So lovely to see my gorgeous girl.' Bea is wrinkling her nose and grinning through her tears. She slips her arm though her daughter's and steers her back into the kitchen. 'What can I do, Sam, to help make breakfast?'

'What would you like?'

'Toast and cereal is fine.'

'I'll show you where everything is.'

Together the two women lay the table, make a pot of tea, and manage to burn three lots of toast out of nervousness and crying by the time Dale comes down with Joe perched on his shoulder like John Silver's parrot and Tony clinging to his hand.

Ralph's turn in the garden restores his composure and all through breakfast he's chatted, asking Samantha about her garden, and Dale about his work. 'All I do in the way of work these days is Bea's business accounts,' he says. 'Apart from that I'm completely idle.'

'That's nonsense. He's busier than I am. He works in the over-sixties drop-in centre in the village on Mondays, he's got choir on Tuesdays. That's on top of helping me out in the shop and feeding us on wonderful veg from the garden.' She squeezes his hand and Samantha marvels at how close they've become. 'I've forgotten to mention the yoga. Go on, Ralph, you tell it.'

'Well. All right. I started yoga to help me relax. Your mother was having all sorts of alternative this and that to help her. Acupuncture, Chinese herbs,' he rolls his eyes dramatically, 'I thought it was a load of nonsense. But whatever it was, she did get better. Visibly, every day. Back on her feet by spring. So I thought I'd try something for my, well, depression – can't beat about the bush, that's what it was. I went to yoga class. I noticed I felt better. Not so sad. Able to cope with Bea and with Sam's going. Anyway. It did wonders. I'm sure you could tell that, Sam. You remember what a wreck I was. Had been for years. Look, I'll give you a little demonstration.'

All through breakfast the boys have sat silently spooning cereal into their mouths without taking their eyes off Bea and Ralph. The trainee grandparents have contained their excitement wonderfully, and let the boys find the right time to make contact, saying nothing to them but a polite good morning. As Ralph kneels down in the middle of the kitchen floor Joe stands up on his chair to get a better view of whatever is about to happen. Slowly, elegantly, Ralph's lean old frame is tilted upside down until he forms a perfect line balanced on his head.

'Wow!' says Tony seriously impressed. 'Wicked!' Joe starts to clap, then sits down suddenly, embarrassed by his own spontaneity.

'Dad,' Joe says in the sort of audible-at-two-hundred-metres' whisper that only five year olds can do, 'what's his name?'

'Ralph, but you could call him Grandad.'

'Oh. Grandad Ralph?'

'Yes, Joe?'

'Can you teach me and Tony to do that?'

'Oh, I expect so. Shall we try after your breakfast has gone down?'

The demanding day full of difficult conversations and more crying doesn't materialise. By noon the boys have learnt, after a fashion, to do headstands and have taken Ralph on a full-scale tropical exploration expedition to the park, with the promise of ice creams on the way home. Bea and Samantha are side by side in deck chairs as if they had never been anywhere else in their lives.

'That Knole sofa is gorgeous!' says Bea. 'The colour of the covers! Oh! Ma had a pair of shoes in exactly that shade when I was a little girl.'

'That material was once the master bedroom curtains in Monmouth Castle!'

'No!'

'Yes! Really. It cost me fifty p! And the sofa I got for fifteen pounds. It was part of a lot with about twelve awful plastic gnomes. We didn't know what to do with them so they rode around in Dale's van for about three months. I think he began to get fond of them. Anyway, he was doing a stone front porch for this lady writer in Bath. She saw the gnomes and gave him sixty quid for them!'

Bea laughed and then squeezed Sam's hand. 'You've got a real eye for colour. Funny, I never thought you cared a fig for all that when you were at home. Full of your rainforest then you were.'

'Yes I know.'

'I didn't give you enough encouragement. You could have gone to Oxford.'

'Not really. I failed the entrance exam in the end. Found out the night I left home.'

'You didn't, Sam. They wrote to us offering you a place. We had to write back and tell them we didn't know where you were.'

'But that phone call Daddy took? It sounded . . . I mean, I was sure they'd rung to say I hadn't got in.'

'No, they rang a few times after you'd left. Asking if you'd take up the place.'

'Oh, my God! All this time I thought I was a failure. And all this time I could have been there, in the jungle. I thought I failed, I was sure I'd failed.'

'Is that why you went?'

Sam just looks at her; is it possible that Bea has forgotten the night she left and what happened?

'Maybe,' Sam says, 'maybe.'

Tired out by their first day as grandparents, Bea and Ralph are dozing in front of a video with the boys. Samantha is trying to think about supper but after twenty-four hours of life-shaking revelations deciding between shepherd's pie and *cannelloni* doesn't seem much of a priority. Her brain is running away with a stream of what-ifs.

What if she had never left?

What if she had known that Bea was alive?

What if she'd known about her Oxford place?

And, most of all, what if the Christmas cards had never been sent and maybe Bea and Ralph had come to find her?

'Shall I get it?' Bea is calling from the sitting room. The phone must have been ringing for some time.

'No, 's all right.'

'Mrs Cassinari. How nice to speak with you again.'

'I'm not going to "speak with you" if you don't tell me your name.'

'Then perhaps I could speak with Mr Cassinari.'

'He's not here.'

'He never seems to be there.'

'I've told him you called. Now why don't you just go away?'

'Mr Cassinari, Dale, definitely wouldn't want that.'

'Who are you?'

'Tell him to call me. It really is rather urgent.'

Beaten to the hang-up again, Samantha almost throws the receiver back onto the hook. She hated to let that little slime ball think he had power over her. Yet here she is standing in the kitchen shaking. What was she afraid of? Violence? Blackmail? Or the unseen, unguessed-at side of her own husband?

Irritation makes the decision about what to eat easy. Shepherd's pie, shoved straight from the freezer to the oven with nothing to do to it but remove her own neatly written date label. Next door in the playroom the plastic killer whale has leapt to freedom and the kids are stirring Bea and Ralph back into action. They'll be tired now, unused to the demands of two small boys. But Sam doesn't rescue them. The phone call has left her sour and resentful, all the 'what ifs' that she's been dwelling on magnified. She takes her parents a sherry and resolutely ignores the weariness in their faces: they can damn well soldier on for a bit longer, it only serves them right for not spotting a fake card when they saw it!

'You boys can go without a bath tonight,' Sam announces to the children. 'You can make peanut butter sandwiches for your tea, and then go to bed.'

'Can Grandpa Ralph and Granny Bea help us?'

'Would you mind?'

'We'd love to!' Bea says, in a 'spirit willing, flesh weak' sort of tone.

'Right. Our dinner's in the oven so I'll go and have a bath.'

Sam shuts the bathroom door behind her and leans against it. There's lavender oil in a little phial on the side of the tub, its label promising to 'relax tension, remove aches'. Sam drips the oil into the running water. 'Never mind tension and aches,' she thinks, 'what about unreasonable anger and unjustified resentment?'

The lavender oil never really had the chance to show its capabilities. Within seconds of getting into the bath Sam was out of it. There had been a crash, a scream that could have cracked diamonds and before Bea had the chance to call her name Sam was rushing downstairs wrapped in rather too small a towel. Joe was on the kitchen floor, blood dripping over his chin and yelling. Bea and Ralph were white and helpless and Tony's bottom lip was begging to wobble. Ralph explained that Joe had fallen off his chair and hit his jaw on the table en route to the floor. There were no limbs at funny angles, his head was still firmly attached to his body, and by the sound Joe was making his chest was undamaged. Sam concluded that it was not a life-threatening situation. She carried Joe up to the bathroom, as much to calm the situation a little as to check on his wound. Sitting on the bathroom chair he still wailed but less enthusiastically.

'Ip hurps!' he said through the rapidly swelling lip.

'Yes, Joe, I know. You're being so brave. Hold this cotton wool tight on your lip while Mummy gets dressed.'

She pulled on the white shorts and vest before remembering that they would probably get bloodstained. But it was too much bother to change now, she had to get Joe to hospital as his lip was bitten right through. A three-stitches job at least, she guessed.

The population of Bristol has had a busy afternoon driving into each other's cars, falling off scaffolding and getting into fights. Ambulance after ambulance pulls up to the big swing-door entrance of the Casualty department. With each new cargo of broken bodies there is a tornado of surgical coats visible through the glass panels of the waiting-room door. It reminds Samantha of the flurry of white when Joe turns his snowstorm paperweight upside down. Whilst the surgical coats and blue uniforms flit across the two little squares of glass, the more domesticated of the accident-prone Bristolians wait quietly on the plastic chairs. They too have had a busy time chopping fingers instead of carrots, trimming toes instead of grass, and cooking skin instead of sausages.

Accidents have caught this roomful of people entirely unawares, and like guests of honour at a surprise party, they've had to come 'as they are'. This is what the waiting room of the after life looks like, thinks Sam. There are three men in work overalls with coatings varying from mud to oil, and different bits of their faces and bodies in makeshift bandages. There's a teenage girl in tennis shorts with a picnic cold pack over her eye, a man wearing a dark suit and a packet of frozen peas on his bald head, and an elderly lady whose hand is bleeding quietly into her floury apron. A distraught woman comes in carrying a screaming toddler, her business jacket and blouse teamed with the jeans and trainers she had half changed into when her son fell off the climbing frame.

Compared with the hurricane of human folly ushered in under the flashing blue lights and the tsunami of breaks, gashes and dislocations around them, one little boy with a split lip is pretty small beer. Samantha wishes she'd taken Joe to the surgery but having waited an hour and a half already, that option is long gone. More urgent and spectacular cases seem to arrive every few minutes and Sam begins to wonder if they'll be spending the night perched on the sweaty leatherette chairs next to the dying pot plants. She wonders if those too have come to casualty for emergency watering. Joe dozes, under the influence of the painkillers Sam administered before they left home. She cuddles him half on her lap and half on the seat beside her, noticing wistfully how long his legs are getting.

Sam can't get up to reach the magazines and every time she looks around to find something on which to fix her attention, she finds her eyes drawn irresistibly to an intriguingly gruesome flap of skin on the knee of the man in shorts opposite her. Every time he shifts position it gapes and wobbles like a proto mouth, and occasionally dribbles a little blood. Three times now he's caught her staring at it and glared angrily across the table of back copies of *Reader's Digest*. The only safe and reasonably absorbing place to rest her eyes is the reception desk where the newly arrived 'wounded' come and go, and the receptionist chats to passing staff.

Her legs are going to sleep under Joe's weight, and she's beginning to notice little tendrils of green snaking their way over the filing cabinets in the reception area. A distinctive shadow on the opposite wall shows that if only she could turn to see it, there would be a toucan sitting on the windowsill behind her. Another ten minutes of this sort of inactivity and Samantha can see that the whole of casualty is going to be knee-deep in leaf litter, and there will be spider monkeys experimenting with the ultrasound machines. Then, out of the corner of her eye she sees Dale, that unmistakable energy moving through the door and up to the reception desk. She frees a hand from under Joe's shoulder and looks up, ready to call and wave to him. But Dale isn't Dale. Twenty years too old and two inches too short for that. He's dressed in a navy overall and he's holding a large dressing to the side of his face. But even without a clear close view of his features, even with the obvious differences in age and height there is something unmistakably Dale-ish about this man that she can't put her finger on. His skin is darker, his hair is grey, he's quite wiry. Yet when he moves there is that same atmosphere of unstoppable energy that is so distinctively Dale's.

She stares as the man gives his details to the receptionist and then Not-Dale walks across to the seats and once again he reminds her of her husband, the way the smell of cut grass immediately suggests summer.

Not-Dale sits at one of the only remaining vacant places, two rows away from the man with the fascinating leg injury. Not-Dale is dressed in a neat navy boiler suit and shiny black safety boots. The sort of outfit that the men who put in the central heating at Lancaster Road wore. His face must be painful because the hand supporting the dinner plate of cotton wool and gauze doesn't even think of moving. Samantha looks at his shoulders, the back of his neck and is disturbed to notice that these apparently featureless body parts are like Dale's, not the same shape exactly but reminiscent of them. She stares and stares at him, waiting for the moment when perhaps he'll take off the dressing and turn towards her wearing someone else's face, not at all like Dale's. But as she looks at him the strange intangible feeling of recognition only grows. Another unfortunate walking wounded comes to sit beside Not-Dale, and although she can see only a tiny corner of his face it seems that it lifts in the total smile she saw first over a cake-shop counter.

Samantha reminds herself of the rows of Lady Di Look-alikes that used to line up regularly on TV, all wearing the same mouth and eyeliner. Resemblance is superficial, she tells herself. But still she's filled with a fizzing sensation that here is a strange and priceless chance, blown to her out of the snow-storm of humanity. She burns her gaze into Not-Dale's neat hairline like Superman's X-ray glance, trying to see if this is the man who left his Italian girlfriend pregnant or simply a genetic fluke who reminds her vaguely of her husband. Maria's words come into her mind: 'Dale don't know about me and his daddy. What he don't know can't hurt him.'

A nurse leans out of the swing doors and reads the name from her clip board. 'Joseph Cassinari?'

At the sound of the surname Samantha scrutinises Not-Dale's seated figure, searching for some clue of reaction to the name. Will the tips of the fingers tremble against the white dressing? Is there some tumultuous emotional struggle under the cotton back of the boiler suit?

'Joseph Cassinari? Are you here?' Not-Dale is very still, but he doesn't turn to look at her. The nurse is about to assume that they've given up and gone home; she calls again, 'Joseph Cassinari?'

'Over here,' Samantha calls, 'just coming.' Samantha gets up and Joe wakes in her arms and begins to wail and struggle. She shifts his weight and walks around the end of the row of seats to pass just inches from Not-Dale's face. He is holding a magazine, looking at it carefully with the one exposed eye, but he doesn't move. With Joe squirming in her arms it's hard to take a good look at him. Between her son's flailing limbs she glimpses the turned-away cotton-covered face once more and can't decide if she is imagining the familiarity of the jaw line. A moment later she and Joe are on the busy side of the swing doors, and the man in the boiler suit shimmers in her recollection, shedding reality and resemblance like water shaken from a wet umbrella, fading as fast as a dream.

Samantha checks one last time on the boys. Joe was streaky-faced with crying and limp with exhaustion by the time they got home and his body raced him into sleep. He lies on his back snoring delicately. Tony is twined with his bedding and burrowed into his pillow, his breathing barely perceptible. Sam stands in the twilight room looking at her children and wondering where they are now, what they can see inside themselves. Their little bodies are so familiar, so completely known to her but under the cover of sleep they could be surfing on the moon or flying with dragons. Usually she likes to imagine the secret internal world of their dream-time adventures. But to-night the illusion of her boys' tranquil appearance is just a reminder of all the uncertainty seething under the translucent surface of her world.

Dale is waiting for her, perched on the edge of the bed. The naked skin of his back is sleek over the muscles beneath and tempts the touch of her fingers. She strokes the close-cropped scalp and somewhere in her mind the iron-grey hair of the man in the hospital flickers like a butterfly wing and is gone again. She sits beside the real Dale and drops her head to his shoulder. He runs his hand under her hair and caresses the nape of her neck.

'Is he OK, Ange?'

'Fine. Flat out.'

'You OK?'

'Whacked.'

'How whacked?' His hand runs under her T-shirt up her bare spine. He's loving his newfound licence to seduce her.

Gently she wriggles away, and takes the wandering hand in her own. 'Dale, who's that bloke who kept ringing up whilst you were away? He rang again today.'

He looks from her face, taking her hand to his lips. 'He's just some bloke I did some work for, hassling.'

'But *who* is he?'

'Nobody who matters.' His hand breaks free and runs smoothly along her thigh to the hem of the white shorts. Samantha's ability to focus begins to disintegrate.

'Well, tell him not to ring then.'

'I will.' Dale buries his mouth in her throat so his voice is muffled by her own flesh.

'I'll finish the work with him pretty soon. Once we've got Lime House sold.'

'Why d'you need the money from Lime House?'

'You know why, Ange.' He sucks the words out of her mouth, and she feels her will slackening under the heat of his lips.

'Yeah, I know, for the business,' Samantha sighs. The texture of the skin of Dale's shoulder under her cheek is beginning to absorb most of her attention, but she clings to her questions for a little longer, whispering them into the hair on his chest, 'But what happened exactly? What went wrong? I thought the loan sorted that.'

'Kind of. But you know bad debts.' He speaks whilst he fumbles with the zip on her shorts, breathing into her hair. 'You get two big customers who don't pay up and you're stuffed if you're a one-man band like me.' Gently, with that relentless steady energy, he pushes her backwards onto the mattress. She knows what he's doing, didn't she hide behind sex this way herself for so long? But being out of control is still unfamiliar, a deliciousness she can't resist. She lets herself go into his hands, like a swimmer slipping into a sea of sweet oblivion. This, she thinks, with vague self reproach, is becoming a habit.

Around five a.m. Samantha's dream life suffers a processing overload. It has popped her mother out of giant orchids, morphed Dale into a representative of almost every group of living organism and banished Samantha into twenty kinds of surreal wilderness. In an attempt to assimilate all her anxieties past and present her subconscious gives up and reverts to a particularly terrifying version of the standard chasing dream, from which Samantha wakes soaked in sweat and crying. Immediately wide awake she goes downstairs to dispel the misery the dream has left with a cup of cocoa and a piece of toast. Framed in the kitchen window, and lit by a pink-light-bulb dawn, she finds a pair of skinny legs in grey sweat pants. Ralph is out on the patio doing a headstand. She moves around as quietly as possible, and then sits down with her drink and buttered toast to look at this strange transformed version of the father she once viewed as hopeless.

From what she can see of him he seems utterly peaceful, surrounded by a stillness that is more than the immobility of his yoga posture. She remembers this tranquillity from long ago, something he had when she was very tiny, pitting the tiny push of her legs against his broad hands. But it got lost, he'd grown uncomfortable in himself, as if his clothes always itched, or his head always ached. Even at their most peaceful times, silently pricking out seedlings in the greenhouse, he had a tension about him, his smile wearing a tight bone corset. By the time she was an adolescent and she judged the world without any shades of grey, she saw him as a cartoon cut-out, two dimensional, inadequate. For ten years he'd existed in her memory like that – a silhouette, something almost devoid of real human form. But from her new perspective beside his inverted legs and neat tanned feet she looks back and sees a man miserable to the point of madness. With a mother like Granny Pearl how could anyone grow up with the emotional tools required for life's trickier DIY projects? He had become a haunted ruin by the time she was seventeen, barely inhabiting his life at all. How, she wonders, did he rescue this warm and peaceful man from that shell of a person?

The legs move, and with a shockingly youthful spring Ralph is on his feet. He stretches, turns and, spying her, smiles and comes inside. He joins her at the table and sits opposite her. In the dawn-quiet house, fresh respectively from meditation and from dreams, Ralph and his daughter are in the same special space outside the normal constraints and awkwardnesses of the waking world. They sit and look at each other without embarrassment, each searching the other's face for clues.

'How did you get to be like this, Daddy?'

'I could ask you the same, Sam. My fierce little girl has grown into a mother, a very good one too.'

Sam is filled with an unexpected sense of relief; as if Ralph has told her that the speck of white she's been steering for really is the harbour light. The boys *are* her rock. If he can see that too it makes it truer. When everything, her past, her man, her ambitions, even her garden, is changing into something else, her love for them is constant. She reaches for his hand and takes a little while to speak. 'Was I fierce?'

'Well, perhaps not fierce. Determined. Frighteningly determined.' He caresses her hand and smiles. 'I rather admired you.'

'D'you remember pushing my feet with your hand, Daddy?' she asks. 'When I was very little?'

'I remember, Sam. Yes.'

'You were like this then. Calm. Sometime long ago.'

'I didn't have my head in the sand then. That was before your mother got ill. She was well then, just like she is now. I grew into an ostrich when she got ill. I let everything that wasn't important occupy my mind, and take me over. Ignored everything that was real and that mattered: her illness. You caring for her. My failure to help. I was too afraid to feel anything.'

'I didn't understand you then. I hated you for the way you were. I'm sorry.'

'Don't be sorry. I hated myself. But when you left I couldn't ignore things any more. There wasn't anyone else to care for Bea. I had to stop being an ostrich and start feeling. It felt like being sliced open, split like a melon. Terrible pain. Terrible. I had to look at how I feared losing Bea. And I had to look at what I'd done to you, how I'd failed as a father. When everything hurts that much, when you've looked at what you fear most, you've nothing left to be afraid of. I just let go of what didn't matter and what I couldn't help.'

'I'm sorry I ran away.'

'Don't be sorry about that either. I'd have my head in the sand to this day if you hadn't gone. We had the cards, Sam. We knew you were safe. That was all we felt we deserved, to be honest. All I felt I deserved at any rate. I think not knowing where you were or what had happened to you would have killed us both. If we hadn't had them it would have been very different. But we did.'

Sam drops her forehead onto his hand. The guilty secret she's lost has been replaced with another, even more precious, a secret she must keep to protect her parents, not herself.

'But none of that matters now, Sam. Bea and I have got you back. That's all there is to it.'

Gently he holds her head upright, pushing his palm against her heavy forehead. 'There now,' he says. 'Don't cry, Sam. That's my strong girl.'

13

Finnian has held onto his curiosity all the way through the bakery delivery, the early morning sandwich rush and the complete outfitting of two large works' picnics. But at each lull between jobs Finnian's unasked questions have hung, white and martyrish, in the air between them. There is no Maria to offer refuge or distraction; she has taken a day out to wrangle over her bakery project. Sam wishes Finnian would just get on with it. She knows he'll give her some sort of third degree because of what Maria said as she was leaving after dinner, on Bea and Ralph's last night in Bristol. 'They are lovely, your mummy and daddy,' she said patting Sam's cheek as she left the house. 'Hey! You know what Finny say when I tell him about them? I tell him your mum not dead. That they come to visit you and he said, "I knew it." Just like that, "I knew it!" Funny, hah?'

At last Tavs is empty for more than a few moments, there is time for coffee and a chat. Sam and Finnian stand, just outside the shop door, sipping self-consciously and facing the road watching the cars in silence. They are as still and wooden as the little carved people who emerge from a weather house. Above them Finnian's pointedly restrained curiosity sits, staring moodily down at Samantha. Samantha glances back into the shop, rather wishing that some tropical orchid would suddenly send a cascade of blossoms over the counter, or a troupe of tamarins might chase over the freezer cabinets. A little distraction from this atmosphere would be nice. But imagination leaks never seemed to happen at Tavs, its realness is too engaging.

She sighs and at last she gives in. 'I'm sorry I never told you the truth, Finnian. About my parents and everything.'

He watches a blue Stag soft-top cruise by, and answers slowly without taking his eyes off its chrome and paint work. 'That's OK. You had your reasons.'

But Samantha can see that it isn't really OK, and that for Finnian, it never has been. His voice contains a note of accusatory irony. She can't blame him for that, he was after all almost the only person who sensed the tissue of invention she surrounded herself with.

'What did Maria tell you?'

'Not a lot. Just that Dale had tracked them down and brought them here from Suffolk.'

'See, I did tell you a bit of the truth. I said I'd grown up in Suffolk.'

'You did so.' He smiles, and softens a little. 'So what's the story?' He leans cozily into the glass and looks at her face for the first time. She knows she must tell as much of the truth as possible.

'I ran away. When I was seventeen. Too scared of how angry they'd be to go back. And the longer it got the scareder I was. I did really think my mum had died though. She was very ill when I left.'

'And were they angry?'

'No. No they weren't.'

'Did they think you were dead?'

'No, they always knew where I was and what I was doing.'

'Private detective, eh?'

'Yeah. Something like that.'

'So they tracked you down but they didn't come and find you? Seems a bit odd.' Finnian's sixth-sense nose is twitching. She'd like to tell him about the cards, about the new secret she has to keep. More and more she finds herself wanting to be rid of it all, to talk and share, but her old habits of self-protection cling like burrs.

'They thought I didn't want to hear from them. It's not so odd. Your family know where you are. They've never come to find you.'

'Well, that's true enough.'

'I don't know what Dale did to get them down here. We didn't talk about that. All I know is that he went to find them whilst he was sorting out stuff about the house I've been left.'

'Right. Right. Yes. That's a great thing, Maria told me about it. Sounds like it'll be worth a packet.'

'Enough to kill the mortgage on Number eleven! And a lot more.'

'Right!' Finnian is still waving his antennae and looks intently into her eyes over the rim of his mug. 'Who was this guy who left you such a handsome legacy?'

'An old eccentric with no family. We shared an interest in plants. He lived near my parents and I used to go and look at things in his greenhouse. He was kind. Encouraging. I didn't know him for long. Just a few months before I left.'

'You must have made a big impression in that short time . . .'

'Oh, I was a right little swot in those days. Latin names of plants, all that. I think he'd never met anyone he could share his enthusiasm with. Bit sad really.' Her tone is nonchalant, artlessly natural but Finnian doesn't miss the tiny shudder she can't suppress at the thought of Lawrence.

He looks at her slow and steady. 'Right,' he says, 'right,' then looks away hurt again by her reluctance to share the truth with him. He sighs and as he goes inside to resume work, he says, 'Well, at least you found your family. I always thought you looked so lost.'

Samantha thinks that for someone who is right about so much Finnian is wrong this time. 'Found' is what she used to be, before Lawrence's letter, before Dale's mystery caller, before Bea's aliveness and Ralph's yoga, when everything was under control. Looking past Finnian to the salamis strung like lianas from trunk-like towers of tins and packets she feels that it's now that she's lost, and in a very unpredictable sort of forest.

*

By the afternoon Finnian is quite recovered from his sense of being somehow slighted by Sam's perceived lack of honesty. Their banter is restored to normal, and has even managed to incorporate some of the details of Samantha's newly revealed history. Finnian has told her several times during the course of the afternoon that she is far too young to be slicing salami.

'You don't get the necessary maturity in the wrist until you're thirty.'

It's the mid-afternoon lull. Very soon Mums will call in on the way to and from school, and then there'll be the rush on that last essential ingredient before closing time. But now it's quiet, and as they lean on the counter sipping juice the man in the boiler suit and the cotton-wool dressing floats back into Sam's mind, and an uncertain sort of connection suggests itself again.

'Has Maria ever talked to you about Dale's father, Finny?'

'Why d'you ask?'

'Oh, I dunno. Probably because my parents have made me think about who Dale's dad might be.'

'It's a funny thing, but you know, she never has. And she talks about everything else. I could probably find my way around the house she grew up in blindfold! But she only ever tells the bare bones of the drama . . . you know she was young and foolish, she was deceived, he left her, she followed him here . . . But no detail. You know. Nothing about the colour of eyes or how they met exactly. Just like, you know, bullet points!'

'Yeah. That's as much as she told Dale. Or at least that's as much as Dale tells me.'

'Ah! You think they both know more than they say?' Finnian wriggles into a more comfortable leaning position ready for the exchange of some choice sweetmeat of information, or stuffed olive of theory.

'It's all a little too sketchy. D'you not think?' he says, 'Suspicious, you know, to think of Maria being deceived! Nobody pulls any sort of wool over Maria's eyes. Never! She's got X-ray vision that woman. I know she was young and all, but not that young. No, I'd say there was a lot more to it than that. I just feel it in my waters.'

Finnian's eyes drift back from the shiny traffic to fix Samantha with an antenna-twitching stare. 'Just like I feel there's a lot more to your story of the guy who left you his house. When are you going to tell it all to me?'

'Someday, Finn. But not now. Have you seen who's coming?' Sam tilts her head towards the cherry-red 1958 Aston Martin that has just pulled into the parking space across the road. A woman, skinny as a piece of baler twine and bouffant-ed to within an inch of her credibility is locking up and crossing the road: Judy Mellors, diamond-encrusted soap star, and one of their most faithful customers is about to make a 'royal visit'. She never spends less than five hundred pounds when she comes from Gloucestershire to stock up on Italian Gourmet delights, and she expects a hundred and ten percent attention for her money.

'Jeeezuz. She was only here a week ago. She can't possibly have got through all the stuff she bought in seven days!'

'We might as well put the closed sign up behind her, the time we'll have to serve anyone else the rest of the day!'

By the time the Aston Martin is packed tight with cheeses, olives, salami and wine it really is time to close. Finnian gloats over the till roll as he cashes up. 'Well, that's a record! She spent seventeen hundred today. I'll ring Maria and tell her. She'll be delighted.'

'I'm dropping in on my way home. I'll deliver the good news.'

'Are you not picking up the boys?'

'I am . . . can I just give Louise a call to say I'll be late?'

'Don't know why you're asking me, you're practically the boss's daughter.'

'Ah well, I have to bow to your experience and age now, don't I. What with the salami cutting . . .'

He throws a tea towel at her.

'Get on that phone, you cheeky baggage!'

Maria's voice floats from the open bedroom window, instructing Sam to let herself in. The house is spotless as always, and still, like a smooth pond or the green shade under an olive tree. Upstairs, in Maria's ruby-red bedroom, Sam is amazed to find Maria in bed. It is three years since she even had a cold. The curtains are half drawn, and the breeze sucks and releases the net through the open sash. Maria is propped up on a slope of pillows wearing white broderie anglaise pyjamas. She looks tiny. Her body is hardly big enough to raise the contour of the sheets and the distance from her face to the peak of her toes seems ridiculously small. Her lively olive colouring has faded to a dirty green and she looks small and broken, like a crushed bird. Maria seems too worn out for serious conversation. Sam's spirits sink. Until this moment she hadn't admitted to herself how much she wanted to share with Maria her nebulous misgivings about Dale's unnamed secrets and fish for information about his mysterious father. She sits on the bed beside Maria, amidst papers covered in scribbled Italian, and Maria's pencilled plans for the bakery.

'Oh, Maria! Why didn't you phone and say you were ill?'

'I'm not ill. I'm OK. Little too tired I think.'

'What's the matter?'

'Nothing. Really. Thank you for coming. Nice to see my girl!'

'Are these the plans for the bakery?'

'Oh yes,' Maria brightens a little, 'just ideas. But you know when you think about the future so much you think about the past too.'

'Were you thinking of home? Of Italy.'

'Not so much.'

'Of Dale's father then?' In the open the question seems as intrusive as a naked blade. She sheaths it quickly in a feeble joke. 'Finnian says he thinks you married a film star in secret!'

'Nnnnah. Finny is a silly queen.'

'Maria. Maria, who is Dale's father?'

'Is no business of yours!' The colour flares back into Maria's skin, and the flesh seems to gather to her bones ready for conflict.

But Sam goes on, quiet and gentle.

'Whoever he is, he's my children's grandfather. It is my business, Maria.'

'Why do you think of this now?'

'Because of my parents. Because, like you say, you think of the future and it makes you wonder about the past.'

'Angie. This the God's truth. I don't know him any more. I don't know where he is. OK?' and Maria's face is so full of sadness and of regret that Sam accepts that at least for now this is all the truth there is to be had.

'OK.'

'But you got more questions, yes?'

'Yes. Why don't you want to talk about what Dale was like, before me?'

This is not a question Maria expected or was prepared for. She is speechless, guiltily frozen for a tiny moment. Then all Maria's forces mobilise, the film star smile, the dolce vita laugh. 'You know that! I told you. You know what he was like. A 'opeless little bugger who give his mamma a lot of trouble. Now. Enough. Go to your boys.' Turning on her smile seems to have cost Maria an enormous effort. She looks greyer, more tired than Sam has ever seen her, so now Sam feels sorry that she's pressed for answers.

'All right, Maria. I'm sorry. I shouldn't have asked when you were feeling ill. Would you like something to eat?'

'No. I will get up, make some soup. Watch TV. Later. You go to the boys, eh?'

'Call me if you need me. If there's anything . . .'

'Yes yes. Go now, eh?'

'Can I call Dale before I go?'

'You know where the phone is.'

'I'll call in tomorrow.'

'No need. I will be in work.' As Sam reaches the bedroom door she remembers the unimparted piece of retail news.

'Maria, Judy Mellors spent seventeen hundred pounds to-day!'

'Nnnnah,' is Maria's only comment.

Behind Dale's voice she can hear the swoosh of passing cars and footsteps on a pavement. He's outside a pizza take-out place in Bury St Edmunds, he says. She tries not to think that cars and footsteps could be the backdrop anywhere.

'But how is she?' Dale is trying to reach down the phone for some tangible proof of his mother's well being. There's a little something more than mild anxiety over Maria's 'indisposition'. Sam can hear it between the words, tiny but obvious as a dropped stitch.

'I can't talk much. She's upstairs.'

'Is she ill?'

'No. She says she's OK. But I think she looks pretty awful. Says she's thinking about the past.'

'Oh. Right.' There, in the warm familiar glow of Dale's voice is that little space, the place where the thread is missing. Dale is too far away for her to find what this break in the pattern means; she listens to it for a moment then he speaks again, 'Look. If you're worried, why don't you get her to stay with us for few days. She'll be taken care of and you won't worry. I just don't want you to worry.'

Everything is what Dale isn't saying. Everything is what Maria didn't say. Everything is not going to get said down a phone.

Sam sighs. 'When are you coming home?'

'As soon as I can get a new windscreen.'

'What?'

'It shattered about fifteen minutes ago!'

'Oh no!'

'Don't think I can get it sorted tonight. I'll head down there the moment it's fixed in the morning.'

'See you then.'

'Bye, love.'

'Bye, Dale. Drive safe.'

A little touch of Louise's maelstrom mind will be a good distraction from the half-formed suspicions, uncertainties and shadows knocking around her own brain. Down the three streets Sam walks to Louise's, she tries to rid herself of the undertow of thoughts that bring her all sorts of unpleasant visions about her husband's true nature and the threat from the Voice on the phone. But whenever reason swims her up to the light, the swirling suspicions of the last few days pull her down again. When she reaches her hand to grasp them they run through her fingers like water.

At home, with only three children to impress, most women might slob around in a dressing gown or even a couple of towels after a bath. But although Louise has a towel around her wet hair when she answers the door, it is the same deep shade of purple as the sarong and vest that package her little slither of a body. She smiles, and welcomes Sam inside nodding and bending in nervous excitement like a displaying bower bird.

'Oh. Right. Hello. Come in, come in. I wasn't expecting you.' She leads Sam into the little kitchen, 'Or rather I was really, but not now. Would you like a drink? Nail varnish?'

Sam is accustomed enough to Louise to understand that acetone cocktail is not what she's being offered; Louise is carrying a pot of clear varnish and has been doing her toenails.

'I could do all your nails for you. It's terribly soothing I find, having nice nails.'

'No thanks, Louise. I can't stay. Dale's coming home. Are the boys OK?'

'Oh yes. I got the tap fixed so I could chase them round the garden with the hose pipe. They got tired pretty fast! They're all asleep in a heap like a litter of wombats or something. Except I don't think wombats have litters. Anyway. I'll take them to school in the morning.'

'Thanks, Louise. That would be great.' Sam suddenly feels tired to her bones.

'Do let me get you something. You look, well. Actually you look terrible.' Louise's apologetic candour makes Sam laugh. 'I'm sorry, Angie. I didn't mean to be rude.'

'No. No, that's OK. I feel terrible.'

'OK. Well. Um, have some toast and honey.' Louise puts down her little pot on the work surface and begins to rummage in cupboards. She gives Samantha the impression that behind the neat façade, her kitchen is chaotic, and finding simple things like bread and honey is a major challenge to ingenuity and powers of memory. 'Frightfully restorative. Just sit down.'

Louise is right about the toast. Sam munches gratefully into a second slice and Louise pours them each a glass of some exotic fruit juice, then sits quite still watching her friend. She is having one of her moments of crystal-clear perception and can see that Sam is more than irritated with the fact that Dale can't get back tonight.

'You don't believe him, do you? That's what's the matter, isn't it?'

Sam has only ever been good at elaborate and efficient fabrication. Direct lying to a bullseye question has always been hard for her. But how can she explain this feeling that has gripped her that nothing is how she has seen it, that Dale's world could be as invented as her own with all manner of snakes writhing underneath?

'Why don't you believe him?'

'I do. I mean. Yes. I do'

'Yes and no. I understand.' Louise speaks slowly, dreamily, almost hooking together facts and theories in mid air. 'You don't believe Dale, because you hadn't told him about your past. So. Now, you wonder what he hasn't told you! Right?'

'Right. Yes I suppose.'

'But you love him.'

'Yes.'

'And he still loves you so?' Louise shrugs eloquently as if to say after love everything else is just icing.

'Dale's up in Suffolk sorting out your inheritance. End of story. Yes?' Louise's narrow earnest face is turned towards her, open and inquiring.

'Yes. Yes. OK.' Suddenly the heavy tangle that Sam has made of her present life seems ridiculous. She has been shying at shadows. Dale is as steady as a rock. Maria is just tired. The phone calls come from a crabby punter. The man in the boiler suit was just that and nothing else. 'No. You're right. I do believe him. End of story. I'm tired. Just tired.'

'Well, long-lost parents popping up from nowhere must be pretty exhausting. God knows, when mine appear from Sussex it's like a visitation from the dead. Go home and go to bed.'

Louise sees Sam to the door quite contentedly.

'We haven't talked about the food for end of term barbie.'

'Don't worry, Angie. I've been quite organised for me. I've co-opted another person onto our committee. Jamie he's called. Single parent with a girl in year three. Ex-chef. So you don't have to do anything. I can see you've enough to cope with. Go and rest.'

'I will. I'll get a cab from the corner.'

Number eleven feels very empty. It's more than the particular type of emptiness that lives inside a family house when all its residents are gone. It's more, too, than the extra space left behind by Bea and Ralph. Number eleven was fashioned to fit Angie and Dale inside their portraits and now that they are both out of their frames, the old house feels changed too. Sam stands in the hall noticing the new quality of this absence, then she walks through the house inspecting its atmosphere.

In the sitting room there are cushions out of place, and books left on the chairs which Sam makes no attempt to tidy. She looks at the room and sees, not the fabric from Monmouth Castle or the way the rug picks up the shades in the curtains, but Bea's stockinged feet curled on the sofa whilst reading a story to Tony, Ralph kneeling on the rug holding Joe's legs in the air, Dale asleep over the Sunday paper. She flicks on the light in the kitchen and the twilight garden disappears into a dusty blueness. This kitchen was made for Angie, obsessively neat, tidying for her life, forever finding tasks to hold back the past and keep the present in its place. Now, the worktops are a little cluttered and the children's drawings have escaped the confines of the notice board and spread their exuberance all over the unit doors. Her home has learned to relax, it has learned to smile. That's why now it feels so empty, because at last it has been able to be so full.

Walking out onto the patio Sam can feel the big exotic plants breathing into the evening air. She takes a long lungful of their green scents and lets it out like a stream of corn pouring steadily from a split sack. She kicks off her shoes and feels the residual warmth in the paving stones. A large iguana is doing the same, lying belly flat on the warmest stones. It looks at her appraisingly and slithers away. This is the form her 'leaks' are taking these days, small scale, subtle, intimate almost, finding their way into the new habitat of her garden. She no longer finds her visions distasteful or unwelcome; she accommodates them, welcomes them almost. She is comforted by the way her home can host them and contain the changes that she is finding so hard and so confusing. If only Dale were here, her rock, her anchor. She could be really at peace and quell all uneasiness and suspicion.

The doorbell rings and Sam leaps towards it: Dale! It must be Dale, as if her wanting him could conjure him out of the air or at least down two hundred miles of road in a windscreenless car. She flings open the door and finds an unnerving version of Dale. Older and smaller, with nicotine-tanned skin. He is dressed in a new tweed sports jacket and light coloured trousers whose pleat is so sharp it could slice cucumbers. He has a nasty burn healing on his cheek.

'Mrs Cassinari?' The voice too is a variant of Dale's, the same warmth but grated by time and cigarettes. 'I know it's a bit late. I called earlier but I didn't catch you in. We met, well, saw each other I think in the hospital last week?'

'Yes. You had a dressing on your face.'

'Burn it was. Yes. You were there with your little lad. Nasty chin injury.'

'I didn't think you'd seen us.'

'I noticed you when they said the surname. Quite unusual.'

'Oh.'

'I was worried about the boy. Because. Well. He's my grandson.'

It's not such a shock really. In fact all Sam can think of to say is 'Yes I know' because really in her heart she'd guessed from the first moment she saw him behind the pad of cotton wool.

Dale's dad is called Gordon, Gordon Armstrong. He's a builder!

'Small scale stuff these days. Not so young as I was,' he tells her. She can't help staring at him. This is Dale's father who should have cuddled his grandchildren, who should feel as familiar to her as Maria. Yet here she is politely offering him tea and calling him Mr Armstrong.

He stands in the middle of the kitchen looking slightly confused. 'It's a lovely home! Not quite what I expected,' he says.

Samantha sits at the table, her legs a little too wobbly to support her.

'Is Mr Cassinari expected home?'

'Dale?'

'Dale. Yes.'

'No. He's coming home tomorrow because his car broke down.'

'Is he away a lot?'

'Not usually. He restores old houses. Sometimes he has a job too far away to come home every night.'

'Your little boy, how's his chin?'

'Healing beautifully. He's with his brother staying at a friend's house tonight.'

'I see.' But Not-Dale – Gordon – doesn't seem to see at all. In fact he seems almost dazed.

'Are you sure I can't get you a cup of tea?'

'No. No. Thank you.'

'Maria, my mother-in-law, she's never mentioned you.'

'No. No, she wouldn't do.'

Samantha is getting over her wobbly legs and beginning to wonder what sort of lunatic she might have admitted freely to her house. She glances around to the open kitchen door and calculates how long it would take her to run through it and vault into Keith and Felicity's garden.

Gordon shifts uncomfortably from foot to foot. 'Perhaps I should go, I was clearly mistaken,' he says. 'Yes, I'll go,' and he turns as if decided, but doesn't move. Samantha puts aside the wall-vaulting escape route and decides that really Gordon looks pretty harmless and quite lost. And if he truly is Dale's father then this opportunity is not to be wasted.

'Look, Mr Armstrong, Gordon. You're my boys' grand-father. I'd like to get to know you a little.'

'Would you mind if I smoked?' Normally smokers are banished to the garden but, under the circumstances, worrying about the smell clinging to the curtains seems a little petty.

'No, not at all.'

Gordon sits at the table and rolls a cigarette and is clearly comforted and calmed by the ritual. He talks as he rolls, without looking up, happier for the moment not to meet her eyes. 'When I saw you at the hospital. When I heard that name.

I knew you had to be Maria's daughter-in-law. And that the little boy was . . . well, my flesh and blood as it were. Dale's son. I don't want to offend you, but you looked worn out. The little one looked like someone had punched him. And I worried. I thought you might be in some trouble. That's why I came. I thought it was about time I helped.' He pulled long on the cigarette and looked up to the ceiling.

'Joe fell and caught his chin on the table. Just an accident.'

Gordon looks at her out of the blue smoke. 'Yeah?'

She nods emphatically in reply. But something about her response is unconvincing and she knows it. Because she fears that they may indeed be in some kind of trouble, and that 'some kind of trouble' is what she has for years felt herself to be in. When she explains that she took her son to the hospital leaving his older brother with her parents, it sounds like a lie, because of all she isn't saying about her parents, about her worries over Dale's 'secret life'. Gordon takes the last toke of his roly.

'You don't smoke?'

'No. Nor does Dale.'

'Doesn't he?' Gordon seems surprised. 'He used to.'

She can see that Gordon is in the habit of being cautious, guarded. Any information he'll give in his own way, not at her request. So she tries to stay calm and accept that this is a process like peeling paint, you just have to pull it off where you can and hope that eventually the whole wall will be revealed.

For the first time since he lit up Gordon looks at her. 'How much do you know about Dale? You'd be too young to have known him when he was a teenager I guess?'

'He was gone thirty when we met. Yes, that's right.'

Gordon fixes her in his sights, leaning closer to her face. 'And he's always been good to you? Never laid a hand on you? Never hurt the kids? Never been in any kind of trouble?'

'Never. He's so kind. Always gentle. He adores the boys.' Samantha is speaking without knowing what her mouth is doing. What Gordon *hasn't* said is disturbing and the flood of fears begins to wash towards her. She throws words towards it like sandbags. 'We've been together for ten years and he's never been anything but a wonderful husband and father. He was with me when both the boys were born; he nurses them when they're ill; he takes them swimming; he brings me tea in bed; he built sand castles with them in Ilfracombe last summer; he built me a shelf for my cookery books; he would never . . . I've never felt . . .' The frenzy of words calls up images of Dale that melt and coalesce into a single impression of her husband, warm and true as a handprint on her heart. The wail goes out of her voice, she takes a deep, deep breath and slows down. 'He's my *Dale*. He'd never never do anything to harm us.'

Gordon's face is pulled into a thousand tight little ropes, his whole self focused on Sam and her words.

'And you swear to me that's true?'

'Yes,' she says, 'yes.' Because no matter what this long-lost father knows about Dale's past, there is nothing he can say that will change her answer.

'Then it's all right. Thank God.'

'But why *wouldn't* it be all right?'

'As long as it's all right it *doesn't matter*.'

'Why wouldn't it be all right?'

Gordon gets up. 'It's not for me to say.' He tucks his tobacco in his breast pocket. He moves into the hall slowly but unopposed, and it feels to Sam as though he's slipping away, as a dream does when you wake.

She wants to hold onto him at the door. 'You haven't told me anything about yourself. You've met Dale before, haven't you? He always said he never knew his dad?'

He shakes her hand warmly but doesn't reply.

'I need to be getting home. I'm glad things are OK. That Dale's making a good job of his life. I was just worried. Responsible sort of. But now I know things are OK. I'd love to meet the boys. Here's my card, the old business one. Just give me a call sometime. You know. If you need me.' He's already halfway down the path and out into the dusk, slipping and slipping out of her grasp. She wants him to stay and tell her all the story, peel off all the years and years of paint that covers the picture.

'What about Maria?' Sam says a little desperately. 'What shall I tell her about you?'

His shrug is youthful, a little shadow of the wildness he might once have had perhaps.

'If you mention me use my middle name.'

Sam stares stupidly at the card clutched in her hand.

Gordon A. Armstrong

'That's how she knew me. It's what my mates all called me when I was young, A for Alan. Alan a'Dale, you know, Robin Hood's mate? It was my nickname.'

'Alan a Dale.'

'Right!'

14

Samantha woke to find that someone had taken a blender to her brain overnight. Everything was in a tangle and nothing seemed to work properly. First the shower temperature fluctuated between volcanic geyser and glacial melt water. Then she fell and twisted her ankle through having put both feet through the same leg of her favourite knickers. Finally, when she made it downstairs she found that the bedside clock had been wrong and she was already late for Tavs. The taxi firm couldn't promise a cab until sometime in the New Year, so she dashed out of the front door and set off to walk to work at a half limp.

'Angela? Do you need a lift?' Maeve called from the driver's seat of their ancient Volvo. She was wearing a navy suit jacket and looked vaguely professional.

'I'm late for Tavs!'

'Oh. I can drop you. Do hop in.'

Gratefully, Sam hopped. But Maeve was so busy being pleased to be helping out that she forgot to tell Sam about the cranberry-chocolate pie hidden under the cloth on the passenger seat. Its gorgeous brown and ruby stain had seeped through to Sam's pale blue skirt within two seconds.

'Oh dear,' wailed Maeve, leaning over at the traffic lights to slide the squashed confection from under Sam's behind, 'it was a birthday treat for one of the partners!'

Sam did not feel particularly sympathetic.

The morning at Tavs took its cue from Sam's arrival with an apparently incriminating brown and red stain on the back of her skirt. Maria had arrived at nine and left again at nine fifteen with little explanation. Finnian was grumpy and hung over, the bread was late and a huge order of olives that Maria had told no one about arrived and made any sort of movement in the shop impossible for half an hour. Things spilled, fell over and leapt spontaneously from shelves. Customers were rude, indecisive, mumbling. Some made a point of combining ignorance with arrogance. A grey-rinsed, pinched-looking woman at the front of a large queue asked for eight ounces of Mortadella and, as Sam was slicing it, leant over the top of the counter and said, 'You stupid girl! Mortadella is a cheese. A hard cheese made from buffalo milk in the South! I don't want that nasty cheap luncheon meat!'

At that moment there was a strangled screech from the back of the shop where Finnian had found the freezer warming the speciality ice creams to blood heat.

The midday rush was just as accident prone as the morning had been. There had been no time to clear away the unexpected olive order and customers had to manoeuvre awkwardly between crates and boxes. Just as Finnian took an order for a large mixed plate of antipasto for an office lunch party, Maria arrived and Sam managed to spill a carton of seafood salad over the salami slicer. It took Maria fifteen minutes to clean all the fragments of clam and octopus tentacle from its various blades and settings by which time the queue for lunchtime sandwiches was out onto the pavement. Normally calmest when the shop was busy, today Sam was like a beginner who didn't know her *provolone* from a round of Dairylea.

'You didn't put the tomatoes in this roll!'

'I asked for *soppresata*, but this is *salami calabrese*.'

'No, sorry, I asked for *focaccia* not *ciabatta*.'

With Maria beside her all Sam could think about was how to tell her about Gordon. Time after time Samantha managed to put the wrong filling in the wrong sandwich, or served the right sandwich to the wrong person. Tavs' regulars were sweetly tolerant, smiling sympathetically, stoically taking their mixed-up lunches without complaint, but some of the less familiar customers got grumpy and argumentative. For the third time Finnian was stepping in to calm an irate punter and remake the sandwich she had ordered, when Dale strode into the shop. He looked agitated and unhappy but was slapping a half-smile on top of it to greet his wife and his mother.

'Hello,' Sam said over the heads of the customers, 'can you hang on, I'm busy.'

'I can't, love.'

'Please! I've got something terribly important to tell you.'

'I just popped in to say I'm back is all. I've got to go, Ange.'

'Dale! I need to talk to you . . .'

'See you later.'

'Dale, you little bugger. Your wife call you. Come back 'ere,' Maria yelled at him over a huge carton of salad. 'Go get him,' she said, snatching Sam's half-made sandwich from her hands.

Sam squeezed past Finnian and round the end of the counter.

'Go! For God's sake, go,' said Finnian, taking the serving spoon out of her hands before it dripped mayonnaise onto a cheesecake. 'If you were less busy it might help!'

'Dale! Wait!' she shouted as he crossed the pavement to his car. 'Where are you going?'

'Got to sort out that punter you've been so bothered about.'

There was something alarming in the way that Dale said 'sort out' that made Sam think of fists, tight wads of cash and the way that Gordon had asked if Dale had ever 'laid a finger on her'. The thicket of confusion that had been blocking her mind all day cleared instantly as if it had been defoliated and she knew that Dale must be told about his father and right now.

'Dale!' But he was in the car before she could tell him that his long-never-found or searched-for dad was a real live builder and decorator called Gordon.

'Dale!!'

Sam ran to where Dale's car was already indicating its intention to pull out into the road. Rashly she leapt for the passenger door and wrenched it open as it was pulling away. The door swung wide, combining its momentum with the moving car, and Sam swung forward and smashed into the bonnet on top of her left arm. There was a nasty little crunching sound and a pain like hot wires shot up from her wrist.

Dale's car stopped, half pulled out from its parking space, and Dale rushed from the driver's seat.

'What the bloody hell did you do that for?' He peeled her off the car and she felt in his touch that he was frightened not angry. 'God, Angie! You could have really hurt yourself!'

It didn't hurt. The pain was swept aside by the way her heart accelerated, like a car pulling out of a nasty bend with a spurt of speed. But her hand looked odd, as if the glue that held it to her wrist had melted a bit and allowed a little sideways slippage.

She looked at it in surprise. 'I have really hurt myself.'

'Oh bugger. I'll take you to Casualty. Come on. What the hell's got into you!'

'I could ask you the same!'

'Yeah. Well. Just get in the car, OK?'

Injuring her wrist was the most help Sam had been to Tavs all day; the queue of customers had forgotten its sandwich orders and had been standing on the pavement enjoying the little drama that she had provided. Meanwhile Maria and Finnian filled rolls, sliced salami and sighed sighs of relief and utter mystification.

And now Dale has done some very out-of-character parking. His car is slanted across two spaces in the hospital car park and the left-hand indicator continues to flash. Dale and Sam sit stony faced and pale. Dale is holding his father's business card as if it were a sacred relic.

'Gordon A. Armstrong. General builder.'

'He knew you, Dale.'

Dale looks at her blankly at first as if her words are in another language. Then their meaning solidifies. 'He knew you when you were a teenager. He asked me things about you, as if, I dunno. As if you'd done something bad, in the past when you were young.' Sam watches a kind of greyness spread through Dale's face.

When he speaks his voice has shrunk to a dry whisper. 'Your wrist,' says Dale quietly, 'we should go into to Casualty.'

'I can wait a bit longer. It's only just beginning to throb a bit. Tell me what he was on about, Dale!'

'Later. I'll tell you later. Let's get you strapped up before it starts to hurt more.'

He's right. As they sit down to wait Sam's adrenaline drains away and in moments all she can think about is the pain of her wrist. Dale lets her lean against him, a crash mat cushioning her fall. He holds her good hand whilst the nurse puts on the plaster. He was like this when she was in labour, quiet and solid. Certain and intimate like her own personal sunrise. But now his face is slack and sad. His eyes have the same lost look they had the day she first showed him the new garden. Behind the smile he gives her to keep her brave he's looking at her face as if she were about to disappear for ever. She wants to comfort him but she can't think what to say.

'I've made you late for sorting out your punter. I'm sorry.'

'It doesn't matter now, Ange. I'll tell you about it later.'

She looks at his sad face and feels once more that there is nothing she could know about him that could stop her loving him. She knows that he is true and good to the core, sweet like a honey pot, right to the very, very bottom.

Tony and Joe used every colouring pen in the box to convert Sam's plaster to an explosion of wiggles and faces and odd-shaped creatures. Sleepily Joe traces them now with one finger as Sam leans over his bed to kiss him good night.

'This is Archimedes and his kittens,' he explains.

'*Her* kittens!' says Tony, butting out of his goodnight cuddle with Dale.

But Joe is above being irritated by Tony's correction. He knows Archimedes is the only Tom cat ever to have given birth. In Joe's view, it's Tony's problem if he can't spot magic when he sees it. 'Here's their whiskers and here's their tails.'

'Night, Joe.'

'Night, Mummy.'

Sam and Dale swap places, shuffling past each other in the tight space between the boys' beds.

'Will Mummy's arm get better?' Joe asks Dale.

Tony rolls his eyes conspiratorially at his Mum, then looks suddenly concerned. 'Your arm will be better, won't it?' he whispers.

'Yes, lovely, it will. It's not even broken. In a couple of weeks it'll be fine.'

'Are we going to see Grandpa Ralph and Granny Bea in the holidays?'

'Yes.'

'Sleep tight, Tony.'

'Sleep tight, boys.'

'Nighty night.'

Out on the landing Dale and Sam stop and hold each other for a moment.

'I'm so tired. I feel eighty-eight not twenty-eight.'

'Let's get a drink, then go to bed.'

'I think I want tea not alcohol.'

'I was thinking cocoa meself. If I had anything to drink after today I'd pass out.'

Sam rests her aching arm whilst Dale potters around the kitchen in companionable silence getting mugs and milk and biscuits. Normally they would take a bedtime drink to the sofa in the front room, but without thinking they sit at the table, opposite each other like penitent and priest.

'So, what was it that you were going to "tell me later"?'

'I don't want to tell you, Sam. I want you to go on loving me.'

'Then tell me how your dad knew you and why he asked me if you've ever hurt me.'

Dale swallows hard, eyes glittering. 'Jeesus. I've cried more this month than I did when I was five.'

Sam squeezes his hand with her one good one, and Dale takes a deep breath. 'I spent all my childhood imagining what he was like, my dad. Inventing excuses for why he'd left her. Why he never came to find Mum. I invented a sort of Steve McQueen type bloke who'd been killed in a terrible crash trying to get to Mum. I invented an English Lord who'd got amnesia and forgotten where to find her. Then when I was older . . .' Dale shrugs, 'I settled for a heartless bastard who'd shagged a girl and left her in the lurch. I dreamt about who my dad might be almost every night of my life, nightmares about axe murderers. Nightmares about what might be in me.'

Sam can't believe how stupid she's been all these years to believe the shrug and bravado that Dale has sold her: '*He's not interested in me so I'm not interested in him.*'

Dale touches the end of the fingers that stick out of the plaster, and looking down at them, goes on; Sam tries not to even breathe, this access to Dale's insides is so rare and precious she doesn't want to do anything to disturb it.

'I always saw there was something behind you that you never told. I let it go because I had something behind me I didn't tell.'

Sam doesn't speak; she is hearing the shredding of canvas and the scraping of layers of oil paint faintly but distinctly in her head.

'When I was at school, I used to get into fights. Boys just do. But I'd get so angry sometimes that I'd sort of black out, and I'd be hitting some kid without even knowing it. The second time I put a kid into hospital I was expelled. I was almost sixteen anyway. I was lucky not to go to boot camp or something. I had the whole psychiatrist do, the police, the social workers, the lot. Mum nearly went mad with it all, I think. It was her idea to get me a job with a stonemason. I think she thought that beating seven shades of shit out of a bit of sandstone might help. But it was the working on my own that did it. He was a nice bloke old Kevin, just let me get on with things at my own pace. I felt calm for the first time in about five years. I didn't get into fights any more. I thought I was over it. Things went pretty well with the job. I did more on the building and restoration side. Then Kev was ill and he asked me to be foreman on a job he was doing in Bath.

'I was eighteen and I had two blokes working for me. One of them was nicking stuff from the client. I caught him. And I don't even remember what happened but I broke his jaw, three ribs and I fractured his skull. He was in a coma for a month. Off work for three years. I got five years.'

It isn't really a revelation to Sam. Although she's never dreamed of Dale being violent, never feared his anger, the feel of him, his atmosphere is suddenly explicable, the way that a picture emerges when you join up the dots. His focused irresistible energy has a tinge of wildness to it, storm power driving a sensible turbine, or an explosion somehow made to run a central heating system. Sam sits quietly taking in her new perspective, then realises that Dale is waiting for her to make some sort of judgment. She can't think what to say. 'Oh' just isn't enough.

'Did you do the whole five years?'

'No. Two and half.'

'Oh.'

'That's where I met my dad.'

Of course. She can see it immediately, that slow way Gordon rolled his cigarettes, the way you'd roll them if that was all there was in your day.

'He just walked up to me in the yard one morning. "Cassinari?" he said. "I used to know your mother." As soon as he said that I think I knew. He was what they call a domestic lifer. He'd killed his wife's lover with a piece of copper plumbing pipe. He did twenty-two years for it. Got out the year I met you.'

'Did he help you, you know, get you through your time?'

'No. Not meaning to anyway. I only spoke to him a couple of times. He told me how he'd brought Mum from Italy. Sounded to me like they made a deal. He got her pregnant so he married her so she could come here and get away from her dad. She divorced him after two years but he'd left by that time anyway. He said he hit her once. That would've been enough for Ma to want to put him six foot under. He married his childhood sweetheart, started a building business. It could've worked OK for him. Struck me as a bright sort of bloke. But he wrecked it. He knew about his temper, his rages. He actually called them black outs. He never did anything about them and he ended up killing the bloke he found in bed with his wife.

'He talked about it all as if it had happened to somebody else. Just smoking all the time. And then he got transferred I heard and I never saw him again. Not ever. Not once. I never told Maria.'

He's been talking to their hands, and now he looks up for reassurance.

'Go on, Dale,' she says.

'He scared me. I could see my life going the same way. I'd thought I'd learned to cope with my demons, chipping away at stone, not speaking to people. And I hadn't. I'd nearly done what he did. Nearly killed someone. I went to the prison shrink the day after he was transferred. I signed up for every kind of bloody therapy, this, that and the other. I did art therapy, I did psychoanalysis, I dunno what else. They loved me. I wanted to be cured. That's pretty rare in prison. After six months all it had done was make me give up smoking. Then I got this bloke, prison visitor. Befriender they called them. He'd been a heroin addict then taken up marathon running. He said, run. When you feel the anger coming on, get a pair of trainers and run. So I used to run round the yard every day. And when I got out

Kevin took me back. Couldn't believe it. I kept a pair of trainers in my bag and whenever I felt that hot-behind-the-eyes feeling, I ran.'

'D'you still run?'

'Yeah. Sometimes. I keep the kit in the back of the truck. I run from work, from a site, whatever. Quite often. But I need it less for my head these days. More for my body.'

'It explains those nice legs. And the bum too, I suppose. I never knew.'

'Course you didn't. I didn't want you to know. I was terrified of you knowing. I thought you'd start to be afraid.'

'Do I look scared to you?'

'No. Beautiful. Not scared.'

He squeezes her hand and fingers so tight it hurts.

'I ran miles after I met you. Even when I didn't feel I needed it. I wanted to be sure you'd never ever see that side of me. I wanted to kill that part of me. If I could have cut off my arm and been rid of it I would have. I wanted to be *all* good, for you.'

Sam can't speak. She knows that feeling so well. She knows its cost. And she knows about the fear it makes. The purpose behind the anonymous voice is apparent now, clear as sunrise, clear as a light switch.

'That man, who kept ringing. He knows about you being in prison. He's been blackmailing you!'

'Yeah. Not too hard to work out I suppose when you know the background. I've done a lot of running because of him. And I've paid him so much money. He's called Maurice Stennar. He got out three years after me. I was in the supermarket with you and the boys in April and he saw me. He waited by the trolley park and came up to me. "Bet your little wife doesn't know where we met," he said. I should have shrugged him off then. Told him I didn't care. But I was so scared of you knowing. I told him I'd kill him if he told you. So he knew just how much money he could bleed me for, right from that moment.'

'How much?'

'Twelve grand. Borrowed off the business. Then I had a couple of late-paying customers . . . and, well, it doesn't take much to wreck a one-man-band business. But Lime House saved my neck.'

'Would you have gone on paying him?'

'For a while. But once I knew about, well, you and your parents I thought I can tell her. I can. It'll be all right. Just not yet.'

'Will you go and see your father?'

Dale shrugs. 'I dunno. Yeah. I will. At least he deserves to see I didn't make the same mistakes.'

'Should we tell Maria?'

'Probably. Maybe. Yes. Yes. I'll talk to her.'

He downs his cocoa. 'Let's go to bed. I don't care how early it is. I've had it.' The porthole into Dale's inner life is closing. He smiles, takes her hand. 'Thank you.'

'What for?'

'For still loving me.'

Maria and Sam are walking up the road on Maria's afternoon off, carrying a bag of shopping between them. They make a pleasing composition, Sam's pale blue dress and Maria's faithful orange. The bag, a cream square with the gold of a loaf sticking jauntily out of one corner and the mauve and crimson of a bunch of anemones at the other. The pollarded trees cast blotchy blue shadows that move over their skin and clothes, changing the pattern of colours moment to moment. They climb steadily up the steeply sloping street, each holding a handle. Each leans outward very slightly giving the impression of some subtle and delicate balance effortlessly held.

'We are a pair of old crocks, no?'

'Well, at least you've got two functional hands, Maria.'

'Angie. What a good girl. Always, always make me laugh.'

'D'you want to rest for a minute, old crock?'

'No. I can do all the way without stopping. Watch me!'

They walk on up the hot pavement, in silence for a few steps.

'OK. Maybe not all the way!'

They put down the bag and stop in a patch of shade.

'Angie? Dale told me about Gordon.'

Sam is not at all ready for this.

'When?'

'This morning. He come for coffee. He took me out of the shop.'

'Oh.'

'So now I guess you know about my bugger son is a jail bird.'

'Not any more he isn't, Maria. I don't care about it anyway.'

'No. No. I know. You love my Dale.'

'Yes. I do.'

'I feel bad about this Gordon. He had big problem. Like Dale. Phhhut . . . explosion when he get angry. But I didn't help. I just kicked him out. I feel bad.'

'You were very young. You had a baby. And maybe you couldn't have helped anyway.'

'Dale says I should see him. He says Gordon is like him.'

'It's up to you, Maria. It was good for Dale to meet his dad again. Laid ghosts, you know? Maybe it could do that for you?'

'What do you think about him?'

'I've only met him once. I think he's very sad. I think he's cured himself, like Dale did. It took him longer and did more damage.'

'You know, I wanted to be pregnant. I *made* him make me pregnant. I wanted out from my father. I was glad my dad chuck me out. I knew he would chuck me out if I was pregnant. What would I do if I stay there? Take care of Mama and Papa. No life for me.'

'Will you tell Gordon that?'

Maria nods. 'He knows. He knows from the start, I think. But maybe I think he cared more for me than nothing. You

241

know? So, maybe, I see this Gordon guy. Old crock like me these days? Lay ghosts before we *are* ghosts!'

They smile, and without speaking pick up the bag and walk again.

'What are you goin' to do, Angie? You going to sell salami all your life? Your mum told me about the University, about your Tropical Rainforest.'

Hearing those words – Tropical Rainforest – from Maria's mouth is astonishing to Sam. She has always seen Maria's world as confined to a single square mile of Bristol, beginning with *antipasto*, ending with *zuccotto*, with Tony and Joe sandwiched in between.

'I know a bit about Tropical Rainforest you know,' Maria says. 'I read about it. It's all bein' cut down, and it's full of animals and all. Trees like the Empire State Building. Parrots, butterflies like big plates. Nnnah. I don't like to think of that bein' gone, ppphtt.'

This is what Sam always used to tell people when she was a girl, when she was still full of dreams, that jungle was important to everyone, and here is the proof; Maria of all people caring about the wanton destruction of biodiversity.

Maria gives her handle a little shake to draw Sam's attention. 'You're very clever girl. You could be a Tropical Rainforest *Professore*. Yes? Yes, I think so.'

Sam loses the rhythm of their carrying and walking for a moment, then pushes down the old passions. Be satisfied with an exotic garden, she tells them, with imaginary iguanas and phantom jaguars, that's all you're going to get . . .

'I don't know, Maria. It was all a long time ago. I've got the boys now . . .'

'You don't have to go and live in the bloody place to study it. Just visit. Eh?'

'There's a lot of dust that needs to settle first. Bea and Ralph. Dale's dad. Lime House to sort out. Your new bakery even! We'll see.'

'*We'll* see. Eh! I hear you say *that* to the boys I know what *that* means! All I need for the new bakery is your money! You can be sleepin' partner, like Dale!'

Once more a well-composed picture, finely balanced with their bag, they round the corner into Lancaster Road. Dale is getting out of the car with the boys outside Number eleven. He walks up the road, snow, blood and ebony in a blue denim shirt, full of inexorable energy, and beaming.

'You haven't been shopping for tonight's dinner, have you?' he says, taking the bag. 'Needn't have bothered. I'm taking both of you out!'

Sam's immediate thought is that they're going to see some new project of Dale's, a crumbling sandstone terrace, or a neglected Edwardian façade. It doesn't occur to her that what he's talking about is dinner in a restaurant. 'Out where?'

'Out to to eat. Somewhere nice. It's a surprise.'

'Well, Dale, you get to be gentleman in your old age, eh? What's the party?'

'Well.' Dale puts down the bag and counts off the day's triumphs on his fingers. 'One: I signed off on the Bath job this afternoon. All the work's done. The client is happy and the house looks lovely. The money's all sorted at last, thank God, and the bloke in Wickwar finally coughed up! Two: a large wodge of cash arrived on the site this morning in a dirty Jiffy bag, courtesy of our friend Maurice who really doesn't want a conviction for blackmail. And three: we've had a very good offer on Lime House as it stands, before any work is done on it. So, heiress-Angela, you could be about to come into a lot of dosh!'

Sam has expected to feel relieved or even excited when the news of the sale of Lime House finally came. She thought she might squeal like a lottery winner, or jump up and down like a four year old with a bag of sweets. She certainly expected to feel lighter, cut free of ever having to talk about Lawrence or his house again. But all she can feel is uneasy; she senses some awful catch to this bargain that Lawrence has left her with, some consequence that she just can't see.

'For a girl with money, you don't look so happy. You can be my investor now!' prompted Maria.

'Oh. I am happy. I mean I'm just shocked. I think tonight should be on me then!'

'No, no, Angie, after Lime House is sold, I'll never be able to treat you to anything ever again. Let me make the most of my last chance.'

'All right. Have you got a baby sitter?'

'Ah!' Dale, unused to planned evenings out, has forgotten the essential component!

'Then I will baby sit. You go, you two!'

'No, Maria!'

'Yes, Maria! I have a big day tomorrow. I took this morning off and was on the phone all afternoon. Phhhew! Finny in a big Queeny strop. My God, do I need sleep tonight. You go.'

'Mum, I really want to take you both out.'

'Don't change habits of a lifetime so fast, Dale. If you such a big shot you take me to Harveys for lunch sometime instead.'

'Well. All right. But stay the night here, we'll be late. I don't want you getting knackered like you were last week.'

'Knackered. If you had gone to Bristol Grammer School like I told you, you would not use this word!'

'I might call my son "a little bugger" instead, eh, Mum?'

In fits and stops they have at last reached the front door of Number eleven, which stands open like a hand to draw them softly inside.

Going out to dinner has not been a part of what Dale and Sam do. The cozy evening in alone, before the boys, and then, with their children, has been their 'thing'. Sam has given Dale idyllic domesticity, and sex that always took place in a bed. It suited both of them: it maintained Sam's cover and control; it gave Dale the feeling of family completeness he'd lacked growing up with Maria and the safety he seemed to crave. It felt good for them to be cocooned together, away from the world. Even this evening, as they got ready inside the cheese-wedge house with Maria and the children around them they've felt cocooned. So it's only now, standing on the threshold of the pearly interior of the poshest restaurant in town that they notice the difference of tonight's situation.

Dale is in a black suit and a plain white shirt. It isn't a style statement, simply his dislike of fuss and his distrust of flamboyance. All the same, he looks handsome, intense, even a little fierce. Sam has scraped her hair back into a clip, exposing her long neck and the line of her shoulders disappearing into the boat neck of a plain dark red dress. Her heels make her almost as tall as Dale so she can look him right in the eye. Her thinness has lost its usual gangly quality and acquired an elegance that Dale has only glimpsed in passing moments before. As they stand with their drinks waiting for their table they each take a sidelong look in the mirror. There they are, Dale and Angie, looking handsome and interesting. They carry with them a kind of dangerous unpredictability that couples with potential have on their first date. It is obvious from one glance that it isn't just the packaging that makes this evening different from all the other evenings they've spent together. Tonight Sam is a young woman with means and newly reawakened ambitions. Dale is a successful craftsman with a reputation for excellence. Not just Mr and Mrs Cassinari out for a night without the kids.

They take their seats at a little round table, and study their menus in absolute silence. Sam chooses the wine because Dale only knows his way around Italian wine lists and she worked on Stayfleurs off-licence counter for two months. They sip Sam's choice, metallic and clean, and chat over their choices of food, watching each other carefully. But then the menus are taken away and there is nothing to act as a distraction. They drink half the bottle before the food even arrives and are eating their starters before either speaks.

'Well. This a is bit daft,' Dale says, spreading his pâté as if he were mortaring a particularly precious piece of stonework. 'Our first meal out in I don't even remember how long, and we don't talk!'

'You look too handsome. I don't know what to say.'

'All right then. Here's what we can talk about. The offer on Lime House.'

'Oh. All right.'

'Airline pilot and barrister wife want country seat for four kids, nanny and ponies. Cash buyers. Want to move in before the winter. Hardly even seem interested in a survey report.'

'We could pay off the mortgage on Lancaster Road and still put a pile in the bank and I could give Maria her money to invest in the bakery. All by Christmas.'

'Or I could do it up for thirty grand more and sell it for another hundred and fifty thousand.'

'I thought you wanted to get rid of it.'

'That was when I was scared I'd have Stennar on my back for ever, when the jobs were going pear shaped, and I thought my wife was about to run off with another man.'

'It's a risk not to sell it when we've got the offer . . .'

'It's not. House like that in that area, it'll always sell. And it's such a lovely project, Ange . . . It's been so neglected. It could be a great showcase for my work, get me more of the really creative restoration stuff. I've only really looked at the outside, the roof, the look of the stonework. But I can tell already. I want you to come and see it.'

The thought makes the taste of the wine curdle in her throat. Standing at the end of the drive was close enough for Sam. Lawrence is still tapping at her mind and she wants him gone. She wants him gone now, at the very least for the duration of the evening. If she tells Dale she wants to sell now, then they'll talk about it all evening. So she pushes Lawrence and his house down under the alcohol and the delicious sexiness of her husband.

'Dale, let's not talk about this now. It broke the ice but now let's just pretend this is a date.'

Dale is ready to argue for a moment, but the unfamiliar atmosphere of the evening seeps through to him again. He looks at Sam's glistening skin, her long mouth, then he picks up his glass. 'I think I was saying how very young you are, wasn't I?'

'Not so young.' Sam swirls the little curl of cream into her soup.

'Younger than I thought. Barely legal when I married you.'

'I was eighteen, Dale!'

'Well, you seemed younger. It was only your experience that convinced me that you were as old as you said you were.'

Sam knows the kind of 'experience' he means. Dale has never asked about boyfriends, about a sex life before he met her, it was all part of the forbidden territory of the past she didn't talk about. But now he's testing the water. For a moment Sam feels a little knock of the old panic, the fear of being found out. Then she remembers that this truth, or part of it, is what she *can* tell him.

'What d'you mean, experienced?'

'You know. When I came round that time. That first time we, you know.'

'And you think I was experienced.' Suddenly Sam knows that this isn't just about finding out for Dale, he's playing. Stroking her skin with his eyes, already in bed with her in his mind. Playing with sex the way they never have before. And she can play too. She leans across the table, touches his hand, and lets one leg slip between his under the starched cloth.

'I'll tell you, Dale, how I got experienced.' She speaks quietly, slowly, sounding consonants soft as kisses. 'I got a book. I was terrified you'd guess about me. Being young, being a runaway. So that weekend I said I was ill? Do you remember? I went to bed all weekend, and I read.' Briefly Sam glances round, then whispers, '*The Joy of Sex*, from cover to cover. Four times. And I decided what I was going to do.'

Dale swallows a mouthful of pâté, and breathes out very slowly. Sam can feel the pulse of tension that runs through his thigh. She spoons her soup, and lets it slither down her throat and spread, warm, into her belly.

'OK. My turn for confessions. But for a bloke what I've got to say isn't much to boast about.' Dale's tone starts as a purr, part of the game. He wipes his mouth and doesn't move his eyes from hers. He drops a hand and caresses her knee. But in two sentences he's not playing any more but telling her secrets more serious than games. 'I was pretty awful-looking when I was a teenager. Acne. Greasy hair. Difficult personality. That part you know about. Busy acting the tough. I knew girls would reject me. So I just kept away. I preferred loneliness to humiliation. And I got used to that, keeping away. After school keeping away from girls got easier. I never met any apart from Chrissie the fat secretary who came in twice a month to do Kev's books. After I came out I just worked. And ran. I went to the pub once a week. I went to the pictures. I went home. I read books, I learnt things . . . I gave myself the education Mum wanted me to take from other people. But I kept keeping away from women. I made out I had lots. Boasted to my work mates. Made it all up. It was just easier, less painful, less messy, less risky. Girls would come onto me sometimes in pubs and I acted cool, told them to go away because I didn't dare show that I had no idea what to do. I told myself that one day I'd have a girlfriend but I wasn't really sure how. I was thirty-one and I'd begun to lose hope. Then I met you. Now or never I said to myself.'

'But. That first time. In my bedsit. You knew what to do . . .'

'No. All I'd ever done was read books, just like you did. But you were the better learner. *You* knew what to do. *I've* only just been allowed to find out . . .'

The soup is cold in the pit of Sam's white bowl. She looks up and falls headlong to the bottom of Dale's eyes.

'Angie, Sam. I've never told anybody this. You were my first. You're the only woman I've ever made love to in my whole life.'

They kiss awkwardly across the table, causing cutlery to fall and other diners to smile indulgently.

'Dale. I love you so much.'

The main course arrives and they eat only half of it. They leave without pudding and totter out into the street to find a taxi to take them, by the fastest route, home, to bed. They leave Maria asleep in front of a flickering TV and climb the stairs by Sam's patented route which avoids the creakiest treads.

Still without speaking, they undress, efficiently, without frenzy as if preparing for immersion in a hot bath after a month in the cold and wet. Then they hold each other, skin to skin with a warmth, a lightness, a sense of freedom that feels like the first step on an empty tide-washed beach. Every touch brings them closer. They have climbed inside the word intimate. They are cuddled and twined within its counterpoint of consonants. So little separates them that they hear every detail of 'intimate's' breathed dialogue of tongue and lips and soft vowels.

They lie smiling in the dark behind their eyelids knowing that nothing like this has ever happened to them before. It is a second and profound loss of some deep virginity. Feeling for her forehead, Dale straightens her hair.

'We've taught each other all we know, eh?'

She nods. 'I'll go and look at Lime House with you, Dale. Let's go tomorrow.'

She wants to lose the last lies, to be as open to Dale as he is to her.

15

The Suffolk air is dry as a stick and hot. It feels to Sam as though it could ignite all on its own. In her childhood, when they burnt the stubbles in late summer, it always felt as if the fire came out of the air and ate the ground. Even the cold feels hot. The glass in her hand burns with it and the ice inside makes a miniature clinking with the tiny tremor of her hand.

She's grateful that Bea and Ralph were in the garden to greet them. It's anonymous out here. The neat square of lawn stretches to the picket fence beyond which is Ralph's veg plot. She can see Dale and the boys moving up and down the rows being guided around runner beans and peas, lettuces and radish by the tall figure in the battered Panama.

Bea comes to sit beside her on the bench, touching her arm with the lightest of fingertips. 'Would you like to lie down, Sam? It's nice and cool inside.'

'No, really, Mum. I'm OK. I just felt a bit wobbly after the car journey. It's lovely out here. Like the Med compared with muggy old Bristol.'

'More to drink?'

'No. I'm OK. Don't fuss.' Bea draws back her hand and presses her lips anxiously together. 'I'm sorry, Mum. I didn't mean to be snappy. I'm really wound up about seeing Lawrence's house.'

'Wait until tomorrow then. We could have the boys for you whenever you like. I've got my assistant running the shop for a couple of days.'

'No. I want to get it done. Get it out of the way.'

'Love, Sam. I don't want to pry. I don't know anything about your friend Lawrence. But I can't help wondering if he had anything to do with you . . . going away?'

'No. No, Mum. You know why I went away. You *know*.' The picket gate at the end of the lawn clicks closed and Tony and Joe come running barefoot over the grass, recovered from their car sickness.

'Oh, here come the men. Better get the biscuits out.' Bea leaps up and goes back into the house, bustling inside her summer frock.

'Better now, my Sam-sam?'

'Yes, Dad. I'm fine.'

'We're having runner beans from Grandpa Ralph's garden for tea,' says Joe, very impressed.

'And lettuce for lunch. I picked it. Look!' Tony holds up a beautiful lime-green cos, earth still sticking to its spindly roots.

'Take it inside to Granny, there's good boys, I think she's got something nice for you in there.' Ralph winks rakishly and the boys run for the back door.

'You sit on the bench, Ralph. I'll grab one of those deck chairs.'

'No, Dale, don't bother.' Sam gets up, knocking her drink off the arm of the seat. 'I'd like to go to Lime House now.'

'Oh, Sam, surely you'll have a spot of lunch first. Bea's got it all ready. Won't take long.'

'I'm sorry, Dad. We'll be back afterwards. I just want to get it over with.'

Dale and Ralph glance at one another and say no more.

'OK then, love. Ralph, I'm sorry about lunch. We'll see you . . .'

'When we see you. Don't worry. We've plenty of entertainments for the boys.'

'Right. I'll, um, say cheerio to Bea.'

'I'll be in the car, Dale.'

'Right. OK.'

*

The car door clunks shut and Dale pulls out into the lane and up the road without a word spoken. The air conditioning gets going at the top of the hill and he speaks, 'So what was that all about? Your poor parents, ready to have lunch with us and you walk out!'

'I'd never been to their house before. It'll be full of stuff from . . . From when I was little. I didn't feel ready.'

'Well, how d'you think they feel, what about that?'

'Oh, shut up, Dale! It's awful going to Lawrence's house. You just don't understand.'

'Right. Bloody right, I don't. I've never understood why inheriting half a million is a bad thing.'

'Shut up, Dale. This is awful, and I'm doing it for you.'

'What's awful about it? This bloke wasn't even a relative. Your parents didn't know him. From what you've said you hardly knew him. But he's left you a fortune. What did you do for this guy anyway?'

'What d'you mean, "What did I do"? Are you saying I was his tart? Didn't you listen to anything I said last night? Is that what you were asking when you asked about my being "experienced"?'

Dale pulls the car into the hedgerow. Turns off the engine and winds a window down. Slowly he lets go of the tension and irritation that have grown over the long tight journey from Bristol and the awkward half hour at his in-laws.

'I'm sorry. I wasn't suggesting that. I can't say I haven't wondered. But not any more. I just don't get why you're so screwed up about all this.'

Sam swallows. She'd like to scream. But it's true there isn't a way Dale can understand just yet. She has to wait a little longer. She must hold everything in very tight for just one more hour. 'You will get it. You will understand. Just remember what last night felt like. What it meant. The whole point of coming here is for you to understand. So you can understand me.' She stabs them each in the chest hard. Dale nods and they drive on in silence, the air conditioning singeing Sam's skin with its cool-hotness.

They get to the gates and Sam shuts her eyes. She can feel the crunch of gravel under the wheels and the flashing of the light through the lime trees on her eyelids. They stop. She keeps her eyes shut until the last possible minute when Dale opens the passenger door and takes her arm,

'Watch your plaster, love,' he says kindly. 'OK, let's look inside. I suppose you don't want to hear the architectural stuff now.'

'No, that's OK. That's supposed to be why I'm here. It might help. Make it easier.'

'Ange. I don't understand this. I really don't. Whatever is going on here? You have to tell me.'

'I will.'

The front steps are crumbling and weedy. It could be fifty years since Lawrence stood here to greet her, not ten. But the neglect helps Sam to get to the front door and walk inside.

The interior is almost unrecognisable. The high arched hallway with its plaster cornices is gone. There is a false ceiling of dirty polystyrene tiles, low enough to reach up and touch; it makes the hallways look like a dentist's waiting room. The floor boards are bare but for dirt and old newspapers. The shining banisters are broken and stand sadly either side of the staircase like rotten teeth. There is a smell of damp and rat poison.

'He must have moved out about the time you left I think,' says Dale, 'this looks like a house that hasn't been lived in for a long time.'

'No. He was here to the end. I want to look in the study first.'

'OK. Shall I come?'

'Please.'

To the right of the hall the study door is missing. Green light comes in through the overgrown bay window and falls onto a floor of shredded rugs. Sam recognises the patterns amongst the dirt and tatters. The bookshelves are empty, the big mirror over the fireplace is like a giant web, with cracks radiating from a central impact. A clock and its glass case lie under the mantle, in several hundred pieces.

'Vandals got in at some point I think.'

Dale tries one last time to be practical, but Sam replies in a whisper, speaking almost to herself. 'No. No, they didn't.' Sam can see, surely as if the mirror could replay what it once reflected. 'No. Lawrence threw the clock at it. It was very special. It had two faces, dark and light. I always told him I didn't like the dark one. We used to look at maps and books on a table in here, and we were always reflected there in that big mirror.' The desk has gone, dragged out over the parquet floor judging by the ruts and scratches left behind. Sam is beginning to sense the trail, a thread of story that she is meant to follow.

'I want to look in the glasshouse.' She doesn't wait for Dale's reply.

Through the dead hallway and down the long bleak kitchen, which is scoured bare of anything, even its old wooden units and cupboards. The walls are naked, the plaster pocked and marked by screw holes and ghosts of shelves. Sam doesn't stop to look or remember leaning here or there with a glass in her hand, perching on the table with a mug of tea. Through the scullery, she's running now the way she used to run when the *Odontoglossums* came into bloom. She slams the door behind her and it loses the last of its tiny leaded panes, crashing under Dale's hurrying feet. Across the little covered courtyard, green with mould and slime where the broken guttering has cascaded years of winter rain over the stone. At last the door of the glasshouse, solid and intricate still, every pane perfect and bearing the smudge marks of some attempt at cleaning. Without waiting for a breath or to gather her wits and strength Sam steps in.

She has expected more ruin. A crumbled mass of glass and iron littering plants, dead from cold then drought. Or a claustrophobic dryness, with crisp brown leaves shattering with every step inside the unwatered greenhouse. But Lawrence's glasshouse is just as it might have been if he had stepped out to make a cup of tea or fetch a sherry for them both. The vents are open wide on this hot day, the watering system has recently been working. The plants are thriving – unkempt and uncontrolled they're taking over. The *Gloriosa speciosa* is now as tall as the roof and there are tangles of bougainvillea and hibiscus. The smell is the same as she remembers it, stronger perhaps because the vegetation now is more dense. The same slow thickening of the air that holds your limbs and stops your mouth. Only the orchids have suffered from neglect. Shrivelled and brown, they've become insignificant encrustations hanging amongst the rampant green.

'I could go away for fortnight in winter and they'd cope,' Lawrence used to say, 'but in summer, even with the misting system I have to water some two or three times a day.' He had a little aluminium ladder that he carried around the greenhouse so he could fuss and tend his plants. She can see him in her mind's eye, on a hot day like this, trickling water into a basket, bursting with shoots of one of his favourites. Smiling down at her from the top of the steps.

'You should definitely see this in the wild, Sam. *Stanhopea*. Extraordinary epiphyte. Its flower spike only grows downwards. You can be the one to find out why!'

The open teak basket swings above her now, containing only the remnants of plant growth and the crisp corpses of dead flowers dangling from its underside.

She pushes her way through the leaves and tendrils that catch and hold her hair and skin, following the old brick paths around to where more orchids used to cascade down from their suspended perches of bark and charcoal. They are still just holding on to life, but their strap leaves are yellowing and the leaf bases are shrivelled. Here is the palm she leant against to look up into the underside of the *Oncidium*, the plant that can flower itself to death and long since has. That was the day Lawrence first touched her with some incomprehensible charge in his skin, like an electric fever sparking under the surface.

At the far end of the glasshouse she finds where Lawrence has spent his time. Clustered untidily under the foliage are the essentials of his life, pared down and brought to this spot, where once they took tea at a tiny wrought-iron table under the trailing leaves and flowers. This is where the desk from the study has been dragged. It stands just off the path, its inlays and veneers dulled and splitting, its sides sagged and curved with neglect. The drawers all slouch half open, bloated and over-stuffed with papers. All Lawrence's favourite books are here too, crammed uncaringly into bright plastic crates – the huge leather-bound volumes of nineteenth-century botany, contemporary gardening texts from all over the world, maps and atlases – all mouldering in the damp. Right against the glass-house wall under a little bower of climbers and cobwebs is a camp bed, with a filthy quilt and pillow. And beneath the whole pathetic encampment, stacked against the glass of the walls, strewn like an understorey of fallen leaves, are empty bottles. They're all the same brand of Scotch whisky that Lawrence always described as tasting of the smell of a peat fire. It's almost funny that Lawrence chose to drink himself into oblivion with something better matched to winter moorland than a bower of pink passifloras. Wherever she looks they reveal themselves, camouflaged by layers of mould, twined in stems, too old to show their glassy shine or swanky label. The bottles are everywhere, drifted around the base of every plant, leaning against every wall or iron strut, piled on each flat surface. Everywhere but the path that leads to the island of the desk, the books and the bed. There must be thousands, num-bering the days since last Sam stood here, plainly recounting the last long, bleak chapter of Lawrence's life and testifying to the stamina of his liver.

She pulls the desk drawers out, wrenching free files,

envelopes, pens, and crumpled papers, a thousand letters that began, 'My Dearest Samantha', and said no more. The last deep drawer is the only one in any order. Almost empty and properly closed, it's free of mould and dryer than the others, quite recently attended to, Sam concludes. Slowly now, less frenzied, she takes out its contents, a small portable typewriter in a neat grey case and a single box file, with a black door that makes Sam think of the dark interior of the confessional box. She opens the file and her own face looks out from a plastic wallet, fearfully locking up Julie's cake shop, hunted and big eyed. There are perhaps a hundred photographs snatched from ten years of her life, by a photographer sitting in a car outside school, watching from a bus stop on the other side of the road, even taken from the inside of a bag as she scanned tins of cat food through the Stayfleurs checkout. Here she draws the grubby curtains of her bedsit, her face indistinct and empty. Here she is with Dale, kissing in the front of his car. Each photo is dated, in a neat controlled version of Lawrence's disintegrated scrawl. At the bottom of the pile are the invoices from a firm of private detectives – Marshall and Musgrove Limited of Yate – held together by a small black bulldog clip. She taps them back into order like a pack of cards and lays them on the desktop. The next layer is a sheaf of flimsy carbons, held by another small black clip. They are copies of badly typed letters each detailing the wording for a communication to be sent to Bea and Ralph Powell . . .

'Dale is self employed. He's doing well. I have a part-time job.'

'Tony will be one this year.'

'Little Joe was born on January the fifteenth . . .'

'Both boys are now in school, and doing well. We're all fine. Please don't attempt to contact me. Sam.'

A sample of the cards chosen by Marshall and Musgroye Limited – glitter-strewn robins, fat Santas and dancing holly leaves – are stapled together under the flimsy carbons.

The bottom of the file, its deepest layer, is a single sheet of paper protected inside a deep blue plastic wallet. This, Sam senses, is some last clue, a message left here by Lawrence, a piece of the jigsaw she didn't have before. It is a letter, on good paper with the logo of an oil company based in Caracas, Venezuela, dated the nineteenth of November, just a month before Sam ran out of her parents' house and didn't go back. Below the printed header are spidery rows of handwritten Spanish, divided by dashes and paragraphs, exclamations and brackets, giving the letter a chatty and informal look in spite of the company paper. The signature is one word, a rapid squiggle that could even be some private nickname. Clearly the writer was used to being understood without having to resort to English, yet Sam finds a translation on the back in green Biro. It's written in laboured capitals, the way Lawrence wrote addresses on envelopes or labels on plants, with the same awkward clarity demanded by forms where each letter must sit in its own little box. His usual hand was no more than a few kinks in a line, incomprehensible to anyone but himself.

Dear Friend,

I was thrilled to hear from you again after so long and to hear that you're thinking of paying us a visit. (The house has a proper guest wing these days, no more difficult nights on a camp bed for you, Lawrence!)

Seriously, Lawrence. I am truly delighted: that business with Amoco burned us both so badly I thought you would never want to come back to Venezuela!

I can arrange what you ask. In fact I've already made a few preliminary enquiries. My friend Professor Villars is doing ecological surveys in Amazonas near Plantanal. He is always looking for keen and knowledgeable people to help. Your young botanist would be very welcome. As for funding I think I can pull a few strings there. The Company would be willing to cover some expenses for a visiting student of such a prestigious

institution as Oxford university (especially if there was a little
good press to be had), although they might need some formal
endorsements from the Institution itself.

I can't believe that such an old dog as yourself is at last
contemplating the bondage of marriage in which I have been
so blissfully bound now for twenty years. But perhaps you had to
find a woman who could understand at least some of your
passions. It sounds as if your young fiancée seems to share your
love for plants. Though why a lovely young girl would bother with
a bit of old leather like you, I can't imagine! Hidden talents, eh?

Do you recall the climber you liked in my garden? I don't
remember the fancy Latin name you gave it. It covers the whole
roof now and blooms for three months a year!

Let me know what you decide. I can help arrange most
things here. As I'm sure you remember,

With best wishes

At the bottom, written with the same green pen, is another
date, in May. Three months ago. Less than a month before the
solicitors' letter arrived on her doorstep. How close to Lawrence's death? She doesn't want to think.

The photographs, the sheaf of papers with the incongruous
reindeer emblazoned on the front and the green-ink translation
lie on the desk, like the exhibits in a court case laid up for the
Beak to inspect. The photos she had already imagined, and the
cards too; who else could have sent them to her parents? But
the green ink spells a reality she never guessed, that Lawrence
too had been escaping into a world of his own dreams. A little
fragment of conversation floats into her memory from amongst
the leaves . . .

'It's always Summer when you come here.'

'Perhaps you'd better escape and come to the jungle with
me.'

'Or perhaps you'd better stay here and then Summer would
never go away.'

259

Was it then he'd decided that she was his possession? That all he had to do was plan and wait and she'd fall off a branch like ripe fruit into his hand?

'Sam?'

It's strange to hear Dale use that name so naturally, as if he always has. She looks up from the exhibits to his face. How long he's been standing next to the desk she doesn't know.

'Why did you call me that?'

'I don't know. It just came out. Angie, what's going on? Why are these photos here?'

'Lawrence had them taken. Look, there's an invoice from the private detective firm.'

'Bloody hell fire. He had you watched. He watched us. Did you know this?'

'Not until I went to the solicitors, to hear about his will. I didn't know but I guessed then he'd been doing this . . .' She pushed the carbons and the cheap Christmas cards towards Dale. 'Look at this.'

Dale flicks through the letters, looks at the cards and takes in the instructions for the annual Christmas message from 'Sam'. 'I don't get this.'

'Lawrence had the cards sent to my parents.'

'So you never did get in touch with them?'

'No.'

'Why?'

'I told you. I thought Mummy was dead. I knew she was dead.'

'How did you know she was dead?'

'I just knew . . .'

'But what about your father? And why did Lawrence send the cards?'

Dale is trying to pull answers from her too fast. She feels attacked and frightened, full of concealment again, in spite of every intention that she brought to Lawrence's house with her.

'Did you tell Lawrence to send the cards?'

'I didn't even know about the cards,' she snaps back at him, defensive, shaking with anxiety.

'Why didn't you say?'

'Because they were so grateful for those cards. I couldn't tell them I'd never bothered.' Her voice is almost a squeal. Convulsively she pushes the letter covered with Lawrence's green capitals over the desk to Dale.

'Fiancée? Lawrence's fiancée? This is you isn't it? You were engaged to this guy. That's why he left you the house!'

'No I wasn't. I wasn't. There was nothing like that. He just imagined there was. He was obsessed, and I never saw it, not then.'

Dale steps back from the desk and takes a deep breath. He looks all around at the artificial jungle, at the litter of whisky bottles then at his white-faced wife. 'Angie,' he speaks quietly, 'Angie, why did you come here with me?'

'To tell you all the truth,' she almost wails.

'OK. OK. Then tell me. All you have to do is tell me.'

'It's so hard. I don't want to remember.'

'I think whatever it is you remember it all the time. You might stop remembering after today. That's what you came for, Ange, isn't it?'

She breathes in the green thick smell of growth and moisture and lets the past in.

Looking back at her teenage self Sam feels like a parent watching a toddler ambling to the edge of a cliff. At this distance of years she can see the danger, the rotten intensity at the core of Lawrence's life, quite clearly. She might even have sensed it herself back then, and shied away like a horse smelling fear. But cocooned in her world of determined dreaming and domestic nightmare, her sensitivity to anything but her own obsession was dulled. Lawrence's hand that looked to the seventeen-year-old Sam as if it was pulling her into the light, was reaching to her as the last anchor to hold him back from the absolute darkness in his soul.

When Tony was a baby he couldn't play peek-a-boo. Once Sam hid, he forgot about her, so there was no joke in disappearance, no irony. Out of sight was out of existence for him, the only things in the world were what he experienced. At seventeen, Sam remembers, she was just the same as her baby son. What was out of her mind, didn't exist. And what was in, did, no matter how unlikely or outlandish. Out of her sight Lawrence walked in the rainforest of her imagination. Her mentor. Her provider. Her means to an end. He had no separate existence, he was a rung on her ladder. She didn't conceive of the real Lawrence and what he was when she wasn't looking. She never questioned why he was never busy when she called, never engaged in anything too demanding to drop immediately. She didn't see the layers of soft dust lying on the fax machine and the telephones. If she had, she might have guessed that Lawrence was a ghost in his own life. This house with its sad memories of his dead mother and his iron-handed father had just waited to draw him back.

Lawrence had told her just enough of his past for her imagination to invent the biography she wanted: a life that was glittering and adventurous, wild and bohemian but somehow romantic and even noble. Building from the same elements now, Sam can see the dead tawdriness of it all. Lawrence had never been the Bond-like figure, playing international business as if it was his private Monopoly board. She sees him now for what he was, a broker without moral scruple, negotiating bastard deals outside of the marital bed of trade agreements. The 'major players' Lawrence had described to her were the shadowy representatives of multinational companies wanting cheap toeholds, and corrupt government officials with 'off the record' development opportunities to offer for personal gain. When business was good, he lived in the best hotels, had company cars, government permits. When it was bad he had to cross borders at night, bribe pilots to fly him from distant airstrips. He must have lost as many fortunes as he boasted of gaining.

Fraser Spence had hated Lawrence's adventures. He hated
the way his son had perverted the stern upbringing Fraser had
been so careful to give him after Margaret died.

Lawrence often mentioned it. 'I got my own back on the old
bastard for those Presbyterian boarding schools. No better
than Buchenwald. He couldn't stand it when I made money.
Disgusting displays, that's what he called all my deals. I made
more money in twenty years than he made in a life time!'

Lawrence once spoke of how Fraser hated Lawrence's botanising trips. ' "Wasteful extravagance," he told me. This man
who regularly kept a suite at Browns. Indicative, he told me, of
a weak mind and diseased will power. "*Just like your dead
mother.*"

'I tried once to win him over,' Lawrence had told her. 'You
know, the olive branch and all that. I thought, well he'll be
dead one day and perhaps we ought to understand each other
. . . I had ten exquisite *Oncidiums* delivered direct to his hotel
room in Kensington. The most beautiful plants you could
imagine, in full bloom. They were like wild animals, as if I
had taken ten beautiful Bengal tigers and had them purring at
his feet like tabbies.'

'What happened?'

'He sent them back to me chopped up in a plastic dustbin
bag. I never saw him again.'

Sam's love of the tales of the countless botanising journeys
must have been wonderful for Lawrence. The joy with which
he described the landscapes and the delight of the search, the
tension of the hunt for a plant electrified her. There was no
doubt of his skill, his determination and his endurance. It was
clear that he had bludgeoned his way through his own physical
and financial limits to find the rarest, the loveliest, the biggest.
But the 'kill', the actual taking of the plant that sickened Sam,
was all to Lawrence. In the end, Lawrence was Fraser's own
true son. Experience was always too flimsy, dreamlike. Possession, no matter how brief, was the only solid satisfaction. What

happened to those plants that Lawrence took Sam can only guess now: hundreds withered in hotel bathrooms from Lima to Kinshasa she suspects. Hundreds traded, illegally mostly, to fund his trips.

Hunting plants became his talisman, a symbol for all his father abhorred and the deformed embodiment of the only affection he'd ever known. When his father died he came home 'to bury the old bastard, dance on his grave and run away again'. But he stayed. Tended his mother's garden, brought some of his surviving trophy plants into the sanctuary of the restored glasshouse. Took a year out. Then another and another after that. He found he still didn't want to leave. Found he couldn't. The day Samantha arrived, what she stumbled on was a man too frightened of the world outside to go back to it.

How had he seen her that first day, she wondered? A miracle. A Madonna with a worshipping face turned up to his *Dicksonias*. A supplicant before the throne of God, something transposed from a Florentine fresco, wrapped in denim and dropped like a fallen angel on his lawn. From that first moment he must have always been waiting for her visits. Inventing her to conform to his fantasies of some sensual redeemer, as she invented him to conform to her visions of herself.

She must have seemed to Lawrence to be leading him on. Her long legs in the shorts she wore on summer days, the baggy jeans, the worn T-shirts. It must have been 'obvious' to him how she 'chose' to display her figure for him, the slimness of her hips, the pointed breasts under the stretched cotton. And her control, her intellectualism, was so artlessly arch. Incomprehensible to Lawrence that she was unaware of her attractiveness. To Lawrence her naïvete was just another hook in his flesh. He would touch her arm, or stroke her neck and she would tense, confused, waiting for it to stop. What had that tension felt like to Lawrence? Experience? An invitation? A half-written contract perhaps? Somehow he had felt in it a reason to write to his friend in Venezuela that he was going to marry at last. A young botanist . . . It was always going to be Summer now, for the rest of his life. Finally he'd felt that his life could be healed, made right through loving Sam. She would remake him. Cut him loose from the claustrophobia of his mother's garden and the repression of his father's coldness. She would recast his tainted passions into purity. Her youth was the gift to wash him clean, his experience was the key to give her her dreams He didn't mean it to turn out the way it had.

The night she gave Bea the pills was the first and only time she called on Lawrence after dark. She landed on his doorstep, desperate and hysterical. Shivering, crying, distraught. Transformed. Every shred of the intense, intellectual shell stripped away. For the first time she must have looked to Lawrence like a woman, not a girl. Out of control. Vulnerable.

He had helped her up the steps and into the hall and she had clung to him, hardly able to see or move.

'Whatever's the matter, Samantha?' he said, and all she could do was cry over and over again.

'I've killed her, I've killed her.' She felt cold. So cold. He had led her into the study, and sat her on the sofa by the fire. Made her drink a large glass of something burning, and alcoholic. And then another. Alcohol was good for shock, for calming the nerves. It would, he told her and himself, be good for her.

At last she was calm enough to take off her coat. Underneath was her old blue dress, too small for her by a year, its fabric worn and its tied front straining. Her white skin had showed at the collar bone, and the top of her spine. He sat beside her on the old leather chesterfield as she wept. Her skin was irresistibly lovely, bloomed like a pearl. Impossible not to touch. Impossible that she didn't want to be touched.

'Now. Tell me slowly and calmly what's happened.' He took her hand and she gripped his fingers.

'Oh Lawrence!' She began to sob again . . . So trusting in him. It made him feel strong.

'It's all right. Just tell me . . .'

'My mum. She's dying of cancer. She's in so much pain.' Her words came in gasps and fits. 'She keeps asking again and again for more painkillers. But I can't give her more than the dose she is supposed to have. But she begs and begs . . .' Once again she broke down. He slipped his arm around her shoulder, the ends of his fingers under the edge of her dress.

'Go on . . .' he said.

'Tonight. She was in such pain. And . . .' her voice dropped to a whisper, 'and I gave her all the pills. I counted them. Two days' worth. All at once . . . She lost consciousness . . . And I came here . . .' She collapsed sideways against him and, awkwardly, he drew her into his arms. 'I killed her. I killed her.'

He buried his face then his fingers in her hair, warm and damp. He wanted to be engulfed by her hair. 'No, no, Samantha. You didn't. You made a mistake. Just a little mistake. You didn't mean to kill her.'

She sobbed against his neck without restraint, without even feeling self-conscious about the tears and snot she smeared on his skin. He held her with such gentleness, as if she were a shadow or a dream.

'I'll protect you, Samantha. You're safe with me,' he said, and how he believed it, how hard he believed he could be that person, the protector, the lover. The saviour and the saved. He stroked her hair, just like a father, just like her own father Ralph had done when she was little and woke in the night. Falling into semi-consciousness Sam had felt the gentleness of his touch as he pulled her into his arms. But quite suddenly the tenderness snapped. As if in pulling her towards him, slipping over the polished leather, he'd found he didn't want to be gentle now.

Right up to that moment he'd believed in his vision. That she could transform him, free him from the past. But all the time hiding inside the sweetness of protection and covert desire, was the same sour old wanting to consume, to use, to burn, to *have*. Deep and ingrained as thirst in a desert the irresistible craving to *take, take, take*, because no one had ever shown him how to give. And here was the ultimate in taking. *Taking* the very *body* of another human being, possessing it by force here on the hearth where the old bastard had stood and lectured his son so many times.

Sam is still standing, leaning over the desk and propped by her straight arms, as if shoring up the last of her strength. She's been speaking for minutes? Hours? Dale's lost any sense of real time. She exudes a forcefield of separateness that keeps Dale from reaching out to hold and comfort her, as he longs to do. She is on the last lap now, and he's ready to catch her as she falls across the finishing line.

'I was exhausted, cold, hysterical and he must have given me the best part of half a pint of brandy. I felt so safe and warm at first. It was the end of everything, but it was all right. He seemed tender. Fatherly. He put me on the settee. I fell asleep, passed out, whatever. I felt him hold me in his arms very carefully. Then he just switched, flipped. Smashed me onto the floor. I don't know what happened. I was face down on the carpet, and he was holding my legs, so my back hurt. And . . . my dress was over my head, and . . . Anyway, I screamed and I screamed. And he didn't stop. And then he turned me on my back. He was so strong. You'd never have guessed it to look at him, quite slight, wiry. Just flipped me over. And he wrapped my dress over my face so I could hardly breathe. Then. Then . . .'

Sam stops to wipe her face. Dale has never looked so terrible. He's aged ten years in as many minutes and is sucking in his mouth to stop himself from losing control. 'Then he did it all again. It seemed like days. Then he sort of fell on top of me. I thought, he's died. I wished he'd died. But he got up. He said "pull your dress down" as if it were my fault. Then I sat up on the floor. I was shaking and bleeding. I was in so much pain I couldn't see straight. *He made me a cup of tea!* Jasmine tea. I sat and drank it. I kept smoothing my dress over my legs. I said,

I said: "You raped me." And he said, "Who would believe you? You're a murderer. A mother murderer. I think we'd both better keep each other's secrets. Don't you?"'

'Oh God. Oh, Angie. My love.' Dale reaches out to her, but she swallows hard and holds up a hand like traffic policeman.

'No. Not yet. I'm not at the end yet. I got up. And he got up. I picked up my coat and told him I was going. I didn't know where. I couldn't go home, and face my dad and see what I'd done. He was right, I was a murderer. I couldn't tell my dad, not *that* dad, not the way he was then. Imagine it. "I've murdered your wife and I've been raped, Dad." But I didn't say that to Lawrence. I just said I'm going. And he said, "You'll be back. You can't do anything without me. All you've got is a few Latin names on your tongue." Then he rubbed my blood into the carpet with his foot, as if it was just bit of fag ash or something. I left him there, and walked off up the drive and hitched to the bus station.' Sam's voice now is less than a croak. It's just a wheeze crushed out of her chest.

'That bastard. I wish he was alive so I could kill him again. He called you a murderer, to protect himself. And then he kept track of you to be sure you wouldn't shop him. Kept your parents away with the postcards. He used all three of you, to keep himself safe.' The utter revulsion in Dale's voice makes the words sound as if he's thrown them up, like a salmonella prawn.

Sam pushes the green-inked translation towards Dale. 'He didn't mean to do what he did. He didn't plan it.' She's barely whispering now, but the silence is so blank around her that the words stand out. 'He did teach me a lot. As much as he could. He did mean to help. And he did want to be able to love me. But he couldn't. He didn't understand how. He didn't even understand how to be sorry. This . . . all this . . . letters, stuff, the house . . . is as near as he could manage. It's all to tell me what happened. All his life I think everything ate him up, his dad, his mum, his money, his plants. Then me. As soon as things took root in him, they grew out of control. He was swallowed by his own insides. I can see how that happens. Can't you?'

She stretches her hand to Dale and he takes it. Their touch is full of the raw force of their two lives, unpredictable in its power, dangerous to release without love.

'Yes. Yes, I can see,' Dale says. They stand arms extended and hands clasped for a long moment, then Dale says, 'Let's go now. Let's get out of this place.'

Dale and Sam walk out through the glasshouse doors, through the deserted kitchen, out of the hall that smells of rats and slam the great door behind them. The sunlight floods their faces and the sweet scent of the last lime flowers of the summer washes them clean.

On a winter night long ago a clock on the mantelpiece of Lime House chimed out the centre of darkness, the midnight hour.

'*I can see why you only have the green tree side showing.*'

Lawrence turned the clock to look into the dark face in the dead tree top. That was what was inside him. Had always been inside him. Had finally claimed him back. Lawrence picked up the clock and threw it at the leering reflection in the mirror that suddenly reminded him horribly of his father.

16

Dale helps his mother up onto the chair like a valet aiding his Liege Lady. She keeps one gloved hand resting lightly on his shoulder, and with the other pats the bursting curls of Giorgio, her young baker from Palermo. He is possibly the happiest person present as the successful opening of Maria's bakery will mean that his escape from the lowest rank in his father's business back home is complete. He stands proudly beside Maria drawing up his thin frame, tall and stiff as if his baker's whites were the dress uniform of the Guards. Dale too has risen to the formality of the occasion, and is wearing his black suit and a charcoal-grey shirt. Flanked by her two vassals, one in white and one in black, Maria, in her royal-blue coat and hat with the black fur trim, could so easily be a stylish European Royal, a Countess from Petersburg, a Duchess from Milan. Balanced now on the chair she delicately removes her hand from the supporting shoulder, ready to gesture to her audience of fifty or more people assembled on the frosty pavement outside Tavs. As she starts to speak her words smoke into the air, catching the sunlight, and her voice carries, clear as the Angelus bell to the farthest members of her audience.

'Dear Friends,' she begins, looking about her at all the familiar faces and smiling, 'today is a great day for me and my family. I always try to bring you the best Italian gourmet tastes. I want for so long to give good fresh bread, baked the way I remember when I was a little girl in Italy. Today with help of my family and Giorgio who come to me from his family bakery in Palermo, I can do that.' Graciously Maria looks from Dale on one side, to Giorgio the other who smiles up at her as if she were the Virgin herself. 'Bread is simple. No?' Maria shrugs as her customers and friends have seen her do a hundred times, and a little murmur of affectionate laughter ripples through the crowd as they see the gesture. Their attention wanders for a moment, but Maria is like a magnet, and in just a heartbeat every single person is focused on her passionate voice, the light in her face.

'Bread is flour and water. That's all. But bread is a big, big thing. Important. We break our bread with our family. With our lovers. Even with our God. Bread means home, and warm and happiness. So I want you, my friends, my good Bristol friends, to have the best of bread. This is what I try to do here.'

The applause is rapturous, tears glitter in many eyes and in one defining moment Maria's new venture embodies the community as it would like to be. Once again Tavs has touched the funny, screwed-up fickle heart of the Bristol middle-class.

'God, how she loves it!' Finny is trying to be cynical but too late. Sam saw him wiping the corners of his eyes on his coat sleeve. There's no time to tease him as they are swept forward towards the smell and warmth emanating from the doors of Tavs Bakery. Sam wonders what Arnold Belling would say if he were here to witness the rebirth of his dingy old shop, selling the whole gamut of the most foreign of muck? Probably stomp through the glass doors and demand a loaf of Mother's Pride! 'Oh, Jeesus in a blue swimsuit, willya look at that!' Finny whispers into Sam's ear as Martina Nova, presenter of 'Cookin' Up A Storm', steps out of a taxi just in time to cut the red ribbon and declare the bakery open. Beaming like a beacon and trailing a film crew, Maria strides in with Martina and Giorgio at her side to sample the first ciabatta rolls from the oven.

'We want to open in time to make special *panettone*, nice for Christmas presents,' Maria sweetly tells the camera, getting herself a few grands' worth of free advertising. Reporters scribble, cameras pop. Tomorrow there will be two hundred orders for boxed gifts of Tavs' special Christmas *panettone*.

It takes two hours for the razzmatazz to die down. People finish their bucks fizz and bread and totter off unsteadily to work. True to form Maria has already rolled up her sleeves and joined Louise and Giorgio behind the counter of the bakery, leaving Finnian to field the extra custom next door, alone.

'Where were you?' Dale comes up to her smiling, a half-finished glass in his hand. 'You should have been down at the front toasting your investment.'

'I was up the back being naughty with Finnian. No, love. All I did was shove in a spot of Larry's dosh. You and Maria, and Giorgio, Gordon and Louise too, you all did the work. Not me.'

He puts a hand on her shoulder, and turns her to look at the bakery, the new shop front, the repainted and repointed façade and brickwork, the new colour scheme that links Tavs and its new partner.

'So what do you think?'

'It's miraculous what you've done in such a short time. You and Gordon have worked like slaves!'

'He can work, I'll give him that, my old dad. Did a great job on the oven.'

'He's not here?'

'No. Only just so much emotion he can cope with at one go. Anyway . . . what do you think of it all then?'

'Well. I love the way you've done the glass front like Tavs and the way you've pointed the bricks and painted the façade that leaf green. I love the statuary on the two balustrades. Kitsch but not too kitsch. I think the plants over the rooftop are going to be sensational next summer. And the terracotta paint work inside is inspired. Is that enough?'

'Yeah. That'll do nicely. Thanks.'

'I've got to go, sweetheart. Lecture in ten minutes and I've an essay to give in.'

'Was that the one about rotting leaves?'

'Sort of. Nutrient recycling in tropical forest ecosystems.' She says it all in one breath, like a spell, or a good-luck charm. The words seem to give her such pleasure that Dale can't help beaming at her.

'OK. Right. Who's picking the boys up?'

'I am. I'll be finished at four and they're booked into after school club until five. I'll shop on the way home. And we've got Barney tonight. Louise has a hot date.'

Sam kisses Dale, leaps on her bike and cycles off to the University, whistling completely tunelessly. He stands for a moment grinning after her stupidly, bathing in one of those total smiles she gives these days, baby-sweet, woman-warm. He turns to the bakery, and goes inside. A bit more work on the stockroom and then the job's done. He'll be free to do a little bit of shopping himself later on.

'What did you learn about today, Mum?' says Tony. He and Joe have been delighted by the fact that since Sam began her botany degree course, they are all in the same educational boat.

'Active transport across the cell wall, Tony.'

'I know what that is,' says Joe proudly, 'transport's like buses.'

'Or bikes.' Tony is sitting on the seat of Sam's bike as she wheels it. The boys take turns all the way home. Today Tony has first turn as far as the end of the alley.

'I thought it was all about flowers, mummy, what you're learning.'

'Well, even flowers are made of cells.'

'So why are they telling you about buses?' Joe is mystified and ready to worry at this anomaly like a terrier at a rat. But Tony has learnt that there are things about what Mummy learns that he just is never going to get, no matter how many questions he asks.

'Look! Joe,' he says offering a distraction, 'I'm getting down early. You can have a long turn.'

'Wow. Thanks!' As Joe climbs up Sam and Tony exchange a smile.

'Thanks, Tony!'

'S'right. D'you want to know what we learned today?'

'Yes please.'

'We did halves!'

'Halves?'

'Yeah, and quarters. And Miss cut up apples and we all had bits.'

They emerge from the alley and cross the road, where two big trees lean over from adjacent gardens and embrace above the pavement. Even in winter, Sam has seen all manner of plants and animals in their branches. Strangler figs and rattans, orchid species like the ones that Lawrence used to grow, even once a *rafflesia* blossom spreading its stinking meat-like petals over the top of the garden wall. One day when she'd lost concentration on Tony's story about the horrors of school dinners, a tamandua had pushed its sleepy, silky-furred little face out of the leaves and looked right at her. But since she started her Botany course she's been on the real path to the jungle; now the two trees contain nothing but the odd crow or a shabby squirrel. Today their bare branches are empty, just a beautiful tangle against the blue sky. Overhead a little party of six parakeets flies high, making for the park. Odd, exotic and out of place they are quite a famous little troupe, and reports of their escape from the zoo's new aviary have been all over the local press.

'They asleep?' Dale turns from the drying-up as Sam comes into the kitchen.

'Yeah!' she yawns. 'Wanted to climb in with them tonight. It's freezing and I'm so tired.'

'Have you *got* to work tonight?'

'Only a bit. I'm sorry, Dale. Just an hour is all. I can have a night off tomorrow.'

Dale turns back to the washing-up, his shoulders showing his disappointment and irritation.

'Oh, *go on* then. Get it done.' He doesn't turn back and Sam slinks up the stairs to the bedroom-turned-study, feeling at once guilty and resentful. He was so keen for her to start this degree, and usually he encourages her to work. Why is he being mean this evening?

She pushes open the door of the little book-lined room and flicks the light switch. Instead of the usual flat white illumination from the ceiling light, the switch tonight has triggered something else. The room is spangled with little green fairy lights, that flash and twinkle. They are draped around the shelves and desk space in a rough spiral that tightens to a nest of leaf-coloured glow. In the centre of the glow are two big white envelopes with her name on the front, and big numbers, one and two. She opens the first, and pulls out a card. On the front is a palmate leaf, a simple hand-drawn shape with the veins carefully traced in pencil. Underneath in Dale's best printing is the Latin name *Cecropia*. Inside more Latin words in Dale's print march round the edge of the card as a decorative border . . . each one in a different coloured ink. The names of giant forest trees, of epiphytic orchids, of ferns and aroids, climbers and stranglers. The whole structure of a rainforest springs up between the letters reflected in their Latin meanings . . .

Dale must have spent hours, days, collecting these from library books. Cleverly, all the plants are South or Central American; he's picked not one from the Old World. Knowing Dale, that must be deliberate. In the centre of the card in neat black handwriting is this message:

It's not Christmas, or even nearly Christmas, but this is one present you have to know about six weeks early because of all the jabs you have to have. (Your bottom is going to be a pincushion, I'm afraid.) You deserve a reward for the hard work of the first term of your course, for all you've been through this year and before. I want you to have your heart's desire. Next time, we'll all go, but this trip is yours. Open the other envelope.

The second envelope is fatter. It contains an airline ticket and a little brochure about the Green Mountain reserve and research centre. It's in Belize. You can go and have a holiday in the rainforest there, just laze about and look at things or you can choose to help with any one of the scientific research projects always on the go. There is a picture of one of the little cabins under the trees over which Dale has written: '*This one is yours, you'll be "mapping tree species and studying height distribution", whatever that is.*'

There's a creak of floorboards outside the door. Sam turns to see Dale peering anxiously into the green light.

'Is it OK? You've been so long . . .'

Dale hangs at the door, his face a little crumpled with concern, afraid that his great surprise present is worse than a flop. Looking at him she is paralysed, she can only stare and feel that nothing she can ever say could be enough. She walks to him slowly. Slowly puts her arms as far round him as she can reach and holds him tight. Tight and long. At last she holds his face between her hands and looks hard into his eyes.

'Thank you. Thank you so much.'

'You will come back?'

'It's a return ticket!'

'You know what I mean.'

'Yes I do. I'll come back. But I'll take part of you with me and leave some of myself behind.'

17

January 28th

My darling Sam,

I was clearing out cupboards today and I thought of you. I found those glow-in-the-dark stars you left for me the Christmas you went to Bristol. You probably don't remember, but they were wrapped and labelled in your room. Dad found them after you were gone. I put them up in the telly room where I was sleeping back then. Actually Ralph did it for me. He put them in proper constellations over the ceiling. Can you believe it? It was the first sign I had that there was still life in him! The second sign was his Christmas present to me that year. Not that we felt a lot like presents! In fact I don't think I opened them until after New Year, but he gave me two fabulous hats. Utterly ridiculous considering the state I was in. I put those on the wall in that room too. They helped me have hope that I could survive. I wore one to the opening of the shop two years later; I'll show you the photos sometime!

But there was something else that made me survive too. I should have talked to you about it before. Bless you, you've hinted at it often enough since we've been back in touch. It's that business with the pills on the night you left. I'm so ashamed of what I asked you to do but I was in so much pain I just wanted it to stop, I didn't care how. I was so grateful to you for giving me all there were left in the bottle.

I was out for more than twenty-four hours. By the time I came round you were gone. I always wondered if you'd gone because you were frightened of what might have happened to me. I worried that you felt it was your fault. It made me determined to live, so you couldn't ever wonder, so that I could tell you that I'm sorry. Sam, you were a child, seventeen. I asked you for something I shouldn't have asked for. And you gave it just because I asked. I've always felt that you missed your chances because of me. I'm so sorry, from the bottom of my heart.

It was a terrible, terrible time for us all, but I have learned to see the good that came from it. My guilt about you made me determined to survive (and the stars and hats of course!); your father turned his life around because he'd failed you and he didn't want to fail me too. And you found Dale and had those boys. And now you've got to go your jungle. It helps to heal everything for me because of that. I can't begin to tell you how much pleasure it gives me to think that at last you are there, in your rainforest. It feels like a final sort of resolution, you being there, living out your ambitions at last.

Perhaps it was only your friend Lawrence who lost out so completely, because you must have meant a lot to him, and you went away. But I'm only guessing, dear. Although I never knew Lawrence, I thank him with all my heart that his legacy has helped to realise your ambitions. I'm sure he'll rest more peacefully if somehow he knows.

This trip is just a beginning, Sam. There's no reason why you can't fulfill all your ambitions to study rainforest. I know Dale will support you all the way, and so will your dad and I. (He's blowing an upside-down kiss to you as I write!)

It's very cold here, snowing in fact. You know what East Anglia can be like with that lazy wind that goes through you not round you. It's so funny to think that on this same little planet, such a tiny distance away really, it is hot and steamy with huge trees growing whilst ours look so small and lifeless. I like to think about that, you being in the Summer as it were and us being in Winter, both at the same time. It's like having a complete set of something, matching gloves, hat, handbag and shoes. Listen to me rambling. Your father will tell me I'm going senile.

Ring me the moment you get back. I want to hear every last detail.

Your Old Ma

January 28th

Dear Mum,

The post is erratic to say the least! Although I feel I've been away for years, three weeks is so short a time. I bet as I'm writing this you're writing to me and our letters will cross! Never mind.

It's half an hour after dawn. I've climbed the ropes and pulleys that lift me up to where the birds fly in the tallest of the trees. They're called emergents in the jargon, 'cos they emerge from above the other trees. Technical, eh! A thread of mist is caught in the canopy this morning. It reminds me of that pale blue chiffon scarf you had years ago. You used to keep it in your dressing-room drawer with Granny's locket.

The canopy is below me up here. It stretches like a green sea as far as the horizon. Actually green isn't a good description. It's just one word and there are a thousand colours in it, all of them woven into the mass of what I call 'green'. (And a few that you couldn't call green, splashes of orange and white where some of the trees are in bloom. No subdued little oak-type flowers here, tropical trees are as subtle as Liberace!) Sea is a good description though, because things jump out into the air sometimes like leaping dolphins, then dive down below the surface. All you see is a flash of colour and then the parrot or whatever it was, is gone, swimming down amongst the leaves again. It's peaceful and mysterious like the sea, but frustrating like the sea too, because you want to get a better look at the creatures that leap out and dive back. I'm glad I'm a botanist . . . at least plants never move much.

The weeks here have seemed so long. I've done so much. I've settled into the routine of work and the homey feeling of my little hut as if I'd been doing it all my life. Don, my boss, is great, he's taught me loads. We spend all day tramping the forest mapping trees, measuring heights and trying to get samples from the canopy. I'm getting very fit. He's amazing, sixty-eight and he can still outwalk me every day.

Dale wrote with pictures that the boys had done of me in the trees. I can hardly look at them without wanting to cry. I miss them so much. But somehow *that* makes *this* better. Perhaps the best part of all will be telling Tony and Joe and Dale all about it.

It's a noisy quiet up here. The sounds of birds and monkeys – howlers – spurt up from where all the animal activity is, underneath the shelter of leaves amongst the high branches. I'm above all that here. This space belongs to the big trees. It's their world, their kingdom. I feel their long slow years and the way they hold all the life that depends on them, quietly without any sort of fuss. Up here it's their pace, the pace of light and of the sky and of the air. I come up here every morning at this time to feel the peace of the trees and to pretend that the world is still all like this, with trees clothing all the planet like a hug. It's funny, but up here I feel closer to everyone I've left back home, as if you and Dad, Dale and the boys and Maria were just waiting below, for me to climb down. It's as if everyone I love, everything I've done or will do is under the same forest canopy, joined by intertwining roots and touching branches, all together in one big, green, beautiful jungle.

I'll ring as soon as I get home.

Love,

Sam